Protected Arms

A NOVEL BY

John Thomas

Copyright

The characters and events in this book are fictitious other than the reference to the US court appeal, *Parker v District of Columbia*. Any similarity to real persons, living or dead, or to actual events, is coincidental and not intended by the author.

Dedication

My wife, Lou, has been my biggest supporter. I have bored her over many dinners with my thoughts, concerns, and content of this book. She never failed to listen. I am blessed to have such a wonderful wife and friend.

JT

Preface

On June 26, 1976, the District of Columbia's City Council passed the Firearms Control Regulation Act of 1975 which banned residents from owning handguns not previously registered in the District. The ban was enthusiastically supported by the Mayor, the police department and the majority of citizens of the District of Columbia. It was considered by many as one of the strictest gun laws ever adopted by any local, city, or state government in the United States. The ban stood for almost 30 years despite the many lawsuits and congressional attempts to invalidate the Act. On February 10, 2003 a lawsuit, Parker vs. District of Columbia, was filed in the United States District Court for the District of Columbia to overturn the law on the basis that it violated an individual's right to bear arms as guaranteed by the 2nd Amendment of the United States Constitution. The case was dismissed. Subsequently, an appeal was made to reverse the dismissal and was argued before the United States Court of Appeals on December 7, 2006. This story takes place before the Court's final decision which occurred on March 9, 2007.

Prologue

Tuesday, January 2, 2007, 10:18 a.m. EST

An opened FedEx box sat on George Henry's desk. It had been sitting there since December 31, 2006. All packages and letters sent to the Law offices of Henry, Chapman and Parker were now screened and opened by security in their basement level mailroom ever since the mail-bombings and ricin incidents at other law firms in the District. Even the *Open upon my death* label on the outside of a smaller box contained inside the larger FedEx box had been ignored as it too had been opened. Security did not care if the sender was dead or alive. Their job was to protect the employees of their firm.

Henry found the contents of the smaller box disturbing. Besides an opened notarized envelope, the box also contained a Ziploc bag revealing a 9mm handgun and two shell casings along with a computer CD. These were not items normally sent to a divorce lawyer.

As Henry read the letter which security had dated and time-stamped, everything in the box made sense. It answered a lot of questions about the previous week's tragic events that dominated the headlines of the local and national news media. As requested by the writer of the letter, the entire contents of the box was to be hand-delivered to either Detective Whitehead or Detective Williams of the Washington Police Department.

Henry read the entire letter twice making sure he completely understood the originator's intent. Then as directed in the letter, he took pictures of it and the contents of the box. Satisfied he had carried out his duties as lawyer and friend of the sender, he called the police.

Chapter 1

Wednesday, December 27, 2006, 7:32 a.m. EST – One Week Earlier

It was just a matter of time before the blue and white oriental jar lamp found its way to the floor. It was bound to happen, especially the way Jim Barnes had staggered, stumbled and teetered throughout the night, drinking and swearing, bumping into anything in his way. The lamp hung upside down by its electric cord with its 3-way light bulb still shining. Amazingly, neither lamp nor bulb had been broken. So far, it had been the only casualty of the night at his well-appointed Watergate apartment. The night had been filled with a medley of pacing, thinking and loud cursing laced with swigs of liquor from an almost-empty liquor bottle that he held tightly by the neck. He was still dressed in his dark blue pinstriped Brooks Brother suit that he had now worn for over twenty-four hours. His normal heavily starched, perfectly pressed white dress shirt was now a maze of wrinkles spotted with liquor stains. He had not bothered to bathe, change clothes, eat, or sleep since leaving work.

Jim looked as bad as he felt. Normally, drinking made him feel happy, friendly and fun-loving. But not this time. Today, he was angry, his mind filled with hate, his behavior borderline psychotic. His rage and venomous thoughts were primarily directed towards his boss, Wayne Peters, who, on Tuesday, had summoned him to the office, censured him for his recent performance, and then placed him on paid administrative leave. Jim had worked for the North American Gun Society (acronym NAGS) for over thirty years, long enough to know that he would be fired at their next board meeting. His loyalty, hard work and past successes for the organization seemed to have been forgotten. He was well aware that his last six months with the company hadn't been his best. But they should have understood his 'lack of focus' as Peters had put it. During that time, he had suffered through a nasty divorce and had buried his mother. And the drinking? No. He didn't have a problem. Everybody at the company drank. Hell, it was part of his job. Maybe he had taken a drink or two during work hours, but it never affected his job. In fact, it helped him take his mind off his problems - his now ex-wife's infidelities, his son's drug problems, and his mother's terminal illness. He would forever be filled with guilt for not having been with her more often as she neared death. But work always came first, very often, to the detriment of his family.

Jim took another swig from the liquor bottle wiping off the excess that drooled from his mouth using the sleeve of his shirt. The liquor no longer created the smooth burning sensation in his throat as it had earlier. He hadn't drunk this much since his college days.

On the coffee table, next to an empty liquor bottle that he'd drained earlier, lay a loaded gun. Throughout the night, Jim's mental state had vacillated somewhere between extreme depression and psychotic rage. In one of his weaker, darker moments, he had retrieved the gun from his safe, thinking that a shot to the head would end all of his anguish. It would be quick. But as he thought about his life, how he had devoted the larger part of it to work, how Wayne Peters had humiliated him and how he *now* wanted to shit-can him, the feelings of self-pity quickly turned into wild-eyed rage. Just the thought of the cold, heartless bastard and his condescending attitude infuriated him. Any feelings of hopelessness and desperation were quickly replaced with a crazed sense of anger. He drained the last ounce of liquor from the bottle, looked at the dead soldier with contempt, and then flung it toward the wall, tomahawk style, fully expecting to see a shower of glass shards. But the bottle hit with a thud, causing only a small abrasion to the sheetrock as the missile fell to the floor, unbroken. Aggravated at his failure, Jim jerked up the second empty bottle from the coffee table and threw it even harder toward the same wall, yelling a series of expletives as he did. Neither the bottle nor the wall could withstand his second and more forceful assault as the bottle shattered, and the sheetrock caved.

He needed to meet with Wayne Peters. Confront him. He had been ambushed yesterday, totally unaware of the .purpose of the meeting. He wasn't going down without a fight. He was going to keep his job, or he would take the whole damn company down with him. He had some very highly damning documents that could potentially destroy Peters *and* NAGS and he would use them if he had to. Even a second-rate reporter would have little trouble becoming a modern-day Woodward or Bernstein were they to get hold of these documents. This time, he felt he now had the upper hand. Peters would have to acquiesce to his demands. A wicked smile began to creep into his face. Yes, he was focused all right.

A man on a mission, Jim grabbed his overcoat and car keys and headed to the front door. The gun that once lay on the coffee table was no longer there. Jim had not forgotten it.

No one heard the slamming of the door as he left, just as no one had heard all the noise coming from his apartment during his all-nighter because he had no nearby neighbors. His apartment was located at the end of the hall on the 8th floor of Watergate's 600 Building. It was flanked on the left by the emergency stairwell and on the right by two vacant cooperative apartments that were owned by NAGS. All three had been originally purchased to house their out of town VIPs and sometimes in-town politicians who needed some 'alone' time. But when Jim lost his house in his divorce, he took up residence in the largest of the three apartments as 'temporary housing' and had yet to vacate - another fact that had not set well with Peters or the board.

The wait for the elevator was brief and the descent to the garage level was quick, never having to stop at any other floor. When the elevator doors opened, the frigid air from the parking garage engulfed the elevator cabin dropping the temperature over twenty degrees. It should have been like a cold, sobering slap in the face but Jim barely winced as he made his way over to his silver S550 Mercedes. All he could think about was Peters and what he was going to tell him.

Chapter 2

Wednesday, December 27, 2006, 8:03 a.m. EST

The twenty minute drive from the Watergate Complex to the NAGS office building gave Jim the time he needed to compose himself and to think about how he would approach Peters. He needed to stay calm, stay on topic, and make his demands. Keeping his job was his primary goal and he would settle for nothing less.

NAGS executive offices were headquartered in a three-story brownstone house located on Massachusetts Avenue in downtown Washington, DC. The organization was founded in 1934 as a non-profit gun rights organization whose initial mission was to teach rifle marksmanship and gun safety. Over time, NAGS morphed into one of the largest and most powerful lobbying groups whose sole mission was the protection of the Second Amendment.

Because of the building's proximity to Dupont Circle, everyone referred to the headquarters' location as the Dupont Circle building. The house was built in 1927, right before the start of the Great Depression, and changed owners three times before being purchased by NAGS in 1953. Many renovations and additions had been made to the building, but all were in keeping with the beauty and charm of the old structure and the surrounding neighborhood. The ceilings were high, the rooms big and the molding ornate. It was beautifully appointed with antiques and antique replicas. Located on the main floor were the reception area, a parlor room complete with a 1926 six-foot Steinway Piano, a breakroom/kitchen area, a small gun museum and two large conference rooms. All executive offices were located on the second and third floors. Wayne Peters, Jim Barnes, three secretaries, a security guard and a small legal staff including the head of legal affairs, two staff lawyers and a legal assistant worked at the Headquarters Building. The rest of the organization, primarily staff lawyers and membership service agents, worked in the larger Bethesda, Maryland office complex.

As Jim pulled through the open wrought iron gates into the side parking lot, he saw only one parked car. Peter's black 2006 Jaguar. The week after Christmas was supposed to be a holiday vacation for everyone. But Peters never took any time off. If given the chance, he would work every day of the year. Work was his passion.

Jim eased his car around the Jag and parked alongside it, totally unaware that he had angled his Mercedes across two spaces, both of which were marked 'Handicapped.' If these were normal times, he would have been horrified at having parked in a handicap spot or spots, as it were. But these weren't normal times. All he could think about was meeting Peters, face to face. How he parked never once entered his mind.

Jim entered the building through the side entrance after deactivating the alarm. He tried to be as quiet as possible hoping to catch Peters off guard. Anything to rattle the man. Peters' office was on the second floor of the building, at the top of the stairs. Using the elevator with its noisy, antique brass scissor gates was not an option. So he headed over to the stairway and held on to the hand rail to steady himself as he made his way up the eighteen steps. When he reached the second floor, his legs were burning and his heart pumping hard. The door to Peters' office was open and he could hear him talking. A quick peek inside found him on speakerphone, head down while typing on his computer. Jim slipped into the room unnoticed.

Peters was a pleasant-looking man in his early fifties. He kept himself in excellent physical condition. He would have looked much younger than his age were it not for his graying hair that he wore in a short, military-styled buzz cut. He was well educated, having an accounting degree from the University of Richmond and a law degree from the University of Virginia. He had risen through the ranks at NAGS to become their executive vice-president, the highest-ranking non-elected board member in the organization. Like Jim, Peters was recently divorced after almost twenty-two years of marriage. But unlike Jim's divorce, Peters' had been amicable. He and his now ex-wife, Norma, devoted most of their time to their careers and mutually agreed that neither had time for marriage. The thought of having children never entered their minds. They were still friends and occasionally met for dinner. When the need for a date at a social or political function arose, they were there for each other.

In contrast, Jim Barnes looked much older than his age and had gained considerable weight in the last few months. Depression played a major role in his weight gain as he overate and over drank. But, then again, drinking and eating were a big part of his job. Being the company's 'Special Events' Coordinator for the last ten years, he was responsible for procuring those impossible-to-get tickets to sporting events, plays, and concerts. He knew most every maître d at all the elite restaurants in DC and could get the best table in the house at a moment's notice. He also hosted gambling junkets, hunting trips, golf outings, Caribbean cruises, parties, and European tours. On occasions, he was responsible for providing evening escort services for a few high profile supporters. On the company's organization chart, Jim reported directly to Peters.

Early on, he and Peters had been the best of friends. But Peters had changed over the years as he moved up the corporate ladder. Friends were important to him but not as important as the company and his career. Peters now felt that Jim had become a liability to NAGS and that fresh blood, new ideas and a total dedication to the 'Cause' were needed. Jim was no longer that person. Too many problems. Too much baggage. NAGS needed someone 'more focused.'

Peters pushed the 'off' button on his phone and finished entering his email. He hit the *send* key, then leaned back in his chair and started to place his hands behind his head when he saw Jim leaning against the door frame with his arms folded and a scowl on his face.

"What are you doing here?" Peters blurted out, somewhat startled as Jim walked toward his desk. "I thought you were supposed to be off … uh… on vacation."

"Vacation, my ass. Administrative leave," Jim said, arrogantly elongating the words.

"If that's what you've come here to discuss, you're wasting your time."

"Well, we *are* gonna discuss it. I've decided that I'm not going on administrative leave. Not now. Not *ever*."

"You don't have that option, Jim. The Board has already…"

"THE BOARD!" interrupted Jim, his calm demeanor quickly fading and his anger returning. "This has nothing to do with the damn BOARD," he yelled elongating the word 'board.' "This is all about you… you're behind all of this. Not the BOARD!" he bellowed treating 'board' as if it were a curse word, all the while, moving closer to the front of Peters' desk stumbling forward as he did.

"Gawd-almighty, Jim. See. You've been drinking again. I can smell the alcohol from here. I think you need to go home, get some rest, sleep it off, and come back after the holidays. Then we can discuss…"

"Go home? What home? I don't have a home anymore. Thanks to that incompetent, half-wit divorce lawyer you pushed on me, I have nothing left. I got fucked just like you fucked my wife."

"What the hell are you talking about?" Peters tried to remain composed. Two people yelling only made matters worse.

"You know damn well what I'm talking about!" shouted Jim, jabbing his index finger into Peters' desk, his face turning red with anger.

Peters stood up and pointed to the door.   With only a slight raise and authoritative tone to his voice, he replied, "I think you better leave. Now. While you still have *any* chance of keeping your job."

"Oh, I'm keeping my job. You're not getting rid of me that easy. I've given over thirty years of my *life* to this place. But… but… if I *do* go down, all you assholes are going down with me. I've got so much bad shit on you and… and on this… this rat hole it'll make Richard Nixon look like a Sunday school teacher. And, by God, don't think I won't use it."

What 'bad shit' was he talking about? wondered Peters. Needing to find out more, he decided to take a different approach.

"Why don't you sit down and we can talk this out like civilized…"

"I DON'T NEED TO SIT DOWN," interrupted Jim, his face becoming redder and all contorted with anger. "I want YOU to send out an email right now to every damn member of the board telling them that…uh… that… uh, you made a mistake. Changed your mind. Whatever the hell you have to say to make this thing right 'cause you're not taking my job away."

"Nobody's taking your job away, dammit! And placing you on administrative leave wasn't even *my* idea. That came from three or four of our most important board members. They are concerned about you. Your recent lack of attention. Lack of focus. They're the ones that wanted you to take a leave of absence. To get your priorities back in order. We talked about that yesterday."

"I've got my *damn* priorities in order, you lying son-of-a-bitch!" yelled Jim.

"You don't need to yell. Just calm down," said Peters softly and slowly, punctuating each word. "You *know* you haven't been yourself lately. I mean, geez, you've been coming in at noon, smelling of alcohol, and trying to conduct business. For God's sake, man, you've been late for appointments. You even stood up Congressman Richards. You know we must always conduct ourselves at the highest possible level. These are people…"

Peters knew immediately he shouldn't have mentioned the Richards' debacle.

"YOU… STUPID… MORON," interrupted Jim, now more belligerent than ever. "You know DAMN well I was at the hospital with my mother. And that asshole, Richards, only thinks of himself, just like you and all the other greedy bastards that work here. You didn't even care that she was dying. All you care about is kissing the right asses. Well, you can kiss my *ass*, you son-of-a-bitch."

"Jim. Jim. I'm telling you to calm down!"

"GO TO HELL!"

The anger in Jim had reached a boiling point. Without thinking, he pulled out the gun from his overcoat pocket. At the time, it seemed the right thing. At first, he pointed it to his head. Then, he pointed it at Peters. His hand was trembling.

"PUT THAT GUN AWAY, YOU CRAZY SON-OF-A-BITCH!" yelled Peters.

"I'm not crazy," Jim said faintly, his voice quivering. Maybe it was the anti-depression meds. Maybe it was the alcohol. Maybe it was simply because he'd just had enough. Regardless of the reason, it had become crystal clear what he had to do. He had gone too far to turn back. He had reached the point of no return. The paper would read 'Murder / Suicide.'

Resigned to his fate, Jim adjusted his aim, pointed the gun at Peters' head, and then pulled the trigger. Nothing happened! In his confused state of mind, he had forgotten to remove the safety. As he clumsily fiddled with the safety, Peters reached down, jerked open his bottom desk drawer, and pulled out a gun, one that he had kept in the event a crackpot got past their security. He quickly removed the safety and fired at Jim. Peters' bullet was right on target, hitting Jim in his chest, knocking him backwards, into a nearby wingback chair, and onto the floor but not before Jim also managed to pull the trigger on his gun. The bullet whizzed past Peters' ear leaving him unharmed. Margie Hamilton, Wayne Peters' secretary, was not as fortunate.

With both men were so involved in their confrontation, neither noticed Margie coming out of the storage vault located behind and to the left of Peters' desk. She had been busy in the far recesses of the L-shaped vault, copying highly sensitive documents. Because the storage vault was fireproof, the door only slightly ajar, and the copier noisily humming away, the voices coming from Peters' office were muted and the words muffled, so she was unaware of the commotion. Only as she neared the door did she realize that a full-blown argument was in progress. As she exited the vault, Jim's bullet struck her in her left eye, knocking her back into the vault against the filing cabinets. It killed her instantly. Jim never saw Margie and never knew that he had killed her.

Jim lay on the floor holding his chest, screaming, "I'm shot. You shot me, you bastard. Call an ambulance! Oh God... Hurry! Hurry!"

Jim tried in vain to sit up. The drinking, his size, and the fact that a major artery had been pierced kept him on his back, struggling like an upside-down turtle.

Peters ignored him. Instead, he ran to Margie Hamilton. Her face was a mess with blood spewing everywhere. He knew she was dead. There was nothing he could do for her.

Jim screamed out again, but this time, not as loud. "Where are you? Where's the ambulance? Have you called 911? Oh God... I'm sorry Wayne. Please forgive me! Wayne? Wayne? Where are you? Please don't let me die! Pleeeeeaaassssssseeeeee..............."

Wayne Peters looked over at Jim Barnes whose life was quickly slipping away and then looked away. Slowly he walked back to his desk and slumped into his chair. His hands were shaking, and his heart was beating furiously causing his chest to heave. Maybe he should have tried to save Jim. He *could* have called 911. He *could* have tried to stop the bleeding. He *could* have at least comforted him, but he didn't. He had done nothing.

Chapter 3

Wednesday, December 27, 2006, 8:21 a.m. EST

WHY! Why hadn't he done anything? Why hadn't he called 911? Or the police? Somebody? Anybody? Why?

Wayne slumped in his chair and stared blankly at his computer screen. He couldn't bring himself to look at either body. He had seen death before but never this way. It was so fast. A living human being one minute and a lifeless body the next. It was surreal. Like a bad dream. Reluctantly, he turned and looked at Margie's body. It was then that he knew why he hadn't called for help or the police. It wasn't that he was worried that he would be charged with murder. No! Jim was shot in self-defense! And Margie. She was shot by Jim. An accident. In truth, it was the harsh realization that this would be the political death of him, his job, and NAGS. They would never survive the onslaught of attacks by the liberal press, the left-wing Democrats, and every anti-gun zealot on the internet if they were to find out that two NAGS employees had been killed by guns at their headquarters. Illegal guns at that. The fallout would be far-reaching. And the lawsuits? It would be a feeding frenzy for the lawyers. They would be all over NAGS like a cheap suit. He could not let that happen. He had worked too hard, too long and had given up too much in his life to let the actions of one crazed employee ruin his career, his company, his life. He thought about his options. Whatever he did, whatever plan he devised, it had to totally distance him and the company from these killings. There could never be any connection of these deaths to NAGS and more importantly, himself. Never.

Just thinking about the situation and what needed to be done had a calming effect on him. Instinctively, he turned to his computer. As he stared at the screen, he began reviewing the events of the previous day. Automatically, he opened up his online organizer/day planner and checked the notes that he had entered about his meeting with Jim. Only he and Jim had been in the office that day. And only a couple of Board members knew that he had planned to place Jim on administrative leave. The only other person who *knew* about yesterday's meeting was Margie.

Poor Margie. With that thought, he glanced over at her lifeless body with her head lying in a pool of blood. *Oh my God!* What was he thinking? While he sat there, strategizing, organizing his thoughts, both bodies continued to ooze blood onto the floor.

Wayne bolted from his seat, rushed out of his office, and headed downstairs to the supply closet located in the breakroom, carefully avoiding the bodies as he passed them. He grabbed a roll of paper towels, a box of trash bags, and a pair of yellow dish gloves and ran back to his office. There, he rolled up his sleeves and slid on the gloves. Any size smaller and they wouldn't have fit. *If the gloves don't fit, you must acquit!* A bizarre thought at a most bizarre time.

Standing over Jim's body, Wayne pushed it a couple of times with his foot like someone would do over a dead animal making sure it indeed was dead; that it wasn't playing possum, waiting to attack. Partially hidden under Jim's coat was his gun. Wayne carefully picked it up, pushed the safety on, and placed it on his desk next to his. Making a conscious effort not to look at Jim's face, he rolled the lifeless body onto the plastic trash bags. To his relief, there was very little blood found under the body as most of it had been absorbed by Jim's suit clothes and large black wool overcoat. The small amount of blood that did manage to seep through the coat was pooled on the hardwood floor. He did a cursory look at the Oriental rug on which the body partially lay. If there were any traces of blood, it was not readily visible having blended in with the color and design of the rug. Regardless, he made a mental note to have *all* rugs in the building cleaned, not just his office's, so not to arouse any suspicions.

With Margie, he couldn't place the plastic bags under her head without looking at her face. As he did, a sudden pang of grief engulfed him causing him to quickly look away. Tears began to well up in his eyes, and his throat tightened. Although not a religious man, Wayne felt a need to pray. *Oh, God! Please forgive me. Tell her I'm sorry. Amen.*

The words, regardless of how few, seemed to give comfort to Wayne. He wiped the tears from his eyes with his shirtsleeve. *OK, get a grip!* He couldn't allow that to happen again. Grief sapped people's energy and their ability to think and act rationally. Shaking his head as if to erase the horror, he looked again at Margie, this time with his feelings in check. Her right eye was still partially open, and her left eye had blood oozing out of it. Her always perfectly coiffed red-dyed hair was now blood wet and blood red. He wondered if she knew what had happened. Did she see the bright light that many say they see when entering death – the ones that were fortunate or possibly unfortunate to experience death, then return to life and be able to tell about their journey?

As he mopped up the blood off the floor and the splatters off the filing cabinets, his mind replayed the events leading up to the shooting. Everything seemed to play out in slow motion. Although he didn't see Margie get shot, his mind visualized the bullet hitting her in the eye, snapping her head back and knocking her backwards into the storage vault. As his mind turned to Jim, he could see him aiming the gun at his face, pulling the trigger and having nothing happen. The thought of it sent chills down his spine. Why hadn't he ducked or tried to shield himself? Or try to grab the gun from Jim? And the safety? What were the odds of someone with Jim's knowledge of guns, who worked with them all his adult life, a trained instructor, failing to remove the safety? He still couldn't believe it. My God what luck! Not that God had anything to do with it.

Wayne used nearly an entire roll of paper towels to wipe up the blood that had pooled around the two bodies. It amazed him as to the amount of blood that came from the human body, especially from someone as small as Margie. As he watched the blood continue to ooze from their wounds, it became quite apparent that if he didn't do something soon, the blood would overrun the bags. The only thing that came to mind was the adhesive tape in the first-aid kit located in the breakroom. He rushed back downstairs to the breakroom where a big white box bearing the symbolic Red Cross hung on the wall just inside the door. Seeing the roll of adhesive tape triggered another idea. A better idea. Like a madman, he began searching through all the cabinets and, to his amazement, found what he was looking for, sitting right next to the coffee filters. One of man's all-time greatest inventions. Duct-tape. He grabbed the tape and returned to his office, shutting and locking the door behind him.

So far he had been able to avoid getting any blood on his clothes. But Jim was a big man. Getting the tape around his body wasn't going to be easy and could get messy. Not taking any chances, Wayne removed his pants, dress shirt, and tie, laid them neatly on his desk, then wrapped his arms and chest with trash bags and secured them with duct-tape. He spent the next ten or so minutes holding Jim's limp body in a sitting position wrapping duct tape around the overcoat covering the bullet holes. The size and weight of Jim's body made Wayne realize he was going to have a major problem getting him out of the office.

Wrapping Margie's wounds with duct tape was much easier considering the location of the wounds. But at the same time it was much more painful as he once again had to look at her disfigured face.

Physically, Wayne was spent. But emotionally, he was running on high octane adrenaline. He needed to get back to his computer. He needed to map this whole thing out. Operating by the seat of his pants wasn't how he worked. That could only lead to mistakes, oversights, inefficiencies. Wasting little time, he grabbed a clean trash bag and filled it with the spent paper towels, the soiled trash bags, and the yellow cleaning gloves. He closed the bag, wrapping a twist tie around it, and then double bagged it. A quick inspection of his boxers and T-shirt showed only a few spots of blood. He felt dirty, in need of a shower. Something to wash away the emotional stains of today's horror.

Chapter 4

Wednesday, December 27, 2006, 8:44 a.m. EST

Wayne dressed while simultaneously surveying his office - his home away from home. He felt invaded. Like someone had broken into his house. Like he had been robbed. Like someone had stolen his good life, his good name, his job, his company. He could not let that happen. Slowly he made his way back to his desk and plopped down in his chair. Tension had begun to build in his head. He rubbed his temples in an effort to fend off the oncoming headache and a possible migraine. He had no time for either, especially a migraine. His hands made their way back to the computer keyboard and he began to log his thoughts. He liked seeing them on the monitor. It made him feel organized and in control. He was well aware of the risks of having such incriminating evidence on his computer, even one that had password protection. But until his plan had been fully implemented and the hard drive destroyed, he would have to take that risk.

Within minutes, he had effortlessly typed in a series of issues/topics, initial questions, a few potential answers and a timeline of events. It was as though he were writing an article for NAGS' monthly magazine, *Rights of the People.* While the subject matter was different, the methodology was similar. Pose the questions, find the answers and produce the document. Only, in this case, the final document would be an action plan complete with dates, times, and checklists – a roadmap for making sure that everything was completed, on time and in the proper sequence. Anal? Absolutely. He had that reputation, but that's what made him successful. In the NAGS' organization, there were few, if any, more skilled or proficient at project planning, resource coordination, and time management than Wayne Peters.

Being conservative by nature and giving himself a two-day buffer, he set December 31st as the target date to have his plan fully operational. That gave him five days. Too fast an operation could be just as ruinous as one too slow.

His first action item was the inspection of his office and its restoration back to its original state. He pulled a lined writing pad and sharpie from his desk to make his notes. As he pushed his chair away from his desk, one of the wheels seemed to go askew. When he looked to find the reason, he spotted a spent shell casing. He picked it up and then began looking for the one from Jim's gun. He found it to the right of the dead man's body. He placed both shells on his desk next to the guns so not to forget. Continuing with the office inspection, he found a few scattered spots of blood on the red Tabriz Oriental that he hadn't seen earlier. But no one would be able to tell if they were blood, wine, coffee, food or whatever. Regardless, he made a note to have all rugs in the office professionally cleaned before January's Board meeting.

The bullet holes were not so easily found which meant they were not readily visible to the casual observer, a deep relief to Wayne. The bullet that passed through Jim was found in a section of baseboard a couple of inches to the right of a leather couch located behind and to the left of Jim's body. Based on its location, the bullet had to have ricocheted off one of Jim's bones. Some dark wood putty would easily camouflage it, but until then, the couch would be moved to hide it. No one would be the wiser. Two notes: Move couch and wood putty from Home Depot.

He found the bullet that hit Margie plugged in the wall in the storage vault, just to the left of a four-drawer filing cabinet. He would move the cabinet to hide the bullet hole until the wall could be repaired. More notes.

With his inspection of the office complete, he returned to his desk and from his written notes updated his action plan and afterward shredded the notes. By using a sharpie pen, there would be no impressions of the written notes on subsequent pages. He then turned his focus to the next action item which was the disposal of the guns. As he looked at the two guns lying side by side on his desk, he saw that they both were the same make, model, and caliber. He immediately knew the source. They had been thank-you gifts from their manufacturer when President Bush signed into law Senate Bill 397 (Public Law 109-92, October 26, 2005) limiting the liability of firearm manufacturers. NAGS had played a major role in getting the bill written, introduced, and passed by the House and Senate. Both guns would need to be cleaned, the serial numbers filed off, and completely dismantled. Wayne decided that they should spend the rest of their days scattered and rusting at the bottom of the Potomac. Until that could happen, they would have to be locked in one of the secure filing cabinets.

The disposition of the bodies was next on his list. What he chose to do with them would dictate the remainder of his plan. He first turned his attention to Jim. By now, every board member probably knew he had been placed on administrative leave. He would be expected to be at the upcoming Board meeting in January to defend himself, fight for his job, cast doubts on Wayne's decision making. So if he wasn't there, where was he? Just as concerning was Margie. There had to be a reason why she didn't go home after work. And who knew she had gone to work?

Wayne first looked at Jim's body then turned to look at Margie's hoping for some miracle answer. One body was bad enough. But two bodies? Both killed on the same day. By guns of the same caliber? Impossible. *Wait a minute! What if Jim offered Margie a ride home and they were carjacked? Both shot and killed!* The thought excited Wayne - at least momentarily. It could have worked if Margie hadn't driven to work. And there was no telling how many people knew that.

"This is the problem with coming up with a solution before all the facts are known," muttered Wayne, out loud.

Retreating to his standard methodology, Wayne began entering questions again. *Who knew Jim and Margie were coming to the office and at what time? When do I have them leaving the office and who left first? Where were they going and do I know? What do I tell the cops?* As more questions came to mind, the stress from not having any answers reignited the dormant headache. Wayne stopped typing and began rubbing his temples. As he did, he closed his eyes, reclined in his chair, and decided to concentrate on one question at a time. First, who might have known Jim and Margie were coming to the office today?

With Jim, it was simple. No one. Not even a crazy person would carry a gun to their office and tell someone what they planned to do. Besides, whom would he call? Certainly not his ex-wife or his semi-comatose drugged out son. Board members? Not a chance. But if he had, they would have called Wayne. So based on what he knew, he felt pretty comfortable that nobody knew that Jim had come to the office. With Margie, there was really no way to tell. She was a widow who lived alone in Alexandria. She was very close to her two sons who also lived in the DC area. And she had lots of friends. Since she *had* to work on a vacation day, more than likely, she would have told someone.

OK. That wasn't so hard. So now, when did they leave the office, who left first, and where were they going? And what the hell do I tell the cops? There were no real answers. Only lies! This was going to be a major cover-up. Just like Watergate. That Watergate even entered his mind bothered Wayne, and he began to rationalize his actions. *This isn't like Watergate. Nixon and his cronies committed felonies – stealing, breaking and entering, and God knows what else. I certainly didn't do any of those things. I shot Jim in self-defense. That's not a crime. So there's no real comparison. This is more about protecting NAGS. Damage Control. That's all. Damage Control.* But as hard as he tried to convince himself, he knew it wasn't true. He was well aware that he could be charged with illegal possession of a firearm, discharging a firearm within the city limits, obstruction of justice, failure to call the police, tampering with evidence, and probably a whole host of other crimes he hadn't even considered. While his crimes weren't the same as Watergate, they could be just as damning.

Wayne shook his head as if trying to erase his negative thoughts.

OK. Focus on the present. Think! Everybody knew that Jim had been drinking a lot. Recently divorced. Recently moved. Stood up a couple of congressmen. Impatient with co-workers and even board members. So I need to send out a memo immediately telling them that I put Jim on administrative leave of absence. Paid. Of course. And if anyone wants to reach him, they can call him at his apartment. If he's not there, then I don't know where he is. I'm not his keeper. And if they ask, I can say that he got very upset when I told him that he needed to take some time off. Missing? Hell, people go missing every day. Yeah. That'll work for him. I just need some time to figure out what to do with his body.

Wayne leaned forward, updated his action plan, and then leaned back in his chair. He closed his eyes and continued his train of thought.

Now Margie. No. She can't go missing. Two people from NAGS can't go missing - not on the same day. Having Jim go missing makes sense. But not both of them. And what about the bodies? Both have gunshot wounds. Suicide? No. It can't be suicide. I shot Jim in the chest. And Margie was shot in the head. No. Margie has to be shot. But by whom? Jim? No! That won't work! What kind of mess have I gotten myself in? None of this is making any sense. THIS IS NOT GOOD! Oh! God! Why did this happen to me? What did I do to deserve this? That stupid, stupid moron. If he weren't already dead, I'd kill him.

The ringing of Wayne's cell phone startled him but came as a welcome relief until he saw the caller-ID. 'Bobby Cell.'

"Oh God, not now! What the hell does he want?" 'Bobby' was Nelson Robert Armstrong, president of NAGS.

Wayne hesitated before answering the phone. He needed to act normal, like nothing had happened. He cleared his throat and slowly flipped open his phone.

"Wayne Peters," he calmly answered.

"Merrrrry Christmas! Hope I'm not interrupting anything," said Bobby, in a singsong, jovial tone of voice.

"No. Just wrapping up a few last-minute things. I… uh… I…" Wayne stopped mid-sentence, a wave of desperation and panic hitting him head-on. He needed help. He needed Bobby.

"Oh God, I'm *so* glad you called. We've got a full-blown crisis here at the office, and I need your help. I need you here. As soon as possible!"

"Well, Wayne, ol' boy. You're in luck. I was already planning on coming this Saturday. I got a hot date lined up for New Year's Eve. One of those gorgeous DC chicks."

"No, Bobby! Not Saturday! I need you here, now!"

"No can do. I guess you forgot that I'm supposed to take Congressman Jensen hunting tomorrow."

"Dammit, Bobby! You're not listening to me. I said I need you here now! Cancel the damn hunting trip," Wayne said loudly and pointedly

"What the hell's going on?"

"I can't tell you. Not over the phone. The future of this company, my future, your future. All could be on the line. I can brief you on this situation when you get here. But you've got to leave *NOW!* And let me know when you take off. Apologize to Jensen for me and tell him we'll make it up to him. Big time. But drop everything and get up here."

"Geez, Wayne. I've never heard you this upset before. This doesn't have anything to do with that little party I gave for Senator Borders, does it?"

"I wish," said Wayne Peters now more calmly. "If this weren't a crisis, I wouldn't ask you to come. But I need you. Tell the congressman that… uh… our DC gun Appeal campaign has run up against some unforeseen resistance, and that you're needed back here ASAP."

"That important, huh?" asked Bobby.

"Yeah. That important."

Chapter 5

Wednesday, December 27, 2006, 9:35 a.m. EST

Wayne was thankful that Bobby Armstrong had called. Getting him involved was the right thing to do. He, if anybody, would understand the situation. It was a career killer – for both of them. Just talking to him had brought about a settling effect on his mental state. Wayne wasn't bipolar, but his mood did an immediate 180 degree turn around - from abject negativity to ebullient positivity. He began to think clearly. Everything seemed to fall into place - what to do with the bodies and the cars; what he would say, what he wouldn't say. Furiously, he hammered away on his computer. He wanted the plan to be completed before Bobby arrived which gave him about six hours. Then once he arrived, recovered from the initial shock of the situation, and, of course, onboard, Wayne would review the plan and if Bobby held true to form, would offer few suggestions, if any at all. Unlike himself, Bobby was a wing-it, reactionary kind of guy. He left the planning to those who did it best. And Wayne was the best.

Chapter 6

Wednesday, December 27, 2006, 11:15 a.m. EST – 10:15 a.m. CST

Nelson Robert Armstrong, one of NAGS' thirteen Board members, was elected president of the organization by the Board in 2000. Bobby (his familiar name) was the most recognizable member of the Board and by far the most popular. During his tenure as president, which traditionally carried a one year term, NAGS membership grew at an unprecedented rate. In 2001, breaking with custom, the board elected him president for a second term. After the 9/11 terrorist attack, NAGS' membership soared to even greater heights and from that time forward, no one else was even considered for president.

Bobby was the perfect spokesman for NAGS. He was born in Texas and grew up hunting with his daddy and granddaddy on his granddaddy's ranch, the Circle A. It was one of the larger ranches in Texas. His family was wealthy, and he took advantage of all the perks that money and power could offer. He was smart, both academically and politically, and extremely popular. He graduated with honors from Highland Park High School and four years later graduated from the University of Texas where he was president of his fraternity and vice-president of the student body. After a year's sabbatical in Europe, he applied for and was accepted at Georgetown University's Law School where his roommate was the son of Texas Senator Edward 'Tex' Keller. The Senator liked Bobby and his aggressiveness. He told Bobby that he had a standing job offer anytime he wanted it. After graduating from Georgetown, Bobby took the Senator up on his offer, working for him in Washington at the Russell Senate building where he learned the 'art' of national politics.

Senator Keller, a former Marine veteran of the Korean and Vietnam wars, lived by the polls. He carefully orchestrated every decision, every meeting, and every appointment by whatever made him popular in the polls. And it worked because he stayed in the Senate for six terms. Being politically astute wasn't the only reason for his long tenure. He took his job as Senator very seriously working long, hard hours for the citizens of Texas with never a hint of scandal, wrongdoing, or any other indiscretion. During that time, he always made himself available to his constituents and community leaders. He also visited local churches, synagogues, mosques, diners, bowling alleys, coffee shops where he listened to his people, and if they had problems, he was there to help. Unlike most politicians, he personally answered all senate related correspondence - even from those who didn't support him. His tenure allowed him to be on the most important Senate committees, one of which was the Senate Armed Services Committee.

It was at one of the parties hosted by NAGS honoring the Senator that Bobby first met Wayne Peters. Wayne took an immediate liking to Bobby, but everybody liked Bobby. Wayne tried to get him to come work for NAGS. But Bobby had other plans. When he left the Senator's office, he went back to Texas to run for the State House. Because of his inherited wealth, he didn't have to work which allowed him to spend every available minute running a door-to-door campaign. With only a couple of months before the election, the polls showed his opponent a few points ahead and their numbers growing. Bobby's hopes of being elected seemed completely dashed when his opponent's teenage son was killed in an automobile accident. Overcoming the sympathy vote seemed impossible. But when the boy's autopsy revealed large quantities of heroin and alcohol, most of the sympathy voters, as well as non-committed voters, moved into Bobby's camp. His opponent spent the last few weeks of the campaign burying his son and defending him against an unrelenting press. Bobby was very sympathetic. Never once did he try to capitalize on his opponent's son's drug use and steadfastly refused to become embroiled in the media's hatchet job. His opponent who saw his short-lived lead slipping away tried to use Bobby's youth and family wealth against him, but it backfired. Bobby knew the demographics of his district. Thirty-five percent of the voters were under the age of 44, and his district had two of the wealthiest cities (Highland Park and University Park) in the U.S. If anything, his youth and wealth helped him. He had learned well from the Senator who accompanied him on many of his speaking engagements. It was good for Bobby, and it was good for the Senator. Bobby eventually won the election with over 60% of the popular vote. His opponent never returned to politics.

Bobby remained a state representative for four terms. But, his political ambitions were higher. He wanted Senator Keller's seat once the Senator retired. He and the Senator had discussed the possibility many times but decided he didn't have the state-wide appeal or name recognition. When he chose *not* to run for a fifth term, all of the major Texas lobbyists came calling. Most of the big names made their pitch. But Bobby wasn't interested. He could make a lot of money as a lobbyist, but he had money. What he wanted was power. It was at a NAGS' political rally in Texas that Bobby saw his future, his access to local *and* national recognition. Within a month, he became Wayne Peters' personal assistant. A couple of years later he was promoted to NAGS' national publicist where he became one of their main featured speakers. He was funny, smart, and looked and talked like Dr. Phil. In fact, he had been asked many times for 'Dr. Phil's' autograph. In 1997, with endorsements from Peters and the Senator who was now his new father-in-law, Bobby was elected to NAGS' Board from the 5th district. In 2000, when the board decided they needed a younger, more aggressive president, they elected Bobby.

Six years later (2006), Bobby's hard work had paid off. His exploratory committee had recommended that he announce his Senate candidacy the day Senator Keller announced his retirement. Currently, the Senator and Bobby were waiting on the outcome of the Parker vs. District of Columbia appeals case. They had good vibes about the ruling, expecting a decision no later than June 2007.

* * * * * * * * * *

Wayne's call had caught Bobby completely off guard. Especially when he said the future of NAGS could be on the line. If that was true, that meant he could say 'adios' to his Senate bid. That couldn't happen. Nothing was going to get in the way of *his* future regardless of what it took, how much money it cost, or who got hurt in the process.

Two hours later, Bobby Armstrong, still dressed in his Wranglers, boots, and wearing his favorite 'LBJ' hat, took off from Love Field in one of NAGS' private jets, a Gulfstream G150 heading for Washington Executive Airport located in Maryland. He was not accustomed to being left in the dark, regardless of the reason. He and Wayne had always kept in constant communications, even in the worst of times - like the Columbine killings, the crazy snipers in the Washington/Virginia area, and the Philadelphia Amish killings. To abruptly cancel a hunting trip with one of Washington's most powerful legislators with no real good explanation was most alarming. Wayne had better have a damn good reason!

Chapter 7

Wednesday, December 27, 2006, 2:32 p.m. EST

Having completed his plan, Wayne scrolled through his work, reviewing it, marveling at his creativity and ingeniousness. *This is good! This is really good. This might actually work!* One of the addendums to his plan was a shopping list of supplies he would need from Home Depot. Using the internet, he located a store on Rhode Island Avenue, only a couple of miles from the office. The trip to the big box store would give him a sorely needed break and a chance to clear his mind. As he printed the list, he heard the faint sound of a phone ringing from outside his office. Shortly after it stopped, his office phone began to ring. *Who the hell is that?* The caller-ID showed it to be his off-hours answering service. They would never call his office unless it was important.

"Hello, Mr. Peters. I hope I'm not interrupting anything, but I have Ms. Hamilton's son, Kyle, on the line. He said he was trying to reach his mom. When she didn't answer her office line, it rolled over to us. Do you want to speak to him?"

Things were happening, sooner than expected. His plan was nearly ready but was he? Could he pull this off? Would Kyle see through him - his deception? There was only one way to find out.

"Sure. Put him through," Wayne said while simultaneously grabbing the shopping list from the printer. "Wayne Peters," he answered, his voice calm and controlled.

"Mr. Peters, I hate to bother you, but I was looking for my Mom. She said she was working today, but her phone keeps rolling over to the answering service. Do you mind asking her to call me when she gets a chance?"

Watch what you say. "Your mother's not here. She was… uh… here earlier today… uh… helping me out, but she's already gone. We got finished much quicker than I thought. Have you tried her cell?"

"Yes, sir. But she's not answering."

Wayne paused a few seconds as if thinking, then said, "I can't be certain, but I thought she said something about going shopping. Kyle, is everything all right?"

"Oh, yes sir. It's not an emergency or anything like that."

"Well, if I see or hear from her, I'll tell her to call you." Wayne paused a moment to reflect on the words he had just said. *If I see or hear from her.* What a sham. No one would ever hear or see that wonderful lady again. Then as if it would soften the sorrow and turmoil that was about to be reaped upon the Hamilton family, Wayne offered, "I don't know if I ever told you what an asset your mother has been to this organization. She's a wonderful person as well as an excellent worker. I don't know how this office would function without her. Kyle, you have been blessed to have had a mother like Margie." *Have had? Quit talking. You're saying too much. Less is better.* Then, as if he were a dummy and a ventriloquist were talking for him, "Let me know if there's ever anything I can do for you or your brother." *Well, how stupid was that?*

After the call ended, Wayne continued to berate himself mentally as he pounded his desk with his fist. Why hadn't he stuck to the plan? He had adlibbed - a sure-fire way of screwing up everything. He couldn't let that happen again. On a positive note, he hadn't detected any panic or worry in Kyle's voice which was good. But it would come. Then the anger. Then the sorrow and grief. And there was nothing he could do about it.

Chapter 8

Wednesday, December 27, 2006, 2:40 p.m. EST

That was really weird, thought Kyle after ending his call with Peters. *Let me know if there's ever anything I can do for you or your brother? The man has never said two words to me and I don't think he's ever met my brother.*

Kyle Hamilton was Margie's youngest son. Moms aren't supposed to have favorites, but Kyle certainly came close – probably because he looked like his late father. Kyle was a tall, brown-haired, brown-eyed handsome young man in his late twenties. He worked for the Office of Personnel Management in Washington writing procedure manuals. Working for the government was not what he had dreamed of doing after he got out of college. He wanted to be a professional golfer. He had the desire, attitude, confidence and the equipment. He only lacked one thing – a really good game. His job with the government paid well, offered numerous advancement opportunities, and lots of time off to play golf – which he did every chance he got. His passion for the game was one of the main reasons, much to his mother's dismay, why he had yet to have a meaningful relationship.

Kyle's office on E Street was less than a mile from NAGS headquarters. It was close enough that he and his Mom would oftentimes meet for a quick lunch, an after-work drink or dinner. He and his Mom had become extremely close after the death of his Dad. He tried to stay in touch as much as possible in case she needed him which was almost never. She had become very independent. When they did go to lunch, they would usually meet somewhere between their two offices, a place within walking distance. She wanted the exercise, wanted to keep in shape – especially since she had met a new friend. And they always went Dutch unless it was to celebrate a special occasions - those red-letter days like raises, promotions, new cars, whatever.

While today wasn't exactly a red-letter day, it had potential to be. Earlier that morning, Kyle had met a girl. A very nice girl. Maybe *the* girl. They had even gone out to lunch together. She was young, attractive, and very sweet. Best of all, she played golf. In fact, she'd been on the University of Maryland's golf team. That's why he was trying to reach his Mom. He wanted to share the good news.

What Peters had said about his Mom having gone shopping would certainly explain why she wasn't answering her cell. She loved to shop. Kyle refused to go with her because she looked at *everything*. She'd fill up her cart and then put most everything back with her practical side showing up just before checkout. *Can't interfere with her shopping.* Kyle smiled at the thought. More than likely her cell phone was in the deep recesses of her pocketbook where she couldn't hear its ring, couldn't get to it, or was in the checkout line and couldn't be bothered. But she'd call him back when she had time. Her phone was her lifeline to her friends and family. She knew more about the features of her phone than most people her age and younger. She was constantly downloading new ring tones, pictures, anything new.

As Kyle sat in his office cubicle thinking about his good news, in retrospect, maybe it was a good thing that he *hadn't* reached her. His past relationships had always been sketchy. Some took off immediately, then fizzled; some took off slowly, then fizzled; and then some just fizzled right out of the gate - with fizzled being the operative word every time. No sense in getting anybody's hopes up. Especially his Mom's.

Chapter 9

Wednesday, December 27, 2006, 2:51 p.m. EST

With his supply list in hand, Wayne headed to his car. Out of fear and caution, he had checked and re-checked the front and side doors of the building making sure they were locked, dead-bolted, and the security system activated. Before leaving the parking lot, he did a quick drive around to the back of the building where he saw Margie Hamilton's car parked in her assigned spot. So typical of her. With no one else expected at the office that day, she could've parked anywhere. But Margie would never do that. She had her assigned spot, and that's where she parked.

Before turning onto Massachusetts Avenue, Wayne checked his rearview mirror to make sure that the wrought-iron parking gates had completely closed. Through the gates, he saw Jim's Mercedes which spanned two parking spaces. So unlike him. Obviously he was not himself. But why did he go off the deep end? He had not been fired, just placed on administrative leave. But even if he were terminated at the January board meeting, he would have been given a huge severance package – probably in the three to five million dollar range depending on the generosity of the board. He would never have to work again. He would have known that. In retrospect, maybe he should have reviewed this with Jim at their Tuesday meeting. Or even today, before Jim worked himself up into a frenzy and went postal. Wayne shook his head. All the woulda's, coulda's, and shoulda's.

Out of habit, Wayne turned on his car radio. It was set to an AM station, and a nationally syndicated conservative talk show was in progress. Not surprisingly, the topic of conversation was the DC gun appeal. Wayne couldn't help but be amused as the host, a fervent supporter of the appeal, belittled a caller who tried earnestly but unsuccessfully to argue against the appeal. The caller was very passionate but obviously very ignorant on the subject. The host seemed to take pleasure in patronizing, berating, humiliating and interrupting the caller to the point where he began stuttering and yelling obscenities then abruptly hung up. Wayne wondered if the caller was one of NAGS' plants from an established network of hired operatives whose mission was to make calls into talk shows like this one and others throughout the country offering their opinions, both pro and con, on gun rights, the DC appeal, and the 2nd amendment. NAGS made certain that the hired callers who championed their agenda were articulate, knowledgeable, and calm.   The callers who were hired to oppose NAGS' viewpoints were to sound emotional, lack basic facts, seem uneducated and easily discredited.   While borderline unethical, NAGS felt these plants provided a public service in educating the masses.

The next phone-in caller to the talk show had just begun to bash the previous caller when Wayne spotted the Home Depot's large parking lot. He had never been a regular customer of the big box store like some of his neighbors who seemed to have a weekend addiction. He had never been a do-it-yourself, fix-it kind of guy. Still, the enormity of the place and all the different things you could buy simply amazed him. Too bad they didn't sell guns or ammo like Walmart and Kmart.

Anonymity was most important so he roamed the aisles looking for his supplies rather than asking any of the clerks where they might be found. He located the majority of the items including heavy-duty plastic tarps, overalls, caps, booties, latex gloves, duct tape, and wood putty in the paint section. Paper towels and large garbage bags were found on the cleaning supplies aisle. The two digging shovels were discovered in the outdoor tool and garden section. The hardest item to find was the rubber boots which were located in one of the most faraway aisles in the store. He had spent more time there than he had planned but, nonetheless, had actually enjoyed himself. A needed, albeit temporary, diversion. With all the paint-related items in his cart, he looked like any other do-it-yourselfer, getting ready to repaint the living room - something that always happened to the unlucky husbands whose wives had seen too many episodes of HGTV.

With no time on his schedule for lunch, Wayne grabbed a Coke and Payday candy bar at the self-checkout register where he paid in cash. This way, there would be no paper trail and no cashier to remember him. He systematically scanned each item as they would be needed according to his plan and bagged them accordingly. Just before scanning his last item, his cell phone rang. A quick glance showed it was Bobby. There was no way he could answer the phone and risk having the customers waiting behind him hear anything Bobby had to say. He let the call go to voicemail.

In the privacy of his car, he listened to the call. There was no urgency in his voice. He said that he was in Maryland and would be at the office in less than two hours depending on traffic and road conditions. He also said he was most curious about the *big* secret. He didn't ask for a return call, so Wayne didn't.

As Wayne drove out of the Home Depot's parking lot, almost simultaneously an old dented, dirty white van with two black occupants pulled into the NAGS parking area.

Chapter 10

Wednesday, December 27, 2006, 3:43 p.m. EST

The white van cautiously made its way into the NAGS parking lot and did a brief stop next to the Mercedes as if to check the car for occupants. Apparently satisfied with what they say, the van eased around to the back parking area, made a U-turn then returned to park in the handicap spot next to the Mercedes. Two black occupants in the van got out and slowly made their way to the side door where the taller of the two, who had a decided limp, made several unsuccessful attempts at entering the proper security code. After failing three times, he reached in his pocket and pulled out a pair of thick prescription glasses. This time he had no trouble entering the correct code and the two entered the building.

Hardly five minutes had passed when Wayne pulled into the parking area. As soon as he saw the van, he knew he had a problem. *What the hell are they doing here?* He parked next to the van and quickly ran into the building. He had to stop them. Get them out of there. *Oh, God! How long have they been here?* He knew it couldn't have been too long or the police would have been swarming everywhere. Once in the building, he spotted an old black man hobbling from the breakroom carrying a big black trash bag.

"Jerome! What are you doing here? Where's Idella?" Wayne asked, almost yelling.

"Merry Christmas, Mr. Wayne," responded Jerome Davis whose voice had a slow and gentle cadence - one that was pleasing to the ear. "Me and Idella thought we'd get you out of the way today. Hope that's awright with you. We just didn't think anyone would be here today, being the holidays and all. I pro'bly shoulda called."

Jerome was a tall, elderly man, in his late 60's. His tall thin, slightly stooped frame was cloaked in a faded blue jumpsuit and a heavy grey Georgetown University sweatshirt that matched the grey in his partially receding hairline. He and his wife, Idella, were the NAGS' office cleaning crew, having worked there for over five years. They had moved from North Carolina eight years earlier after the textile mill where they had worked for over 25 years shuttered its doors.

Wayne could hardly focus on Jerome or what he was saying as he searched the room and the stairway for Idella. *Oh God! Where is she? I've got to stop her!* She had keys to every office - including his.

"So where's Idella?" Wayne asked again as calmly as possible even though his heart was racing and his eyes darting everywhere.

Jerome could see that Peters was upset and distracted. It was very unsettling. He had never talked to him like this before. Everyone at NAGS, especially Wayne Peters and Margie Hamilton, had always been very kind to him and his wife.

Jerome set the trash bag down on the floor still holding on to the red plastic tie cords.

"Uh… Mis… Mister Wayne…" But before Jerome could finish his sentence, Wayne heard Idella's voice coming from the breakroom. Singing. It was beautiful music to his ears.

"Oh, I just wanted to wish you and Idella a Merry Christmas," said Wayne, his voice now calm and pleasant, more in keeping with his normal demeanor and a welcome change by Jerome.

"Thank you, Mr. Wayne. Thank you. Me and the missus 'preciate that," said Jerome as Idella waddled over to his side.

"Merry Christmas, Mr. Wayne," sang out Idella, her voice filled with joy. She and Jerome had been married for over forty-five years and were a modern-day example of the 'Jack Sprat' nursery rhyme.

"And Merry Christmas to you, Idella," responded Wayne.

"Jerome, I'm sorry if I seemed out of sorts today," said Wayne sensing the need to explain his earlier apprehensive manner, "but we… Jim, Margie, and I… we're trying to wrap up an important project. This is a sensitive matter and we need some *quiet, alone* time." Wayne placed his hand on Jerome's shoulder as an act of friendship. "Matter-of-fact, I'm surprised that Jim or Margie didn't come down and ask you to come back later. So neither of you have seen them? Jim or Margie?"

"No, sir. Ain't seen hide n' hair of them, but we ain't been upstairs yet." Then looking at Idella. "How 'bout we come on back tonight? That way, we don't get in y'all's way."

"No, Jerome. Not tonight. You can catch us next week. In fact, I insist. Regardless of what some people think, I'm not coldhearted, especially at Christmastime. You should be home with your family. So why don't you and Idella pack up, go home and enjoy the rest of the holidays. With Jim, Margie and me the only ones working today, we won't mess things up too much. I promise," said Wayne, forcing a wide smile on his face.

"That's mighty kind of you. Mr. Wayne. Some extra time off would be nice, 'specially with our young'uns in town. Leave us get our stuff, and we'll be on our way."

Having heard everything, Idella rushed back to the breakroom, put up the cleaning supplies and met Jerome at the side foyer. As they were about to leave, she turned to Peters.

"Mr. Wayne, I got a note that I wants to give Miss Margie. She made me and Jerome a plate full of homemade cookies and fruitcake last week, and if you don't mind, I'll just run it up to her desk. I won't bother her if she's there."

"I can do that for you Idella. I'll make sure that Mrs. Hamilton gets your note. I'm sure she'll appreciate it."

You're sweet to do that Mr. Wayne but I ain't so feeble that I can't do it myself."

Before Idella could take her second step, Wayne moved to block her path holding his hand up like a school crossing guard stopping traffic.

"Idella, I'd appreciate it if you let *me* do that," groused Wayne, his raised voice frightening her.

"I'm sorry, Mr. Wayne. I'm sorry," she whispered handing Peters her note then quickly backing away, her head bowed.

"I didn't mean to upset you, Idella. Or you, Jerome," apologized Wayne, looking first at Idella then Jerome. "It's… It's just that we are under a lot of pressure here trying to wrap up a big campaign. I hope you'll understand and forgive me. I will personally make sure Margie gets your note."

"I'd appreciate that," replied Idella, satisfied with Wayne's contrite answer. "She's such a good Christian lady. She's helped me and Jerome many a time when we were a little short if you know what I mean. You tell her that I love her, OK? And y'all all have a Merry Christmas holiday."

That's all he needed right now. Someone telling him what a wonderful woman Margie was. Wayne took the note from Idella, slid it into his pocket then waited at the side door until they had left. With the door ajar, he watched Jerome toss the garbage bag in the dumpster then join Idella who was waiting in the truck.   Only when he saw the truck leave the parking lot and the gate close behind it did his heartbeat begin to slow back down to its normal rhythm.

Chapter 11

Wednesday, December 27, 2006, 3:57 p.m. EST

For ten minutes, Wayne remained at the side door watching the gate making sure Jerome and Idella didn't return. Once he felt quite certain they weren't, he ran out to his car, grabbed the bags of supplies that he needed and rushed back into the building. He secured the side door, then made his way back up to the second floor taking two steps at a time. As he approached his office door, his gait slowed to a crawl. He knew the horrors, the unthinkable, that lay behind it - his Pandora's Box. Eventually, he had to face it. There was work that needed to be done before Bobby arrived. Slowly, he fished his keys from his pocket. His hand trembled as he unlocked the door. Once inside, he immediately locked the door behind him and checked to make absolutely sure it was locked. He placed the bags of supplies on his desk and pulled out the painter's coveralls, shoe covers, and latex gloves. The coveralls and the shoe covers were a one-size-fits-all and easily covered his suit pants, shirt and his Salvatore Ferragamo black Oxfords – a much better solution than stripping to his skivvies and covering his body with trash bags. From the box of latex gloves, he grabbed a couple and slipped them on.

He quickly reviewed his plan making sure he knew all that had to be done before Bobby arrived. Bobby's buy-in was crucial. Without it… Wayne couldn't finish the sentence in his mind as there was none. He shook off the negative thought and began by searching Jim's clothing for his keys and wallet. He placed them on his desk next to the two handguns. He then spent the next two hours 'mummifying' the two bodies by rolling each one up into one of the clear plastic tarps then sealing them with duct tape. Once he finished, he slid the bodies into the storage vault along with the garbage bags containing all of the blood-stained paper towels, the used booties and latex gloves.

Afterward, he returned to his desk and collected the guns and shell casings, placed them in a large envelope, and then stored them in the back of one of the storage vault's secure filing cabinets - the ones that have combination locks. Lastly, in an effort to delay rigor mortis, he set the vault's thermostat to its coldest temperature before closing and locking its air-tight door.

The whole process of dealing with Jim's and Margie's bodies had been exhausting to him, both physically and mentally. Rather than return to his desk, he leaned against the vault's door trying to gather his thoughts. From there, he surveyed his office. Everything seemed back to normal. No evidence of the earlier debacle. Nothing to suggest that this had been the worse day of his life. Without warning, the questions began bombarding his brain. Why didn't he see it coming? Could he have prevented it? Could he have said anything that would have calmed Jim? And why couldn't Margie have walked out of the vault ten seconds later? Or earlier? Or not at all? Why didn't he call the police? Did Jerome or Idella sense anything wrong? And the stupid things he said to Kyle, would he think anything was awry? And Bobby? What if he wouldn't help? *Oh, God!*

Eyeing the cut crystal decanter on his credenza, he headed over to the table, poured a short bourbon and water then quickly downed it – a jolt of liquid courage. Wayne had never been a heavy drinker. But if ever there was a time that warranted getting totally wasted, this was it. However, sanity prevailed. Getting shit-faced was not part of the plan. He poured himself a second, much weaker drink then he headed to his office door where, once again, he visually inspected the room for anything odd or out of place. Satisfied, he unlocked the door and left it ajar so hopefully he could hear Bobby when he arrived. While nursing his second drink, he carefully removed his coveralls, folded them, and placed them back into their original Home Depot bag. They would be needed again - later. That was part of his plan.

Chapter 12

Wednesday, December 27, 2006, 5:40 p.m. EST

Quarter-size snowflakes were just beginning to fall as Bobby arrived at the NAGS headquarters building. He hated the snow. He loved Texas and its warmth. As was his custom, he over-tipped the taxi driver who quickly opened the back door. The driver's face could hardly contain his very wide and extremely grateful smile. Bobby grabbed his suit bag and dashed up the front steps of the old brownstone. Since receiving Wayne's call, he'd had more than seven hours to consider all possible issues and concerns facing NAGS. Nothing came to mind. Nothing that was so secretive, so important that the subject matter couldn't be disclosed over the phone. Nothing that was so important that he *had* to leave a United States congressman high and dry with little explanation, and fly to Washington without even the hint as to what was wrong. Bobby was pissed. He expected to see Wayne opening the front door the moment he exited the cab seeing how nervous and anxious he sounded over the phone. But he wasn't there. Nor was he in the foyer pacing back and forth or at the top of the stairs waiting in anticipation of his arrival.

Bobby dropped his suit bag on the foyer floor and flung his overcoat and 'LBJ' to a nearby chair. His Levi's, plaid shirt and leather boots screamed 'Texas' which he loved. Wasting no time, he headed up the steps to Wayne's office where he found him sitting at his desk with a drink in his hand and staring intensely at his computer screen. He was so deep in thought that he didn't hear Bobby enter the room.

"Well," said the Texan in a loud, sarcastic voice that tinged with anger, startling Wayne, catching him off guard for the second time that day. "Just so you know, I've been worrying my little head off for over seven hours. Seven *long* hours thinking that we've got some major catastrophe on our hands. And there you sit. Drinking. What the hell's going on?" Since Wayne never drank at the office unless it was for a celebration of some kind, he understood Bobby's frustrations.

"Bobby!" said Wayne, rising quickly from his chair. "Thank *God* you're here." Before Bobby could utter a response, Wayne ran around his desk and instead of shaking his hand, began hugging him most vigorously. Feeling the startled Texan stiffen, Wayne quickly released him.

"What the hell's wrong with you?" barked Bobby. "Are you crazy? So what's so damn secretive that you couldn't tell me over the phone? I left Congressman…"

"I shot Jim Barnes," said Wayne, interrupting Bobby's tirade.

"You WHAT!"

"I shot Jim. Killed him."

"OK. Now you're pissing me off."

"Bobby, I'm not kidding. See for yourself."

Then Wayne turned his back to Bobby and walked over to the storage vault and unlocked it. As he did, Bobby eyed his every movement.

"He's in here," said Wayne, pulling open the vault's door.

Bobby did a quick glance at the lump on the floor and then back at Wayne. "OK. No more fucking jokes. What's really going on?"

"Bobby. Take a closer look. This is no joke. Believe me."

Cautiously, Bobby walked over to the open vault and peered in, looking down at the two plastic-wrapped bodies.

"OH MY GOD! YOU DID!"

Curiously, Bobby moved closer to get a better look at what appeared to be two mannequins rolled up in clear plastic sheets. Even through the opaque plastic sheets, he could make out Jim's face in the larger of the two roll-ups.

"OH GOOD GOD! THIS IS BAD!" bellowed Bobby now fully realizing that this was no joke. "Who's… who's the other one?" he stuttered pointing to the smaller of the two wrapped bodies.

"That's Margie Hamilton."

"You killed the Hamilton woman, too? Why? What the hell's going on here?" asked Bobby, horrified at the sight and alarmed of the situation. Maybe he was next. Is that why Wayne had called him to Washington? To kill him, too? Had the stress of the Appeal campaign finally gotten to him causing him to flip out, go postal?

"Where's the police? Why didn't you didn't call the police?"

"I… uh…"

"Look. I don't know what you did, why you called me or why you haven't called the cops but I'm calling them now!" interrupted Bobby pulling out his cell phone while cautiously watching Wayne's every move.

"Wait! Wait! Wait!" Wayne pleaded as he watched Bobby slowly back away from the vault. "Just give me a chance to explain. Then if you still want to call the police, I won't stop you."

This was *not* what Bobby had expected. Not in his wildest dreams. He looked skeptically at Wayne, then punched in 911 on his cell and stopped before pushing the 'SEND' button. Instead, he held his thumb over the button making sure that Wayne could see that he was prepared to push it should the need arise. Keeping full eye contact, he slowly positioned himself between Wayne and his office door - just in case he needed a quick exit.

"OK. Explain. I'm listening."

Wayne knew that Bobby had a short fuse and attention span, so he wanted to be brief as possible. "Jim came to the office this morning, drunk, mad as hell, and acting like a crazy person."

"So you shot him?"

"No. Well yes. I shot him. But please… let me finish. Like I said, Jim came here all drunk and crazy. He worked himself up so much that instead of talking about his situation, he pulled a gun on me and actually tried to shoot me. Luckily for me, his safety was on. So while he fumbled around trying to unlock it, I pulled my gun from my desk and shot him first."

"So why'd you shoot Margie?" asked Bobby, confused.

"I didn't shoot her. Jim shot her. Just as he was hit, he shot at me but missed and hit Margie in the head as she came from the vault."

"That crazy son-of-a-bitch!! I wish I'd been here and I would have shot him myself. So why didn't you call the police? It was obviously self-defense," said Bobby, feeling somewhat relieved. Unconsciously, he cleared the 911 numbers from his phone and put it back in his pocket. He wasn't sure why he was relieved, especially with two dead bodies in the room. Maybe it was the fact that he wasn't about to be the third.

"I considered it. Real hard. But think about it, Bobby. The press would skewer us alive. Their pages would be filled with stories, pictures, and editorials about two of our employees being killed with guns. Illegal guns, at that. Our careers would be over. NAGS might not survive the onslaught. And if the press didn't kill us, the lawsuits would. I didn't think we had any other choice."

Bobby wasn't prepared for this. What had happened here was worse than anything he could have imagined. He looked at the two dead bodies then at Wayne who had a look of desperation about him - something he had never seen before. He carefully considered his options, his career, his future. Truth be known, he didn't care what happened to NAGS or Wayne for that matter. But his Senate bid. That's what mattered. And it would all go down the tubes if NAGS' reputation (which also meant his reputation) was ruined.

After mulling it over in his mind for a few minutes, Bobby answered, nodding his head as he did. "I think you did the right thing, calling me, and not calling the police. You're right. We'd be crucified. Run out of town. We probably couldn't get a job shoveling horse shit if this hit the fan."

"So, what do you think?"

"What do I think? I don't think I have a choice. I think you need help. Look at that *lard ass*," fumed Bobby, pointing to Jim's body, livid about the sudden upheaval in his life. "There's no way you can move that crazy, son-of-a-bitch out of here by yourself. You need me. So what do we do with the bodies?"

Wayne headed over to the credenza and poured a drink for Bobby and refreshed his own, mostly with water.

"I've had a lot of time to work on a solution and have put together a plan."

"And why am I not surprised? Why can't we take the bodies over to the Potomac and dump them in the river? Zip. Zip. Zip."

"It's not going to be that easy, Bobby. We can't have both Jim and Margie go missing at the same time. That would be too coincidental, raising suspicions."

"Yeah. You're right. Didn't think about that. So what do we do? What's your plan?" asked Bobby as he settled into one of the two burgundy-leather wingback chairs angled toward each other and facing Wayne's desk.

Wayne moved over to the other wingback and got comfortable.

"You want the detailed or the condensed version?"

"Do you even need to ask?" Bobby wasn't a detail person. He lived by briefs and summaries. Cliff notes were his mainstay in college.

"So Margie will be a carjacking victim. We'll place her body in some dark alley, near Capital Street and park her car a few miles away. I'm guessing it'll take a day or two for anyone to find her body and maybe another couple of days for the police to make an identity depending on how soon she's reported missing. And that won't be us since she's not due back at work until after the first of the year. This should keep us out of the loop. Totally uninvolved." Wayne paused for a second. "So what do you think so far?"

"I like it. It's simple. Believable."

"Well, here's the best part. Margie was a member of NAGS. We use her death to rally support for the Appeal. We say that if Margie had been able to carry her handgun for protection, she would have been able to defend herself and would be alive today. We could even use her picture at our rallies… assuming we get her family's buy-in."

"Oh my God, this is ingenious. Absolutely perfect," Bobby exclaimed, vigorously nodding his head in approval.

"It's most important that we have the timing right before we start using her. I'm thinking that just before the funeral, while Margie's still on everybody's mind, we hold a press conference to denounce the violence in Washington and call on everyone for their support of the Appeal. Then afterward, we hit the internet, airwaves, media, politicos. Anybody and everybody with our 'Margie' campaign. The Appellate Court won't know what hit them. I don't see how in good conscience the court could deny it."

"This is *so* like you. So well thought out that if I didn't know any better, I could almost swear that you even planned the shootings. So what about Jim? What do we do with that asshole?"

"Jim's not going to be so easy," replied Wayne, feeling troubled by Bobby's remarks about him having planned the shootings. But he let it slide. "The plan is to keep him alive for the next few days then have him go missing."

"Alive?" interrupted Bobby. "How the hell are you going to do that? He's deader 'n a doornail."

"Let me continue. Then you'll understand. We can't have both Jim and Margie carjacked. Too coincidental and certainly not believable.

Nor can we have a carjacking and a suicide, not on the same day. And suicide victims usually shoot themselves in the head. I shot Jim in the chest. So we'll have to make it look like Jim's still alive. I've already sent out an e-mail to all of the board members telling them that I've placed him on administrative leave. That we'll discuss the issue at the January's board meeting. I've also sent out a similar e-mail to the office personnel so they won't expect him back at work. For the next couple of days, Jim will seem to have totally isolated himself from the outside world, obviously embarrassed over his job situation. His landline will be off the hook, and his cell phone turned off so it appears that he's not taking any incoming calls. Then we'll have him surface again. Maybe Saturday or Sunday. That's when 'he' (Wayne finger quoting *he*) will send out an e-mail to you and the other board members complaining about my callous treatment of him but not respond to any replies. Then sometime next week, he'll start sending out emails again. This time sounding even more distraught than ever over the prospect of losing his job… saying that he's too old to start looking for another job and criticizing me for doing this to him. Then, he'll accuse me of causing Margie's death. That I worked her too hard. That I wasn't caring. That I made her come into work that day. That I should have known that Washington wasn't safe. Then the emails will stop. He'll vanish. Go missing, never to be seen again."

"Yeah. Kinda like Jimmy Hoffa. So where do we dump him?"

"I thought we could bury him at our hunting lodge. In the barn. We can control who and when it can be used. Then sometime in late January, we'll have the barn's floor paved. Nobody will ever find him. That's my plan."

"I like it. I like what you've done. It's well thought out. Just what I would expect. So when do we do this… you know… dump the bodies?"

"Tonight, when it's dark and when there's little traffic. I don't think we can wait any longer. I've got the temperature in the vaults set to its lowest, but it's not a refrigerator, so I'm worried about the bodies decomposing. Once that happens, there's no way we could ever explain that smell."

"Good point. So what do we do now?"

"We need to get a rental car. One with a big trunk. And we need to move Jim's car around to the back of the building. That's it. Then we wait for dark."

"Wayne, I hope you don't think I'm being cold-hearted when I say this, but I feel excited… pumped! I can't wait to get started. This could be the most fun I've had since college days. I'm sorry about Jim and the dead lady, but you know what they say. Shit happens."

Chapter 13

Wednesday, December 27, 2006, 6:02 p.m. EST

Shit happens? While Bobby drove the driver of the Enterprise rental car back to the rental office, Wayne continued to reflect on what Bobby had said. That he was looking forward to it. Excited about it. Pumped. That it was going to be fun. Only Bobby could trivialize something as tragic as death. Especially Margie's. Maybe bringing him in to help was a big mistake. But there was no turning back now. As tactless and thoughtless as his comments were, it was also his strength. Nothing seemed to get to him. Not even something as serious as death. But, who was he to criticize Bobby? After all, it wasn't Bobby's idea to use Margie's death as a rallying point for their Appeal campaign. Or using her family to further NAGS' agenda. Maybe he was worse than Bobby. But fun? No. There was no place for fun in this plan. This would be all business.

At his computer, Wayne looked over his plan one more time making sure that every detail of their impending evening's mission was committed to memory. A checklist would have been helpful, but that wasn't going to happen. There could be nothing in writing linking him, Bobby or NAGS to the two deaths. Even the Home Depot shopping list, innocuous as it was, had concerned him. So he hand-shredded it and tossed in an outside trash bin at the store. Their greatest exposure, other than the two bodies still in the vault, was the action plan on his computer. But all his files, as well as his computer, were password protected. No one, not even the IT department, could access his computer without his authorization – a benefit of being the executive vice-president. Regardless, once this whole ordeal was over, he would erase the files, then remove and destroy the hard drive. That was the last item on his action plan.

By the time Bobby pulled into NAGS' parking lot driving a white Chevrolet Impala, Wayne was ready to go. He was wearing his previously worn white coveralls over his dress clothes and black rubber boots in place of his black loafers. To minimize or eliminate boot prints, he also wore shoe covers over the boots. Latex gloves covered his hands, and a painter's cap donned his head. Laid out on his leather couch was an identical outfit for Bobby.

Placed on his desk was Margie's handbag, which he had found in the bottom right-hand drawer of her desk. Alongside her handbag or pocketbook as Margie called it – a throwback to her southern heritage - were two key rings - her GM car keys on one ring and her office and apartment keys on another. Finding them had been an ordeal. The bag had more pouches than a mob of kangaroos, some zippered, some not, each a resting place for all the things that most women required - lipstick, compact, hairbrush, nail file, lip gloss, hand cleaner, Kleenex, Visine, hand lotion, Advil - a mini-CVS in a bag. Hidden among all of that stuff in her bag were recent church bulletins, her thick wallet, and her cell phone with messages that would never be returned.

For whatever reason, maybe curiosity or maybe just trying to kill time, Wayne pulled out Margie's wallet and opened it. Besides a few credit cards, health insurance cards and her NAGS membership card, he found an insert with sleeves filled with pictures. He slowly leafed through them. They were mostly pictures of her two sons and her late husband. He also saw a picture of Margie at a Christmas party with a distinguished-looking gentleman by her side, the two holding hands. The photo was dated only a few weeks ago. He knew of the gentleman and the Christmas party as that's all Margie had talked about for days on end. It was at a fancy country club, and she wanted to have the perfect dress. She wanted to make him proud.

As he flipped to the next picture, suddenly, without warning, the guilt that he had so successfully suppressed for the last nine hours sucker-punched him, invading his whole body. His hand shook as he looked at a photo of Margie all decked out in her hunting gear, rifle in hand, standing next to him and the Senator from Georgia. She was happy and alive. This was so wrong - what he was doing. So wrong.

Chapter 14

Wednesday, December 27, 2006, 6:42 p.m. EST

"Don't you look sweet!" laughed Bobby, his sudden appearance interrupting Wayne's anguish. "You plan on doing some painting around here?"

Wayne quickly folded Margie's wallet and shoved it back into her handbag.

"Don't laugh. I've got a matching set that has your name on it," he answered, pointing to the couch.

"What's all those brown spots on yours… Oh jeez. That's blood, isn't it?"

Wayne looked at the spots then gave him a quick nod while wondering why he hadn't thought of getting spares.

Bobby followed Wayne into the office and began slipping into his coveralls. "I pray to God we don't see anybody we know," he muttered, almost laughingly.

Wayne ignored him.

While Bobby struggled to pull on the rubber boots, Wayne filled him in with the plans for the evening, keeping it short and to the point. Bobby would drive Margie's car and follow behind Wayne in the rental car. Both bodies would be in the trunk of the rental car. They would drive over to Capital Street and dump Margie's body in one of several possible alleyways that Wayne had committed to memory. Afterward, they would drive her car into Maryland and then leave it abandoned with the key in the ignition in one of Prince George County's high crime areas. Next, they would drive to NAGS' hunting lodge in Virginia, bury Jim's body in the barn and return to Wayne's Georgetown townhouse. The estimated time to complete all tasks, including drive time, was five to seven hours which meant they could be back in Washington as early as midnight depending on how long it took to dig the grave.

Bobby listened but had no questions, suggestions or changes. He relied heavily on Wayne's acute attention to detail and planning expertise. That was Bobby's management style. If you had good people, you let them do their job. And Wayne was the best, successful at everything he did. Especially planning. There were no reasons to challenge Wayne or his plan.

Once Bobby was dressed and looking like Wayne's twin, the process of moving the bodies to the trunk of the rental car began. This came none too soon as rigor mortis was setting in. Wayne's earlier decision to move the bodies to the vault and to lower the temperature had proved to be a wise one.

Moving Margie was no problem. She was small in stature and light in weight. As if moving a rolled-up oriental rug, each man simultaneously hoisted her body up onto their shoulder and carried her down the steps stopping at the breakroom long enough for Wayne to flip off the breaker switch to the automated outdoor security lights. Even though this meant they would be working in the dark, it allowed them to move the bodies without fear of being observed through the wrought iron parking gates. With Wayne in the lead, the two men moved from the breakroom, out of the building through the side entrance and down the steps to the rear of the rental car. Then like a couple of pallbearers, they gently lowered Margie's body into the trunk and shoved her as far back as possible to make room for Jim's body.

Wayne had a different plan for moving Jim's body. Its size and weight precluded them from moving it as they had with Margie's. Instead, they rolled the body onto an area rug they had brought up from the main foyer. The rug had been flipped so that the soft wool-pile was face down making for less resistance as they pulled the body out of the office and onto the elevator. Once they reached the main floor, they slid the body out of the building and onto the side entrance landing. From there, the two men lifted the body off the rug, lugged it down the steps and heaved it into the trunk. Before it was over, both men were breathing hard, gasping for air. Wayne wondered if Bobby was having fun now.

Before returning to the building, Wayne moved the remainder of the recently purchased supplies from his Jag to the backseat floorboard of the rental car. Meanwhile, Bobby carried the rug back to the foyer, retrieved his boots from Wayne's upstairs office and returned to the foyer where he made himself comfortable in one of its overstuffed chairs, eagerly anticipating the evening's activities. Wayne had no time for rest. He reset the electrical breaker that controlled the security lights then ran back upstairs where he closed and locked the storage vault.

After checking his computer to make sure it was turned off, he surveyed the office looking for anything unusual or out of place. All appeared to be in order. Then for the next few minutes, he paced, fidgeted and constantly checked his watch, waiting until it was time for the night's activities to begin.

At 6:55 p.m., the old Regulator on the wall just outside his office began to chime. The antique clock was five minutes fast. That was Margie's doing. When she wound the clock every Monday, she added five minutes to the time to make sure she was never late to any meetings or appointments. Her absence was going to be hard on everyone - especially Wayne.

On his way out of the room, he grabbed his overcoat, Margie's handbag, her keys, and the bags of supplies which also contained his dress shoes. Before closing the door, he once again glanced around the room. The big spacious office seemed so normal with everything in order. It had always been a place where he could find refuge. It was his sanctuary. But it would never be the same again. Never. Staring blankly into the room, he slowly slid his hand down his office wall flipping off the light switch. He eased the door shut and locked it, turning the doorknob two or three times to make absolutely sure it was securely locked.

Downstairs, he found Bobby, sitting in the foyer, whistling and fiddling with the brim of his 'LBJ' in a trance-like state as if he didn't have a worry in the world.

"I see you thinking. You have any questions?" asked Wayne.

"Nope. I'm good. Just making sure everything's set in this little ol' pea-brain of mine."

"So are you ready?"

Bobby stood up and looked at Wayne with excitement in his eyes.

"Oh yeah. Showtime."

Chapter 15

Wednesday, December 27, 2006, 7:04 p.m. EST

"Quit bugging me, Nate!" Jamie Barnes half yelled into his cell phone. "I'll get you the fuckin' money… just as soon as I can reach my old man."

"Dude, I ain't playing around. You either git here by eight, or I'm selling the shit to another garbage head. I got bills to pay."

"I'll be there! I'll be there! Just please don't sell it to somebody else! Please!"

Jamie slapped his cell phone shut. He hated begging Nate. So degrading. Even worse, he hated having to beg his old man for money. Money he needed for drugs. But he had no choice. It wasn't like he didn't have any money. He had plenty. Almost $120,000. An inheritance from his grandfather. But his Dad had complete control over it - a stipulation in his grandfather's will until Jamie turned thirty, 892 more days. But who's counting. Until then, he would have to endure his old man's chokehold.

By most accounts, Jim Barnes was very fair to his son. From the inheritance fund, he paid all of Jamie's living expenses, medical coverage and gave him some spending money. It wasn't until Jamie needed that extra spending money, which seemed to be happening more and more often, that his Dad took issue. However, Jamie's constant badgering, pleading and harassing was stronger than his Dad's resistance. So eventually, he would give in but not without lecturing his son on the evils of drugs or the value of working. Those were his Dad's two favorite topics. Jamie was 27 years old, but his old man still treated him like he was 16. Jamie didn't need the sermons. He knew the evils of drugs. Hell, he should. He had been using them for over 13 years. He had been in and out of treatment centers so many times that he could write his own treatment plan. Drugs were his life.

But they hadn't always been. Growing up, Jamie was a normal, happy-go-lucky kid. He was a decent student, hardly ever gave his parents any grief, played sports with his buddies, attended church when his parents occasionally did, even tried Boy Scouts. He did all the right things. Then one day, not long after his 14th birthday, all that changed when one of his best friends dared him to try some weed with him. After that, he was hooked. He wasn't trying to get away from anything. He wasn't stressed about school. He wasn't depressed because he didn't fit in. He wasn't hiding a different sexual orientation. He wasn't whacked out because he hated his parents. He just found that he liked weed. Too much. After a while, when weed's kick wasn't enough, he turned to stronger drugs. He would do almost anything for drugs – run drugs, sell drugs, and steal from his parents. Anything to get his drugs.

After Jamie turned 21, on the advice of his psychiatrist, his parents kicked him out of the house hoping that tough-love would somehow straighten him out, make a man out of him. Hardly two months had passed when his dad, while driving in downtown Washington, saw Jamie, filthy looking and obviously homeless, on a street corner with a sign, begging for money. It was like a knife to the heart. Against the wishes of his wife, Jim moved his son into a spartanly furnished old house near Catholic University, bought him a three-year-old Honda Civic and gave him a little spending money. In return, Jamie was to get a job or go back to school. That never happened. What did happen was an ever-widening rift in Jim's marriage which ultimately ended in divorce. But Jamie didn't care. Not about his parents, his appearance, the old, dumpy house he lived in. Only drugs. He knew that he had driven the wedge between his parents. His mother believed in tough love. His dad believed in sermons, believed that he could talk his son into giving up the thing he loved most. His dad was a perfect enabler. They had two opposing philosophies on parenting. A deadly combination in a marriage. Before drugs, Jamie would have cared. But now, he didn't.

He needed drugs. He needed money - for Nate, cigarettes, and gas. That's why he wasted little time in getting over to his Dad's Watergate apartment. Time was of the essence. He guided his 1992 Cadillac Sedan de Ville into one of the three Watergate parking spaces. The oversized car completely filled the spot and its elongated rear-end extended well into the smallish driving lanes. He no longer owned the Civic - a casualty of his cocaine days. Currently, his drug du jour was crack. As he exited the car, he took notice that his father's car wasn't in its usual parking space. But that didn't necessarily mean he wasn't at home. It only meant his car was either parked in someone else's space, in an unassigned space or possibly at a bar where he had been drinking and forced to take a cab home. Jamie didn't like what was happening to his Dad, but, hell, it was his life.

Other than the girth, Jamie looked like his dad. Drugs and his mother's metabolism kept his body gaunt. While he no longer looked completely homeless, his dress was anything but neat or clean as he wore the same shirt and jeans a week at a time. His dirty brown hair was long and usually pulled back into a ponytail. And he shaved about as often as he changed clothes. The long stares he got from the Watergate tenants because of his unkempt appearance no longer bothered him. He was there for one purpose. Money.

While Jamie waited impatiently in the garage for the elevator to arrive, he continued to call his Dad's cell phone and the apartment phone with no answer. The more he called, the angrier he got.

"Why the hell is he ignoring me?" he muttered to himself. That was not like his Dad. They had their differences but he had never shut Jamie out of his life. He was always there for him, in the good times, that were few, and the bad, which seemed to rule Jamie's life.

Once the elevator arrived, he shoved his phone back into his jeans pocket and ducked inside the cabin, pressing the floor button non-stop until the door finally closed. Most of the time, he rode alone as other potential riders refused to be enclosed in the same space - as though he had some kind of contagious disease.

Before the elevator door was completely open, Jamie was out and rushing down the hallway to his dad's apartment. With no regard to whether his father had company, was eating dinner, taking a nap or anything, he began pushing the doorbell numerous times with his left hand while simultaneously knocking loudly on the door with his right.

When no one came, he began yelling at the door. "Come on, Dad. I know you're in there. Open up. Please. Open up." As his demands turned to pleas, he looked at the doorknob, fully expecting to see it turn. Nothing.

Frustration was setting in. Jamie pulled his cell phone from his jeans and checked the time. There wasn't much left. After making sure no one was in the hallway, he pushed his ear up against the door to listen for voices, footsteps, running water. Anything. But heard nothing. Nor did he see any sign of movement when he looked through the peephole in the door. He flipped his cell phone back open and punched in the quick-dial number for the apartment. Through the door, he could hear the faint ringing of the phone. When the call went to voicemail, he canceled it and punched the quick-dial number for his dad's cell. It too went to voicemail. Oddly, he could also hear its muffled ringtone coming from the apartment. *What the hell's going on? Where is that fucker? God, I hope he hasn't stroked out on me. That would really fuck things up.* He took a quick look up and down the hallway. Seeing no one, he pulled out a key to the apartment and let himself in, softly closing the door behind him. His father never knew that Jamie had the missing duplicate set of keys to his apartment, desk, office, and lodge, thinking they had been misplaced or lost when divorce forced him out of his house.

Once in the apartment, Jamie glanced into each room looking for his dad. He was relieved not to find him. As good of a liar he was or thought he was, he had no credible explanation as to how he had gotten into the apartment. Even more important was *not* finding his old man lying on the floor, dead. He needed his dad. After all, he was the only one who actually cared for him *and* he had the money. But something wasn't right. Lights had been left on in the apartment, and, even stranger, the living room had been trashed. This wasn't like his old man. First of all, he was very frugal. TVs, lights, computers were always turned off when not in use. The thermostat was set to 68 in the winter and 72 in the summer. Left-overs ruled. Secondly, he was a neat-freak. Everything in its place and a place for everything. Beds made. No dirty dishes left in the sink. Dirty clothes in the hamper. But Jamie didn't have time to dwell on the whys. More than likely, his dad must have had a major argument with somebody - maybe his mom - and he just wigged out.

With no more time to waste, he walked straight to the safe. It was located in a walk-in closet inside his dad's office, a converted bedroom just off the main foyer. The combination to the safe had been an unintended gift from his dad. It was a day that Jamie would never forget. He had come by to get some money from his dad. After an unusually short five minute sermon, his dad walked over to his desk, opened the top drawer, momentarily gazed down at its contents and then walked into the closet returning with two twenties and a ten. Jamie took the money, gave his dad a big hug and left. Only as he relaxed that night in his raggedy pizza-stained recliner with a joint in one hand and a beer in the other did he realize what he had seen. His dad didn't know the combination to his new safe! He didn't have it memorized, and that's why he looked in the desk drawer! The combination had to be in that top drawer! The next day, learning that his dad would be at a Chamber of Commerce luncheon, he slipped back into the apartment, opened the desk, and sure enough, there sat the safe's manufacturer's tag with its combination just waiting for him to copy. He could hardly contain himself - especially when he discovered how much money his dad kept in the safe. There were hundreds, no thousands of dollars in stacks of ten, twenty, and fifty dollar bills. He stopped counting after seven thousand dollars. The temptation to take a thou or two was overwhelming, but he resisted not wishing to kill the golden goose. He decided to limit himself to fifty dollars each visit figuring that with his newly found cache and the money he could sweet-talk out of his dad, he could manage. Sometimes good things happen to bad people.

Jamie's hand shook as he turned the safe's dial. Normally he was very proficient in opening the safe, usually in less than 30 seconds. But tonight, he was already on his third attempt, his mind preoccupied with fear. Fear that his dad might walk in on him. Fear he might miss Nate. It was the first time he had ever entered the apartment without knowing his dad's whereabouts. When the last tumbler fell into place, he jerked down on the safe's handle and yanked open the door, pissed at how long it had taken.

His jaw dropped in disbelief as he looked at the contents in the safe. *What the hell is this? Where's the money. Oh God! Where's the fuckin' money! Don't tell me he took it!* Instead of stacks of money, there were stacks of red-roped, brown fan folders. Afraid that he had just lost his personal ATM, he began feverishly raking the folders out of the safe - two and three at a time until all but a few lay on the floor. That's when he saw the money. It was still there. Hidden behind the folders. His frayed nerves quickly calmed and his rapid breathing normalized. A smile returned to his face as he removed three or four stacks of ten's and twenty's from the safe. He then pulled two twenty's and a ten, each from the middle of different stacks just in case his OCD father might be logging the serial numbers of the first bill in each stack. He counted the money, making sure he only had taken $50, then folded it, kissed it, and shoved it in the left side pocket of his leather coat. Methodically, he replaced the stacks of money in the safe in the exact order he had found them just in case his dad kept track of their positions. *Gotta think like the old man!* Then he picked up four or five folders, jostled them straight and started to place them back in the safe but stopped. *Oh Jeez! What am I thinking?* Unlike the money that he systematically removed and then replaced back into the safe, he had no clue how to restack the pile of folders that lay around him in a jumbled mess. Had there been an order? If so, was it alphabetical, numerical, date sequenced, relative importance, or just random? Trying to stay calm, he examined the outside of the folders he was holding. Travis was hand-written on one, Stewart, on another, then Richards, Timmons, Vincent. It had to be alphabetical. He would have to go with that. Glancing at the time on his cell, he still had thirty-five minutes. Enough time unless his dad walked in. If that happened, it wouldn't matter what order the folders were in. Working through the alphabet as fast as his mind would allow, Jamie sequenced the folders then placed them back into the safe. He closed the door and returned the dial to the exact position as he had found it. Again, just in case.

It had been an ordeal. His shirt and hair were soaked with perspiration, but his mission was a success. He smiled knowing that his dad would never know.

Chapter 16

Wednesday, December 27, 2006, 7:11 p.m. EST

With Bobby following close behind, Wayne slowly drove down Massachusetts Avenue, turned left onto Mt Vernon and then left onto New York Avenue. Except for an occasional glance into the rearview mirror to check on Bobby, his eyes never left the road. He stayed with the flow of traffic, stopped fully at each traffic light, never tried to beat out any yellow lights and never tailgated anyone as he drove over to the Capitol Street area. The death grip he held on the steering wheel seemed to fuel the tension that occupied his neck and was now invading his head. Every turn of the steering wheel felt stiff and mechanical. This was the part of his plan that he dreaded the most. Driving around with two dead bodies in his trunk. Tomorrow couldn't come soon enough. Until then, he and Bobby were at their greatest risk.

Using MapQuest and Google Earth, Wayne had earlier identified five possible sites to dump Margie's body, all within a mile of each other. He didn't like using or thinking of the word *dump,* but that's what they were doing. Margie deserved better. For security reasons, Wayne elected not to use GPS. Instead, he had the directions to all five sites committed to memory.

While stopped at a red light within a mile of the first site, he grabbed his cell phone from the cup holder and pressed Bobby's speed dial number. He answered immediately.

"Talk to me." His voice was unusually calm, cheerful, but somewhat muffled by some background music.

"What the hell's that noise?" asked Wayne, irritated that Bobby wasn't all business considering the gravity of the situation.

"Noise? Man, that's music. I'm telling you, that old lady has some decent CDs. Listen." Before Wayne could say anything Bobby had already placed his phone next to the speaker for a few seconds then pulled it back to his ear. "In case you didn't know, that's 'Chasing Cars' by Snow Patrol. She's also got some Kelly Clarkson, Daniel Powter, Matchbox ..."

"Bobby! Listen to me," interrupted Wayne who took offense at his cavalier attitude and at having called Margie an old lady. "We don't have time for music. We *must* remain *focused* on what we are doing. This is no time to be acting…"

"Normal?" interjected Bobby. "You think we need to ride around like what? A couple of goobers? This is normal. Music is normal. People will sense when things aren't normal and I know that from firsthand experience.   You act normal, and everything *is* normal." Then, to satisfy Wayne, he turned off the music.

"You're right. It's just that I'm totally out of my comfort zone. You know I've been through some tough situations. But this."

"Hey. It's no big thing. All we got to do is stop, unload our cargo, and leave. You know. Zip. Zip. Zip. We'll be done before you know it."

Maybe it was the words Bobby had said, or how he said them or the casual tone of his voice, but somehow it relaxed Wayne. Like he was talking to someone who had the 'Been There. Done That,' T-shirt. The light turned green, and Wayne drove through the intersection still talking to Bobby. His death grip on the steering wheel had relaxed, and the muscles in his neck no longer demanded the constant twisting, circular motion of his head to ease the tension.

Wayne turned left off New York Avenue and slowed to about ten miles per hour. "We're coming up on the first site. Be there in about a minute. It's this next left. Keep a lookout for anybody. Anything. If it looks clear, we'll circle around and make the drop. Also, keep a sharp eye out for any security cameras. If we see anything, we'll move on to the next one. Oh. And keep your cell open."

Wayne turned on to one of the secondary streets where snow-covered cars were parked along both sides of the road. Large warehouses and aggressively fenced-in self-storage facilities populated the area. He slowed almost to a stop, eyeing one particular building on his far right.

Bobby blinked his headlights and yelled into his cell. "Wayne! Wayne! We got activity at 9 o'clock."

Wayne turned his head one hundred eighty degrees to the left and saw a couple of men jostling with each other in a side alley. It could have been a fight or the two of them could have been just horsing around. It didn't matter. Site one was scratched. No Zip. Zip. Zip there.

"I see 'em. Good job. All right, let's try the next location. It's straight ahead, four blocks, then take a right and immediate left. Just follow me." He laid his open cell phone down on the passenger's seat and sped up to just under the speed limit.

The next site was perfect - an old warehouse with a small parking lot on the side and an alley behind the building. There were no security gates blocking the parking lot, no visible security cameras, and no human activity. The building was illuminated only by a street light and a flood light at the entrance to the alleyway. Wayne drove slowly past the site then circled two more times. Before he reached the entrance to the parking lot, he grabbed his cell off the seat and whispered, "Bobby! Bobby? Do you hear me?"

"Barely."

"If it looks good this time, I'm going in. Watch my back."

"Ten-four," answered Bobby, whose senses were fully heightened by the sheer excitement of the situation.

Wayne set his open phone on the passenger's seat and slowed to a stop at the entrance of the parking lot. This had to be it. One more time around the block and Bobby would probably blow a fuse. He cautiously checked the entire area one more time. Seeing no one, he flipped on his right blinker and turned into the parking lot. He slowly drove the length of the building and then turned into the alley behind the building. As directed, Bobby drove in behind him, made a U-turn, and then drove back to the entrance where he parked Margie's car at a forty-five-degree angle blocking both entry and exit lanes. He turned off the car's headlights but left the engine running, the heater blasting, and the music off. Parked at this angle, he had an unobstructed view of the street and sidewalk. If anybody came his way, he would know.

Wayne drove to the end of the ally and stopped. Other than a big dumpster at the end of the alley, he saw nothing that would cause him to abort the operation.

"Bobby, you still there?"

"That's the plan."

"Everything looks good here. You see anything?"

He checked up and down the street before answering. "You're good on this end. I'll honk twice if I see anything."

Anxiously, Wayne surveyed the dumpster area one more time, looking outside each of the car windows. Seeing nothing, he placed his phone on the passenger's seat and turned off the headlights. He pulled down the bill of his cap, popped the trunk, grabbed one of the newly purchased flashlights from his Home Depot bags and exited the car, leaving the motor running and the car door open. The only sounds he heard were the ever-present sirens blasting away in nearby neighborhoods, the humming of his car's engine, and the crunching of virgin snow under his feet as he slowly circled the dumpster checking out the site.

Satisfied, Wayne walked briskly to the rear of the car. Before lifting the trunk lid, he looked behind him at the alley's entrance one more time to make sure no one was there. Paranoid. Yes. But who wouldn't be? In a couple of minutes, it would all be over, and they would be out of there. Seeing nothing, he lifted the trunk lid, and the trunk light came on.

"Oh no! No! What the hell was I thinking?" muttered Wayne to himself.

Peering into the trunk, he saw Jim's body laying *ON TOP* of Margie's. The situation completely unnerved him. How could he have overlooked something so simple and logical as to which body should be on top? Could there be other holes in his plan?

Like a madman, he began jerking and shoving on Jim's body, trying to reposition it so he could get to Margie. After a few minutes of futile effort, he began beating on Jim with his fist and flashlight, taking his anger and frustration out on the plastic tarp.

"You stupid, stupid son-of-a-bitch! I hate you! I hate you!" He spat out each word in disgust.

Once he had calmed himself, he tried to regroup and rethink the situation. He needed Bobby's help. He ran back to the car and picked up his cell.

"Bobby! Bobby! You there?"

Bobby was adjusting the curve on the bill of his cap when he heard Wayne's voice coming from his cell phone that sat in one of the cup holders. He quickly snatched it up.

"What's the matter? Everything OK?"

"I need you back here. I can't get Margie out of the car. We put that damn lard-ass on top of her. Hurry!"

"On my way!"

Bobby snapped his phone shut and tossed it onto the passenger's seat. He turned off the engine and quickly exited the car, slamming the door behind him. He ran as fast as he could considering the snow and the oversized rubber boots he was wearing. Once in the alley, he could see the silhouette of a frustrated man, standing at the back of a car with his hands on his hips, shaking his head.

When Wayne saw his help approaching, he immediately felt the need to apologize for his oversight.

"I can't believe I didn't think this through. Once I opened the trunk…"

"Forget it. Shit happens. Let's get ol' fat boy out of here so we can get the hell out of Dodge." While Bobby remained unflustered and sympathetic towards Wayne, deep down, he took pleasure when Wayne's plans, which always had every 'i' dotted and every 't' crossed, went awry, and they had to improvise, which was Bobby's planning methodology.

Both men grabbed Jim's body, which now seemed heavier and stiffer than before, pulled him to the edge of the trunk then let him fall to the snow. After rolling him away from the back of the car, they pulled Margie's body from the trunk and, with Wayne leading, carried her over to the dumpster and laid her on the ground. With the adrenalin pumping in both men, Wayne's from anger and Bobby's from the sheer excitement, they easily hoisted Jim's body back into the trunk.

"You need me anymore?" asked Bobby.

"Yes. Help me get her out of this damn thing," he whispered, jerking at the duct tape that encircled the dead body's tarp.

Once the shroud was removed, Bobby headed back to Margie's car. Wayne wadded up the tarp and tossed it in the trunk. He then bent down next to Margie, gently removed the tape that covered her eye, or what was left of her eye, and tossed it in the trunk. He hated leaving her there - in the cold, in the snow, next to a trash dump, in a dark alley behind an old cinder block building. She didn't deserve this. Nobody deserved to be treated like this. *Well… maybe Jim.*

He slowly backed away from Margie never letting her disfigured face leave his sight until he had reached the back of his car. Could he ever forget what he had done? Would he forever mentally castigate himself for leaving her in this hellhole? Almost trancelike, he closed the trunk, got back into his car and started backing out of the alley then suddenly slammed on the brakes when he saw Bobby in his rearview mirror furiously flailing his arms back and forth over his head as a signal for him to stop. Before he could get his side window down, Bobby was at the side yelling at him.

"It's gone. My fucking car's gone!"

"What? What do you mean?" asked Wayne in total disbelief. His plan was unraveling right before his eyes.

"Someone stole my fucking car!"

"Margie's car? You've got to be kidding! I can't believe you left it running!"

"No! I don't think I did. But I must have left the keys in the ignition. I can't remember. I was too busy trying to help *YOU*!" snapped Bobby. "So what do we do now, huh?"

"Shut up and let me think!" Wayne snapped back. He didn't say anything while his mind methodically stepped through his plan. Meanwhile, Bobby paced back and forth in the snow, kicking it every so often, furious at Wayne and himself. More than once he found himself checking the entrance to the parking areas as though the car would miraculously reappear.

Then Wayne looked at Bobby and smiled. A big smile.

"This is perfect! Don't you see? Everything's fine. In fact, it's better than fine. We wanted the car to look like it was stolen and damned if it wasn't. Bobby, I could kiss you! Are you sure *YOU* didn't plan this?"

Both men began laughing, almost uncontrollably because this was how Bobby *did* plan things. Nothing written out or methodically planned. Just spontaneous. It also helped that no harm had been done. Their next stop was the NAGS hunting lodge. As they drove away from the warehouse, leaving Washington, DC, the snow began to beat down on the car with flakes the size of white rose petals. Bobby saw the flurries as a blessing in disguise as it would cover their footprints and tire tracks. Wayne saw the snow as a funeral spray that would cover Margie's body as she lay in state next to the snow-capped dumpster - a sight he would forever remember.

Chapter 17

Wednesday, December 27, 2006, 8:23 p.m. EST

Less than twelve hours ago, Kyle Hamilton didn't even know Miss Katie Chandler. Had never seen her. And now, he sat directly across from her, gazing into her gorgeous dark brown eyes. Van Morrison's *Brown Eyed Girl* came to mind. Without a doubt, she was the most beautiful woman he'd ever met. Their first date was a 'Hey, you wanna grab some lunch' suggestion from Katie where each paid their own way. So technically, maybe it wasn't a date. But they enjoyed each other's company well enough to meet for drinks and dinner after work. A real date.

Katie, who also worked for the US Government as a GAO (Government Accountability Office) accountant, had met Kyle that morning at a mandatory half-day new-hire diversity seminar where he was one of two volunteer instructors and she was one of twenty-two attendees. Katie sat on the first row, third seat from the left and accordingly was the third person to introduce herself to the rest of the class. As part of their introduction, the lead instructor had each participant tell which area of the Government they worked and something interesting about themselves. It was the least boring part of the session that otherwise had everyone struggling with fanny fatigue, nodding heads, and droopy, if not closed, eyelids.

Kyle immediately zeroed in on Katie as she stood and talked about her job as a CPA for the GAO. He was impressed by her easy manner and poise. She had a soft and natural beauty that complimented her friendly demeanor. Her brown eyes were a perfect match for her stylish short brown hair. When she told the class that she played on the boys' high school golf team and then on the University of Maryland's women's golf team, Kyle was hooked. As an instructor, it was his job to listen to each participant as they introduced themselves and make them feel comfortable since, for most, this was their first job. While the majority of the attendees had unexciting, non-descript jobs, their private lives were anything but. One new hire had climbed Mt. Whitney with his dad. Two had served in Iraq. Another had been an intern to the Chief

Justice of the Supreme Court. One had been a sorority sister of Jenna Bush. And another raised llamas. But to Kyle, all paled in comparison to Katie's golf accomplishments.

Once all the attendees had introduced themselves, each instructor did the same. Chris Adams, the lead instructor, meticulously and enthusiastically explained his job and its responsibilities making it seem like he worked in one of the most important sectors of government. Then, just as passionately, he delved into his current training regimen for an upcoming Ironman race to be held the following year in Louisville, Kentucky. Kyle took notice as the entire class seemed to be in awe of Adams' physical attributes. Even with a long sleeve shirt on, his muscles were obvious to anyone with eyes. Kyle made a conscious effort to never stand next to Adams at these seminars as the duo looked like a 'before and after' picture from a muscle magazine. As Adams spoke, Kyle couldn't help but gaze at Katie to see if she was as impressed with him as was the rest of the class. She was. So when it was Kyle's turn to introduce himself, he quickly glossed over his job responsibilities and jumped right into his impending volunteer work at a Nationwide Golf tournament to be held at the Country Club of Woodmore in Maryland. No one seemed to be paying the least bit of attention except Katie.

At the session's first break, Katie made her way over to Kyle and formally introduced herself. She was most interested in his volunteer work at the Nationwide Golf tournament as her parents had been members of Woodmore for more than twenty years until they resigned when their health started failing and they could no longer play golf. The two hit it off right from the start, and at the second break, they sought out each other again. The breaks gave them little time to talk, so Katie suggested lunch after the seminar which in turn led them to agree to meet for dinner at J. Paul's - a restaurant/bar located in the Georgetown area.

By 6 p.m., the restaurant was crowded and noisy, being one of the more popular hangouts in Georgetown. The bar was filled to near capacity with the regulars claiming their seats early. It wasn't unusual to find politicians at the establishment filling the air with lies, half-truths and embellished truths. Neither Katie nor Kyle seemed to care or notice. The conversation between the two was very relaxed and natural. Over the next couple of hours, he learned that she lived in Georgetown, only about four miles from his apartment. Her father had retired from the Government after 43 years of service and her mother was a former schoolteacher who had quit teaching to be a stay-at-home mom when she became pregnant with Katie. He discovered that Katie had considered the LPGA tour after graduating from college but her practical side prevailed. Instead, she chose the business world and moved to Atlanta to work for a large accounting firm passing the CPA exam in the interim. She loved her job and loved living in Atlanta with all the streets named Peachtree but decided to move to Washington to be near her parents after her younger and only brother was killed in Iraq.

It was only when Katie asked about his parents that he remembered that he had yet to hear back from his Mom. While it was unusual for her not to call or text him back, he understood. More than likely, she was either preoccupied with her new 'man' friend or involved with friends at her Wednesday night church supper. He would call her tomorrow. Maybe have lunch together.

Chapter 18

Wednesday, December 27, 2006, 9:07 p.m. EST

Hidden among the hemlocks, pines, beech and oak trees in a valley of the Bull Run Mountains, near the quaint town of Middleburg, Virginia lies the NAGS hunting lodge. It was originally built in 1915 by William Henry Jackson from logs cut from his 500-acre property. Shortly after Jackson's death in 1958, his heirs sold the property to NAGS who used it as a place to bring their most generous and influential supporters to hunt, fish, ride horses, drink, or just relax. While the original structure was never changed, it was upgraded many times to include the latest conveniences. The lodge was not fancy – not like some of the nearby regal horse farms. But for what it was intended, it was nice enough. Other than occasional guests, the lodge remained vacant with no permanent caretaker on the grounds. Whenever NAGS did have people visiting the lodge, they would bring in local help to clean, cook, chauffeur and whatever else was needed. The property was gated, and the lodge was only partially visible from the frontage road during the winter months.

Drive time to the lodge from downtown Washington, D.C. was about an hour depending upon the traffic and weather conditions. Despite the snow and Wayne's refusal to drive above the speed limit, they still made decent time getting to the lodge. The time on the road was filled with lots of talk and laughter with Bobby doing most of the talking and Wayne, the laughing. The light banter between the two men helped keep Wayne's mind at ease and off Jim's body that occupied the rear trunk. Even so, Wayne was mentally exhausted by the time he turned into the gated driveway that led to the lodge.

As their car neared the main building, the motion-sensors immediately activated the security lights in surrounding trees, the area spotlights and the lodge's front porch lights. Wayne pulled up to the barn that sat to the left of the lodge and did a three-point turn. He backed the car as close to the barn as possible, leaving enough room to swing open one of the two large doors. The barn doubled as a garage and storage area. Soon, it would serve a third purpose. Wayne killed the engine, popped the trunk and both men quickly exited the car.

The plan was simple. Move Jim's body from the car to the barn, dig a grave, dump the body into the grave, fill the grave back up with dirt and leave. But the plan had issues right from the start. Wayne and Bobby struggled to get the body out of the trunk as it seemed to get heavier and stiffer every time they had to lift it. Once out of the trunk, they dragged the tarp-covered body into the barn. Wayne returned to the car and grabbed the two shovels while Bobby found the light switch. When he returned to the barn, he saw Bobby bent over, staring at Jim through the tarp.

"This is really weird. I've never seen a real dead person that wasn't in a funeral home. It's almost surreal. He looks so relaxed. Death doesn't seem to be as bad as you think… as long as it's not you."

"Well, it could have been me," replied Wayne as he threw one of the shovels to Bobby. "Let's find a spot and get this done." He didn't want to think about 'what could have been.'

Step two of the plan ended almost as soon as it began with both men trying about a dozen different spots searching for ground soft enough to be shoveled. But regardless of how hard they tried, the ground was frozen rock solid. Two inches was the deepest that either could dig.

"You got a plan B?" asked Bobby. "It's pretty damn obvious this isn't going to work. If not, I say we dump his fat ass out in the woods and let the wolves or bears eat him unless you've got a better idea." Bobby eyed Wayne while leaning against his shovel as he waited for a response.

Wayne had no plan B. It never occurred to him that the ground would be frozen in an enclosed barn. This was embarrassing just like the earlier debacle in the alley. Not wishing to seem unprepared for this unseen event, he quickly addressed the situation.

"Actually, I do have a backup plan. We dump the body behind the barn and… uh…," he said haltingly as he quickly formulated a replacement plan. "and later this week or next, we rent a couple of portable gas heaters from Home Depot, buy a couple of pickaxes and come back and finish the job."

Bobby didn't remember him saying anything about a plan B but wasn't surprised by his alternate plan knowing how painstakingly anal he had been about everything else.

"Hell, maybe he'll be eaten by the time we get back. Either way, we got a plan. Let's get ol' fat boy behind the barn and go inside for a drink. I could use one," he replied, tossing his shovel down to the frozen ground then grabbing the closest end of the rolled-up corpse.

Wayne shook his head while grabbing the other end of the load. "Bobby, we don't have time for a drink. We gotta get back to Washington. We have an early day tomorrow."

Bobby abruptly dropped his end causing Wayne to do the same. "Look, dammit," he snapped. "I'm not asking to get shit-faced. I want one lousy drink. *One*. It's been a long, rough day. Nothing seems to be going as *planned* and I want a fucking drink."

It surprised Wayne how quickly Bobby's attitude changed – and just over a drink. But it *had* been a rough day and alienating his only ally over 'one lousy drink' was stupid. So to keep peace in the family, he acquiesced.

"You're right. We both could probably use one. But keep in mind we still have things to do back in Washington."

Whether amends had been made or not, both men, almost simultaneously, picked up the body and without saying a word, began lugging it to the back of the barn. It took all their strength to move it down and around the barn, up against the building and onto a pile of snow. Jim was no longer a person to them - just an action item on Wayne's plan.

As the two men hustled back to the lodge, Wayne was mentally running through a checklist of things to be done and changes that needed to be made to his plan. Bobby, on the other hand, was only thinking of the Jack Daniels that awaited him.

Once they reached the front porch of the lodge, Wayne began checking each pocket of his coveralls for the key to the front door while Bobby paced back and forth behind him, feverishly rubbing and blowing into his hands, trying to keep them warm. After what seemed an eternity, especially to Bobby who was now mumbling curse words under his breath, Wayne found the key stuck in the front pocket of his suit pants. The key unlocked both the deadbolt and doorknob. As he pushed open the door, a loud shrill erupted throughout the lodge.

Wayne rushed into the lodge, flipped on the lights, and quickly entered the security code into the keypad located above the light's switchplate. **1 9 3 4**. The year NAGS was founded. But the annoying sound of the breached security system continued.

Figuring he'd entered the code incorrectly, Wayne punched in the security code again trying to satisfy the alarm but with no luck. With each rejection, the punching became harder and more furious.

Bobby watched Wayne jabbing his finger into the keypad. It was obvious from the number of failed attempts that he didn't have a clue what the code was. Trying to help, he yelled, "HAVE YOU TRIED **1 7 7 6**?" Emphasizing each digit. That was the security code for the office.

"YES. YES," yelled Wayne. "Nothing works. I've tried everything… everything I can think of."

"Un-fucking-believable," mumbled Bobby shaking his head.

Exactly forty-five seconds after the initial alarm sounded, an even louder siren began to wail. Then the phone in the kitchen began to ring. Wayne knew the drill. It was the security company. This had happened at his own house when his now ex-wife forgot their security code. If you don't answer the phone, the local police will pay you a visit. He couldn't let that happen. As Wayne ran to the phone, Bobby closed the door hoping that would stop the maddening noise. It didn't.

As expected, the call was from the security company – Gates Security. The representative was all business explaining that they had been alerted that the alarm had gone off and wanted to know if everything was all right.

"Yes. Yes, it is," answered Wayne and then with as much authority as he could assert over the phone, "I'm Wayne Peters, executive vice-president of North American Gun Society. We own this property. For whatever reason, our passcode is *not* working. But everything is OK. Would you mind turning off the alarm? It's loud enough to raise the dead."

"What is your security password?"

"I don't know. I've never had to use it."

Holding his hand over the phone's mouthpiece, he turned to Bobby.

"You know the security password?" He shook his head.

"Try NAGS," he quickly added. "Or Dupont Circle…"

Neither worked.

"Can I please speak to a Mrs. Hamilton?"

"She's not here. I'm her boss. Why do you ask?"

"Thank you, Mr. Peters." Then the representative hung up.

About that time, the siren stopped. All was quiet again.

Wayne whose face had turned ashen hung up the phone and turned to Bobby. "The police are coming."

"Great. So what do we do now? You got a plan?" asked Bobby, clearly agitated.

"Give me a minute to think!" Wayne had no plan because his original plan had not taken into account that Bobby *had* to have a drink. That they *had* to go into the lodge. His plan allowed for just enough time to bury Jim and then head back to Washington. This was all Bobby's fault. If they had stayed on plan, none of this would have ever happened. But it did. And he wanted to tell Bobby. But he didn't.

"We don't have a fucking minute," barked Bobby. "So here's what we're gonna do. You get rid of the incriminating stuff that's in the car and I'll cover up the holes in the barn. If you get finished before I do, come help me. And vice versa."

Wayne wanted more time to think everything through. Make sure they didn't have any loose ends. But, there was no time. So, dutifully, he set about doing his task. He grabbed all the Home Depot supplies from the back seat of the car and headed to the barn where he found a storage cabinet just inside the door. Bobby, who was busy sweeping the small piles of dirt back into their holes, stopped long enough to give Wayne the thumbs up. Neither spoke. By the time Wayne returned back to the barn with Margie's wadded up tarp and the used duct tape, he found Bobby setting the broom and shovels next to the storage cabinet.

"Where are you putting that?" asked Bobby, referring to the tarp.

"I don't know."

"Then give it to me. I'll take care of them. You back the car into the barn. That should cover most of the holes. Then meet me in the lodge."

Bobby was barking orders like he had a plan. But Wayne knew he was winging it just like he always did. A case in point - the forgotten footprints in the snow from when they had carried Jim's body to the back of the barn.   Proper planning wouldn't have overlooked this potential show-stopper. Wayne pushed the doors open wide enough so that their earlier tracks were erased. He backed the car into the barn, grabbed Bobby's boots, the painter's caps, and his loafers and ran back into the lodge. There he found Bobby stoking a newly built fire in the fireplace while nursing a drink. The sight of the half-filled glass unleashed his pent-up feelings.

"You just couldn't wait, could you?" asked Wayne as he began pulling off his overalls. "You just *had* to have a drink. And with the police coming? What's wrong with you? We'd have been on our merry way back to Washington with my plan still intact if you didn't have to have a drink. But *nooooo.*"

Bobby's gut reaction was to challenge Wayne, fight back, defend himself. But this would only escalate a bad situation. Instead, he decided to reason with the man.

"Wayne. Listen to me. You need to lighten up. I'm just trying to help. I know you get all hot and bothered when your plans go off-kilter but if I can see the tension in your face and how uncomfortable you are, so will the cops. What we *want* the cops to see is just a couple of overworked guys getting away from the salt mines. Just having a little fun away from the office. OK?"

Wayne thought about what Bobby had said earlier about acting normal and he was right. But acting normal in abnormal situations wasn't his strength. Planning was. With no time to plan, it was best to rely on Bobby's strength. Instincts.

"Yeah. You're right. I don't know what I was thinking. I guess I kinda overreacted. But you know I can't help it. I don't like leaving things to chance. I like plans. It's in my DNA. So when things go askew, like today… like right now, I'm not good at altering everything in midstream without doing the proper planning, knowing the consequences and unintended consequences. Like, have you thought about what we would say or do if the police looked behind the barn? I know I haven't."

"If they do, then we're fucked. But don't get alarmed over something that's probably not going to happen. It's not like we're a couple of ne'er-do-wells. Anyway, what's the worst that can happen? We get the chair. Or maybe the firing squad? God, I can see the headlines now! Come on Wayne. They're not going to look out in the back of the barn unless we act nervous or suspicious. All they're gonna do is check us out and make sure we're not a couple of strays. That's all."

As Bobby talked, Wayne removed his boots and slipped on his loafers.

"What do you want me to do with these?" asked Wayne who only now realized that Bobby had already removed his work attire and they were nowhere in sight.

Bobby grabbed them and went into the kitchen where he shoved the boots into the oven and the caps and overalls in the microwave. Wayne watched him as he did.

That's perfect he thought. No one would ever look there. But he wouldn't tell Bobby otherwise he'd get another lecture on how spontaneity trumps detailed planning. He didn't need that. Not now.

"So I'm thinking I should do all the talking. Is that OK with you?" asked Bobby, pulling on his boots as he did.

Wayne nodded his head in agreement. Then, as if on cue, both men donned their overcoats, Bobby covered his bald head with his 'LBJ,' and they headed outside to the porch to wait for the men in blue.

Chapter 19

Wednesday, December 27, 2006, 9:47 p.m. EST

The door had hardly closed behind them when they saw the flashing blue lights of the patrol car making its way up the snow-covered gravel driveway. Soon they heard the crunching of the snow and rocks beneath the tires. The car stopped about twenty feet from the porch. The driver of the car pointed a high beam spotlight toward Wayne and Bobby causing them to shield their eyes with their hands to avoid the glare. The two patrolmen cautiously exited the car. Neither had their guns drawn. One looked to be in his late forties, maybe early fifties and the other most likely in his early twenties. Both were very neatly dressed, looking like Marine Drill Instructors. The younger one stayed behind the door on the driver's side as the older one approached the porch.

"Hi officers," said Bobby, coming down the steps to greet them, hand extended. Wayne remained on the front porch.

"Sir. Could you please return to the porch and keep your arms by your side," said the older patrolman in a commanding voice.

"Oh. Yes, sir!" replied Bobby as he returned to the porch. He could see that Wayne was starting to get an uneasy look.

"I'm Sergeant Frankel, and that's my partner, Corporal Geddings." The older patrolman pointed back to the younger patrolman who tipped his hat. "The security company called us regarding a possible break-in. Can both you gentlemen show me some identification?"

"Yes, sir. I'm Robert Armstrong, and this is Wayne Peters. Sorry to have you guys come all the way up here. My friend and I are up here for a couple of days of needed rest. Maybe get in a little hunting. A little R&R. Getting away from the old salt mines if you know what I mean."

The sergeant didn't respond but waited patiently while Bobby and Wayne searched for their driver's licenses.

"If you two don't mind waiting here, this shouldn't take but a few minutes," said Frankel as he took the licenses from the two men and returned to his patrol car without waiting for a response.

The younger patrolman, Geddings, stayed outside the car keeping an eye on the two men. Shortly, the sergeant began talking to someone on his two-way mobile radio, nodding his head from time to time, as if in agreement. Wayne and Bobby waited in silence. The younger patrolman couldn't help staring at Bobby. And Bobby knew why. The patrolman was trying to figure out where he had seen him before. His Dr. Phil curse. Wayne tried to act calm but kept nervously rubbing his hands together. After a few minutes, Frankel placed the mobile radio unit back in its cradle, said something to the young corporal, and both men headed over to the porch.

The sergeant looked at the picture on the first license and handed it to Bobby then, by default, gave the second one to Wayne.

"Do you mind if we look around?"

"No. Not at all. Come inside," said Bobby stepping aside so the two patrolmen could enter first. Instead, the older patrolman ushered Wayne and Bobby in first, following directly behind them. The corporal brought up the rear. Once inside, the sergeant stayed with Wayne and Bobby in the main room while the corporal did a cursory check of the bedrooms, bathrooms, and closets. Nothing was said among the three men while the corporal did his search. All in all, he was gone for about five minutes.

When he returned, he nodded to his superior. "Everything looks to be in order."

Wayne hoped the look of relief on his face was not obvious to the officers. Bobby's expression never changed.

"Mr. Peters, Mr. Armstrong. I'm sorry if we've inconvenienced you, but we're only doing our job. Next time you or anybody else comes up here, make sure they know the passcode. That way, we don't have to make an unnecessary trip. If it happens again, the owners of the property will be charged a fee. One last thing. You mentioned hunting. If you two don't have a current Virginia hunting license, don't even think about hunting here. We don't take kindly to people who break the law."

After his little lecture, Frankel and his partner returned to their squad car. Bobby and Wayne returned to the great room, both in real need of a drink, and quite relieved that the patrolmen had not checked the kitchen appliances or behind the barn – especially behind the barn.

"Well, we dodged a bullet there, no pun intended," said Bobby as he headed to the bar to refresh his drink.

* * * * * * * * * *

"Those two city boys sure acted nervous," said young Geddings as he pulled on his seatbelt. "And that dude with the cowboy hat. Seems like I seen him somewhere before. Did you get that feeling?"

"Yeah. He did look familiar. But you'll find that in this business, everybody looks familiar," growled Frankel as he drove away from the lodge.

"So what do you think they were really up to?"

"They were up to no good, that's what. It was flat out obvious that those boys weren't up here to hunt anything, except each other's pecker. You see that dude in the cowboy hat? Reminds me of a movie I saw a whiles back. Called *The Midnight Cowboy*. You're too young to have seen it. It was a story about a cowboy who was a man whore. He liked both men and women. Now that I think about it, didn't you see how that cowboy was eyeing you? Hell. He was probably thinking how he'd like to pull on that little weenie of yours."

"You better shut your mouth or I might have to tell your wife about how Amy's always hugging on you," laughed young Geddings. Then more seriously, he continued. "I know I seen that one flamer… the one with the cowboy hat. I seen him somewhere before but I just can't place it. I might have to do a little digging when I get back to the office. I mean after we git ourselves a doughnut." Both of the men laughed at the comment they had heard and made a million times. It didn't take much to make them laugh.

Chapter 20

Wednesday, December 27, 2006, 10:12 p.m. EST

Bobby was now on his third drink. He sat in one of the leather armchairs in front of the fireplace trying to get warm and forget how close they had come to getting caught. He couldn't believe that Wayne didn't know the passcode or that it had been changed. That was his job. Such a simple thing. But oftentimes it was the simple things that wrecked good plans. This couldn't happen again. Regardless of how thorough Wayne's plan appeared to be, he would monitor it more closely in the future.

Wayne, on the other hand, was still nursing his first drink. He was standing with his back to the fire, deep in thought. Wayne looked at Bobby, who continued to gaze at the fire. He knew what he was thinking. They had worked together too many years not to know. What had just happened was extremely unsettling and he knew Bobby would start second-guessing him, at least until he felt comfortable with the plan again. Then he would back off. That was Bobby. He didn't like to plan anything, but he sure liked to be in charge.

Finally, Bobby spoke up. "What a fucking Chinese fire drill! We were mighty lucky tonight. But we can't afford to depend on luck anymore. We have to do a better job of anticipating the unexpected."

"Well, uh… I think we handled it quite nicely. Especially you," stammered Wayne, playing to Bobby's ego. "No way I could have pulled this off by myself."

"Hey. We got through it. That's all that matters. But I gotta tell you, I'm a little antsy about leaving ol' fat boy unburied. I think we need to get back here tomorrow or Friday at the latest and get his ass in the ground. I believe that's what you told me, wasn't it? Your plan B?"

"Yes. This week or next. That's my plan B."

"And what about those portable heaters? Where did you say they can be rented?"

The second-guessing had started.

"Home Depot," Wayne replied, clearly agitated. "But then, again, we've already discussed that."

"Well, I've got to tell you, I'm a little nervous about this whole damn thing. I don't like being caught off guard, not like we were tonight."

"Things will go a lot smoother from here on out. You'll see. And if we're going to stay on track, we need to leave ASAP."

Once the fire was extinguished, the light turned off, the door locked, the Home Depot supplies back in the car, and the barn doors closed, the two men were back on the road to DC. Needless to say, the alarm was not set.

Chapter 21

Wednesday, December 27, 2006, 11:37 p.m. EST

Kyle returned to his apartment after the best day of his life. He and Katie had lost track of time, enjoying each other's company, talking more than eating. The next thing they knew, it was after eleven o'clock, and Katie had to work the next day. Kyle was off the rest of the week - one of the perks of working for the Government. Any other red-blooded American would have tried to take Katie home and stay the night. But he wasn't that type, and after nearly six hours of getting to know Katie, he knew she wasn't that type either. Relationships had to develop before they could become intimate. Kyle walked Katie to her car, and that's when things became awkward. He didn't know whether to shake her hand, hug her, or walk away. But Katie knew. She gave him a gentle kiss on his lips taking Kyle completely by surprise, leaving him speechless. So sweet, yet so intimate.

He was a happy man going home. He cranked up his radio as loud as he possibly could. The station was playing the old American Idol's exit song, 'You had a Bad Day' by Daniel Powter. He loved the song and joined right in singing it to the top of his lungs. He was totally drunk with happiness. It was a great song, but it surely wasn't meant for him tonight. No. He hadn't had a bad day. It had been a great day!

As he opened the door to his apartment, he could hear the phone ringing. It stopped before he could get to it. The message count showed that he had three messages. None from his Mom. The first two were hang-ups, most likely telemarketers. The third was from Katie who had called from her cell phone on the way home. She wanted to thank him for the wonderful evening and hoped she hadn't been too forward. She wondered if they could meet tomorrow for lunch. And could he please call her tomorrow morning, early, before she went to work. Six-thirtyish. If he was awake.

Tomorrow morning. If I'm awake? Kyle doubted he would get any sleep. He hadn't been this excited since the day his Dad took him and Aaron to the '86 Masters, the Sunday round when Jack Nicklaus overcame a five-shot deficit to win his 6th Green Jacket and become the oldest winner of the tournament. They had been on the bank of the 16th hole when Nicklaus almost holed his tee shot. His Dad told him that if there was a golf course in heaven, he hoped it was as beautiful as Augusta National. Kyle missed his Dad. He wished he could have met Katie. He would have loved her. But at least his Mom would get to meet her.

* * * * * * * * * *

Jamie was happy, too. He had made his connection with Nate and life was good. Since his Dad had not seen him today, he could go by again tomorrow, get his sermon, and get some more money. Yes. Life was good.

Chapter 22

Wednesday, December 27, 2006, 11:57 p.m. EST

The trip back to DC was interrupted by a brief stop at a 24 hour IHOP. Bobby needed food. This was not part of Wayne's plan but he decided not to fight this battle. They had hardly entered the restaurant when the hostess and customers at nearby tables thought that Dr. Phil had entered the room. Even though he denied being the celebrity, they didn't believe him, asking for his autograph and advice. Bobby ate it up, both the food and the attention. Even Wayne relaxed. It gave him time to think about the passcode debacle.

Once they were back on the road, Wayne turned to Bobby and said, "I know who changed the passcode and why. It was Margie. She had it changed after the break-in at the lodge a couple of months ago. Whoever did it knew the passcode. We *all* got emails telling us about the changes."

"If I got an email, I don't remember it. I probably get a hundred a day. Unless it was from somebody *important,* I don't read it. But *you* should have," Bobby said, sidestepping any blame. He was going to make a great Senator.

"I'm sure I did. Obviously, I forgot."

"By the way, wasn't it Jim's boy who was responsible for the break-in? Should we be worried about him mucking up things at the lodge again?"

"We never really found out who did it but everybody sure *thought* it was Jamie, you know, with his drug problems, and all. But I don't think he'll be a problem."

"And his old man wanted to kill you because you fired him? Jeez."

"I didn't fire him. I put him on administrative leave of absence."

"Semantics. His ass was grass at the next Board meeting. But why would he want to kill you for that? He had lots of money, even with the divorce. He didn't even *need* the job, especially with what the board would have given him as severance pay."

"I know. But something made him snap." Then reflecting on what Jim had said at their last and fatal encounter. "You know. He also accused me of having an affair with his wife. Maybe that's what put him over the edge."

"Yeah. That would do it for me. So did you, you know, fuck her?"

"*Oh nooooo. No.* I heard the rumors just like everybody else, but it wasn't me. She's nice looking but not that nice. But no. Not me."

"The man doth protest too much, methinks," said Bobby, paraphrasing a familiar line from Shakespeare's *Hamlet,* then laughed.

Uncomfortable with the direction the conversation was heading, Wayne switched topics in midstream and began talking about his plan B, making it up as he went. Mentally, he reswizzled Thursday's schedule using Bobby's 'shoot, ready, aim' methodology. He explained that they would have to move Jim's car tonight instead of tomorrow as originally planned. This would give them enough time to return to the lodge to bury Jim and still remain on schedule for everything else.

Bobby agreed.

As they approached Washington, Wayne explained in detail what they were going to do when they got back to the office. It was quite simple. Wayne would drive Jim's car to the Watergate apartment parking garage while Bobby followed him in the rental car. Bobby was then to circle the Watergate complex a couple of times then park near the garage's Virginia Avenue emergency exit and wait. Wayne would park Jim's car in the garage and then meet Bobby at the emergency exit. Afterward, they would return to NAGS headquarters to get Wayne's car and then drive both cars to Wayne's townhouse in Georgetown. That was it. Simple and straightforward.

Chapter 23

Thursday, December 28, 2006, 12:21 a.m. EST

Once the gates to the NAGS parking lot opened, Wayne drove the rental car up next to Jim Barnes' Mercedes and parked. Both men quickly exited the vehicle. Bobby circled the rental car and slid into the driver's seat where he laid his head back on the headrest and closed his eyes. It had been a long day - for both men. Meanwhile, Wayne rummaged through the Home Depot bags in the back seat of the rental car looking for the box of latex gloves. Once he had his hands gloved and before closing the door, he heard the sound of heavy breathing coming from the front seat. In that short span of time, Bobby had dozed off. Wayne envied, yet detested his cavalier attitude and his obvious lack of concern. He purposely slammed the rear door shut, the loud noise causing Bobby's head to jerk forward abruptly awakening him. Seeing it was Wayne, he sat straight up and shot him a 'bird'.

The gesture was wasted on Wayne as he never saw Bobby's middle finger rejoinder. Instead, he headed over to Jim's silver Mercedes where he climbed in the spacious luxury car, started the engine and waited for the car to heat up. As he did, he checked the seats and glove compartment looking for anything that might be connected to that morning's confrontation, like extra ammo, gun cleaner or even a suicide note, just in case Jim had planned on killing himself. He found none. As he looked around the inside of the car, he saw that it was spotless. No leftover water bottles, hidden French fries, candy wrappers or fast food sacks. Jim was known to have always kept a clean car just like his apartment and office. That would have to be changed. If Jim were depressed, upset, angry, cleanliness wouldn't be high on his list.

Wayne looked over at Bobby in the rental car to make sure he hadn't fallen asleep again. He saw Bobby smile and this time give a thumbs up. Wayne nodded and slowly drove out of NAGS' parking lot, headed for the Watergate garage with Bobby following close behind.

Once the two men reached the Watergate apartments, Wayne turned into the garage while Bobby continued straight ahead to begin circling the complex. NAGS' parking spaces were located on the third sub-level floor. Wayne drove down the three levels and parked in the first of NAGS' three parking spots. He easily found the emergency stairs and climbed the steps, two at a time, until he reached the street level exit. When he opened the door, he immediately realized that it opened onto New Hampshire Avenue, not Virginia Avenue. He had mistakenly gone up the wrong set of steps. Again, a part of his plan, however trivial, had gone awry. Angry and frustrated at himself and now needing Bobby to come pick him up, he pulled out his cell and tapped Bobby's speed dial number.

After about four rings, the call went to voicemail. "Hello. You've reached…" Wayne quickly canceled the call and tried a second time. Again, voicemail. He slammed the phone shut and jammed it in his pocket.

"That stupid moron! Why doesn't he answer the damn phone?" he mumbled to himself as he began a quick walk down New Hampshire Avenue toward Virginia Avenue.

Once he rounded the corner at Virginia Avenue, he saw Bobby, double-parked in front of the garage's Virginia Avenue emergency exit – waiting for him, just as planned. He stopped, pulled his cell out of his pocket and began waving it wildly over his head as he marched towards the car, screaming, "Answer the damn phone, you stupid idiot."

As he approached the car, his front foot hit a slick, icy spot on the walkway causing him to fall backwards into the freshly fallen snow. Embarrassed and now even madder, he scrambled to his feet only to see Bobby, in the car, laughing. The son-of-a-bitch was laughing! He brushed himself off, staring angrily at Bobby as he did. Maybe it was the screw up at the lodge, or at the dumpster, or here at Watergate or possibly the whole cover-up in general, regardless, he just lost it. Or as Bobby would later say, he went ape-shit.

"What the hell's wrong with you?" yelled Wayne as he jumped into the car slamming the door. "Why didn't you answer me?"

"Huh? Answer you? What do you mean?"

"Your cell phone, you stupid idiot. Your phone. I called you twice! Three times! Whatever. Why didn't you answer?" Wayne rarely showed emotions. But tonight was different. He had lost his composure which never happened. But nothing was going right. Nothing. Everything seemed to be falling apart. And then there was Bobby - laughing. That was the last straw.

"You must have dialed the wrong number, asshole. See for yourself," responded Bobby, angrily, as he began searching his coat pockets, his pants pockets then the car for his phone. "Oh shit! I don't have it." He thought for a few seconds. "I must have left the damned thing in the old lady's car."

"Great! Just great! So now whoever stole the car has your phone. Unbelievable! What about anything else? Anything that could identify you, me… us?"

"No. Not that I remember," Bobby replied trying to recall what, if anything, he had left in the car. "I think that's it. My phone. Oh yeah… and the old lady's handbag."

"Would you quit calling her *the old lady*? IT'S MARGIE. And *think* is not acceptable. I want to *know* if that was it. If that's all you left," demanded Wayne.

"What the hell's wrong with you, buddy? First, you call me a moron and then an idiot. I oughta take my white ass back to Texas and let you handle this whole damn mess yourself. You got yourself into it. Maybe you should get yourself out. Without me."

Bobby was fuming as he jerked the car in gear and jammed down on the gas pedal, causing the tires to spin in the snow as they sped off.

There was a long period of silence before Wayne spoke, having regained his composure.

"It's not your fault, Bobby. I'm sorry. I'm just so stressed out that I'm not myself. And now this. What if the police finds the guy who stole Margie's car and he has both your phone and Margie's? That's gonna point directly to you, me and NAGS."

Bobby understood Wayne's fear. And it wasn't like he wasn't afraid. NAGS was the stepping stone for his Senate bid. He had more to lose than Wayne or anybody at NAGS. But unlike Wayne, he understood how criminals worked having served on the Texas House Committee on Juvenile Justice and Family Issues for a number of years. So he tried to calm Wayne.

"Look, man. I understand your frustrations. You're not in your element. This isn't your day job. But *listen* to me. The car is not an issue. Neither are the phones. The car is probably in a chop shop where they've already stripped it for the parts. Almost impossible to trace. And if not, they've changed the VIN and sold the car. Probably out of state. And the phones? They were probably sold in the first hour. They don't keep them long. Too easily traced. They'll be sold overseas. So tomorrow morning, I'll call Verizon and tell them my phone was stolen. That'll take care of that. And the car? I'm not worried and neither should you. I say we call it a night. Go back to your house, get a drink and get some sleep."

Wayne looked at Bobby not knowing whether to believe him or not. Finally, "Are you sure? You're not bullshitting me, are you?"

"Believe me. I know what I'm talking about. The alternative is to call my cell phone and when someone answers, say, 'Hey, can I get my phone back?   You can keep the car. We don't need it. We got one already." Then he laughed.

Wayne laughed. That's all he could do. Bobby was right. There was nothing they could do about the phone. Wayne prayed it wouldn't come back to bite them in the ass.

Chapter 24

Thursday, December 28, 2006, 5:50 a.m. EST

Kyle was already wide-awake when his alarm clock went off. His mind seemed to be working in overdrive thinking about last night's date with Katie. And that sweet kiss!

He quickly rolled out of bed, turned on the light, and headed, to the kitchen where he waited patiently for the coffee to brew. One day he was going to buy himself a real coffee machine with a timer! Once it was ready, he poured himself a large mug, then added two packets of sugar and a little pour of cream. His coffee had always been on the weak side, more like colored water. Aaron, his brother, called it the essence of coffee.

From his kitchen, he could see the living room of his one-bedroom apartment. Just what you would expect from an unmarried 28-year old male. The focal point of his 'man-cave' was a 36" Sony Trinitron TV, perfect for watching golf, college football, the Hoyas, and the Redskins. In the cabinet under the TV sat his Sony CD/DVD player and a Samsung receiver that connected his surround system to anything that had sound. Completing his manly lair was a large brown leather couch and matching recliner complete with built-in armrest beer holders. A 4x6 dark green rug lay on top of the off-white apartment-grade wall-to-wall carpet. It doubled as a putting green during the winter months and rainy weekends. With the exception of the large framed litho of the 12th green at Augusta National that hung above his couch, the stark white walls throughout his apartment were completely bare. It wasn't everyone's taste and style, but it was home to him.

Kyle drained the last ounce of coffee from his mug, checked the time (6:10 a.m.), and poured himself another cup. He picked up his phone and settled in his recliner in anticipation of his call to Katie. Automatically, he checked his messages. He only had Katie's phone message from last night. The others he'd deleted. Surprisingly, he didn't have any texts from his Mom. Nor had she returned his calls. This was so unlike her. She was an early riser. She had time to call or text him. Questions began to fill his mind. *What if she's sick? What if she's fallen? What if she's had a wreck?* Immediately, he called his Mom's apartment and then cell phone. Both went to voicemail. He left messages on both. *Probably in the bathroom,* he thought hopefully.

He checked the time once again. 6:18 a.m. Continuing with his morning routine, he retrieved the *Post* from outside his apartment door, laid it on the kitchen counter next to his sad, two-foot fake Christmas tree, reheated his coffee in the microwave, and turned to the Sports Section. He hardly ever read anything else in the paper. He didn't like reading about wars, fires, murders, robberies. So he didn't. Nor did he watch the news on TV for the same reasons. Aaron called him an ostrich. His Mom read everything in the paper. All the home-invasions worried her, so she kept a gun at her apartment. Aaron also had a gun. Gun ownership was legal in Virginia. But Kyle felt that his Big Bertha – an oversized golf club, a driver – was all he needed. A good wop to the privates with old Bertha would stop any intruder. Besides, neither he, Aaron nor his Mom had ever had a break-in. So why worry?

It didn't take long for Kyle to finish reading the paper. The Redskins sucked and golf season was in hibernation. Only the Georgetown Hoyas basketball team captured his attention. They were winning but the season was early.

The time was now 6:29 a.m. As far as Kyle was concerned, that was six-thirtyish enough. He looked at the note with Katie's phone number and began dialing it. His fingers trembled as he did. He hadn't been this nervous since his first real date - the junior prom. Back then, he hung up at least ten times before he got up enough nerve to complete the call. But Katie was different. He was nervous and excited, not nervous and scared.

Katie answered after the two rings. "Good morning, Kyle Hamilton."

Her voice was just as sweet as he remembered.

"I hope I didn't wake you," he responded.

"Good heavens, no. I was drinking my coffee and thinking about the wonderful time I had last night. I hope I didn't talk your ear off."

"It's funny you say that because I was thinking the same thing about me."

The conversation with Katie went on for just a few more minutes. It was so easy, so natural with nothing forced. The conversation ended with them setting a lunch date at Luigi's - a popular DC pizzeria.

Kyle was on top of the world. He loved the way she said both his names. Like he was somebody important. He had dated only a few women in his life. Until now none were special nor had there ever been any chemistry or spark. Maybe it was his fault. Maybe not. But this was different. He couldn't wait to see her, to hear her talk, to see her smile.

After he'd hung up, he realized he'd left earlier messages with his Mom asking her out to lunch today. He immediately called his Mom's apartment. Voicemail. Then he tried her cell. Same thing. He left messages on both canceling their lunch date saying he'd explain later but that it was a red-letter day.

That she hadn't answered his calls for two days was concerning. That she hadn't returned his calls or texts was even more disturbing. His thoughts turned to his brother, Aaron. Maybe he knew where she was. He hated calling Aaron – for anything. Aaron always made him feel like an idiot, always patronizing him. But this was about their Mom, so maybe this time, he'd be civil.

Aaron answered his cell phone on the first ring. All of his calls went straight to an earbud which seemed permanently attached to his head.

"Aaron here." His brother's standard curt answer. He did not tolerate idle chit-chat.

"Hey. It's me, Kyle. Do you know where Mom is?"

"OK. Let me get this straight. You called me at 6 a.m. to ask where Mom is. What the *hell* are you thinking? Why don't you just call her?"

"I have. I've called her apartment and cell phone, both last night and early this morning, and she doesn't answer."

"Well, try them again. I gotta go."

"Wait! Wait! Don't hang up. You know Mom always calls us back. In fact, she gets on us when *we* don't. I don't like the fact that it's been two days."

"Kyle! Listen! You need to understand that Mom has a life. We all have a life. Life is not just golf. Have you ever thought that she might be with that boyfriend of hers? Look. I've got this huge deal that I'm working on, and I'm the only one who can do it. It's *got* to be done by tomorrow.   You can't even *imagine* how important this is. But if Mom calls me, which I doubt, I'll tell her to call you. And if you're that worried, why don't you go over to her apartment and check things out for yourself. You got the time. You government people can take off anytime you want. I can't. I gotta go." And he hung up.

That was Aaron. No time for small talk. And no time for family. But maybe he was right. Maybe he should just go over to her apartment and check things out for himself. She lived only about four miles from his apartment by way of the Mount Vernon Trail. He could jog over. The view of the Potomac River and Washington from the trail was spectacular, even in the dead cold of winter. And… it would help pass the time before his lunch date with Katie.

Chapter 25

Thursday, December 28, 2006, 6:05 a.m. EST

At precisely 6:05 a.m., the final measures of Debussy's classic, *Claire de Lune*, came wafting from Wayne's clock radio gently breaking the silence in his dark magnolia green bedroom. Setting the alarm had been completely unnecessary as he had tossed and turned all night, with the image of Margie's disfigured face haunting him, preventing him from garnering any sleep or rest. Reluctantly, he sat up on the edge of his four-poster bed with his feet dangling above the bed steps and turned on the bedside light. Everything about yesterday's awful events seemed so unreal. And the questions? They wouldn't stop. Had he done the right thing? Should he have called the police? Should he have gotten Bobby involved? And what about Bobby's cell phone? Should he be worried about it or forget about it like Bobby said. And what about his plan? Was it going to work? Had he forgotten anything else? And, most troubling of all, why did Jim have to bring that damn gun to the office? If he hadn't, they probably could have settled things like two normal people. Then Jim would be alive. Margie would be alive. And life would be good.

Wayne would have preferred staying in bed, hoping everything would go away. But that wasn't going to happen. He had to get moving, work his plan and pray nothing else would go askew. Slowly he made his way to the bathroom. If he looked anything like he felt, then *shit* came to mind. Once he had flipped on the bathroom's light and glanced at himself in the mirror, he was spot on. He did look like shit. The dark bags under his eyes were reminiscent of Jim's, yesterday, in his office. *Best I stay away from guns today.* Normally a morning person, he found himself moving like an old man.

Wayne was a creature of habit with few changes in his morning routine. He flossed, brushed his teeth, and then took his meds. From inside the connecting walk-in closet, he slipped on his bathrobe, his bedroom slippers, and then returned to his bedroom where he turned on the TV, changing the channel from Fox News to a local station. He sat down on the bench located at the foot of his bed and watched apprehensively for any news about a dead woman's body being found. But the only deaths reported were drug and gang-related, none involving women. Even as he made up his bed, he continued to listen but nothing about a dead woman found in the Capitol Street area. He wasn't sure if he was relieved or not. He turned off the TV then headed down the hall to the guest bedroom. The lights were still out, and Bobby was sound asleep, snoring heavily. Nothing ever seemed to faze the man.

"Bobby! Wake up! We need to get a move on. We've got a lot to do today."

"Huh? Huh? What time is it?" he asked as he quickly threw back his covers.

"It's about 6:15. We need to get on over to Margie's and Jim's this morning."

Going to Jim's apartment had been part of Wayne's original plan but not going to Margie's. Last night, while undressing and hanging his clothes, Wayne found in his coat pocket the handwritten note given to him by Idella, NAGS' cleaning lady. Before going to bed, he placed it on his bedside table believing it could somehow be used to his advantage. When he saw it again this morning, an idea popped into his head. He never liked mental modifications to any plan. Too many risks. But the note from Idella seemed harmless enough and could be used to corroborate NAGS' story that 'Margie was at work that Wednesday morning but had left early. And that he (Wayne) had given Margie the note before she left.' The operative word being 'left.' However, the note had to be found. Hence the trip to Margie's apartment to place it in a conspicuous place. This would give physical proof that Margie had returned to her apartment after work. Furthermore, this could limit NAGS involvement in any investigation.

Unlike Wayne, Bobby was moving fast. "Margie's and Jim's. This morning. I gotcha. But I need some java. You got some made?"

"On the kitchen counter along with cups, cream, and sugar. By the way, nothing's been on TV this morning about Margie. So things are going as planned," Wayne replied, with a forced smile.

"That's good. That's good. But I expected that. By the way, this is a great bed. Best night's sleep I've had in months. I'm going to have to get me one of these mattresses. Who makes it?" He then searched the foot of the bed looking for a manufacturer's label.

I toss and turn all night, and Bobby gets his best night's sleep in months. What the hell's wrong with this picture?

Wayne ignored his question. Instead, over a cup of coffee, he briefed Bobby on the morning's agenda. First, they were going over to Margie's apartment to leave Idella's note. Next, they would go by Verizon to report Bobby's cell phone lost or stolen and get him another, and then on to Jim's apartment. Nothing too difficult. Not like the night before.

Once Wayne declared coffee time over, both men returned to their bedrooms, showered and dressed. Wayne walked out of his bedroom within twenty minutes wearing a neatly pressed pair of khaki's, a nondescript sweatshirt and a National's baseball cap. Nothing that would attract any attention. He grabbed his briefcase which contained Idella's note, keys to Jim's and Margie's apartments and headed down to the kitchen where he heard Bobby stirring his coffee. He too was already showered, dressed and ready to go.

"What the hell is that?" Wayne asked, looking at Bobby and almost laughing.

"Coffee. What'd you expect?"

"No. That thing." Then he pointed to Bobby's head. "That thing on your head. That thing that looks like a dead rat."

"Hey. Don't you go bad-mouthing my new hairpiece. It cost me over two hundred bucks. I ordered it online back in Texas. I felt I needed something to change my looks in case I wanted to go somewhere unnoticed, incognito. You know. When I didn't want to look like Dr. Phil. Like today. This way, I blend in with the crowd. So, what do you think?"

"Bobby, it's bad. It's beyond bad. It's even beyond Chuck Norris bad. Beyond Charlton Heston or Burt Reynolds bad. An ax stuck in your head would be less noticeable. I can't believe your wife would ever have let you buy that thing, much less let you wear it out in public."

"She doesn't know anything about it. But there are lots of things she doesn't know about me. Some things are best-kept secret if you know what I mean."

Wayne knew what he meant. Everybody but Bobby's wife and father-in-law, the Senator, knew that Bobby had the reputation of being a rounder - a womanizer.

"So yes or no?" Bobby replied as he sashayed around the kitchen showing off his new mullet.

"I'll go get you a cap."

Even when things were at their worst, Bobby had a way of lightening the mood. As Wayne made his way back to his bedroom to get Bobby a ball cap, he couldn't help but laugh. Today was going to be a better day. It had to be.

Chapter 26

Thursday, December 28, 2006, 6:38 a.m. EST

The caller-ID displayed Vernon Martin's name, Lt. Daniel Whitehead's boss. It wasn't a call Daniel could ignore even though it was interrupting his daily morning regimen of push-ups, crunches and pull-ups interlaced with thirty minutes on the treadmill or elliptical, depending on the day. His gym was a re-purposed 2nd bedroom in his apartment. He found it cheaper to rent a two-bedroom apartment and buy his own gym equipment than to rent a one-bedroom and join a local athletic club. Furthermore, he didn't have to compete for the equipment with the first-and-only-timers, the professional narcissists, the meat hunters (players and cougars) and soccer moms. When he trained, he had only one purpose in mind - to be more physically fit than his opponent - the criminal.

Dutifully, he answered the call, already knowing he wasn't going to like what he heard.

"Whitehead, how much you got on your plate?" The question was one of courtesy because Vernon Martin, a captain in the 5th District, Washington D.C.'s Police Department, knew his team's workload and he wouldn't have called Daniel unless he was about to dump another case in his lap.

"More than I can handle," Daniel replied, trying not to sound irritated as he grabbed a towel to wipe the sweat from his lean but well-toned body. Cutting short his morning exercise didn't bother him. Cutting short the only time of the day that offered him quiet solitude did. It was during this alone time – just him and his exercise routines – that he could digest everything that had happened the previous day and to try to make sense of it all. It gave him the opportunity to tie up loose ends. That wasn't going to happen today.

"How 'bout one more?" More of a rhetorical question than a request.

"Sure. What you got?" Was there any other acceptable response?

"This one's different. Not one of our usual gang killings. It's an elderly female, Caucasian, nicely dressed, lying by a dumpster with a bullet hole in her head in the North Capitol Street area. Not your usual victim for that part of town."

"Who's with her?"

"Couple of our street guys. And the two guys who found her."

"Are they suspects?"

"No, I don't think so. They're with the garbage company. They're going to stick around until you get there. You gotta pen handy?" Vernon then gave the lieutenant the exact location of the body and the names of the two patrolmen. "I'm guessing the media is probably already on their way if they're not already there. I want you to handle them. How soon can you get there?"

"Twenty, thirty minutes. How about Wrinkles? Have you called him?"

"No. You do that."

"I'm on it."

"Daniel, keep me in the loop. I have a bad feeling about this one. Real bad."

"Will do."

Vernon Martin hated his job on days like this. If the victim had been some addict or some punk, it would have been business as usual. It would have been just another statistic, a blip on the screen on the eleven o'clock news. But this was different. This one would have all the suits on his ass especially if she were a tourist, or even worse, one of Washington's elite. Washington was such a political town when it came to where the buck stopped. If his gut feeling was right, he was going to need his best person on this case and Lt. Daniel Whitehead was that person.

Chapter 27

Thursday, December 28, 2006, 6:54 a.m. EST

The sky was dark and overcast making it impossible to tell if morning had broken. Under the glow of a street light, Wayne and Bobby scraped the accumulated snow off the front and rear windshields of the rental car whose motor was running and heater blasting full throttle. Had he not been so mad at Bobby last night, Wayne would have probably remembered to park his car on the street and let Bobby park the rental car in the single car garage thus avoiding all the scraping and the time it took to thaw the window. That didn't happen. And for some reason, Bobby said nothing about the miscue. Either he didn't realize the oversight or was giving Wayne a pass. Regardless, Wayne was glad there was no confrontation. Once the icy residue on the windshields had melted and the car was drivable, the two men headed over to Margie's apartment. Heavy layers of snow clouds filled the sky giving credence to the TV's forecast of two to four inches of new snow. Despite the forecast, the weather didn't concern Wayne, who drove while Bobby rode shotgun. As planned, the Chevy was equipped with snow tires and a backup set of tire chains in the trunk. If all went as scheduled, they would be back at NAG's HQ by no later than 10 a.m. Forty-five minutes was allocated for the trip over to Margie's including a brief stop at a McDonald's drive-thru for a couple of cups of coffee and sausage biscuits. Wayne could just as easily have skipped the fast food, but Bobby insisted on stopping saying that if he didn't eat something, his blood sugar would drop and he couldn't be held responsible for his grumpy or irritable behavior.

As they neared Margie's apartment complex, good fortune came their way as a car pulled out of a parking space in front of the building. In the Washington metro area, vacant parking spaces, like honest politicians, were always a rarity. Wayne quickly claimed the spot to the dismay of the driver directly behind him and expertly paralleled parked the car. Wayne lowered the volume of the radio and stared out at the apartments. He had known Margie for over ten years, five of which she had been his personal executive secretary, and yet, he had never been to her apartment. He didn't even know where she lived! Was he that insensitive? Was he that callous? *It's a two-way street. She could've invited me!*

"What're you thinking about?" interrupted Bobby, seeing that faraway look in Wayne's eyes. Neither man had talked much on the trip over. Wayne was mostly preoccupied with the news on the radio listening for anything about Margie while Bobby spent most of his time leisurely devouring his and part of Wayne's sausage biscuits, savoring every morsel as if it were the finest pork sausage he had ever eaten.

"Uh… just what all we have to do this morning," lied Wayne, not willing to share his guilt-ridden thoughts of Margie.

"You sure you can do this? 'Cause, if not, I can."

"No. I'm good. While I'm gone, see if you can find a nearby Verizon store and call them." Wayne handed his phone to Bobby. "See what needs to be done about your stolen phone. Got it? Stolen. Not lost. Stolen."

"I got it the first time. Don't treat me like I'm a fucking retard!"

"Sorry. I didn't mean to come across like that." Then, while not really looking for any suggestions but simply trying to ease the moment, Wayne asked Bobby if he could think of anything else besides leaving the note. Anything that would make it appear as though Margie had returned to her apartment after being at work.

"How about lunch?"

"Lunch! Is food all you think about? You just ate *your* biscuit and half of mine!"

"If you'd just shut your yap and listen. I'm *talking about* you doing something at the apartment to make it look like she ate lunch there."

The thought had never crossed Wayne's mind. It was so normal, ordinary and brilliant. "Bobby. That's good. Really good. I like it. You're a damn genius." Besides giving credit to where credit was due, stroking Bobby's ego kept his mind in the game.

"You got that right, Bubba," confirmed Bobby. "What I'm thinkin' you should do is leave a half-empty glass of watered-down Coke and maybe a knife with some mayo or peanut butter or something like that in the sink."

"Great idea! That's… that's so perfect."

"And if you have time, make a couple of sandwiches for me, will ya?" laughed Bobby.

Wayne rolled his eyes and shook his head in feigned disgust - their brief verbal altercation now behind them.

"I'll be back in about fifteen, maybe twenty minutes. Look inconspicuous and work on getting…" Rather than finish the sentence, Wayne immediately shut up knowing he was about to get in trouble again. Instead, he grabbed the note from his briefcase, got out of the car and headed straight for Margie's apartment complex, never looking back at Bobby. If he was pissed, he didn't want to know.

Chapter 28

Thursday, December 28, 2006, 7:13 a.m. EST

Daniel Whitehead had no trouble contacting Wrinkles. Wrinkles was short for Wrinkle Butt. It's what everybody called Johnny Williams, Daniel's homicide partner of three years. The nickname was no secret to Johnny. In fact, he found it amusing and wasn't offended when people addressed him by the moniker. No one ever owned up to being the source of the nickname, but Johnny always suspected an earlier partner - a young, ambitious detective named Jason White (now with the CIA).

There was probably no other detective team on the DC police force whose partners were so opposite. Daniel, age 31, was 20 years younger than Johnny. Daniel was athletic, trim, good looking. Johnny was soft, overweight and dumpy looking. Daniel was aggressive, always seeking high-profile cases - the ones that required research, dedication, and long nights. Johnny just wanted to retire with the maximum police pension possible, so he was putting in his time.

Daniel arrived at the crime scene to find the area cordoned off with yellow crime scene tape. Two white patrol cars with their red, white and blue emergency lights flashing formed a 'V' at the alley's entrance to keep curious onlookers, including the press, away. Standing behind the tape were two patrolmen and two other men dressed in green jumpsuits. The garbage-truck driver and helper. As he walked from his car to the crime scene, one of the patrolmen saw him and came to meet him.

"Daniel, I'm glad it's you."

"Thanks. Jer (Jerry Markham. Literally, one of DC's finest). Those the two guys who found the body?"

"Yeah. That's them. They're pretty shook up."

"I can imagine. They provide anything helpful?"

"Not really. The driver said he spotted the body as he was about to empty the dumpster. At first, he thought it was a couple of bags of garbage… you know… because of all the snow on top of it. He and his helper got out of the truck to pick up the 'bags' (the officer air-quoting the word). That's when they discovered it was a body instead. According to the driver, it scared the ever-loving shit out of both of them."

"So they called 911?"

"No. The driver called their dispatch who called 911."

"Do you know if they picked up or moved the body?"

"I figured you'd ask me that   Yeah. The two men said they picked it up but dropped it immediately when they saw it was a body. So it's probably not far from its original location. For the record, the two men were wearing work gloves so their fingerprints shouldn't be found anywhere around here. "

"That's good. Do you know if they emptied the dumpster?"

"No. The dispatcher told them to sit tight 'til we got there. Not to do anything. And that's what they did."

"Well, they did the right thing. Have you verified their names and addresses?"

"Yep. On my report."

"Did they see anybody or anything suspicious?"

"No. Nothing unusual."

"What about the wagon (referring to the Medical Examiners, aka ME)? You get a chance to call 'em?"

"They're on their way."

"You do good work, Jer!"

"Thanks."

"Now if you can keep the vultures outta my hair."

"No problem."

The media had not arrived yet, but the blitz could be expected at any moment. Johnny would be their contact point. He was really good at giving out just enough information that allowed the media to do their job but nothing more.   Nothing that would compromise the investigation. The less the public knew, the better the investigation. That was his and Daniel's philosophy.

Daniel looked over at the victim from behind the yellow tape. He then looked at the dumpster, the truck, the driveway, the surrounding buildings. He tried to take in everything. It was pretty obvious there probably wouldn't be any useful footprints or tire tracks – not with the snow last night, and the unintentional contamination done by the two workers and dump truck.

He lifted the yellow tape up and over his head and walked slowly to the victim, slipped on a pair of latex gloves, opened his notepad and began writing down his first observations.

Female, Caucasian, late fifties, early sixties, reddish hair, most likely dyed, about five feet tall, nicely dressed in a black pants suit. Pretty much the same as what his captain had told him. *Gunshot wound to the left eye. Black blood matted in the victim's red hair. No visible signs of a struggle. No visible scratches. Rigor Mortis had set in. Death was probably sometime yesterday. But what was she doing here? A robbery? A carjacking?*

"Yo! Danny boy."

It was Johnny. No one else called him Danny boy.

"Well, it's about time."

"The 'Hot Now' sign was lit at the Krispy Kreme, so the line was unbelievable. I had to wait forever. You'd think I'd have some kind of priority with all the business I give 'em."

"At least you got your priorities straight. Doughnuts first, then work. So where's the coffee?"

"What? I look like some kind of take-out service?" responded Johnny, laughing. "So what's got the captain's panties in a wad?"

"He's not getting good vibes on this one?"

"So now he's a psychic?"

"For what it's worth, I think he's right on this one. Let me get some pictures then I'd like you to take a look at the victim and tell me what you see."

Johnny excelled at 'reading' a crime scene. He was once the best detective on the force. He had hoped to make the rank of captain. But he never could handle the politics. He said what was on his mind and that sometimes caused the suits to go crazy. Johnny eventually settled into just doing his job as a detective, marking his time until retirement. But his mind was that of a true detective when you could get him to use it.

Johnny slipped on a pair of latex gloves and waited as his partner snapped pictures from every possible angle. The pictures complemented their notes and eliminated any possible lapse in memory. They would later compare these pictures to the ones they got from the Department of Forensic Science (DFS).

Once the photo shoot was finished, Johnny moved in closer to the body, crouched down on his haunches and began his initial assessment of the victim and the surrounding area.

"It appears that the victim was moved… recently. Do we know who moved her?"

"Yes. The two guys from the garbage company that found her. Standing over there (Daniel pointed to the two men in the green jumpsuits). They tried to pick her up thinking she was a bag of garbage. When they realized it was a body, they dropped her where she is now. I figure she's pretty close to where they found her."

After only a few minutes, Johnny stood up and turned to Daniel.

"Well, I do see a few things. Probably nothing that you didn't already see."

"Maybe. Maybe not. Besides the obvious, what'd else you see?"

"First, I don't think the little lady was shot here. Too little blood on her, around her or on the dumpster. Second. I don't think it was a robbery. Possibly a carjacking, but definitely not a robbery. Look at her right hand. She's still wearing her wedding ring, and it's not from Walmart. No crack head is going to leave that stone behind even if he had to cut her finger off. Third. She's probably widowed, not divorced. Hence the ring on the right hand, not her left hand. Fourth. She's not wearing an overcoat. Why wasn't she wearing an overcoat? You steal an overcoat, handbag and leave a big ol' diamond? That doesn't make sense. 'Course none of these things ever make sense at first. But that's what I see."

"Well, you saw more than I did. Like her coat. I didn't even notice that it was missing. And the widow thing. How'd you know that?"

"Well, if you were an old fart like me, hitting the bars, looking for women, you'd know things like that."

Seeing that the media was getting restless and getting in everybody's way, Johnny made his way to the head of the alley to greet the ever-increasing crowd. Rumors among the Fourth Estate were heading in all directions and needed to be corralled. While Johnny answered their questions, Daniel met with the two witnesses and briefly questioned them. But they offered no real information regarding the why, where, when, who or what - the five W's in solving the crime. He then checked in with the forensic team that had arrived and was setting up shop. He briefed the team on the status of their investigation and then got out of their way to let them do their work. He and Johnny would talk to them later, once the team had enough time to do their preliminary evaluation. The DFS's final report wouldn't be available for at least three weeks unless the lady turned out to be someone important or special. If she were, that would change everything.

As he walked up to the front of the alley, he could see and hear Johnny holding forth. The reporters were taping everything he said while cameramen shot videos of him and the forensic team behind the yellow crime scene tape dusting for prints, checking for footprints, taking measurements. Anything that could be used on the news reports. They knew not to take any images of the victim. Journalism hadn't reached that low point... yet. The homicide would be made public on the noontime and nightly TV news reports with the reporters' 'live, first on the scene,' 30-second report and would hit the morning newspapers tomorrow.

"Don't they ever get tired of asking the same old questions," said Johnny as he met up with Daniel. "And do you know what they get paid? Hell, I could've retired ten years ago on what they make. And a couple of those boneheads had the nerve to snitch my last two doughnuts. Hell, they should be buying 'em for us. I swear they're nothing but a bunch of ... of... friggin' prima donnas."

"Wrinkles, do you even know what *prima donna* means?"

"Yeah. It means they're assholes."

The two detectives split up the remainder of their tasks. Johnny would canvas the area looking for possible witnesses and surveillance cameras while Daniel met with the workers from the nearby warehouse.

The building fronting the alley was a tile distribution warehouse. Unfortunately, there were no outside surveillance cameras. Obviously, tile was not high on thieves' priority list. Daniel only had to interview six people, including the manager, as business was slow this time of the year. During their peak, the company employed as many as sixty people. He briefly interviewed each one, making notes as he did. Every employee, at one time or another, had been in the alley that day because they all entered and exited the building through a back door that opened into the alley. None saw anything unusual including the smokers and the one employee who had emptied a box of discontinued tile samples into the dumpster. All of the employees had left work between 5 and 5:30 p.m. the day of the crime except the manager. He had stayed until about 6:30 p.m. and didn't see anything out of the ordinary as he left. That meant the body had to have been dumped there between 6:30 p.m. and approximately 6 a.m., the time that the dumpster workers found the body. Daniel thanked the manager and workers, gave each one his business card, and returned to the crime scene.

He found Johnny talking to his buddy and lead DFS agent, Benjamin Franklin Archer, aka 'Bennie' to his friends. He had been around almost as long as Johnny and looked it. The bags under his eyes were large and dark and his 'looks like I just got out of bed' curly white hair was covered up by a 'DC Police' ski cap.

"Bennie, find anything significant, like a ladies coat?" asked Daniel.

"No. But we weren't looking for one. Oh, I see. The victim doesn't have one on. That's strange. I don't think I would have ever noticed that. I guess that's why y'all are the detectives. One thing I can tell you, the victim wasn't from this part of town. I figure she was carjacked."

"That's kinda what we were thinking," said Johnny. "Somehow, though, my gut tells me there's more to this than just your ordinary carjacking. If you see anything out of the ordinary, can you call us? Me and Danny boy are already feeling the heat from Vernon, and we don't even know who the victim is."

"You find any cameras?" asked Daniel, his question direct to Johnny.

"There's a couple at the entrance of an off-site storage complex across the street. Maybe we can get some useful videos from them. I'll check with the owner when we get back to the office and have them sent to you, Bennie."

Both detectives thanked Bennie and his team and made their way to their car. There was a lot to do at the office – on this case and the other cases that seemed to bog down over time. And time was the most important part of any case. The sooner they began work on the case, the better the odds of finding the person or persons responsible – especially while the tracks were still fresh, everybody's memory was still good, and the perpetrators were still nervous, and apt to make mistakes.

Chapter 29

Thursday, December 28, 2006, 7:24 a.m. EST

Margie's apartment building was a 16 story red brick high rise located in an area of Alexandria, Virginia called Old Town. The complex was much more luxurious than Wayne had expected with many of the apartments having sunrooms facing the Potomac. As he approached the main entrance, he noticed a security code box fronting the double doors. He had Margie's apartment key but didn't know the security code. He had no plan B for this. The flaws in his plan were killing him not to mention the thought of having to tell Bobby. As he was about to head back to the car, he saw his plan B - an elderly man, using a walker, entering the building. Without skipping a beat, Wayne fell in behind the old man and tailgated him into the building keeping his face down so not to have it videotaped by the overhead security cameras. No one seemed to notice or care. Once inside the lobby, he saw a bank of elevators on the far wall. Halfway between him and an open elevator door sat a security guard reading the newspaper. Remembering Bobby's earlier advice to act normal, Wayne walked nonchalantly but quickly past the elderly man, past the security guard who never once looked up from his paper, and into the open elevator cabin. He quickly pressed 10 and then watched the elderly man struggle desperately to make it to the open elevator only to see the doors close in his face. Wayne promptly dismissed his rudeness as a necessary part of his plan – no witnesses.

Wayne walked out of the elevator into an empty 10th-floor hallway. The door to the emergency stairwell was to his right. He used the stairwell to walk down to the 8th floor where Margie's apartment was located. Not going directly to her floor was part of his newly altered plan. Before exiting the stairwell, he slipped on a pair of latex gloves and pulled down the bill of his cap. When he opened the door to the hallway, he spotted in the elevator's landing a young couple holding hands, forehead to forehead, whispering. Before they could turn to see him, Wayne shoved his hands in his coat pockets to conceal the latex gloves. The couple looked at him only briefly then resumed their prior activities. Margie's apartment was found almost immediately, the second door on the left. But instead of stopping, Wayne walked passed it and on down the hall towards the elevators so to appear as if he were heading to another apartment - just in case the young couple looked at him. But they were too preoccupied with each other to pay him any attention.

As he neared the young couple, the elevator doors opened, and the couple hurriedly made their way into the 8x8 cabin. As soon as the metal doors closed, Wayne raced back to Margie's apartment, unlocked the deadbolt, the door lock, and swiftly entered her residence closing the door behind him. He was greeted by the soft glow of light shining from a room just beyond the foyer. He flipped on an overhead light and surveyed the apartment. Straight ahead was the living room with an adjoining glass-enclosed sunroom. To the right of the living room was the dining room. And to his immediate right was the kitchen and mini-laundry closet. All of the rooms were painted in a soft pastel yellow giving the apartment a warm, comfortable look and feel.

When he entered the living room, he saw the source of the soft glow. Margie's Christmas tree, obviously on a timer. He suddenly felt the urge to leave. To turn and run, his good conscience trying to take command. *What the hell am I doing here!* He felt weird, like an intruder, a burglar, a trespasser violating Margie's space. But corroborating their story was an important part of his plan, so he pressed on, pushing the negative thoughts from his mind.

Once in the middle of the living room, he gazed around. The apartment was so Margie. There were pictures everywhere. Most of the pictures were of her late husband and two sons taken at different times and stages of their lives, just like the ones on her desk at the office. Even though he had never been here, he remembered when she moved to the apartment. She had been depressed the whole week before the move. She was leaving behind the home that had blessed her with so many wonderful memories. Where she had raised her two boys. Where she had spent so many Christmases and Thanksgivings. Where she had her small vegetable garden. And where her husband had lived and died. But the house had become too big for her, too much to handle, too expensive to maintain, and she refused to be dependent upon anyone - including her sons. They had their own lives to live. She had bravely made the transition from wife and homemaker to widow and executive secretary and accordingly, the transition from homeowner to apartment dweller. It had taken her a while, but she seemed comfortable with her new life. Wayne wondered why he hadn't helped her with the move.

His stomach began to ache with the thought of losing Margie. If *he* felt this bad, he could only imagine how her sons would feel.

One of the centerpieces in the living room was a burl walnut secretary/desk. He stopped to admire the desk. He appreciated fine antique furniture. He guessed the piece to be from the mid to late 19th century. Unlike most period pieces that are used primarily for decoration, this was a working desk. There were letters and bills stuck in many of the desk's pigeon holes. A small laptop lay open on the desktop - a perfect place for Idella's note. He pulled the note from his coat pocket, unfolded it and laid it on the laptop's keyboard where it could be easily seen. Checking his watch, he saw that nearly ten minutes had passed. His nerves were under control and he was no longer scared, but he needed to wrap things up. He headed to the kitchen to make 'lunch.' There was no need to turn on the overhead fluorescents as the light from the foyer provided sufficient illumination. Moving with the speed of a hungry teenage boy, he found everything he needed - a small salad plate and tea glass in the overhead cabinets, a knife in a cabinet drawer, a loaf of bread in a small pantry and mayo and a pitcher of tea in the fridge. He grabbed a slice of bread and ran his hand back and forth over the crust so that crumbs would fall onto the plate. He then pulled off a small piece of the crust and placed it on the plate. Next, he stuck the knife in the jar of mayo making sure a small amount of mayo was left on the blade. Both plate and knife were placed in the sink. The final step of 'lunch' was to pour a small amount of tea into the glass and dilute it with some tap water to make it appear as if it were ice tea. He set the glass in the sink next to the plate and knife. He hated to admit it, but Bobby's idea of 'lunch' was brilliant. Checking the time, less than fifteen minutes had passed. He swiftly returned all the food items to their original locations. Then instead of leaving the remains of the leftover piece of bread in the trash, he stuck it in his coat pocket. *I'll give this to Bobby.* Wayne smiled. This hadn't been so bad after all.

Moving from the kitchen, Wayne surveyed the other rooms in the apartment. He wasn't sure what he was looking for, but he felt he needed to do just one more thing - something little to further validate their story. On the left side of the living room was a door to a small bedroom with two twin beds. It was very clean and showed little signs of daily use - obviously the guest bedroom. The door to the master bedroom was on the right side of the living room and to the left of the dining room. In keeping with the rest of the apartment, there were pictures of Margie's family atop the dresser, chest of drawers and night tables. The large queen-size four-poster bed gave Wayne an idea. Whenever his ex-wife, Norma, would come home after work, she would take off her shoes, lay down on the bed for a few minutes and take what she called her power nap. Wayne assumed that older women, like Margie, would probably do the same. So he lay down on Margie's bed being careful to keep his feet off the bedspread. He stayed there for a few seconds. When he arose, he looked at the bed. It was ruffled up enough to appear that someone had slept there but no one would be able to tell the size or gender of the person.

He was through. And it had been so easy. And with no pre-planning whatsoever. Mishaps? There were no mishaps because with no planning, what happens, happens and you adjust. This was Bobby's 'shoot from the hip' methodology. Thank God it worked this time.

Chapter 30

Thursday, December 28, 2006, 7:45 a.m. EST

Looking at his watch, Wayne realized he had now been gone for over twenty minutes. He needed to leave now or Bobby might get worried and do something stupid.

As he walked out of the bedroom, he heard the doorbell, then someone knocking on the door in the 'shave and a haircut - two bits' cadence.

Wayne froze.

Seconds later, two or three more knocks - this time much louder but with no cadence.

Oh, God! Who's that?

Wayne prayed that the visitor was either a friend or neighbor. If so, with no one answering the door, they would soon leave. If it were Bobby, he would probably continue to knock until he finally realized that Wayne had left or wasn't going to answer. Regardless, he wasn't answering the door. He promptly turned off the light in the bedroom and tiptoed into the adjoining bathroom closing the door behind him while simultaneously flipping on the bathroom light. A door to his immediate left was to a walk-in closet. He would have to hide there – no choice. He flipped on the light in the closet and flipped off the one in the bathroom. The closet was typical of most women. It was filled with clothes of all varieties, handbags, and shoes. Lots of shoes with most still in their original boxes. Behind the door, hanging on a rod that ran the length of the closet, were Margie's long dresses, pants, and blouses with many covered in clear plastic dry cleaning bags.

When he heard the faint noise of three more quick knocks, he flipped off the closet light and quickly but silently moved behind the closet door pulling it as far open as the door allowed. He positioned himself between the wall and the hanging clothes, keeping as many of the clothes in front of him as he could. *If it's Bobby, I'm going to kill him.*

Wayne's anger soon turned to fear. Fear like he had never experienced before as he heard a man's voice inside the apartment. And it wasn't Bobby's.

"Yo! Mom!! You home? It's me, Kyle"

Kyle shut the door behind him and walked into the living room, looking in the kitchen as he did.

"Hey, Mom! You here?"

With no answer, he headed to her bedroom. She wasn't there, but he found the bathroom door closed. Maybe she was in there and just hadn't heard him.

Tapping lightly on the door, Kyle called out again. "Mom. You in there? It's me, Kyle."

With no answer, he knocked once more and then tried turning the doorknob. It wasn't locked. Slowly, he pushed the door open.

"I'm coming in! Cover yourself!"

He flipped on the bathroom light as he entered and looked toward the shower-tub. He was relieved not to find his Mom there, in all her glory, drying off or possibly even worse. Like laying on the floor dead like Aaron had found their Dad. Maybe that's why he was the way he was. Maybe finding Dad that way had hardened him, made him fear closeness. That way he wouldn't feel the hurt so bad the next time. But Kyle knew that hurt never takes a vacation. Not for those you love.

Beads of sweat that had formed under Wayne's cap began to seep down his face and across his tightened lips. The plastic laundry bags that covered Margie's dresses and provided Wayne's cover seemed magnetized by the salty liquid and tried desperately to shrink wrap his face. Only by looking straight up was he able to save his face from a suffocating plastic veil. But even with this adversity, Wayne remained invisibly quiet, breathing only when it became necessary. From the time Kyle entered the bathroom until he left, Wayne kept his eyes closed perhaps thinking that if he couldn't see Kyle, maybe Kyle couldn't see him. His heart was pounding so hard it was a wonder why Kyle hadn't heard it. The amount of time spent in the bathroom and closet was less than a minute, but to Wayne, it seemed forever. He had never been this scared in his life – not even when Jim pulled the gun on him. It made him think. What would he do if Kyle found him? He hadn't planned on this. But the whole trip had never been part of his original plan. Why had he veered from it? Why had he thought that something like breaking and entering could be done extemporaneously? No planning, whatsoever. Like Bobby would have done. Why hadn't he just called the police in the first place? Were NAGS and his job that important? *Yes. Yes, they are.* NAGS was his life. What would he do without NAGS? He'd have nothing. Now he knew how Jim Barnes felt.

Kyle flipped off the light to the bathroom and pulled the door closed. Heading down the hall back to the living room, he pulled out his cell phone and called Aaron.

"Aaron. It's me, Kyle."

"What do you want now?" he answered impatiently.

"Mom's not here… at her apartment. I came by just like you said and she's not here."

"Kyle, I don't have time for this. Listen to me. Mom's probably with her boyfriend. Check that out. But don't be surprised by what you find." And he hung up.

Butthead.

Kyle knew Aaron was right, like always. He went over to his Mom's desk in the living room, flipped on the small candlestick lamp and started looking in the drawers for her address book. He found her familiar pink and white stripe address book in the top drawer and started scanning through it looking for a name that might ring a bell. His Mom had told him her new friend's name, but he had forgotten it. The search was fruitless as his Mom had lots of friends, so there were lots of pages. Closing the book, he subconsciously ran through the alphabet hoping one of the letters might jostle his memory. It was a technique his Dad had taught him. It worked about 60% of the time, but not this time.

Aaron would know. He always remembered everything. Reluctantly, he flipped open his cell then immediately closed it. He couldn't bear to listen to Aaron's patronizing voice again. His Mom's friend's name had to be somewhere in her desk. His eyes immediately zoned in on the note sitting on his Mom's laptop. Excitedly he picked it up, did a quick read and returned it. No help. Just a note from someone named Idella - probably someone in her church. Her emails would have been a big help but her laptop was in shutdown mode and he didn't know her password. He checked out all the little cubby holes in the desk but found nothing except paid and unpaid bills. And he found nothing useful in the desk drawers. All they contained were old trip memorabilia - Hawaiian leis, voided passports, trip diaries, maps and everything else under the sun except the name of his Mom's new boyfriend.

Resigned to his fate, he pulled out his cell again and pressed the speed dial for Aaron.

"Hey, Aaron. It's me, one more time."

"*What, dammit!*"

"Real quick. Mom's friend. What's his name?"

"You mean her boyfriend?" he said disparagingly, emphasizing the word 'boy.'

"Yes."

"Winston. Winston Blackwell. The *third!* Don't call me again!" Then he hung up.

It should have made Kyle mad, but it didn't. He knew the thought of any man dating his Mom made Aaron extremely jealous. Aaron wanted his Mom to be happy but not if it meant someone trying to replace his Dad.

Kyle went back to the address book. No Winston Blackwell there. Not under 'B' or 'W.'

Meanwhile, Wayne remained motionless, his back pressing hard against the wall of Margie's closet. From the heavy winter clothes he wore, the suffocating weight of Margie's clothes and the anxiety caused by fear, he was now completely drenched in sweat. He had already fought off one sneeze caused by beads of perspiration taking up residence in his left nostril and was working hard to fight off a second sneeze that seemed imminent. On a positive note, having avoided Kyle's detection had boosted his confidence. His fear was slowly subsiding. He began thinking more clearly. He needed to hear Kyle. Hear what he was saying. Hear where he was in the apartment. And most importantly, hear when he left the apartment. Quietly, he pressed his ear against the closet wall. All he could hear was some muffled words. He prayed Kyle wasn't talking to security or worse, the police. Then a thought occurred to him. A really bad thought. What if his cell rang? What if Bobby lost patience and tried calling him? Or if anybody tried calling him? Then he remembered, he'd left his phone with Bobby! *Oh, thank you, GOD! Thank you!* But just as soon as he had dismissed that thought, another bad one occurred. He had been gone a lot longer than he had told Bobby he would. So what if he came up to the apartment and began banging on the door, looking for him? *Oh,*

God! Please don't let that happen. I don't need this! An uneasiness began to permeate Wayne's mental state with fear ebbing and flowing like the ocean tides.

Kyle returned his Mom's address book back to her desk. He mentally kicked himself for not asking Aaron if he knew Blackwell's telephone number. But calling Aaron again? NOT going to happen. Then he remembered his Mom's blackboard in the kitchen, next to the landline. Maybe she'd written the number there! In a flash, he had turned the corner to the kitchen and was looking at the board. He had to smile at its message:

MERRY CHRISTMAS!!!!   HAPPY NEW YEAR!!!

The trip to the apartment had been a total bust. Yet he wasn't worried about his Mom. Aaron was probably right. Most likely she was at her friend's house.

Even without his ear to the wall, Wayne heard the front door slam. After five minutes of total silence to make sure that it was Kyle going out and not someone coming in, he pushed aside the sweaty plastic laundry bag and exited his hidden sanctuary. He saw no one in the bedroom. A quick visual sweep of the living room revealed the same results. Relieved, he walked swiftly but quietly to the front door. Like in the closet, he pressed his ear against the door to listen for voices or movement in the hallway. He heard nothing. He then visually checked for anyone through the peephole. Seeing nothing, he unlocked the deadbolt, jerked open the door and looked up and down the hall. The coast was clear. Quickly he stepped outside pulling the door shut behind him making sure all locks were engaged. Wasting little time, he sprinted down the hall, out the emergency exit and down the eight flights of concrete steps, taking two at a time. In record time, he found himself outside the building on the opposite side of where he had parked. But that was OK. At least he was out, the trip was a success and he had not been discovered.

Chapter 31

Thursday, December 28, 2006, 8:09 a.m. EST

The cold air felt good to Wayne. A strange and eerie feeling came over him – a kind of a high. A feeling he had never felt before. He had to tell Bobby what happened. It was scary, yet invigorating. It certainly wouldn't have been, if he had been caught. BUT HE WASN'T. Walking at a brisk pace, the once steamy hot sweat that encompassed his body now had a chilling effect. Without being obvious, he quickly made his way from around the back of the building to the parking place where he saw the car but no Bobby. Rushing up to the car, he saw him in the passenger seat with it tilted as far back as it could go. Sleeping! Wayne banged twice on the door panel as hard as he could causing Bobby to wake with a jerk. His wide-eyed head twisted left and right looking wildly for the source of the clamor. Then he saw Wayne standing outside of the car, laughing!

"Funny. Very funny. Asshole," yelled Bobby through the window and flipping him a 'bird'.

This time Wayne had seen Bobby's indignant gesture but ignored it. He ran around to the driver's side of the car and quickly jumped in, talking excitedly as he did.

"You're not going to *believe* what happened!"

"What? Where?"

"In the apartment."

"Something happened in the apartment?"

"Let me get the hell out of here, and I'll tell you!"

Bobby quickly returned his seat to an upright position while Wayne pulled out into the street. His hand automatically went to the heater control where he turned it up full blast.

"So what happened?"

"Get this. One of Margie's sons, Kyle, walked in on me."

"You're shitting me. What'd you say to him?"

"Fortunately, I was in the bathroom and was able to hide in the closet. He never saw me, but I thought I was a goner. I was sweating bullets the whole time. I don't know what I would have done or said if he had found me. But he didn't. It was really kind of…"

"Fucked up?" Bobby interjected.

"No. I was going to say exciting, almost thrilling. Like nothing I've ever experienced before."

"God, you've led a sheltered life," returned Bobby. Wayne recognized the boasting tone in Bobby's voice - the one that suggested that experiences like this had been commonplace in his life.

Bobby turned to Wayne. The expression on his face turned serious.

"We need to think about this. What would you do *if* somebody found you out?"

"I dunno. I guess we go to plan B," shrugged Wayne.

"And what's plan B?"

"I don't have a plan B for that. I've never really thought about getting caught."

"Well, I have."

"Really? So… if you had been in that closet and Kyle found you out, what would *you* do?"

"I'd deal with it."

"Deal with it? What do you mean?"

"I mean I'd deal with it." There was a silence that seemed to last forever. "Wayne, I'm messing with you. Quit thinking about it. What's next on the schedule?"

"Let me think." But it was hard for Wayne to think now. What Bobby had said had unsettled him.

"Well?"

"Oh yeah. Verizon. Did you find a Verizon store?"

"There's one on 'F' Street, a couple of miles down from the office, but they didn't answer my calls. Probably not open. I say we go get some coffee. There should be a Starbucks near Verizon. I can call them again from there."

'Sounds good' came out of Wayne's mouth but his mind was still thinking about what Bobby had said, *I'd deal with it.*

Chapter 32

Thursday, December 28, 2006, 8:30 a.m. EST

Kyle's jog back to his apartment was much faster than the trip over to his Mom's. He loved running in the wintertime with its brisk cold air. The mixture of the body heat and the winter's frigid air made for an invigorating, pleasant run, whereas the summer with its stifling, humid heat was only for the brave. He didn't jog very often in the summer.

On the way back, all he could think about was Winston Blackwell and how to locate him. Jogging seemed to clear his mind. All sorts of ideas popped into his head. Like checking with his Mom's apartment manager to see if Blackwell lived in the same complex. Or checking with his Mom's church to see if he was a member. The thought of Googling Blackwell's name also came to mind. As a long shot, he considered calling Mr. Peters to see if Blackwell worked for NAGS.

Kyle's apartment, unlike his Mom's, didn't overlook the Potomac. It overlooked other apartment buildings and parking lots. The apartment building was equipped with the two slowest elevators in Virginia. At least that was the consensus of those living there. Not wishing to wait for the sluggish lifts, he headed over to the emergency stairwell and jogged up the six flights of stairs to his apartment. He could feel the burn in his legs as he reached the last landing. After stopping a moment to catch his breath, he dragged himself into his apartment, into the kitchen for a bottle of water then over to the sofa where he crashed. Once he drained the Dasani, he pulled his cell from his sweatshirt pocket and checked for any messages or calls he might have missed. Nothing. And again, his calls to his Mom's phones went to voicemail. This was getting very frustrating and repetitive. She had never been this inaccessible. Winston Blackwell III was his best bet. He pushed off his running shoes using only his feet then pushed off his sweaty socks using his big toes. It was an art that most guys learned at an early age. He grabbed his laptop off his leather footstool and logged on. Googling the White Pages, he entered Blackwell's first and last name. No city, state or zip. Seconds later, he was looking at a screen filled with Winston Blackwell's but only one Winston Blackwell III with a Chevy Chase,

Maryland address - a suburb of Washington, DC. Hopefully, this was the guy.

Kyle grabbed his phone and punched in Blackwell's number only to have the call go to voicemail. Mr. Blackwell had a distinguished sounding voice, almost like a radio announcer or a preacher. The fact that neither Blackwell nor his Mom answered their phones and assuming it was the right Blackwell, it was quite possible that Aaron was right. They were somewhere together having fun. He left a brief message telling Mr. Blackwell who he was and to please return his call. He placed his phone in one of the beer holes in his sofa arm and stared at his computer screen, pondering his next move when his cell rang. He immediately recognized the number.

"Hello, Kyle Hamilton. This is Katie. Are you busy?"

Kyle couldn't help but smile as he heard her voice. As he talked, he slid his laptop onto the sofa and stretched his legs up onto the footstool.

"Not for you. Just finished my morning jog."

"Well, I've got good news. My boss said that I could have the afternoon off. Are we still on for lunch?"

"Absolutely. I can hardly wait." Kyle's phone beeped in mid-sentence letting him know of an impending call. This *had* to be his Mom.

"Katie, can you hold just a minute? Someone's beeping me. It's probably my Mom. I really need to speak to her." Kyle hoped Katie didn't sense the anxiety in his voice.

Kyle hardly heard her reply before quickly answering the incoming call.

"Well, hello!" he answered with a tone of voice that said *finally*.

"Hello. This is Winston Blackwell. Could I please speak with Kyle Hamilton?" asked the caller whose deep resonating voice Kyle immediately recognized.

"This is he. Thank you for returning my call," responded Kyle, his hopes of finding his mother rising by the second. "Are you by chance a friend of my Mom, Margie Hamilton?"

"Yes I am."

"Thank goodness. Mr. Blackwell, the reason I called is that I have been trying to reach my Mom for the last couple of days, uh… and hoped she might be with you," stammered Kyle, somewhat embarrassed.

"No, Kyle. She's not with me. In fact, I've also been trying to reach her. We were supposed to have dinner together last night. But when I came over to pick her up, she never came to her door nor did she answer her apartment phone or cell phone. So then I checked with my sister, Abigail. She and Margie go to the same church. But she hadn't heard from her since Tuesday night.   I am very worried about your mother. I don't believe she would have canceled our dinner engagement without calling me. She's not that type of person. And I would have called you if I had known your number."

This was not good. This is *not* what he wanted to hear. His mother would never stand *anybody* up. Not unless it was an emergency. She didn't have an impolite bone in her body.

Blackwell continued. "I was just about to call her apartment's main office and have their security people check on her when you called. If I'm not overstepping my bounds, I think we should do that."

The anguish in Blackwell's voice was most noticeable adding to Kyle's worry.

"That's not necessary. I've already been to her apartment this morning. She wasn't there. I also called my brother, and he hasn't seen her either. I'm not sure what to do next. I'm kinda at a loss. Do you think she could be doing something for the church?" asked Kyle, searching for *any* reason to account for her prolonged absence.

"Possible. But that wouldn't explain why she missed our dinner engagement. If you'd like, I'll have my sister call the church and some of their mutual friends," replied Blackwell. Then after a brief pause, "One other thing and I hesitate to say this, but you might want to check the hospitals and possibly the police."

"I don't know why I didn't think of that. You know, maybe she slipped on some ice or fell in her tub! If you call your sister, I'll call the hospitals and… and the police."

Then suddenly, Kyle remembered that he had left Katie hanging.

"Mr. Blackwell, can you please hold for one minute? I'll be right back."

Kyle quickly switched lines, but Katie had hung up. He couldn't blame her. It was so rude of him to leave her hanging like that. He would have to explain what was going on and hope that she would understand. He switched back to Blackwell.

"I'm sorry Mr. Blackwell. I had completely forgotten that I had left a friend on hold. But getting back to Mom, if either of us find out anything, we'll let the other one know."

"Let's pray that we hear from her soon." And the call ended.

Kyle liked Mr. Blackwell, even though he had never met him. He seemed concerned and caring. He knew his Mom wouldn't date anyone who wasn't. His thoughts returned to Katie. His fingers couldn't dial her number fast enough.

"Hi, Katie. This is Kyle. I am really sorry for leaving you hanging on the phone like that. I'm not usually that rude. I can't believe I did that. I just lost track of time. My mind…"

"Kyle, it's OK. Is everything all right?"

"I think so. Just some family issues."

"Anything I can do?"

"No. I think everything is fine." Kyle felt if anything were wrong, Katie would want to know and help. But now wasn't the time. And he wasn't 100% sure anything was really wrong. "Luigi's still fine with you?"

"Looking forward to it, Kyle Hamilton." She then hung up the phone.

Katie made him feel good. This is probably how his Dad felt about Mom when they first started dating. Dad had always told him that he would know when he found the right person. That if it didn't feel right, it wasn't. Kyle laid back with his hands behind his head, mentally revisiting his date with Katie, her phone calls, her voice, her upbeat positive attitude. She was the one. He had that feeling.

Chapter 33

Thursday, December 28, 2006, 10:18 a.m. EST

While Bobby was in the Verizon store getting his new phone, Wayne sat in the car, the heater running full blast, thinking about the events that had already occurred and what changes needed to be made to his plan. As he thought about the issues with the lodge's security system, it made him realize that they also had an exposure with the security system at the headquarters' building. There were security cameras around the perimeter of the building and in the parking area. Every activity in those areas had been recorded including Jim and Margie going into the building but never coming out. And he had completely overlooked it! A major, major oversight in his plan. That evidence *had* to be erased. Like today! And Bobby could never know that it was not on his original plan. That meant they would have to put off going back to the lodge to bury Jim. He would blame that on the side trip to Verizon. It troubled him that he had overlooked something with such potential damaging consequences. It seemed like everything in his plan was going haywire. First, the stolen car, next, the fiasco at the lodge, then the near-disaster at Margie's apartment and now the Headquarters' security system! What else had he missed?

The ride back to the office was quick. Other than a brief mention of the security fix that had to be done at the office, little was said between the two. Bobby kept himself busy setting up his new phone while Wayne drove and worried. Once they turned into the parking lot and headed into the building, the events of yesterday filled Wayne's mind. Would he ever forget the fear that engulfed him as he stared down the barrel of Jim's gun, his quick and deadly response, Margie's unfortunate death, the two mummified bodies dumped in the back of the car, Margie's lifeless body tossed beside a garbage dumpster, and Jim's body frozen in the snow behind the barn?

Even worse was the haunting feeling he had when he passed by Margie's desk and into his office. The memory of her lifeless body, her blood-laden hair and her hollowed-out eye with blood oozing down her face sent chills down his spine. Not surprisingly, there was little sorrow for Jim Barnes, only anger. While Wayne internalized, Bobby was whistling, obviously unfazed by yesterday's tragedy. Didn't he care? Didn't this bother him? Was he that callous?

"Are you that happy? Your whistling is annoying."

Bobby stopped whistling and looked Wayne dead in the eyes. Wayne fully expected him to lash out, take him to task. But instead, he seemed to understand. He placed his arm around Wayne's shoulder and spoke to him like a father giving counsel and advice to a son.

"Look, Wayne, I know this has to be hard on you, coming back today to your office with everything that went on yesterday. But you… we have got to move on. Stay with your plan. What happened, happened. Can't go back and change it. We can either let it smother us, or we can put it aside. I plan to put it aside, get past this, and move on with my life. It doesn't benefit you or me to dwell on the past. Things we can't change. Our life is NAGS. If you're having second thoughts, you need to stop. I'm telling you, it'll get better with time. Believe me."

"It's… it's just that I worked with Margie every day. You didn't. She was more than a good worker. She *made* this office. It's hard for me to believe that she'll never be back. It's hard putting her out of my mind. I keep seeing her alive at her desk, smiling and happy and then, suddenly, she's dead, lying in the storage room or in the trunk of the car, wrapped up in that awful tarp or worse, lying next to the trash dump. This is too much. I'm not sure I could have handled this alone. I don't know what I would have done without you. You've been a rock. You've kept me going."

"All right already. You're gonna make me blush. I didn't do anything for you that you wouldn't have done for me. We're a team, you and me. So let's quit dwelling on the past and get on with fixing that security thing."

Wayne walked over to his desk and booted up his PC. He wasn't sure how to 'fix the security thing.'

"All I know about the security equipment is where it's located. But I don't think it could be that complicated," said Wayne.

"Can't be. Not if old Ernie's in charge," added Bobby. Ernie Carter, a retired DC policeman, was NAGS' security guard for over fifteen years. When not on vacation, lunch, smoke break or at the doctor's office, he would sit in the lobby and keep watch on everyone who came through the door unless he was 'resting his eyes' which seemed to be more often than not.

"Ernie wasn't in charge. In fact, he probably didn't even know we had surveillance equipment. Not unless it was in the breakroom or the restroom." Wayne forced a smile. "No. Margie handled all security-related issues."

"Like at the lodge?" reminded Bobby.

Ignoring Bobby's last snarky remark, Wayne motioned for him to follow along as he walked into the 'L' shaped storage vault, all the way to the back and around the 'L'.

The security equipment was sitting on one of the built-in shelves with its keyboard and monitor on top of the processor. The monitor displayed four different areas outside the building - the front door, the driveway, the back door and side parking lot, and the rear parking area.

"So there's no video surveillance inside the building, just these four areas outside?" asked Bobby as he closely watched the video monitor.

"No. That's it. I guess no one ever thought we needed any surveillance inside since we have so few people here, and we're gone most of the time. Plus we have ol' Ernie watching out for us." Wayne smiled; Bobby didn't. The joke had run its course.

"Good. Which means there was no video of what happened *in* your office. That's really fortunate."

Both men hovered over the security system unit. Wayne pressed a couple of keys, and nothing happened.

"How can we tell if anything is being recorded?" Asked Bobby as he watched the monitor. "Surely it doesn't record everything 24/7."

"I wouldn't think so. The recording system is probably motion-sensitive. Why don't you go out to the parking lot and I'll see what happens."

Bobby left the vault and walked out to the parking lot. As he left the building, he looked up at the camera and gave Wayne a slight wave and a big Dr. Phil grin. After a quick walk around the parking lot, he returned to the vault. Wayne was busy pushing buttons, nodding his head as he did.

"You got 'er figured out?" asked Bobby.

"Getting there. OK. Here's what happened. When you walked out the back door, 'REC' appeared on the portion of the monitor for that camera location. When you moved to the car, 'REC' appeared on the monitor for the camera pointing to the driveway. So I was right. The system only records whenever there's any motion."

"That makes sense. Do you know how to erase yesterday's recordings?"

"I think so. I found a 'FILE' tab on the 'MENU' screen, and one of the options is 'DELETE.' Assuming that we can delete a portion of the tape, should we do that or delete the entire tape? Remember Nixon and his 18-minute gap?"

"You're right," agreed Bobby. "I say erase the whole fucking tape."

"It's not a tape. It's a hard drive. These things are actually computers."

"Oh for crying out loud. Don't get technical on me. Just erase the damn thing."

Wayne selected the 'DELETE -> ERASE ->DAYS -> ALL' options. It worked just like his computer. As the disk was erasing, a '%Completion' bar appeared. When it reached 100%, a message appeared indicating the job was complete.

"Well, that wasn't so hard." Wayne punched in a few more keys, and the display returned to monitoring the four outside areas.

"Hey. I just thought of something. Why don't you call Margie and ask her if she could come back in tomorrow to help us with the Appeal campaign? Tell her that I just flew in."

"What the hell are you talking about? " Then as if a light came on. "Oh, I get it. Great idea! Great idea. I should have thought of that."

"Yeah. Put that in your plan. Put a note by it saying I thought of it!" Bobby said proudly.

Both men headed back to Wayne's desk where Wayne called Margie on both her apartment phone and cell phone, leaving messages on each requesting that she come back to the office on Friday and to call him at the office or on his cell phone if she couldn't make it. He apologized profusely for the inconvenience, especially since it was the holidays.

"I like that. A really good idea," said Wayne as he hung up the phone. Then checking his watch, he continued. "How about an early lunch before heading over to Jim's apartment? We're going to let him buy today. At least his credit card is. You have a preference?"

"I say Chinese… in honor of last night's Chinese fire drill at the lodge." Then turning somewhat serious, he continued. "Before we go, how 'bout printing me a copy of your plan. I think it'd be easier on both of us if I knew ahead of time what the hell we were doing and when. Like I didn't know we had to do this security thing until we left Verizon's. I thought we were going back to the lodge to put old lardass in the ground. As it is, I'm just kinda hanging around, waiting for my orders."

"Yeah. The Verizon's trip put us behind schedule so I'm having to rethink, replan a few things."

"Well, I'd still like a copy."

"You think that would be wise? A printed copy? What if it were to fall into the wrong hands? We'd be dead meat."

"You think I'm *that fucking* irresponsible?"

"No. No. Nothing like that. I guess I'm just paranoid. Have a seat. Let me make a few changes, and I'll print you out a copy."

While Bobby paced, Wayne carefully adjusted his plan, adding the security oversight then scheduled Jim's burial and all associated action items as a Plan B addendum. Once the changes were completed, he printed it, stapled it then handed it to Bobby on their way out to lunch. He hoped his facial expressions didn't show his concern with Bobby having a printed copy. And yes, Bobby was *that fucking* irresponsible.

Chapter 34

Thursday, December 28, 2006, 11:12 a.m. EST

Corporal Ray Geddings wasn't a morning person. Never had been. He had almost flunked out of the police academy because of its early hours - so for him to be at work before noon was quite unusual. But today, he was eager to get an early start – at least for him.

"Well, look who's here?" asked Amy, administrative assistant/secretary of the Middleburg's Police Department. "You must have heard that we were having a free lunch today?"

"We're having free lunch? I hadn't heard that. What's the occasion?"

"You coming in early."

"Huh? How'd they know I was coming in early?"

"Good heavens, Ray. Don't be such an idiot. I'm just kidding."

"So, uh, no free lunch?"

"No, Ray. No free lunch. Why're you here so early? You know you can't clock in 'til 2:45. No overtime. Remember?"

"Yeah, I know. I just wanted to check out a couple of dudes that were up at the old Jackson house last night." (The NAGS lodge was originally built by William Henry Jackson. In small towns, the locals often called the older houses by its original owner's name – regardless of who lived in the house. In this case, the NAGS lodge was often referred to as the Jackson house.) "Me and Al were called out on a possible security breach last night."

"Yeah, I saw the report this morning. Looks like their alarm went off. But it appears they checked out OK. Why didn't the Sheriff's department handle the call? It's their jurisdiction."

"Should've, but they were tied up with a big wreck on 66. They called and asked us to help."

"So what's to check out? Y'all did that last night."

"Yeah. I know, but somehow I feel like I seen one of those fellas before. Can I get a copy of the report?"

Amy nodded and pulled the report for Geddings who then headed to his desk and signed on to his computer. The first thing he did was to check the NCIS for a Wayne Peters and then for a Robert Armstrong. Nothing.

Next, he checked for any state criminal records. Nothing. Then he checked for any traffic violations. Nothing. Why did he think he recognized the one in the cowboy hat? Maybe Al was right. Maybe they all look like somebody they'd seen before. As a last resort, he googled Wayne Peters' name. Geddings almost fell out of his chair. He'd hit the jackpot. There were over 400,000 hits for Wayne Peters. Next, he googled Robert Armstrong. Same thing. But even more hits.

"Amy! Look here. Quick!"

"Why? Ya find something?" Amy asked as she rolled her chair over to look at young Geddings' computer screen.

"Those dudes are famous. Look at the number of hits for this Armstrong dude. And almost as many for Peters."

"See if there's a picture," she asked.

Geddings clicked on the first hit which was the Wikipedia website. It had a picture of Bobby and a brief biography. There were numerous web links including ones to NAGS, Wayne Peters and the Parker vs. District of Columbia lawsuit.

"That's him. That's the cowboy. He had on this big Texas cowboy hat. Al figured him to be a man-whore, kinda like in the movie, uh… *Goodbye Cowboy* or something like that."

"Well, I can see why you thought you had seen this guy before," offered Amy. "He looks just like Dr. Phil. Print that website and one of the other guy."

Geddings printed two copies of Bobby Armstrong's info and then 'googled' the Wikipedia site for Peters which also had his picture and biography. He printed two copies of Peters' info. He kept one copy of both men's bio's and gave the others to Amy.

Amy first looked at Wayne Peter's picture and read his bio.

"This Peters fella *is* somebody important. He's an executive with NAGS." Then flipping the page, she read Armstrong's bio. "Good

Lord! This Dr. Phil looking guy is the president of NAGS. Say, aren't you a member?"

"Hell yeah, I'm a member. Just like every other red-blooded American. But I never seen him before 'til last night. Boy, was I wrong about those two guys. I just had this feeling that they were up to no good. Guess I was *way off* base."

Chapter 35

Thursday, December 28, 2006, 11:22 a.m. EST

Punctuality was a Hamilton family trait, so it wasn't unusual for Kyle to arrive early at Luigi's. Plus he wanted to beat the lunch crowd so he could get the perfect table for him and Katie.

The delicious aromas of the freshly baked lasagnas, pizzas, and other mouthwatering Italian dishes greeted him as he entered the restaurant. Luigi's was definitely the right choice. No Italian restaurant was complete without the red-checked tablecloths, and Luigi's was no exception. The only thing missing was old straw basket Chianti wine bottles with white candles. Generally, by noon, the restaurant would be jammed as would all of the other good restaurants in the surrounding area. But today, with many of the government and corporate workers using up their remaining vacation days (use it or lose it), the restaurant was only partially filled. Kyle requested one of the empty window tables and was immediately seated. The window afforded him a view of everyone coming up 19th Street.

Even though it had been less than twelve hours since he had last seen Katie, Kyle was most eager to see her again. Without realizing it, he found himself scrutinizing every woman that passed by his window as he searched for her. Their heavy coats, hats, and scarves covered most of their features causing him to give the ones with approximately the same body size as Katie an extra look. Some of the women thought he was ogling them and were flattered. Others either ignored him or quickly looked away in contempt. The anticipation was killing him. Katie was so unlike most of his other dates where he could hardly wait to get back to his apartment – alone. He loved the way she looked at him, her smile, the way she said his name. Everything about her.

Once he was seated, he checked his phone for any calls. There were none. He then set it to vibrate and placed it on the table in front of him. There was no reason to call his Mom. He'd left messages on both her phones multiple times. Thinking back to this morning, it had been a godsend to have found Mr. Blackwell. As he had suggested, Kyle called every major hospital in the Washington metro area but came up empty-handed. He also called the local police and spoke with an officer in Missing Persons. No one matching his mother's description had been found in either the local or NCIS reports – dead or alive. The officer suggested waiting at least another day to report her 'missing' unless she had Alzheimer's or suffered from dementia. Kyle assured the officer that his Mom was sound of mind but, as suggested, would wait another day.

Katie arrived a few minutes past noon. She saw Kyle peering out the window, but he didn't see her as he was looking down 19th Street, not up 19th Street, the direction of her parked car. She watched him for a few minutes. She really liked Kyle. He was the genuine article; what you saw was what you got. And she liked what she saw. He was so unlike a lot of her dates who were 'skirt-chasers' – interested in only one thing.

She walked closer to the window, tapped, then waved. A big smile appeared on Kyle's face when he saw her. He quickly rose from his chair and headed to the front entrance to greet her.

"I'm sorry I'm late. I actually had work to do this morning. You know it takes a lot of time trying to add more red tape to our bureaucracy."

"Hey. I'm the king of red tape. Nothing passes through my office that we don't add a circular path so that the public always ends up back at the beginning – having to start all over again. It's the American way." It was always fun to make light of the federal government. After all, it was such an easy target.

Service at Luigi's, like most restaurants, was unpredictable – sometimes excellent, sometimes not so good. But the food was always excellent. It was worth any type of service. Today, the service was excellent. The waiter was jovial, attentive, and talkative. Maybe it was the holiday spirit, maybe it was the lighter-than-usual lunch crowd, maybe it was the anticipated tip, or maybe he was just a good waiter. Regardless, neither Katie nor Kyle cared. They decided to split a pizza with Kyle ordering pepperoni and Katie ordering 'garbage' style. Neither one hardly ate as both seem to prefer talking and listening. The conversation was never forced or strained. They talked about the food, their work, college, golf, Washington, and their families - but primarily their families. It was hard for Kyle to talk about his Mom and not feel a burning pit in his stomach. He hoped his concern about his Mom didn't show, but it did.

"Kyle? Is everything all right? You get this distant, somewhat disturbed look when we talk about your Mom and you keep looking at your phone."

Kyle wasn't sure he wanted to involve Katie or if she would even *want* to get involved. . After all, they had only known each other for just a few days. But if she had a problem with her Mom or Dad, he would want to know and would want to help. He felt that Katie would be the same. If not, then maybe she wasn't the person he thought she was.

"You remember that I mentioned that we had a family problem when we talked on the phone this morning, you know, when I so rudely left you hanging?"

"You weren't rude. And I do remember you telling me that you had a problem, but I thought you said everything was fine."

"Well, I don't know if it's fine or not. I don't even know *if* it's a problem. But it *is* about my Mom. I haven't been able to get in touch with her since Tuesday. I've tried calling her apartment, her cell phone, her office, even her special man friend. Nothing. I've even called the hospitals and the police. Nothing. This is so unlike her."

"Oh. Kyle! You should have told me. I'd be worried, too. Have you checked her apartment? I mean have you been to her apartment. Maybe she's fallen ill… or worse."

"Yes. I went by this morning but she wasn't there. And Mr. Blackwell, her man friend, went by last night. They were supposed to be going out to dinner. But she didn't answer her phone *or* her door."

Katie could see the concern in Kyle's face and didn't want to say anything to upset him anymore.

"Let me think... So… While you were at the apartment, did you try calling her cell to see if she'd left it there by accident or maybe on the charger? And what about her car, does she have an assigned space and if so, did you check to see if it was there?"

"No on the phone and I didn't check on the car. I guess I'm not really thinking all that clearly."

"Kyle, you're not a detective. You've got a lot on your mind. Don't be so hard on yourself."

"I think I need to go back over to the apartment. Check out a few more things. You can come if you want. I know this isn't what you had in mind on your day off, but…"

"Kyle Hamilton. What kind of woman do you think I am? This is your Mom we're talking about. If this were my parents, you'd do the same. But… Before we go, let's call her one more time just in case she's home. I don't want to meet her for the very first time by coming in unannounced."

Kyle was so glad he had told Katie. She had jumped into the fray, head first. Just like he thought she would. She was definitely a keeper.

Chapter 36

Thursday, December 28, 2006, 12:50 p.m. EST

"Good Lord!" exclaimed Bobby as he and Wayne entered the living room of Jim Barnes' Watergate Apartment. "What a mess! Look at this place!"

"I see it!" replied Wayne, stunned at the condition of the room. Anyone who knew Jim Barnes knew he was a neat-freak.

Bobby circled the living room, stopping at the wall where the two broken liquor bottles lay. "This is un-fucking-believable! He must have been *really* pissed."

"Well, I guess you'll believe me *now*," offered Wayne. "I'm telling you, the man went off the deep end. That's the only way I can explain it."

"Yeah, I can see that."

Wayne set the leftover carry-outs from the Chinese restaurant on the living room coffee table and returned to the foyer where he set his briefcase down on the credenza. In his briefcase was the box of latex gloves. He slipped on a pair, grabbed a handful more, and gave them to Bobby figuring that would be enough to get him through the next couple of days. Bobby placed his briefcase next to Wayne's, slipped on a pair of the gloves, and dumped the rest into his briefcase. He then pulled out his copy of Wayne's action plan and scanned a couple of pages before throwing it back into his briefcase. Wayne tried not to let Bobby's nonchalant handling of such a sensitive document upset him. But it did.

"OK. So the plan is to make the apartment just look like Jim felt," said Bobby. "Angry, despondent and possibly suicidal. Looks like we can go ahead and check that bad boy off. He's already taken care of that one. What's next?"

"Not so fast. He certainly made a good start. But we'll still need to add a few more things besides these half-empty Chinese carry-out cartons. Like maybe some fast-food wrappers and bags, half-eaten pizza, pizza boxes and a few more empty liquor bottles. Things like that."

Wayne continued. "The next thing on our agenda is mail. Email, phone mail, and U.S. mail. Do you mind going downstairs and check Jim's mailbox while I check his phone and computer?"

Bobby looked confused. "I thought we weren't doing any of that stuff. I thought Jim was supposed to be incommunicado."

"That's the plan, but seeing how out of sorts he's been as of late, we can't chance him dropping the ball on anything important. *Especially* anything to do with our Appeal campaign. So I want to check *all* his communications and respond as though I were Jim."

"Gotcha. Makes sense. I'll go get the mail and while I'm out, I'll put my suitcase next door if that's all right with you."

"Actually, that won't work. Use the apartment two doors down. If you're next door, you might have heard Jim's tirades. We don't need you in a position to explain why you did nothing. Why you didn't look in on him to see what the hell was going on."

"That makes perfect sense. The less involved we are, the better."

Bobby picked up his suitcase and walked out the door leaving his briefcase on the credenza, still open and his copy of the action plan in plain view. Wayne fought the urge to take the plan to Jim's shredder and destroy it.

Instead, he headed directly to Jim's office. On his large mahogany desk sat his laptop, still open but with the screen in shut down mode. Wayne sat down on the edge of the large burgundy leather chair, grabbed the computer mouse with his gloved right hand, pressed the leftmost button and the NAGS' sign-on screen appeared. With any other employee's computer, Wayne would have needed the assistance of the CIO to reset the password which would have created an unwanted exposure. But Jim was a creature of habit who rarely changed his computer password or, for that matter, the password on any other device or application unless forced. And Wayne had worked long enough with Jim to know that his password was a combination of his son's name and birthday. He keyed in the password, clicked on the Lotus Notes© icon and Jim's in-basket appeared.

Wayne scanned through the first three pages of Jim's inbox and found that only the emails for the last two days had not been opened. Then starting back at the first page of the inbox, he clicked on the first unopened email. It was a thank you note from a Georgia congressman for the Super Bowl tickets along with a request for an invoice from

NAGS so they could be reimbursed. A similar email was from a Nevada congressman also thanking Jim and also requesting an invoice. New ethics legislation was on the table that prevented members of Congress from accepting free tickets, trips, etc. So NAGS and other registered lobbyists had to work around the new upcoming laws. NAGS would accept payment from the congressmen for the face value of the tickets, not what was actually paid to obtain tickets, then turn around and send the legislator a campaign contribution of that same amount. Reimbursement of travel expenses was much more kludgy, but NAGS always figured a workaround, be it a seminar, class, fund-raiser, whatever.

Wayne sent replies to both congressmen letting them know that an invoice would be forthcoming and thanked them for their continued support. As he continued down the inbox, he saw three emails from Congressman John Richards. Richards was chairman of the Judiciary Committee and a personal friend of two of the three judges on the U.S. Court of Appeals. The judges were the ones making the decision on the DC weapons ban appeal. Richards had always been a major ally of NAGS. Accordingly, NAGS rewarded him most generously with their support, both monetarily, up to the legal, muddy limit, and non-monetarily with NAGS backed fund-raisers, mailings, and special events. It was at the congressman's last NAGS sponsored fund-raiser, in his home state, probably his most important event of the year, that Jim no-showed. Richards was furious and demanded that he be fired. It was the proverbial final nail in Jim's coffin giving rise to him being placed on administrative leave.

As he nervously opened Richards' emails in the order received, he hoped that none were bad news. They needed Richards, his support and his influence, in the worst way. The first email was a note thanking Jim for the two Super Bowl tickets. In the second, he asked for two more tickets, and the third, which was more of a demand, he requested four tickets, not two. *Greedy bastard!* Wayne forwarded Richards' request to his email address. He would make damn sure that Richards got his four extra tickets.

Scrolling down to the next page of emails, Wayne found a couple from NAGS' board members - both declining any knowledge of the board's request to have him placed on administrative leave. In fact, both messages were very supportive and complimentary. The emails were dated Tuesday evening, December 26th. *Omigod! What'd he tell them?* Wayne clicked on Jim's out basket. There were only two notes sent that were dated December 26th or later. The first was a broadcast message sent to all of the board members, time-stamped at 5:48 p.m., December 26th. Wayne moved the mouse to the email, opened it and read the following:

To the Board members of North American Gun Society:

Dear friends,

After over 30 years of loyal service to NAGS, my job is in serious jeopardy. I have been placed on administrative leave by Wayne Peters. The reason? According to Mr. Peters, LACK OF FOCUS!!!! I have always put NAGS first, even at the expense of my family's health and well-being. In the last six months, I have lost a mother to pancreatic cancer and a wife to divorce. Yet I continued to work 10 hours a day, six and seven days a week except during the times when my mother was critically ill and subsequently at her funeral. I also took off a couple of days for my divorce hearing. I would hope that the board would agree that the time-off was warranted and was not unreasonable. But according to Wayne Peters, some board members have made some complaints about me and that he had no other choice but to place me on administrative leave; that his hands were tied. You know that I have always done what NAGS and, more specifically, Wayne Peters have always asked – on time and with excellent results. If any of you have had issues with the way I conducted business for NAGS, please let me know what they were. Otherwise, I hope I can count on your support at the next board meeting.

Your friend,

Jim Barnes

Wayne re-read the note. It was perfect. Jim was begging for his job. You could sense his desperation from the note. He was pulling out all the stops - using his mother's death and his divorce. Now all Wayne had to do was to send a couple of follow-up emails to the board from 'Jim' sounding even more distraught. Then a couple from 'Jim' to Wayne, the first spewing hatred and disdain, and the second, a 'woe is me, I'm no good to anybody' kind of email. Then Jim would go missing. It was perfect.

Wayne couldn't help but smile. He scrolled down to the next email that Jim had sent and began reading. The smile was gone.

What the hell is this?

From the mistyped words, it was easy to tell that Jim was drunk, really drunk. It was not what he expected. It was a letter to Wayne, and Jim was not begging. He was demanding!

'you thiink you can fire me well think again!!!!! i got the flies nobady can fire me. not ever YOU. HAve a nice day aashole.'

Wayne was perplexed.

What the hell's he talking about? Why didn't I get this email?

Wayne looked at the date again and then the email address. It was time-stamped Wednesday, December 27, 4:10 a.m., the morning he was shot. And the email address was to Wanye.Peters@nags.org. Wayne had never received the letter because the email address was invalid.

Wayne read the letter again.

What does he mean that he has 'the flies'? Oh shit! He means files.

Wayne heard the front door slam shut.

"Yo! Mail Service," said Bobby with a 'not a worry in the world' tone of voice.

"We could have a big problem here."

"What do you mean?" he asked dropping the box of mail at the base of the desk.

"Come. Look at this email!"

Bobby moved behind Wayne, stooped down and slowly read it.

"What's he talking about?"

"He's saying that he has our files and that he's going to use them against us."

"What files is he talking about?"

"You know. The *files*!"

"Oh shit. Are you sure?"

"It's gotta be. What else could he be talking about?"

"How could Jim get to those files without you seeing him go into the vault? I know you didn't let him go in there after you fired him, did you?"

"Dammit, Bobby. I didn't fire him. And no. Jim left immediately after our meeting."

"Could he have come back after you left work?"

"God, Bobby. You sound like a prosecutor," snapped Wayne as sweat began to bead on his forehead.

"Wayne, if those files get into the wrong hands, that could be just as devastating as the mess we're in now."

"I know. I know. But yeah, I guess Jim could have gone back to the office after I left. But there's no way of knowing since we erased the security video. The best thing for me to do is run back to the office and check the filing cabinets. Like right now."

Without waiting for Bobby's concurrence, Wayne headed out of Jim's office. Before he reached the door, Bobby's new cell phone rang. Wayne stopped in his tracks.

"Who's that?" he quickly asked, his face now frozen with a look of concern.

Bobby pulled his cell phone from his pocket and looked at the number and quickly returned it to his front pocket. "It's my New Year's Eve date. Some bimbo I met in DC a while back. Probably trying to see if I'm still coming to DC. She can wait."

"Do you think this date is a good idea right now with everything that's going on? What if your wife finds out about it? We don't need any more conflicts."

"That ain't gonna happen. Leslie's out of town with her dad. She and the Senator are in Africa on some sorta mission trip for the church. She's been there for about a month. Won't be back for about another two weeks. And I need this distraction. Especially now. And from the look on your face, you could use a little fun, yourself. You still getting it on with your ex or better still, how about Jim's ex? You still fucking her?" asked Bobby, trying to change the conversation.

"We've already discussed this. And I don't think this is the time or place for that kind of discussion. I gotta go."

Wayne stood in thought for a few seconds, making sure he wasn't forgetting anything.

"While I'm gone, go through the mail. But make sure you put on some gloves."

"Got some in my briefcase!" yelled Bobby as Wayne left the apartment. *Anal son-of-a-bitch.*

Chapter 37

Thursday, December 28, 2006, 1:36 p.m. EST

Soon after Wayne left, Bobby dead bolted the door. He walked over to the credenza, opened his briefcase, pulled out a pair of latex gloves and headed back into the office. He sat down behind the desk, slipped on the gloves and began opening envelopes from the box of mail. They were Christmas cards. Without reading them or seeing who sent them, he flicked them toward the wastebasket. One went in; the other landed close by. *Good enough for government work.* His laugh was followed by a big sigh. *I better call the bitch back before she does something stupid.* Bobby pulled his cell phone from his pocket and dialed his last caller. The phone rang once before a woman answered.

"Robert! Where *ARE* you?"

"I'm here in Dallas with Congressman Jensen. We're out hunting. I told you that last week."

"I'm sorry. I forgot. I got worried when I couldn't reach you last night. Your phone kept going to voice mail and I… I…"

"My phone got stolen. Kinda hard to answer when someone else has your phone."

"Robert… uh… I think I did something stupid… something you told me not to do."

"What?"

"I called your house. I know I shouldn't have but I was soooo worried. I think I woke your housekeeper."

"Oh shit. You didn't tell her your name, did you?" asked Bobby, trying to remain calm.

There was no answer.

"Elaine, *did you tell her your name?*" snapped Bobby.

"I'm not sure. I don't think so. I don't remember. I think I just hung up. I'm sorry, baby. Please don't be mad at me. I'm sorry," Elaine pleaded. Her voice was trembling.

Bobby tried to calm himself.

"Did you use the phone I gave you?"

"Yes, baby. I would *never* call you on any phone except that one."

"*Thank God,*" Bobby uttered under his breath. Bobby didn't want NAGS prying into his personal business, and he certainly didn't want his wife to get suspicious. The cell phone he had given her was one listed under his Texas office's name. Any calls from her would appear to be calls from his office.

"You're still coming this weekend, aren't you?" she asked, almost pleading.

"Be there Saturday. No. Sunday morning, bright-eyed and bushy-tailed. I'm looking forward to it."

"Me too. I really, really need you. I can't wait for you to get here. To be next to me. Can you stay with me this time?"

"No can do, baby. I gotta work on that gun appeal. So I'll need to stay close to the office."

"But it's New Year's Eve!" pleaded Elaine.

"No, baby. Not this time. Maybe next time."

"Then can we go somewhere fancy next time, like the Willard Hotel? Please say 'yes.'"

Bobby's eyes rolled as he shook his head.

"I was thinking we could spend the evening alone at your place. Not at some hotel with a thousand other people. You know, cook some lobsters, have a nice bottle of wine or two, get in the hot tub... naked."

Bobby couldn't afford to be seen with her in DC. Too many eyes and ears. If this got back to his wife, she would dump him, and that would end his political career. Bobby needed his wife and her father, the Senator. Nothing was going to get in the way of his career, not even a good piece of ass. With all that was happening at NAGS with the cover-up and the Appeal campaign, he didn't need any 'Elaine' problems.

"Just as long as I'm with you, I'll be happy," sighed Elaine. Bobby could hear the disappointment in her voice.

"Look, I gotta run. I'm getting the evil eye from Congressman Jensen. You know how demanding he is. See you Sunday."

"Goodbye, honey. I love you."

Oh shit! I love you? This was not what Bobby had in mind when he started seeing Elaine.   She was needy.   Her husband was a workaholic who had been very negligent, especially when it came to her physical needs.   Bobby just happened to be the one she latched on to fulfill those needs – a fuck buddy.   He loved the sex, but 'I love you'? This was starting to get out of hand.   She definitely had to go.   *After* the weekend.

Chapter 38

Thursday, December 28, 2006, 1:48 p.m. EST

For the second time that day, Kyle stood at the door of his mother's apartment. As before, the ringing of the doorbell went unanswered as did the knocking that started light and got progressively louder. He was not expecting his Mom to answer as they had not seen her car in its assigned spot.

"I don't hear anything, do you?" Katie whispered.

Kyle pushed his ear up against the door, listened intently, and then shook his head. "No. Not a thing."

As a last resort, he looked into the door's peephole. He knew that he couldn't see into the apartment, but was hoping to see his Mom's eye in the peephole, looking back. There was no eye. Having waited long enough, he unlocked the apartment door, and he and Katie walked in. He flipped on the overhead foyer light.

"Mom! Hey Mom. It's me, Kyle. Mom?" After waiting a few seconds, he turned to Katie and shook his head. "She's not here." There was an uneasiness to his voice.

"Try calling her phone. See if she answers or it rings here," suggested Katie.

Just like the last two days, the call went to voicemail and they heard no ring. If the phone were in the apartment, it was turned off, the ringer was off or its battery had no charge. Kyle slapped his phone shut and shoved it back into his jeans pocket.

Margie's kitchen was just off the foyer. Kyle did a cursory peak but saw nothing unusual. He then led Katie through the living room to the master bedroom. He flipped on the light and while he checked around and under the bed, Katie checked the bathroom. Other than the rumpled bed which normally would have been made military style where you could bounce a quarter off of it, neither found anything out of the ordinary in either room. Kyle stopped to think. Had the bed been this way on his earlier visit? He couldn't remember.

"Maybe she packed a suitcase on it," suggested Katie. "Where does she store her luggage?"

With Katie following, Kyle walked back through the living room and over to the guest bedroom. The luggage was found in the closet which ruled out an away trip.

"Does your Mom keep a calendar?" asked Katie. "She might have written down something that might be helpful."

"Yes! In the kitchen! On the back of the pantry door."

The calendar was opened to 'December.' Penciled in for Wednesday, December 27th was 'Work.' Underneath that, in ink, was 'Dinner 7 pm –WB.' Winston Blackwell. Written on Saturday, December 30th and Sunday, December 31st was 'Dinner – 6:30 WB' with a couple of hearts next to 'WB'. Those were the only entries for that week. While it was no help in locating his Mom, it did confirm her interest in Blackwell and their planned Wednesday night dinner date that never happened.

As they were leaving the kitchen, Kyle noticed dishes in the sink.

"That's weird," he said then picked up the knife from the sink and smelled the white substance on its tip.

"Mayo. That's really weird."

"What's weird?"

"Everything in this sink. Mom is allergic to mayonnaise or any mayonnaise-based dressings. She only kept mayo for me and Aaron, and maybe guests. Not only that, she would never leave a dish in the sink unless the dishwasher was running. And even then, she'd rinse it." They both looked inside the dishwasher. There were no dirty or clean dishes. "You know what else is weird? There's only one plate. That doesn't make sense. I hate doing this but, I'm gonna call Aaron. Maybe he got worried and came over. I doubt it. But someone was here."

"Is it all right if I look around the apartment while you call? I'm not trying to be nosy, but maybe I'll see something you didn't. You know, a new set of eyes."

Kyle nodded and Katie wandered off into the living room as he began to dial. She headed first to the Christmas tree that she'd seen earlier but was too busy checking out the bedrooms to stop for a look. The lights were off, controlled by a timer switch. Even still, she was able to see the decorations. Each one seemed to tell a story. Just like her mom and dad's tree, it had that warm and fuzzy feel, not a 'department store' look and feel.

As she moved about the room, she noticed all the pictures on the tables and walls of Kyle and who she assumed was his Mom, Dad, and brother, Aaron. Family was everywhere in the apartment - just like at her home and her parent's home. And she like that.

Moving to an antique desk, she zeroed in on the note from Idella and read it. It was so sweet and kind; it almost made her cry. She set the note down and continued to peruse Margie's desk. Next to the apartment phone, she saw an old answering machine with a blinking light which meant she had unanswered messages. Her exploration was interrupted as she heard Kyle walking into the living room holding his cell phone away from his ear, shaking his head and mouthing, *He's no help.* Aaron was so loud Katie couldn't help but hear his gruff voice.

"...............Good God, Kyle. Give it a break," barked Aaron. "She probably made lunch for that Winston fellow. Why don't you call *him* and quit bothering *me.*" The phone went silent.

Katie shook her head. "Is your brother always that nice?"

He laughed as he slipped his phone back into his front pocket. "Actually, he was in one of his better moods. So did you find anything?"

"Your Mom's answering machine. It was blinking. Maybe there's a call on it that'll be of some help."

Without thinking, Kyle gave Katie a quick 'thank you' kiss on her cheek causing his face to turn embarrassingly red.

Without hesitation, she turned, faced Kyle, and kissed him tenderly on the lips, softly saying as their lips parted, "You're a good man, Kyle Hamilton."

No longer embarrassed, Kyle gently pulled Katie closer to him and returned her kiss. She responded by slipping her hand behind his head and kissed him back with such feelings that it sent chills down his spine. In all the years of dating, he had never had a kiss like this – one with true feelings and emotions. Simultaneously they broke from their embrace, and as they did, they saw the sweetness in each other's face. There was neither embarrassment nor guilt.

"OK. Now where were we?" she asked, and they both laughed. The tension in Kyle's face seemed to fade. Katie was good for him.

"The answering machine. We were going to listen to the messages on Mom's answering machine."

The number nine flashed on the answering machine indicating it had nine messages. Kyle pressed the 'Play' button. Of the nine messages, Kyle had left three, Winston Blackwell, two. Wayne Peters, one. Gates Security, one. And two hang-ups.

"Kyle, the message from that Peters guy, he asked your Mom to call him back if she could come into work tomorrow. Maybe we should call him and see if she called him."

"Great idea. But can you believe they'd ask her to come into work, again? I mean they made her work yesterday, at least part of the day. She was supposed to have the entire week off!"

"Are they normally that demanding?" she asked.

"Oh no, not really. Mr. Peters, Mom's boss. She really likes him. She's never said one bad word about him other than to say he's real particular. Like a micromanager, but how many bosses aren't?"

Kyle punched in NAGS' main number on his cell and the call was answered almost immediately by a lady at NAGS' answering service. She, in turn, called Peters' office which went unanswered. When Kyle asked if she could try his cell or home number, she said it was against policy unless it was an emergency. He thought about it for a second then said it wasn't. The last thing he wanted to do was embarrass his Mom. Instead, he left a voicemail asking Peters to call him back.

Kyle looked at Katie, thinking about what the answering service had said. *Is this an emergency?*

Chapter 39

Thursday, December 28, 2006, 2:18 p.m. EST

It was quite obvious that a number of folders were missing from NAGS' security vault, given the gaps left in the file drawer. Upon closer inspection, Wayne discovered that Jim had been very selective in the folders he had taken - only NAGS' supporters with the highest profiles: Senators, congressmen, judges, corporate CEOs, lawyers. And all were male. He figured that fifteen to twenty folders were taken. If their contents were ever made public, it would permanently destroy the lives, careers, and families of those men involved and in the process would also destroy NAGS. In all the years that NAGS had been collecting its pictorial and financial blackmail, they had never had reason to exploit its value. But Jim had ruined everything. It was imperative that Wayne find the folders before they fell into the wrong hands.

A thorough search of every filing cabinet in the vault turned up nothing. He then rushed up to Jim's third-floor office hoping that by some miracle the folders were hidden there. But again, he came up empty-handed. The folders weren't anywhere in the building, and he knew it. As Wayne slowly walked back down to his office, he tried to think of what Jim might have done with them. The Watergate apartment was the obvious answer. He had to have hidden them there. But, then again, what if he hadn't? What if he'd mailed them to someone? If so, to whom? Certainly not his ex-wife or his imbecile son. Maybe a Board member or even worse, a reporter. But none of those possibilities made sense. As long as Jim had the folders, he could bargain from a position of strength. He could keep his job. Even demand a large raise. Jim couldn't afford to lose his leverage. It wasn't logical. But Jim hadn't been logical. If he had, why did he bring a gun to the office?

His thoughts were interrupted when he heard the phone in his office ringing. *Maybe it's Bobby. Maybe he's found them!* He dashed to his desk but by the time he got there, the phone had stopped ringing, and the light message indicator began blinking. The voicemail was from Kyle Hamilton asking for a callback. Wayne carefully considered what he would say as he dialed Kyle's number. There could be no more mistakes.

The phone rang once before Kyle answered.

"Hello, Kyle. This is Wayne Peters. Sorry, I missed your call, but we've been in conferences all day."

"Thank you for calling me back and I apologize for interrupting anything, but I was wondering if you'd heard or seen my Mom today?"

"No, Kyle, I haven't. I'm sorry. In fact, she hasn't returned *my* calls. That's not like her, not to return my calls."

Kyle felt like a student talking to a teacher. Peters' voice was so professional, so mature.

"And so you haven't seen or heard from her since yesterday?"

"No, Kyle. I haven't."

"Do you know a person by the name of Idella?"

"Yes, I do. She and her husband, Jerome, clean our office. They were here yesterday. Why do you ask?"

"We found a note from her at Mom's apartment. So she must have seen Mom."

Yes! Perfect! Just as I planned! "The note. Yes, I remember the note. Idella gave it to me and I gave it to your mother. That was sometime yesterday, right before she left. Kyle… Are you saying *you* haven't heard from your mother since yesterday?" asked Peters using his 'concerned' voice.

"Tuesday was the last time I talked to her. Tuesday morning."

"Have you checked to see if she's gone out of town or maybe staying over with friends?"

"Yes, sir. As much as we can."

"Let me think. What about your brother? Maybe he knows where she's hiding." Wayne politely laughed.

"No, sir. He doesn't know where she is either. I'm really concerned."

"Kyle, I didn't mean to make light of the situation. But if you're that concerned and you've reached out to everyone she knows, then, if I were you, I would try the hospitals, and maybe even the police. You might consider filing a missing person's report."

"Actually, I've already checked the hospitals and called the police. Neither the police nor the hospitals could help. The hospitals didn't have any 'Jane Doe's' as they called unidentified women patients and the police told me that I had to wait 24 hours before filing a missing person's report."

"As much as I'm a stickler for following rules, I think you should go back to the police. If you need any help in getting past the red tape, you can call me here, at the office, or my cell." Wayne proceeded to give Kyle his cell phone number. "Margie means a lot to us. She's more than an employee. She's like a mother to all of us here at NAGS."

"Thank you, Mr. Peters. And thank you for your offer to help. I may take you up on it."

"Please do. I hate to go, but I really do need to get back to work."

After saying their good-bye's, Kyle slowly closed his cell phone and turned to look at Katie. She could tell by the worried look on his face that he was thinking the worst. She knew the best thing to do was to continue their search.

"No luck. She's…"

Katie interrupted Kyle. "I heard. I'm sorry, Kyle. Mr. Peters seems nice."

"Yeah. He is," he replied, looking at Katie but not really seeing her, his mind searching for what to do next.

"I think I'll call Mr. Blackwell and see if he's had any luck."

Katie remembered Kyle telling her that Mr. Blackwell was his mother's man friend. He answered the call after only a couple of rings.

"Kyle! I was just about to call you." The tone of Blackwell's voice was grave. "Have you located her?"

Blackwell's last words were not what Kyle wanted to hear. That meant he hadn't located her either. Another dead end. "No, sir. I've been back to her apartment. Nothing. And I've called every hospital in the phone book. Nothing there, either. I also called the Alexandria police and they said they hadn't found anyone matching her description. I'm at a loss."

"Kyle, I don't want to be an alarmist but…" There was a long pause before Blackwell spoke again. "There was a report on television today at noon about a homicide in Washington. They gave no real description of the victim other than it being an elderly, white lady. She was found somewhere near Capitol Street. Being that part of town, I doubt that it could be your Mom, but I think you might want to call the DC police and check it out."

Kyle was shaken. Why hadn't he called the Washington police? He could barely speak. When he did, it was almost a whisper.

"Yes sir. I will. I'll call them right now. Good-bye."

"Call me back," replied Blackwell. But Kyle had already hung up.

"What's wrong?" Katie asked, seeing Kyle's hand slowly press the off button on his cell phone.

"I need to call the Washington Police. They've found a body of a woman... murdered. Mr. Blackwell saw it on TV. She was found somewhere near Capitol Street. He thinks we should check it out."

"Capitol Street? I'd say chances are pretty remote that it's your Mom."

"I know. But I think I need to call them."

He dialed 411 who in turn dialed the Washington D.C. police department. Kyle started with the Missing Person's Department. After giving the officer all the preliminary information about his Mom including her description, he asked about the woman's body that had been found earlier that morning near Capitol Street in hopes that it had already been identified – and as someone other than his Mom.

"That homicide would be handled by the Fifth District," said the officer. "This is the First District but if you'll please hold I'll look at the case file and see if the description of the deceased in any way matches your mother's description."

While Kyle paced back and forth, the officer checked the homicide report on his computer. Based on the information he saw, he concluded that the description of the dead woman closely matched the description of the caller's mother. The officer picked up the phone and spoke very calmly so not to unnecessarily upset the man.

"I'm sorry but the description in our report is very generic. I would suggest that you go to the Fifth District and fill out a missing person's report there. All districts will have access to that report and will contact you if they find your mother. While you're there, I can have the detective assigned to the Capitol Street homicide meet you. I think that's your best option. Bring a recent picture of your mother if you have one. Can you come in today?"

"Yes, sir."

The officer gave them the address of the police station and then continued.

"I'll call the station, find out who's assigned to the case and let them know you're on your way. Just go to the information desk and tell them that Lieutenant Michaels sent you from the First District. Tell them you need to file a missing report. Tell them that you want to speak to the detectives assigned to the Capitol Street homicide. That'll get you to the right person."

"Thank you," Kyle replied as he finished writing down all the pertinent information. "I'm on my way."

Turning to Katie, "I've got to go to the police station."

"I heard and I'm going with you." She then lifted his trembling hand and kissed it.

Chapter 40

Thursday, December 28, 2006, 2:40 p.m. EST

The caller-ID on the landline in Jim's apartment office displayed 'Jamie' as it rang. It startled Bobby, who was still busy going through Jim's mail.

What the hell does that idiot want? he thought after he saw the name.

Everybody at NAGS knew Jamie Barnes and his reputation. Bobby ignored the call. The phone rang again. Jamie again.

Give it up, you stupid moron!

Moments later he heard a different ring coming from another room in the apartment. Bobby got up and headed toward the sound of the ring. He found the source coming from a cell phone stuck between two sofa cushions in the living room. The caller-Id was Jamie. The phone was Jim's. Bobby switched it off and tossed it in his briefcase and headed back into the office. He wondered if Wayne had even considered the phone or its disposal in his plan.

He had hardly walked into the office when he heard three quick rings from the doorbell. Then four or five quick, loud knocks on the front door.

"Dad! Open up! I know you're in there. I can hear you!"

Oh shit! He must have been standing right outside the damn door when he called. That stupid, stupid fuck!

Bobby knew he had no choice now but to open the door. Heading for the door, he pulled off his latex gloves and placed them in his pocket. *OK. Why am I here? What the hell do I say about Jim? Where is he supposed to be?*

"Hold your horses! I'm coming," shouted Bobby, trying not to sound angry, which he was.

"Dad! Why are you avoiding… er… oh! Mr. Armstrong?" stuttered Jamie, surprised at who had opened the door. "Where's my Dad?"

"Hi. Jamie. Come on in. Your dad's not here. Uh… he's out running some errands. I think he went to Office Depot… Office Max… whatever. Then he's heading over to the office to pick up a few things. We're working on a project together. I'm not sure when he'll be back," he stammered noticing Jamie eyeing the living room. "Oh, the mess. Yeah. We had a big party here last night. A blast. Hadn't had a chance to clean it up."

"A party? Last night? Here?" Jamie asked as he walked into the living room giving it the once over. *Why's that bald-headed asshole lying?*

"Yeah. A bunch of guys came over last night for a few drinks. Well, a lot of drinks. Couple of 'em got carried away. You want me to call the office to see if your Dad's there? I can't call him on his cell phone. He left it here."

"No. That's OK. He didn't happen to leave me any money, did he?"

"If he did, he didn't tell me about it. How much was he supposed to leave you?"

Jamie had a fish and all he needed to do was to reel him in.

"Usually he leaves me fif… sixty dollars, you know for food and all. But I think he said he could advance me eighty this time 'cause of some extra expenses this month."

"Let me see what I've got." *Anything to get rid of the idiot.* Bobby reached into his back pocket looking for his wallet then realized he'd left it on Jim's desk.

"Oh shit. Wait a minute. I got to get my wallet. I always take it out when I'm sitting down. Keeps the spine straight otherwise it screws up my sciatic nerve."

Bobby could see that Jamie didn't care about his sciatic nerve. Just the money.

"I'll be right back. Wait here."

Bobby headed into Jim's office with Jamie following close behind totally ignoring the *wait here* request until Bobby stopped, half-turned, and gave Jamie a *Don't follow me* look. Not wanting to piss off his potential benefactor, Jamie immediately backed into the foyer but not before seeing all the trash strewn on the floor in his Dad's office. Even with his screwed-up mind, he felt something wasn't right. Whatever was going on, he hoped it wouldn't interfere with him getting his money. Not to appear too anxious and to keep out of Armstrong's sight, he moved over to one of the two chairs that sandwiched the credenza and plopped down. The mound of latex gloves in the open briefcase immediately caught his eye. *What the hell's going on here? Why is Dad...*

Before he could finish his thought, Armstrong returned with money in hand.

"How about a couple of fifties?" asked Bobby. He figured a hundred would keep him out of their hair for a few days.

"Thank you, Mr. Armstrong. Thank you very much. Now I can get some groceries." He quickly folded the money and put it in his jeans front pocket. He never once looked Armstrong in the eye so not to give away the real intent of the money. This didn't go unnoticed. It was a sure-fire indicator of guilt, deceit, evasiveness, misrepresentation, lying.

"Oh. And tell my Dad that I'm sorry I missed him. Tell him if he'd like to go out to dinner tonight or tomorrow night, I'm available." Jamie was lying and it came so naturally. He had no intention of having dinner with his Dad, tonight or tomorrow night. Not with a hundred bucks in his pocket. His plans only included Nate and his bag of mind-altering drugs.

"I'll let him know you came by. But I can tell you that he's not available tonight. In fact, he's unavailable through New Year's. Tonight, we're taking some bigwigs out to dinner. The rest of the week, we're *all* huddled up here in the apartments working on a big project. 24/7. We'll be having food brought in so we can stay focused on our work."

"I understand," replied Jamie staring down at his worn-out sneakers. "I'm sorry if I interrupted your work. It was nice seeing you again."

As Jamie left, he couldn't help but glance over to the open briefcase with the latex gloves that seemed so out of place. Bobby took notice of Jamie's momentary hesitation then realized he had left his briefcase open. Jamie had to have seen the gloves. And what about Wayne's action plan? Could he have had time to peruse the document while Bobby was getting the money? He quickly dispelled the thought. There was no way Jamie would jeopardize his chance for money. That would never happen. He shut the door behind Jamie and set the deadbolt. He then went over to his briefcase and checked its contents. Nothing looked out of place or missing. He hoped so - for Jamie's sake.

Chapter 41

Thursday, December 28, 2006, 3:05 p.m. EST

"Hey Wrinkles," yelled Lt. Daniel Whitehead across the room as Johnny Williams returned from the breakroom. "We might have a possible ID on the Capitol Street body."

"How so?"

"A guy by the name of Kyle Hamilton just called Missing Persons over at First. He's headed our way. He said that his mother has been missing for a couple of days. The officer said the description given by Hamilton matches the description of the dead woman. He said this Hamilton guy actually made reference to the Capitol Street homicide."

"Hmmm. Interesting. Not only a possible ID, but also a possible suspect," replied Johnny as he munched on a Snickers bar.

"What's the status of those surveillance tapes?"

"I called the building's owner, and he's gonna have them pulled. One of the guys from DFS is picking them up either today or first thing tomorrow."

"Hey speaking of DFS, your buddy, Bennie Archer faxed a copy of his preliminary findings."

Daniel picked up his fax then sat on the edge of his desk facing Johnny who had eased himself into his chair, leaned back, put his feet on his desk and placed both hands behind his head.

"Just in case you might want to read along, your copy's on your desk under your feet along with the pictures of the victim taken at the scene by the DFS and the close-ups taken by the ME at the morgue." (ME is the acronym for Medical Examiner.)

"No. No. You read. I want to listen and think."

"If I see you nod or close your eyes… Anyway, there's a lot that's on this report we already know. The victim was a Caucasian woman between the ages of 50 to 60. Her hair was dyed a reddish-brown. She had hazel/blue eyes. Height 5 foot 3 inches. Weighed about 125 pounds. She had no birthmarks or other identifying marks or scars.

Archer said that the woman had been dead for at least 18 to 24 hours, so death occurred somewhere between 9 a.m. and 3 p.m. yesterday. Death was most likely caused by a gunshot to the head, through her left eye. Appears to be done by a handgun, 9mm or larger. No bullet was found in the body and no casings in the area. The woman wasn't sexually assaulted. No traumas, lacerations or unusual marks on the body other than a small bump on the right side of her head. Nothing under the fingernails. The victim wore a large diamond ring on her right hand. No other jewelry except some inexpensive earrings. The victim's clothes most likely came from somewhere like Macy's or Hecht's. There were bloodstains on the upper portion of the back part of her dress as well as dried blood in her hair. All type O. There was some adhesive residue on the victim's hair and over her left eye socket and face. Archer surmised that it came from some kind of tape, like duct tape or medical tape, most likely to stop the bleeding. There were no fingerprints found or identified at the scene or on the body. No personal property that could identify the victim. No tire marks other than the ones made by the dump truck. No footprints other than the ones made by the two employees of the trash company. He said the final autopsy, DNA and dental records would be coming later." Daniel looked up from the fax. He saw Johnny, wide awake and thinking.

"So based on all of that, we're still at square one unless this Hamilton guy makes a positive ID," offered Johnny.

"That's what I told VM right after I got the call from First." (VM stood for Captain Vernon Martin, Johnny and Daniel's boss.) "He wasn't real happy with our progress. Said the media's all over him like a cheap suit. They want an ID of the victim. Soon. Wrinkles, you got any ideas? You think this was just a run-of-the-mill carjacking?"

"Well, that's what it appears to be, Danny boy. But there are too many pieces to this puzzle that makes me want to say no. First. The ring. No decent carjacker would kill their victim, then keep the body for over ten hours and not steal the ring! That doesn't make any sense. Second. The adhesive residue you mentioned over her eye and face. I don't know any carjacker that would take the time to stop the bleeding. They shoot and leave. Third. Why move the body? And why keep the body? That doesn't fit the MO of any carjacker I've ever known. And finally. The coat. Bloodstains on the dress indicate she wasn't wearing a coat when she was shot. So I don't think she was shot outside or in her car. Otherwise, you know, she'd be wearing a coat. But I've already said that."

"Makes sense. But you haven't told me what you think happened."

"I dunno. Could be there's a big estate or lots of insurance money. I think we need to look inside. Maybe this Hamilton fellow. Maybe a relative. What about you? What do you think?"

"Maybe a jealous lover. From her pictures, she probably looked real nice for an older woman."

Johnny removed his feet from the desk, sat up and grabbed the DFS report. He flipped to the pictures and studied them for a couple of minutes.

"Danny Boy, I hate to shoot down your theory, but this woman did not die at the hands of a jealous lover. Where's the proof, you say? As an *older,* single man, I can tell. This woman had class."

Chapter 42

Thursday, December 28, 2006, 3:09 p.m. EST

"Aw shit. Not again," muttered Bobby as his cell phone rang. "If it's that fucking bitch again, I might go shoot someone *myself*."

'Wayne' popped up on his caller-ID.

"Wayne! Where the hell are you? You find the files?"

"Still at the office. I found most of them but, yeah, he definitely took some. Until I finish going through them all, I won't know which ones are missing. What about you? Find any?"

"I didn't know I was supposed to be looking for 'em. I've been working on the mail. By the way, you remember how you said that Jim's son wasn't going to be a problem? Well, you got that all wrong."

"What do you mean?" blurted out Wayne.

"The doofus came here, right after you left, looking for Jim. Wanted some money. Probably for drugs. Anyway, I gave him a hundred bucks just to get his sorry ass out of here."

"Good. That should take care of him for a while."

"Oh for God's sake, Wayne. That hundred bucks will be gone before you get back to the apartment. I've got a feeling that we're going to have to keep feeding that piranha until this thing is over. How much longer are you going to be?"

"Not much. But I'm gonna stop at a liquor store on the way back. Buy a few bottles of Jack Daniels using Jim's credit card. You know, make it appear that he's still with us, still drinking. It's part of my action plan."

"If you mention that damned action plan of yours *one more time...* Just get your ass back here as fast as you can," ranted Bobby, slamming his phone shut and then tossing it on the desk.

He finished scanning through the rest of Jim's mail separating out the important from unimportant. The unimportant ones were dumped in the trash can. The important ones were set aside for Wayne to handle.

He then began his search for the missing folders, starting with the file drawers in Jim's desk. Every folder in the drawers was a standard letter-size, manila-colored basic folder. The folders he was looking for were the brown flap-style with a tie cord. Even so, he inspected every folder just in case Jim had moved the contents to a less obvious folder. All he found were bills, divorce papers, estate documents, and other miscellaneous papers.

He leaned back in his chair with his hands clasped behind his head and began to think about the situation. If he had the folders and wanted to hide them, where would he put them? Certainly not in his office at NAGS headquarters. That would be the first place searched. Unless the folders were close at hand, he'd have no leverage. They had to be somewhere in this apartment in a locked and secure place. Like in a locked filing cabinet. *That's it!* NAGS wouldn't allow Jim to bring sensitive work documents to his apartment unless he could put them under lock and key. The two filing drawers in the desk only had personal documents and were not locked. So there had to be another filing cabinet here in the apartment. Bobby did a 360 look around the office seeing nothing but office furniture, an alcove leading to the bathroom *and a closet!* He rushed over to the door, pushed it open and BINGO! A four-drawer filing cabinet and a safe.

He flipped on the overhead light and checked the filing cabinet. It was unlocked, a clear violation of company policy. He did a cursory look through each of the drawers but saw only standard letter-size, manila-colored basic folders, no brown folders. One by one, he searched through the contents of each folder but found only normal, business-related documents. Not what he was looking for. They had to be in the safe.

He pushed down on the safe's door handle but, as expected, it was locked. Moving faster than he liked, he found the model and serial numbers of the safe along with the manufacturer's name. On Jim's computer, he googled the manufacturer's name, found their customer service phone number and in less than ten minutes had the combination on its way. He was full of himself as he dialed Wayne's cell phone.

"You find 'em?" asked Wayne answering the phone on the first ring.

"No. But maybe. I found a safe. But it's locked. I..."

"Omigod," interrupted Wayne. "That's great! But you said it's locked. How are we gonna get it open without bringing in a locksmith? And that's not going to happen. Too much exposure."

"You didn't let me finish. I called the safe company, told them I was Jim Barnes. Gave them his email address and they said they could send out the combination today. They're going to FedEx it. They hope to have it here by 10 a.m. tomorrow."

"Excellent. But how'd you know to do that?"

"Let's just say I know. Now, get back here as fast as you can."

Wayne's spirits were lifted. The folders had to be in the safe. Other than waiting on the combination from the safe company, they were back on track, except for Jamie. He hadn't counted on having to deal with him. Jim rarely ever talked about him. He would have to amend his plan. Make sure the boy had money. Wasn't that all druggies wanted? More money for more drugs. Bobby had to be pleased with the way most things were going.

But Bobby wasn't pleased. What if the folders weren't in the safe? What if Jim had given them to somebody? And what about Jamie. Today wouldn't be the last time he'd show up, unannounced. He might be a crack-head but even he'd know that something wasn't right if his dad wasn't ever here when he came by for money. And Jim. They still hadn't buried his fat ass. There were way too many loose ends. If things went awry one more time, they were going to do things his way. And there wouldn't be any action plan. Just action!

Chapter 43

Thursday, December 28, 2006, 3:14 p.m. EST

Kyle hardly spoke as he made his way to the police station driving as fast as weather conditions allowed while at the same time trying not to make Katie nervous. But she wasn't watching the road or the traffic. She was watching him – and the anguish on his face. She prayed silently for his Mom's safety and for him.

After parking the car but before getting out, he turned toward Katie. "What if it's her? What if she's …"

Katie could hear the fear in his voice. She grasped his right hand with both her hands and then kissed it tenderly.

"Kyle… *we* can do this."

There was lots of activity in the building as they headed for the information desk. Neither had ever been to a police station. It looked nothing like the ones they'd seen on TV. There was no yelling or screaming and no crazy people running around. It was very organized and business-like. Kyle found the attending officer and told him that a Lieutenant Michaels from the First District had sent them. That they were there to file a missing person's report. After a few minutes of paper shuffling, the young officer handed Kyle a clipboard with multiple forms to be filled out. He also told Kyle that the detectives working the Capitol Street homicide case wanted to talk to him and would be down shortly. He then directed them to a row of chairs where the young couple sat.

Kyle had hardly finished the first document when two men approached them, one young and the other one much older. He and Katie anxiously arose from their chairs.

"Hi. I'm Detective Daniel Whitehead, and this is Detective Johnny Williams. You must be Kyle Hamilton."

"Yes sir," Kyle replied as he shook hands with the two detectives. "And this is Katie Chandler, my uh…"

"Girlfriend," Katie said, matter-of-factly and then she too shook the detectives' hands.

"I'll take that," said the young lieutenant as he reached for the clipboard in Kyle's hands. "We can finish it upstairs. Please follow us."

Daniel and Johnny's office was actually a small cubicle in a large open room. The cubicle was just large enough to contain two desks that were shoved together, facing each other. Two desk chairs, two temporary visitor chairs, and four filing cabinets completed their office. The desks and filing cabinets had stacks of dogged-eared folders sitting on top of them, all very orderly. On every wall, there were numerous awards, citations, and pictures. On the wall closest to Whitehead's desk was his college diploma in Criminal Justice from the University of Maryland. On the wall next to Johnny's desk hung a picture of a much younger and thinner Johnny Williams all decked out in his new D.C. police uniform and standing next to a highly polished squad car.

Daniel moved the two visitor chairs away from the wall and closer to the side of his desk then motioned for Kyle and Katie to sit. Johnny then asked if they would like something to drink - coffee, Coke, water - which they refused. Kyle was anxious, and the detectives sensed it.

"Thank you for coming in. Mr. Hamilton, it's my understanding that it's your mother that's missing, am I correct?" Daniel asked as he sat down behind his desk. Johnny stood at the filing cabinet behind Daniel's desk, drinking his now-cold coffee and observing.

"Yes, sir. And it's Kyle. You can call me Kyle."

"Kyle, I see that your mother's name is Margaret Irene Hamilton."

"Yes, sir. But everyone calls her Margie."

"So how long has she been missing?"

"Two days. The last time I *saw* her was Christmas. We spent the entire day with her..."

"Excuse me for interrupting which I tend to do if I hear something that needs clarification, but by 'we,' you mean you and Katie?"

"No, sir. I mean me and my brother, Aaron."

Daniel was writing as he continued to ask questions. "And Christmas was the last time your brother, Aaron, saw your mother?"

"Yes, sir. As far as I know."

"No other siblings? What about your father?"

"No, sir. Just me and Aaron. And our father is dead. He died 12 years ago."

"I'm sorry to hear that. When did you last *talk* to your mother?"

"The day after Christmas. Tuesday morning. That was the last time."

"Do you have a current picture of your mother?"

"Oh Geez. I was supposed to bring one. I'm sorry."

"I see we didn't give you enough time to complete these forms. Can you give us a brief description of your mother? You know, age, approximate height, weight, color of her hair, color of her eyes, any distinguishing marks you might know about, like birthmarks."

"Yes, sir." Kyle hesitated for a moment to think. "Mom's…uh… she's 62." He was embarrassed that he didn't immediately know his Mom's age. He continued. "She's a little over five feet tall. Maybe five two, five three. I'm guessing she weighs somewhere around 110 pounds. She's small, not overweight. She has reddish colored hair. It's probably gray or white, but she dyes it red. And her eyes are blue. I know I'm prejudiced, but I think she's a very beautiful woman."

The two detectives both noted that Kyle spoke of his mother in the present.

"What about birthmarks or any other distinguishing marks?"

"None that I know of."

"Glasses. Does she wear glasses?"

"Only when she drives."

"What kind of car does she drive and do you know the number on the license plate?"

"It's a new Buick of some kind. I don't know the license. I can get it."

"That's OK. We can get those records."

"I see," continued Daniel as he perused the first page of the *Missing Person's* document. "that your mother lives in the Mt. Vernon Towers Apartments on First Street, in Alexandria. So why didn't you go to the Alexandria police?"

"I tried to file a report there yesterday but they said I had to wait 24 hours. That she'd probably show up. But she hasn't."

"So why didn't you go back to the Alexandria Police?"

Kyle sunk back into his chair. His eyes were now focused on Lt. Whitehead's desk nameplate and he began to nervously rub his hands together. Slowly he said, "I was talking to Mr. Blackwell. He's a friend of my Mom's. Anyway, he said he saw on TV that a woman was killed somewhere near Capitol Street. I just wanted to make sure it wasn't my Mom. So I called your main number, and the officer there told me I should come here. That I could file a missing person's report here and that I should talk to y'all."

Katie could see that Kyle was struggling with his emotions. She reached for his hand and held it tightly to reassure him.

"What is Mr. Blackwell's full name and what is his relationship with your mother?" asked Daniel.

"Winston Blackwell, the third. And like I said, he's just a friend of Mom's."

"By friend, do you mean boyfriend?"

"I don't think so. They just met. He's the brother of a good friend of my Mom's from church."

"Has your mother had a lot of boyfriends?" asked Daniel.

The question hit Kyle the wrong way. In a somewhat loud but controlled voice, he answered, "Mr. Blackwell is the first person my mother has dated since my Dad died. She's gone out with friends from church but usually in groups. But she has never, ever been romantically involved with anyone. I, personally, don't see what this has to do with filing a missing person's report."

Daniel always hated asking that question. Needless to say, Kyle's answer pretty much shot down his *jealous lover* theory just as Johnny had. Regardless, they would still check out this Blackwell fellow.

"I'm sorry. I didn't mean to upset you. We're just trying to cover all the bases. I hope you understand."

Kyle nodded his head. The detective was only doing his job.

Daniel then looked at Johnny. He could tell by his look that it was time. By now they both felt quite certain the victim was Margaret Irene Hamilton. They hoped they were wrong. But they would know instantly from Kyle's reaction once he saw the picture of a woman with a bullet hole for an eye lying lifelessly on a table in the morgue. It was either his mother, or it wasn't. Johnny moved from the filing cabinet to stand close to Kyle. Daniel pulled some of the least offensive pictures from his folder.

"Kyle, I have some pictures I want you to look at. They're of the victim that was found near Capitol Street. I apologize that we have to ask you to do this, but we both need to know if this is your mother."

Kyle nodded his head in agreement as the young detective placed the first two photos on the desk in from of him. Katie looked at Kyle as he glanced down at them. He was not prepared for what he saw. His hands began to tremble, and his chest started to heave.

"Oh no! Oh, please God, no! No! No! No! No! No! No! Why God? Why?" cried Kyle as he cradled his shaking head in his hands. Tears were streaming down his face.

Katie instantly knelt down in front of Kyle and tenderly caressed his hands and stroked his hair as she, too, began to cry. She had never met Kyle's Mom, yet there was a part of Katie that already had. The sting of death was so vicious.

Johnny Williams was all too familiar with this scene. It was the cruelest part of the job. Instinctively, he placed his large hand on Kyle's shoulder. Daniel opened his desk drawer, retrieved a box of Kleenex and offered it to the young couple. He then walked back to the filing cabinet where Johnny had just left and stood there looking into space. Kyle Hamilton was not a suspect. He was a victim just like his mother. It was obvious that Kyle's grief was not contrived or forced but truly heartfelt. He looked at Johnny who was fighting back the tears. He could never conceal his emotions. They were always out there for anyone to see.

For a while, no one said a word.

Finally, without looking up, Kyle spoke. "I… I don't know what to do. How did this happen? Who did this?"

"Kyle, I'm deeply sorry. We don't know what happened except that she was shot. I can assure you we will get whoever did it." After a brief pause, he continued. "Are you *absolutely* sure the woman in these pictures is your mother? Do you need to go to the DC Morgue to view the body? We can drive you."

"No. I'm sure," he said so softly that Daniel had to strain to hear his answer. Once more he looked at the pictures praying he'd made a mistake, but it was no mistake. "I need to call Aaron. I've got to call him now. He needs to know."

"Do you need a phone?"

He didn't answer. Just shook his head.

As Kyle pulled his cell phone from his front pocket, Daniel headed to another cubicle where he sat down at the PC terminal. Katie turned her chair so to face Kyle and sat down as close to him as she could. Tears were still streaming down her face. Small smudges of mascara underscored her brown eyes.

Johnny moved to the back wall of the cubicle, out of sight, but where he could hear the conversation between Kyle and his brother. While he had no way of hearing both sides of the conversation, by listening to Kyle, he hoped to make some sort of assessment of his brother's initial response to his mother's death. Johnny had been involved in too many cases where inheritance and insurance money were the root cause of the crime.

Kyle's hands trembled as he punched in Aaron's speed dial number.

His brother answered almost immediately.

"Aaron here."

"Aaron. It's me, Kyle," he whispered, his voice quivering.

"Oh good God, Kyle. No. I haven't talked to Mom. No. I haven't seen her. No. I don't know where she is. Can you please…"

"Aaron," interrupted Kyle, crying as he spoke. "She's dead. Mom's dead."

There was dead silence on Aaron's end of the phone as he listened to his brother sob uncontrollably. He had heard him. His Mom was dead. But there were no tears, no anguish, no grief. He had been preparing himself for this day since his Dad died. He had learned long ago how to suppress his feelings, his emotions. He would never be hurt again.

"What happened?" he asked sharply once he heard the sobs subside.

"She was sh… shot," Kyle stuttered finding it extremely difficult to finish the sentence.

"What do you mean she was shot? Who shot her?"

"I don't know."

"Have you called the police?"

"We're at the police station now. We're talking with two detectives."

"Are you *absolutely* sure it's her?"

"Yes. The detectives showed me some photos of her. It's Mom."

"That's not acceptable. Where is she now?"

"She's… she's at the morgue," he said, his voice quivering as he thought of his sweet mother lying on some cold metal slab.

"Don't you think we should go to the morgue and make a visual identification of the body to make sure you didn't make a mistake?"

"No. I'm sure it's her. I've seen…"

"Well, if you're not going, I am. You probably couldn't handle it anyway. Let me speak to the detective."

Kyle looked around and saw Johnny Williams standing behind him leaning against one of the filing cabinets. Aaron's intense interrogation had helped Kyle to gain some control of his emotions.

"Detective? My brother, Aaron, wants to speak to you."

Johnny nodded and reached for the phone. Kyle was glad to hand it to him.

"This is Detective Williams. I'm so sorry about your mother. Our…"

"Who did this?" interrupted Aaron. "Have you arrested anybody?"

"No sir but we're doing everything in our power to find the person or persons…"

Interrupting again, Aaron shouted, "You damn well better. Where's her body. I want to make sure that my brother hasn't made a mistake. I can't believe that you use photos as a positive identification. That's so wrong. So incompetent. So lazy."

Johnny had never met Aaron Hamilton but already knew he didn't like him or his attitude. Unlike Kyle, his older brother either had no feelings about his mother's death or else they were very deeply hidden. Unknowingly, Aaron had made himself a prime suspect. Johnny gave him the address of the morgue then handed the phone back to Kyle.

"Aaron. What do we do next?" asked Kyle, his eyes beginning to well up again.

"If you're right, we bury her, Kyle. We bury her. You get your act together. I'm going to the morgue. Let's hope you've made a mistake."

Before Kyle could say 'goodbye,' Aaron had already hung up. He flipped his phone shut and placed it back in his jeans. He looked up to see that Detective Whitehead had returned to his desk.

"My brother wants to make sure I haven't made a mistake, so he's going to the morgue. Is that OK?" asked Kyle looking first at Williams, then Whitehead.

"Yes," responded Daniel. "I called our Medical Examiners just before you arrived. They said they were almost finished with the external examination. I'll call 'em back and let 'em know that your brother is coming so that they'll know to hold off on starting the autopsy."

Before the young couple left the police station, they agreed to meet with the detectives at Margie's apartment the next morning at 10 a.m. Aaron's presence was also requested.

The day had been filled with so much pain and sorrow for Kyle. Throughout the whole ordeal, Katie had been right by his side. She had been comforting, supportive, understanding, sympathetic and loving. It had not hit him yet that his Mom would never meet her.

Chapter 44

Thursday, December 28, 2006, 3:49 p.m. EST

"So. What do you think?" asked Daniel after finishing up his call to the ME.

"What do I think? No way Kyle's involved. But his brother? A real piece of work. I think we need to look real hard at that self-centered, arrogant asshole."

"Wrinkles, you gotta stop sugarcoating your feelings."

"Yeah. Yeah. What about the DMV?" asked Johnny, still fuming over Aaron's callous comments.

"Done. Got her license, make of car, VIN, everything. Put it on NCIS. Called DFS and let them know. That particular model car has OnStar*. So if it hasn't been deactivated or chopped, there's a good chance they'll have it located before your next break."

"Well, I'm heading to the breakroom now, so they better work fast."

Daniel agreed with Johnny regarding the Hamilton brothers' involvement. But both would be thoroughly investigated since nearly eighty percent of all homicides were committed by relatives, friends or acquaintances of the victim.

Chapter 45

Thursday, December 28, 2006, 3:52 p.m. EST

Wayne almost burst through the apartment door. He could hardly wait to tell Bobby the news. He set the two bottles of Jack Daniels and his briefcase on the credenza, next to Bobby's briefcase, and headed into Jim's office, yelling out, "They found her!"

"What?" asked Bobby, engrossed in a porn site he had pulled up on Jim's laptop.

"I said they found her. Margie. They found her. I heard it on the radio just a few minutes ago. They said that they haven't identified the body, but they reported it as a carjacking. Boy, I'm telling you, this is working to perfection." A big, satisfied smile crept across Wayne's face as he pulled a pair of latex gloves from his pocket and slipped them on.

"By the way, Jim got an email from the safe company saying that FedEx had picked up the letter with the combination and it should arrive here tomorrow morning around ten. I sure hope those folders are in the safe for our sake. If not..."

"I'm sure they're there. They've got to be," answered Wayne trying to stay positive.

"Well, the folders aren't our only problem. I've been thinking about Jamie. I'm worried that he could blow this thing wide open. He's a loose cannon. You never know what he's going to do or when. We gotta somehow get him out of our hair."

Wayne looked at Bobby's head, considered a bald joke, but instead quipped, "Well, let's just kill the son-of-a-bitch. Rub him out, as they say."

"Now you're talking. That crackhead needs to go. What's one more killing? After all, drug deals go bad every day."

"Bobby, I'm kidding."

"Well, I'm not. Next time that fucker shows his face around here, I'm gonna take him out."

"Are you crazy? I... I..." Wayne was speechless.

"Oh, for God's sake," interrupted Bobby. "I'm just pulling your chain. But we've got to come up with something to keep him at bay 'cause I get the feeling that he comes by to get money from his old man quite often. I don't know what drugs cost any more, but…"

"What do you mean you don't know what drugs cost anymore?" interrupted Wayne. "Have you ever done drugs?"

"Are you that naïve? I probably tried every drug known to man back in my college days. Still do a little pot when I'm stressed. Ah, jeez. Don't tell me you've never tried any wacky-weed?"

"No, Bobby. I've never done *any* drug. At least none that was *illegal!*"

"Well, you ought to hit the bong every now and then. It'll loosen up that tight little ass of yours."

"I don't want to talk about this anymore," countered Wayne, shaking his head. This was a side of Bobby he had never seen. "But since you're so damn knowledgeable about all this drug stuff, what do you think we ought to do with Jamie other than feed him money? I mean seriously."

"I would have thought that would have been part of your plan. Since, obviously, it's not, I'll have to think about it, but I do know we *can't* keep giving him money, whether it's for drugs, food, whatever. At some point in time, he' gotta wonder why his old man's never here or why we're the ones always giving him the money."

"You're right about that. I'm sure if we put our heads together, we can come up with something."

"Well, we better and soon or *I* will deal with it," said Bobby, emphasizing 'I.'

What Bobby said, how he said it, and the look in his eyes was very disturbing to Wayne. Quickly changing the subject, he asked, "Have you checked Jim's voicemail?"

"Nope. Didn't know I was supposed to."

Wayne walked over to the desk phone and dialed AT&T voicemail. So guests could easily receive voicemail, the password was either *NAGS812, NAGS813* or *NAGS814* based on the apartment number. Wayne entered *NAGS812* and then switched to speakerphone. There were five messages; three were hang-ups, one from a Board member asking for a callback, and one from Jim's ex-wife. She was furious, threatening to send him to jail if she didn't get her alimony check by Monday.

"Oh no!" said Wayne, completely surprised by Jim's failure to meet his financial obligation to his wife.

"I bet you didn't see that one coming when you wrote your plan. But I'm gonna give you a pass. I don't think anybody would. FYI, I saw the check on Jim's desk when I was doing his mail. I guess since he was dead, he wasn't able to drop it off." Only Bobby was laughing at his attempted humor.

"We need to get an email off to her *now* and tell her that we… he… Jim will put the check in her mailbox today. That he just forgot to mail it."

Before Bobby could answer, Wayne pulled the laptop over toward him, clicked off the porn site and typed out a quick note to Jim's wife.

When he finished the email, he looked at Bobby who was examining the check. Both men started to speak at the same time.

Bobby: "Do you…" Wayne: "This actually…"

"You first," said Bobby.

"Well, I was going to say that this actually works to our advantage and fits very nicely into my plan. The email from Jim. The check in the mailbox. All show that Jim is still alive. The email that I wrote was very curt. Nothing to show his current state of mind. I can drop the check off when I go home tonight. Oh! She just responded!"

Fine.

He turned the computer back around to Bobby for him to see.

"Boy, she's pissed," said Bobby. "And you don't want to set her off." He then handed the check to Wayne. "Jim really got screwed. You see what he's paying that bitch? $12,000 a month. I don't know who his lawyer was, but he must be a real loser."

Wayne chose not to comment since he had been the one to recommend the lawyer. Instead, he took a seat on the nearby leather sofa to think, while Bobby returned to his porn site.

Shortly, Wayne spoke up. "We need to make a copy of that check so we'll have a copy of Jim's handwriting just in case we… he needs to sign something. Are you good at forging?"

Bobby pulled a legal pad and pen in the front drawer. "Give me the check." After a few attempts at signing Jim's name, he placed the check next to his last forgery attempt.

"What do you think?"

Wayne pushed off the sofa, walked over to the desk and looked at the signatures on both documents. They were almost identical.

"Bobby? It's a perfect match! I'm amazed! How did you do it so quickly? With so little practice?"

"Bubba, when you're in politics, lying and cheating are not the only things you learn."

Wayne was also learning. Learning that there was a less sanitized version of the friendly, lovable, moral Nelson Robert Armstrong, president of NAGS than anyone knew.

Chapter 46

Thursday, December 28, 2006, 4:06 p.m. EST

Using the GPS and radar detector on his BMW, Aaron drove as fast as he could to the DC Morgue. He made it there just before closing. On the way, he kept mulling over in his mind what Kyle had said. *Mom's dead. She was shot. The detectives showed me some photos of her. I'm sure it's her.* The more he thought about it the madder he got - at the police and his brother. Especially his brother. The cops had asked Kyle to make a positive identification from some pictures! Something this important? From some photos? How could his brother be so stupid and the police so callous and inept? The pictures he saw could have been anybody - a crack addict, prostitute, homeless woman, whatever. Yet he made a positive ID. What a moron. So stupid. Never the one to make waves. And working for the government, for crying out loud. All he cared about was golf and the Redskins. Probably didn't have two nickels to rub together unlike himself who already had over two million dollars in investments and was working on his third. His thoughts were interrupted by a call on his cell. Kyle. Naturally. He let it go to voicemail. He had had enough of his younger brother. Then considering that it might be a call to abort the trip, he listened to the message. Wrong! Instead, a meeting with the police tomorrow at 10 a.m. at his Mom's apartment. A complete waste of time. Probably just as pointless as the trip to the morgue.

Only two parking spaces were available on the street in front of the morgue - both handicapped. Unrepentantly, he parked in the first one, grumbling that there were way too many spaces for the handicap. As he walked away from his car, he made sure he had enough clearance from the car parked behind him so he wouldn't have to worry about the bumper of his brand new 2007 750Li BMW getting dinged.

Once inside the building and through security, Aaron was told that someone would come for him, to please wait. Waiting was not one of his strong suits. After a short while, the door to the right of the elevators opened and a young, black female attendant, carrying a clipboard, entered the lobby and walked directly over to him. She was dressed in blue scrubs with a name tag identifying her as LaShaun. Before she could speak, Aaron introduced himself in his normal curt manner, explained why he was there and asked how long it would take – that he had a deadline to meet on an important project back at his office. She pointed to her name tag and politely introduced herself. She told him that she'd been expecting him. Having worked at the morgue for over five years, she was used to dealing with all kinds of people who were first-time visitors. No one wanted to be there. And they all behaved differently. Having to identify a dead body produced a myriad of responses and behaviors, especially if the deceased was a loved one. Some needed sympathy and compassion; some needed silence and understanding; some just needed to talk. Having someone to listen was optional. With Aaron, everything was very business-like and professional. She had him produce his driver's license to verify his identity. Satisfied, she then neatly wrote the information on the visitor's log which Aaron signed.

The morgue was in the basement - one floor down. Aaron was given the choice of the elevator or steps. They took the steps. As he followed her down the stairwell, he couldn't help but think again of what Kyle had said. *I'm sure it's her.* His words were then followed by his own thoughts. *Oh God, what if he's right!* Before any more thoughts, negative or otherwise, came to mind, LaShaun was badging into the second of three large storage rooms.

The room area was pristine with everything being made of stainless steel. And it was cold, extremely cold, just as he imagined. The young attendant looked at her clipboard then walked directly to one particular storage drawer and slowly pulled it open. She pulled back a white sheet to reveal the face of the corpse and stepped back so Aaron could see. She always made a mental note of how family members, relatives or friends viewed the body. Aaron hesitated at first, looking at LaShaun. She motioned him up to the drawer. He took a deep breath, moved up to the drawer and looked at the body. He fully expected to see some stranger. The sight of his mother laying there, her face mauled as though someone had taken a pickaxe to it, was almost more than he could bear. Slowly, he backed away; his eyes transfixed on what was once the most beautiful lady he had ever known. But tears did not come. His emotions had been locked away for so long that all he could do was stare at the body and then at LaShaun.

"That's her. That's my Mom. Margaret Irene Hamilton," Aaron said without feeling. Then he left.

Slowly, Aaron climbed into his car, closed and locked the door. Everything that happened from the time he saw his mother's dead body until now was nothing but a blur. He didn't remember signing the release form, walking back up the stairs to the lobby or even hugging LaShaun before leaving the building. Nothing. He sat there silent with his head tilted back and his eyes closed. Suddenly, he started banging both hands on the steering wheel, shaking his head violently and wailing, "NO! NO! NO! OH GOD! NO!" Tears began streaming down his face. The harder he fought his pent-up feelings, the more he cried.

He hadn't always been this cold-hearted. It happened years earlier after his Dad died. He cried for weeks. He couldn't eat or sleep. School was out of the question. As much as his Mom consoled him, the preacher prayed for him, and the counselor listened and advised, nothing worked. Then one day, the tears stopped as well as the caring, the feelings, the emotions. Everything simply dried up. It worked until today.

After wiping the tears from his eyes with the sleeve of his coat, Aaron slowly pulled his cell phone from his coat pocket. He pushed his speed dial. After the phone in his Mom's vacant apartment rang four times, her recorded voice answered. Once the recording finished, Aaron whispered into his phone, his voice quivering, "Mom, I love you." Then he hung up.

Chapter 47

Thursday, December 28, 2006, 4:47 p.m. EST

Daniel hung up the phone and looked at Johnny who was furiously keying on his computer, his brow furrowed in deep concentration. The call to Daniel had been from the North Carolina State Highway Patrol (NCSHP) with the good news that Margie's car had been spotted on I-85, heading south. That they planned to blockade the southbound lane at an interchange, outside of Durham and expected an arrest within the hour. The promise of him and Johnny swooping down and capturing their prey would now have to be left to others. He knew Johnny would be disappointed, but that wouldn't curb his enthusiasm.

"Wrinkles? You got a minute?"

"Huh? Yeah. Anything for you Danny boy. I was just checking out the Hamilton brothers."

"You find anything?"

"Nothing. Nada. Not a damn thing. I even checked their driving records. Spotless."

"Well, some good news. The North Carolina Highway Patrol. They've located Margie's car. They expect an arrest hopefully within the hour."

"That *is* great news! And so fast! I guess those southern boys are good for something other than just ferreting out moonshiners."

"I'll let them know you said that the next time they call. Speaking of which, we need to call Kyle. At least now we have some good news to go along with the bad. You or me?"

"You do it. You know what the Carolina boys said, and I'd just be fumbling, bumbling around, as usual. Plus you're better at it than I am."

Daniel gave Johnny the 'OK' sign and started dialing.

* * * * * * * * *

Kyle answered the phone immediately expecting it to be Aaron. He turned to Katie and whispered, "*Detective Whitehead.*"

The detective sympathetically informed Kyle that Aaron had confirmed the identification of their mother's body. He then told Kyle that her car had been located in North Carolina and that an arrest was expected shortly.

"So, it'll be over soon?"

"Not just yet. Not until we've had a chance to question whoever's in the car. Kind of a wait and see. But we'll keep you informed. There's one other thing. If you could get us a list of your mother's close friends, relatives, business associates, housekeepers, and their telephone numbers, it would be very helpful in our investigation."

"If you're about to make an arrest, why do you need that?" asked Kyle, totally baffled.

"Sometimes the occupants in the car are not the ones who stole it. So until we know for sure, we have to continue with the investigation based on the evidence we have."

"I don't understand."

"Kyle, there are some loose ends… inconsistencies, if you will, in this case that I'm not at liberty to discuss. At least, not at this time. I hate to seem so evasive but sometimes we must if we want to solve a case."

"I understand," Kyle said outwardly, but inwardly, was totally confused. He would do what Detective Whitehead asked.

"One more thing. You may start getting calls from reporters if you haven't already. Please decline to comment on the case at this time. You can tell them that you don't feel like talking about it now. Maybe later. And do not tell them *anything* that we've discussed. Some reporters have been known to create stories from the smallest of information, just to have a story. And this can be detrimental to our case."

"Yes, sir. Don't worry. I won't say anything."

Kyle hung up the phone and relayed to Katie everything Detective Williams had said. She, too, was puzzled by the request for a list of Margie's friends and relatives. They speculated for a while as to its purpose, but nothing came to mind.

They had hardly started on the detective's list, with Kyle dictating and Katie, who had the better penmanship, writing, when there was a knock at the front door. Kyle looked at Katie, rolled his eyes and headed for the door. Through the peep-hole, he saw Aaron who had never been to his apartment. But, to be fair, Kyle had never been to Aaron's. They had not been close. Not since their Dad died. He quickly opened the door.

Aaron looked terrible. His eyes were red, swollen and sad-looking. When he saw Kyle, he broke down crying. Kyle grabbed him and hugged him as tears began flowing from his eyes as well. The sight of the two brothers embracing, crying, setting aside their differences and hostilities was too much for Katie to bear. She, too, began to cry. Feeling the two brothers needed time together and alone, she found her coat and handbag.

"I think I should go," she whispered to Kyle as she slipped on her coat.

Before she could slip past the two brothers, Kyle reached for her arm. "Please don't go,"

Aaron, who had not seen Katie when he entered the apartment, quickly apologized. "Kyle, I'm sorry. I didn't know you had company. I should have called. I'm just not thinking straight. I'll leave."

"No! Don't go. Either of you! Please!" pleaded Kyle.

The urgency of Kyle's voice gave Katie reason to pause. He needed her. She couldn't leave him. She wouldn't leave him.

"Yes. Please stay," echoed Aaron, trying to look at Katie while at the same time wiping the tears from his face with his coat sleeve. There was a slight quiver in his voice as he continued. "We'll both stay. I'm Aaron, Kyle's brother." Automatically, he extended his hand to her in his normal business-like fashion.

She ignored his hand and, instead, gave him a Margie Hamilton-like hug. "I know who you are. And I'm Katie Chandler, Kyle's girlfriend." Aaron had not been hugged in so long that he felt awkward hugging her back. But the warmth and sincerity of her embrace made his return hug seem natural.

Family tragedies can bring families together or can tear them apart. Margie's death had reunited the two brothers and, for that, their mother would have been pleased.

Chapter 48

Thursday, December 28, 2006, 6:53 p.m. EST

What the hell? thought Jamie as he watched Wayne Peters and Bobby Armstrong get into his Dad's big, silver Mercedes and drive off. Where was his Dad? He had waited impatiently for over an hour in an obscure area of the Watergate parking garage for everyone to leave the apartment. They were *all* supposed to be going out to have dinner with some bigwigs. That included his Dad. But his Dad hadn't left with them. *Surely they wouldn't leave him there alone. Maybe he rode with some other dudes. Met them at the front entrance.* Tonight was his best, if not last, opportunity to get some real cash from the safe for the New Year's. Knowing his luck, he resigned himself to the fact that his Dad *had* stayed at the apartment, eating some takeout, and working on that stupid project. He'd have to beg him for another fifty or sixty dollars. And he'd get it even though his Dad probably knew about the hundred from Armstrong.

There was no response to his knocks on the apartment door. And his call to the apartment's phone went to voicemail. Jamie's spirits were raised. After a quick look to the left and then right, he entered the apartment. Other than a table lamp in the foyer, he expected the apartment to be totally dark. As his Dad would say, '*A penny earned is a penny saved.*' But the place was lit up like a Christmas tree. His Dad would never leave on that many lights whether he was at home or not. So where was he? Jamie did a quick search of the apartment but found it vacant. It was decision time. Leave or stay? Take a chance on getting caught pilfering the safe and losing his personal ATM forever? Or get enough cash to ensure himself a very happy New Year? Making good decisions had not been his strong suit lately. He pulled his phone and called his Dad's cell. It went directly to voicemail. And he went directly to the safe.

The vibration of his cell phone in his hand made Jamie jump. *Oh shit! It's Nate.*

"Boy, when you coming? I ain't got all day." Drug dealers were always nervous. Always in a hurry. Jamie didn't like Nate, but he trusted him. At least he trusted him not to be a Narc. Other than that, he was scum.

"Give me about an hour. I gotta withdraw my money first. But I'll be there. Just don't leave. And if you got any extra speedballs, I'm good for it. You know me."

"Yeah. I know you all right," replied Nate. He knew Jamie all too well. He was always late, always had an excuse, always lying. But he always had the money. "I'll get you some speedballs but you gotta know it's strong. Gotta be careful." Nate didn't want to lose one of his better customers.

"No problemo."

"Don't call me again on this number. I've got a new one." Nate made a habit of changing his cell phone every week or two. Just as a precaution. And he never met any of his customers in the same location twice. Too risky.

"Hold it! Let me get something to write on," mumbled Jamie as he searched his Dad's desk for pen and paper. He saw a yellow legal pad and grabbed it. Strangely, his Dad's signature was written on it multiple times like he was practicing it. *What the hell! Now, this is really weird!* Something wasn't right, but he didn't have time to figure out his Dad's recent strange behavior. He tore off the last sheet from the legal pad and using a nearby pen scribbled down Nate's new cell number, folded it, and stuck it in his wallet. The buyer and seller ended their conversation.

Jamie headed over to the safe and quickly opened it. Sweat began to collect under his arms. The folders were stacked just as he had left them. This time, he carefully grabbed a handful and set them neatly on the floor. He repeated this process until all the folders were removed. He then removed $200 from the stacks of money being careful to take only one fifty from four different stacks. This was more than normal, but being this would be his last trip to the 'bank' this year, he needed to make sure he had plenty. Hopefully, his Dad would never know. Jamie replaced the stacks of money and folders as he found them, closed the safe and headed out to meet Nate. Better times were ahead.

Chapter 49

Thursday, December 28, 2006, 7:35 p.m. EST

How's that rib-eye?" asked Wayne as he eyed his glass of 2004 Opus One Cabernet Sauvignon. It was the perfect, albeit expensive, complement to his sizzling butterflied filet.

"Excellent. I'm telling you, you just can't beat Ruth's Chris. Best steak house around - even in Texas. I'm glad you thought of it."

As Bobby spoke in his Texas brogue, a number of restaurant patrons stared at him, each wondering if he were Dr. Phil. One male patron even got up on the pretense of having to go to the restroom, went out of his way to walk by Wayne and Bobby's table to get a closer look, then shook his head as he headed back to his table, disappointing everyone who was watching. Regardless, Bobby ate it up.

Over a second bottle of Opus One, Wayne discussed NAGS' role in Margie's funeral. His plan assumed it would be open to friends, relatives, and co-workers. But whether it was a public or private funeral, NAGS would offer to pay for all expenses. They would also send a large but elegant floral arrangement with a card signed by the entire HQ staff expressing their deepest sympathies. If the funeral were public, every employee at the Dupont Circle office would be expected to attend. If the funeral was held on the weekend, or Monday, New Year's Day, all hourly employees attending the service would be paid double time. Every employee attending would receive a $25 mileage allowance. And if any employee wished to send a personal flower arrangement, their cost would be reimbursed in full. Wayne would represent the organization if the service were open to eulogies. He was prepared to deliver a passionate tribute that would leave nary a dry eye in the church. All of this was in Wayne's plan. The one that Bobby had yet to fully read.

Bobby agreed to everything, offering only a toast to Wayne's meticulous planning.

Next, Wayne brought up the need to hold a press conference. His plan was to hold it at 11 a.m. in front of NAGS headquarters on the day after Margie's body had been identified. Based on the latest news reports that would be tonight, tomorrow or Saturday at the latest. Once the body was ID'ed, someone from NAGS' legal staff would invite all local TV stations, radio stations, and newspapers to the conference. Bobby would serve as spokesperson. Having this opportunity immediately caught Bobby's attention as he loved working the crowds and seeing his face on television and in newspapers. He would do almost anything to enhance his name recognition. Having NAGS' president hold the news conference would emphasize its importance and their concern about their employees. But most importantly, Bobby could subtly interject '*If only Margie could have had her gun*' into his remarks which hopefully would give the press their headline for their next edition.

As Wayne pulled out Margie's bio for Bobby to review, his cell phone vibrated in his coat pocket. Normally, he would have ignored the call. He always thought it rude and inconsiderate to talk on the phone in front of guests and, in this case, other diners. But it was a local number, one that seemed familiar but not one immediately recognizable. Concerned that it could be related to the news of Margie's death, he politely answered the phone and then took a sip of his wine. He almost choked on it when he heard Kyle Hamilton's voice. He was not expecting to hear from him nor prepared to talk to him.

"Hello. Mr. Peters? This is Kyle Hamilton. I hope I'm not interrupting anything."

"Hello Kyle," answered Wayne. "No. No. You're not interrupting anything."

Hearing Kyle's name made Bobby stop midstream as he was about to help himself to another serving of the au gratin potatoes. Instead, he leaned in close to Wayne's phone and tried to listen in. Other patrons who once were excited at the possibility of dining with a celebrity now looked disdainfully at the pair and of their total disregard of dining courtesy.

"Sir. I thought you should know that my… uh… my Mom's dead," he said, his voice quivering.

"What? Oh my God!!" Wayne replied, his voice filled with surprise. Seeking a little privacy, he turned his back to Bobby and the other restaurant patrons. Even though he was well aware that she was dead, hearing the words coming from her son stunned him, so the surprise in his voice was real. "When?" he stammered.

There was a slight pause as Kyle regained his composure. "We think yesterday, but we're not sure."

"Oh, Kyle. I am so, so sorry. Margie. She was like a mother to me." Wayne's voice was very genuine, very saddened. If he were an actor, it couldn't have been better. "Is there anything we can do for you or your family?"

Bobby frantically punched Wayne's shoulder trying to get his attention. When Wayne angrily turned around, Bobby held up his hands in the form of a 'T' indicating he wanted his attention. He quickly pulled out his copy of Wayne's action plan from his briefcase along with a pen and scribbled *'Ask how she died!!!!!!'* then shoved it in front of Wayne.

Wayne saw the note and realized his error. He nodded to Bobby and mouthed *OK*.

Kyle continued. "Well, actually there are a couple of things. Aaron and I have been working on Mom's funeral plans. Right now, we think the service will be on Monday but won't know for sure until tomorrow. We were wondering if you wouldn't mind being one of Mom's pallbearers."

"I would be honored to be a pallbearer. It's the least I can do. Keep me informed as to the date and time."

When Bobby heard the word 'pallbearer,' he mouthed *Yes* while simultaneously pumping his fist.

"I will," answered Kyle. "And one other thing. If possible, can you get me a list of Mom's co-workers and their phone numbers? I need this by 10 a.m., tomorrow, if possible."

Looking quizzical, Wayne replied, "I can do that. Is this for the funeral?"

"No, sir. One of the detectives asked me for it."

"Why? How did your mother die?" Wayne asked.

"She was shot during a carjacking."

"Oh! My! GOD! I am so sorry. I assumed she had a stroke or a heart attack. This is terrible. Terrible!" lamented Wayne.

Bobby nodded his head in approval and mouthed *Good*.

Wayne then changed his demeanor, acting angry. "Dammit, Kyle. If she'd been able to carry her gun in this drug-infested city, she might have been able to defend herself. Do they know who did it? Have they arrested anyone?"

A double thumbs up from Bobby.

"The detective asked me not to discuss the case with anyone. But I'm sure he meant reporters. He told me that they're about to make an arrest."

"That's great. So why does he want a list of our employees? That doesn't make sense. Not for a carjacking."

"I don't know, sir. All I know is that he wants a list of Mom's relatives, close friends, co-workers, whatever. He said something about there being some *inconsistencies* in the case. That's all I know."

Wayne's face turned ashen, and his heart raced as he heard the word 'inconsistencies.'

"I'll call you tomorrow morning before 10 with the list. I can either fax it, scan it or drive it over to you. Just let me know. Again, I am so sorry about your mother."

"Thank you, sir. I do appreciate that. I want you to know that my Mom thought the world of you. You were always very good and kind to her. And thanks for your help. Goodbye, sir."

Bobby could hardly wait to speak. "Wayne. That was a perfect lead-in for our campaign." He continued to talk as he cut a big piece from his rib-eye, "I could hardly hear a damn thing he said, but what I did hear, it didn't sound like he objected. I say full steam ahead. Damn the torpedoes. This could be one of our best campaigns ever." He drowned the steak with a big swallow of wine. "Where's the waiter. I want to order another bottle."

Wayne wasn't listening to Bobby. His mind kept playing over and over what Kyle had said: 'Inconsistencies.' What *inconsistencies*? There were no *inconsistencies*.

"Bobby! Stop talking and listen to me. We may have a problem."

"What kind of problem? I thought you did great. You were sincere, concerned. And you got our campaign…"

"Dammit, Bobby. You're not listening. Kyle asked me for a list of Margie's co-workers. He said the detective wanted it because of some *inconsistencies* in the case. I don't know what he's talking about. There can't be any *inconsistencies*."

"Un-fucking-believable! I *knew* something like this was going to happen! Everything in your plan is so mechanical and so regimented that nothing's natural," Bobby said loudly, throwing his napkin onto his plate. "So what do we do now? How does your fucking plan deal with *inconsistencies*?"

"I don't know. I...."

"Well, I'm beginning to think it's time to scrap everything and let me have a go at it. I certainly couldn't do any fucking worse."

Wayne was upset enough from what Kyle had said. But Bobby was making it worse. They had to stick to their plan. Any deviation from it could be devastating. Maybe another bottle of wine would help. At home. Alone.

Chapter 50

Thursday, December 28, 2006, 8:48 p.m. EST

"Wrinkles! You in bed?" asked Daniel who was calling from his office. He took a slug of his lukewarm coffee from his University of Maryland mug and sat back in his desk chair waiting for Johnny's retort.

"Will be as soon as I drink my prune juice and put on my Depends. How old do you think I am? Never mind. Don't answer that. What's up?"

"Just wanted to let you know that things went really good down in North Carolina. Evidently, there were two cars traveling in tandem. They were able to secure both cars and arrest the two drivers. Both males. There were no other occupants. I was told they talked faster than a tobacco auctioneer. Problem was, nobody could understand them. So we don't know if they are the ones that carjacked Margie or not. The folks down south are bringing in a Spanish interpreter, but he won't be available until tomorrow morning. Meanwhile, they're videotaping everything. They've also called in a couple of Spanish-speaking attorneys to make sure no one's rights are violated."

"Probably illegals. Next thing you know, they'll be taking our job at half the pay and working twice the hours," said Johnny laughing at his own comment. "Did the Carolina boys give you any idea when we'll get a copy of their case file? I'd be really interested if there was a woman's coat in the inventory."

"I'll check the fax machine before I leave, but I doubt if they've had time to send it. They told me not to expect anything before tomorrow or possibly Saturday," he answered.

"Don't tell me you're still at the office?"

"Yeah. I'm still here. I was trying to get a few emails out to the boss. Gotta keep him up to date. From day one, he told me he had a bad feeling about this one."

"Well, I guess ol' cue ball got that right. Hey, with you still being at the office making us old grunts look bad, I assume you already know that the Hamilton lady worked for NAGS as Wayne Peters' executive secretary."

"Yes. Mr. Second Amendment himself. We'll definitely have to give him a call tomorrow."

"Looking forward to it," echoed Johnny. For over 30 years, guns had been banned from the streets of Washington D.C., and now all of that was about to be reversed mainly due to the efforts of people like Wayne Peters and his organization – NAGS. It was very controversial – even within the ranks of the DC police force.

"Look, the main reason I called you tonight is that your forensic buddy, Bennie, left me a message saying that they had reviewed the surveillance video from the storage unit. He said that they found something very interesting and would like to show us tomorrow morning. Asked if we could meet at our office at 7. He asked if I thought, and I'm only repeating what he said,,, he asked if I thought you could drag your fat ass out of bed that early."

"That sounds like something that old fool would say."

Chapter 51

Friday, December 29, 2006, 12:58 a.m. EST

"**M**aamaaa!!!! I loooooooovvvvvvvve you. Maaaaaaama. Pleeeeessssssseee don't hate me. I loooooooooovvvvve youuuuuuuu."

The loud voice coming from the front porch startled Elaine Barnes, awakening her from her much needed sleep. Since her divorce from Jim, she was having trouble sleeping through the night. And now thanks to the loud wails from her rebellious son, tonight would be no different. Jamie had done this on at least three other times since her divorce, so this wasn't a new experience – just one she wished to forget. As much as she'd like to ignore him, she knew she couldn't or he'd eventually wake the entire neighborhood, if he hadn't already. She considered calling the cops and having him put in jail, but her maternal instincts wouldn't allow it. Jamie wasn't there for money, only love, and forgiveness.

She blamed Jim for Jamie's drug problems. If he had been at home more, had taken more interest in their son, he probably wouldn't have turned to drugs. But his job was too important, too demanding. He spent most of his time either out of town or out on the town with his Washington bigwigs and important donors. And when he *was* at home, he was at the country club, either playing golf or cards. He never seemed to have time for Jamie much less his once faithful wife. Even when Elaine discovered Jamie's drug problem, Jim refused to believe it, saying he knew all the signs of drug use and Jamie wasn't a user. She called him an ostrich, always putting his head in the sand which didn't help their son or their marriage. In the end, their son's drug use created a chasm between the husband and wife that could never be bridged. Toward the end of their marriage, Jim would have nothing to do with Elaine. He ignored her, both physically and mentally. When their divorce became final, they hadn't had sex in over two years. He now disgusted her - his weight, his looks, his voice – everything. And the fact that Jamie looked like a smaller version of his father contributed to her contempt.

"Maamaaa!!!!   Puleeeeeeeeessssssssssse let me innnnnn.   I looooooovvvvvvvvve you. Maaaaaaama. I missssssssss youuuuuuuu."

Elaine jerked off her eye mask, threw it towards her bedside table, flipped on the lamp and then tried to focus her eyes as she looked at the time on her alarm clock. *One AM!! God Almighty!* She grabbed her terrycloth robe from the foot of the bed and angrily slipped it around her small, well-toned body. She then stepped into her matching slippers and headed downstairs. By the time she got to the front door, Jamie was holding onto one of the front columns, heaving his guts out. Elaine didn't want to touch him. He had vomit running down his shirt and on the front of his open jacket. It was Jim's fault. She knew the son-of-a-bitch must have given him too much money. And Jamie had spent it all – on drugs. When Jamie saw the front porch light come on, he wiped his mouth, turned, smiled, and opened his arms for a mother's comforting hug.

"Don't' touch me, you son-of-a-bitch! You stay here. And quit that yelling. You're going to get me kicked out of the neighborhood!"

Jamie silently obeyed as he leaned against the front door sidelights. His glassy eyes kept opening and closing like shades on a window as he waited for his mother's return. He needed his mother and her love but, right now, he'd settle for sleep.

When Elaine returned, she was carrying a plastic garbage bag in one hand and some wet paper towels in the other. Jamie immediately grabbed for the paper towel trying to help.

"Would you *stop* and let me do it," she snapped as she wiped the vomit off his face and shirt. "Why do you keep doing this to me? God. When are you going to grow up?"

"I'mmmmmmm sorrrrrrrrrrryyyy Mama. Puuulllllleeeeeeeeessssssse don't ha…haaate me. I loooooooooovvvvvvvvvve you."

Jamie's eyes kept rolling to the back of his head as he talked, freaking Elaine out.

"Quit doing that, Jamie. That's disgusting. Now GET inside and go up to your room and take off your shirt so I can wash it. DO NOT, and I repeat DO NOT go into the living room. Do you hear me?"

Jamie nodded his head, smiled again and then staggered into the house.

Elaine continued her tirade as she helped pull him into the house. "That damn father of yours. I've told him over and over again not to give you any money. I hate him. And I hate *you* for doing this to me."

"Noooo Mama. Puuullllleeeeeeessse doonnn't hate meeee annnnddd Daddddddyyyyy. He didn't giivvve meeeeee deee monnnney. Missssserr Aaaaammsssstonnnnng did."

"What? What are you talking about? Did your father tell you to say that?" Elaine didn't believe Jamie. Not for one moment. Since the drugs, Jamie had become a habitual liar. He told lies even when the truth served him better. She knew it couldn't be Bobby. He was in Texas hunting. Bobby would never lie to her.

As Jamie plodded along into the house toward the steps leading up to his room, Elaine left him and headed back to the kitchen and a phone. She was going to make Jim's life a living hell. She dialed his apartment. The phone rang until it went to voicemail. "Pick up the phone you stupid son-of-a-bitch." A second try and a call to his cell phone had the same results. Voicemail. "Fuck you, Jim Barnes. Fuck you. Fuck you. Fuck you."

Elaine walked upstairs and into Jamie's room. He wasn't there. *Oh my God. Please, not in the living room on my new couch!* She hurried down the steps flinging off one of her bedroom slippers as she did. She quickly retrieved it on the bottom landing, slipped it back on and rushed into the living room. He wasn't there. Elaine started searching the house and found Jamie in the guest bedroom lying completely naked across the bed with his clothes in a pile in the middle of the floor.

"Wake up, Jamie," snapped Elaine as she shook the boy's face. "Wake up!"

"Huh?"

"Where's your father?" she barked as she turned on the overhead light.

"Huh?" Jamie held his hand over his eyes trying to shield them from the blinding light.

"I said, where's that fucking father of yours?"

"Donno. Assss Misserr Arrrmmmmmmmmstto.......zzzzzzzzzzzzzz." Jamie passed out and began snoring heavily.

Elaine went back to her bedroom and using her landline dialed Jim's apartment phone and then his cell phone one more time, each to no avail. She then sat on the edge of the bed thinking what her lying, drugged-out son had said. Twice he had mentioned Bobby's name. Why would he do that? Why would he even think to bring up his name? He hardly knew the man. And he was too stoned to make it up. Surely he couldn't know about her and Bobby. No one knew. Not even that fat, stubby detective Jim had hired to follow her every move before their divorce. She and Bobby had been very discreet, rarely going out together. Bobby said there were rumors within NAGS that she was seeing someone, but no names were ever mentioned. And even now that she was divorced and could do whatever she pleased, their relationship still remained a secret. Bobby had too much to lose if their affair became public. She could wait. Bobby was worth waiting for.

Elaine reached for the cell phone that Bobby had given her. She always kept it with her, or on her bedside table. She hesitated for a second, thinking of what to say, why she was calling. She didn't want to make Bobby mad again. This was so stupid. Bobby was in Texas. Hunting. Jamie was stoned. He must have gotten everything confused. She would tell him the truth about what Jamie had told her, and they would both laugh about it, and then if she were lucky, he would talk to her. Maybe he'd tell her how beautiful she was. Tell her that he couldn't wait to be with her, to hold her, to kiss her. Elaine got goosebumps thinking of how Bobby made love to her. She looked at her alarm clock. It was only a little after midnight – Texas time. He should still be awake. Confidently, she hit the speed dial for Bobby's cell phone. *Jamie's such a fucking liar!*

Bobby awoke to the loud ringing of his phone. Automatically, he reached to turn off his alarm clock. But the ringing persisted. It was his cell phone. He rose with a jerk thinking it might be Wayne with another problem. The caller-ID on the front of his cell phone read 'Staff E.' He immediately recognized it as Elaine.

What does the bitch want this time?

Bobby looked at the time on his phone before he flipped it open. *1:22 a.m.*

"What?" he asked, still half asleep.

"Hello, sweetie." She answered timidly hoping she wasn't upsetting him.

"Elaine! It's one fucking thirty in the morning. What the hell do you want?"

Bobby's yelling flustered Elaine and made her mind go blank. Everything she had mentally practiced was forgotten. All she could think about was what Bobby had just said, 'one fucking thirty in the morning,' not 'twelve fucking thirty in the morning'!

"I'm sorry. I didn't mean to wake you. How's your hunting trip?"

"You woke me up to ask me about my fucking hunting trip? Are you crazy, woman?"

Elaine started crying. "I'm sorry. I shouldn't have called. It's… It's…"

Bobby, now more calm and composed, interrupted her. "I'm sorry I yelled at you, honey. I'm still half asleep plus I got a lot on my mind. But the hunting's been great. Jenson didn't shoot a thing. Good thing he didn't take lessons from Dick Cheney."

"I'm glad you're having fun. Is there any chance you'll get here before Saturday?"

"No can do. I can't leave the congressman. You know that."

Elaine's mind couldn't help but wander back to Bobby's 'one fucking thirty in the morning.'

"I understand. It's that I'm always thinking about you. I'll hang up and let you get back to sleep. I'm sorry if I woke you. Oh, and I'm sorry my son was such a bother. How much money did you give him? I want to make sure I pay you back."

"I dunno. Maybe a hundred bucks. Don't worry about it. I…" Bobby now realized what he was saying. *That conniving bitch!*

"YOU FUCKING LIAR!" she screamed. "YOU'RE WORSE THAN MY SON!" Lowering her voice, she continued. "Now thanks to you, he's lying on my guest bed, naked, and stoned out of his mind. I want you to get over here RIGHT FUCKING NOW and get him out of my house. And if you see that sorry-ass excuse for an ex-husband of mine, you tell him that if I don't get my money by this weekend, I'm gonna call the cops. Have his ass thrown in jail!" Her voice was trembling with anger.

"OK. OK. Don't get your panties in a wad. We'll take care of it. I'll be there in about twenty minutes."

"Good. So why *did* you lie to me? Are you seeing someone else? Is that it? Someone younger and prettier? I'm not good enough for you anymore? Is that it? Well, wait until your wife hears about us and believe me, I *will* tell her. After that heifer and the Senator get through with you, you'll be lucky to get elected dog catcher. Now get your ass over here!" Without waiting for a response, she slapped the phone shut and hurled it toward her dresser mirror, shattering the mirror but not the phone. Then she cried.

Bobby slammed his phone shut. *That fucking bitch! No one talks to me that way! No one! Especially her!* Bad thoughts were racing through his mind as he threw on his clothes. This complicated matters. And unfortunately, Elaine had the upper hand. A call to his wife would ruin his career. That couldn't happen. That wouldn't happen. He definitely needed to see her.

Chapter 52

Friday, December 29, 2006, 1:53 a.m. EST

Elaine Barnes lived in one of the more affluent neighborhoods in Georgetown. Her house was only fifteen minutes from the Watergate complex where Bobby was staying and, coincidentally, only a couple of miles from Wayne Peter's townhouse. Because of the proximity to Peters' residence, Jim Barnes always suspected him as the one having the rumored affair with his wife.

Elaine Barnes' house was an elegant Federal-style structure built in the early forties. Soon after she and Jim bought it, they had the house completely renovated. They both enjoyed entertaining and hosted numerous parties at their home, many for NAGS. Until their divorce, none of their many friends and neighbors knew they were having marital problems. But they all knew of Jamie's drug issues. When they filed for divorce, it was the shock and talk of the neighborhood. When the divorce was final, Elaine walked away with everything she wanted, including their paid-off house.

At one-thirty in the morning, there was little traffic to hinder Bobby's trip time. Even the lightly falling snow couldn't impede his dash to Elaine's house. When he turned Jim Barnes' big Mercedes into the driveway, he saw an old Cadillac parked there with the driver's side door open and the interior light on. It had to be Jamie's. The car's left front tire rested on the snow-covered lawn. From what Elaine said of Jamie's condition, it was a wonder that he hadn't taken down the mailbox or a couple of shrubs when he drove in.

Bobby approached the house using the light from the front porch as a guide. None of the Christmas wreaths that adorned each window were lit. As he passed by the old Cadillac, he saw the keys still in the ignition. *Good way of getting that car stolen!* He left the keys in the car, and quietly shut its door. The closer he got to the porch, the fouler the air became. The putrid smell of vomit almost made him gag. He checked the walkway, the porch steps, and the porch as he made his way to the door, making sure not to step into the vile debris.

Elaine had left the door unlocked. So without knocking, he walked in and closed the door behind him, leaving on his leather gloves and overcoat. This was not going to be a social visit.

"Elaine?" he yelled out.

"In here." The voice was coming from the living room, a place he was intimately familiar with. He walked toward the voice and the faint light ahead. When he entered the room, he saw her silhouette as she stood in front of the fireplace with a drink in her hand. She had the gas logs turned up as high as they would go. She liked the dark of the room and the light of the fire. She and Bobby had made love in front of that same fireplace the day after her divorce. Jim never knew and never would.

"Where's Jamie?"

"He's in the guest bedroom on the first floor. Just follow his foul smell. If you get lost, it's the same room where you stayed the night you got too drunk to drive and Jim made you stay over. You know… the room where… where we first made love." Tears began to flow from Elaine's eyes as she remembered the night. "You know, I actually believed you loved me. God, I was such a fool."

Bobby had come to know Elaine well enough to realize that she had a textbook case of bipolar disorder. One moment, loving, hugging, syrupy sweet. Then, out of the blue, a complete 180 degree turn in mood and behavior. Right now from the tone of her voice, he knew that she was vacillating between wanting to make love and cutting his balls off. He wanted neither. He was on a mission.

From the light of the fire, he could see Elaine take another swallow from her drink. Most likely Jack Daniels straight up. Something she learned from Jim.

"I'm sorry, Elaine."

"You're sorry? For what? That I found you out? That you just lost the best fuck you'll ever have?"

"Just that I'm sorry. I better go get Jamie. Can you make some coffee? I'm gonna try to get some down him."

"Whatever," she said curtly. It was obvious that he wasn't there to talk. She could try, but why bother? It was over. Everything. Her hopes of him divorcing his wife and marrying her. Her hopes of becoming the wife of a US Senator. All gone and why? She had been used. All she had been was a receptacle for his boy-sized penis. Well, he would live to regret his decision to dump her.

Elaine wiped the tears from her eyes with the sleeve of her nightgown. Her sorrow quickly turned to anger. "Anything to get you and him the hell out of my house." She slammed the unfinished drink on the mantle and huffed out of the living room, through the dining room, and into the kitchen. Unfazed, Bobby walked over to the fireplace, picked up her unfinished drink, and drained it. He felt warm inside and out. He was ready.

He quickly made his way down the main hallway to the guest bedroom. On the wall to his right, just before the guest room, he found a light switch that controlled four small sconces in the hallway. He flipped it on. A secondary hallway that ran the length of the back of the house gave him a partial view of the lighted kitchen where he could see Elaine's movements. He only had a few minutes before the coffee was ready. The light from the hallway was enough to see Jamie, in all his glory, lying on the bed. There was no movement or sound from him except an occasional snore. His smelly clothes lay in a pile beside the bed.

Bobby pulled off his leather gloves, slipped them into his left coat pocket, and then, from his right pocket, pulled out a pair of latex gloves. Making as little noise as possible, he slipped them on. He then removed his shoes, coat, shirt, and pants and placed everything on one of the two wing chairs in the room. Knowing he had very little time, he quickly found Jamie's pants and shoes. The pants were a tight fit and couldn't be fully buttoned or zipped. But that wasn't necessary. The shoes, however, were a perfect fit. The smell and sight of Jamie's vomit-laden shirt were more than he could stand so he shoved it aside with his foot. And instead, he grabbed Jamie's leather jacket which lay under the shirt. It was a better fit. He zipped it to the top and raised his hands above his head to check his range of motion. It was more than adequate. Checking the pockets of the jacket, he found Jamie's cell phone. He placed it on top of his own clothing. He would need that later. Once he was completely dressed in Jamie's clothes, he moved back to the hallway looking toward the kitchen to locate Elaine. Fortunately, she was still there, pouring the brew. He smiled. Everything was working to perfection. He then silently returned to the living room, his eyes adjusting to darkness with every step. He tiptoed over to the fireplace and pulled the brass fire poker from its set making sure it didn't clang against the remaining pieces. Until tonight, the poker had never been used. It was merely for show. Tonight, it would be used in a way that the manufacturers had never intended.

For his best angle of attack, Bobby moved to the wall in the living room closest to the columned dining room. Elaine wouldn't be able to see him as she entered the room. He made sure there were no mirrors or anything that would give off his reflection forewarning her of his location. Looking at the poker, he turned the hook so that it pointed down as he gripped it.

"Elaine? Where are you? I've got Jamie in the living room. Hurry up with that coffee!"

"I'm coming. I'm coming," she yelled from the kitchen, hurrying as fast as she could, careful not to spill anything. "Oh, Shit! Don't let him sit on my new couch. He's liable to throw up again."

"I've got my eye on him. He's OK."

Elaine was carrying a serving tray containing three mugs filled with hot coffee, a little glass pitcher of cream, a sugar bowl, and a prissy stirring spoon as she walked from the kitchen through the dining room then into the living room. It would be the last trip she would ever make from her designer kitchen. It would be her last effort at being a good hostess. Mentally, she questioned why Bobby had not turned on any lights. It was her hope that maybe he had changed his mind and was waiting for her with open arms. Even though she was mad at him, she would take him back. She would forgive him. She could never harm him. She loved him.

The blow to the head was quick and forceful. It was a perfect strike – a bull's eye. The hook of the poker lodged deep into Elaine's brain. She never saw it coming, and her voice was silent as she fell to the ground. Coffee and blood splattered everywhere – on the wood floor, the interior Corinthian columns that were decorated with red Christmas ribbons and bows, the Oriental rug, the new couch, and all over Bobby. He had to twist and turn the poker to remove it from the skull. Blood gushed out of her brain as he jerked it out. Leaning over the body, he took aim with the hook at Elaine's temple. With another forceful blow, the hook slammed deep into her head again. More red blood poured from her head. Satisfied she was dead, he jerked the poker free from what remained of his ex-lover's head. Before leaving the lifeless body and returning to the guest bedroom, he intentionally stepped into the blood that had now formed a corona around her battered skull.

With the bloody poker under his arm, the empty cocktail glass from the mantle in his left hand, and a half-emptied bottle of Jack Daniels from Elaine's liquor cabinet in the other, Bobby calmly walked out of the living room, down the hall, and into the guest bedroom. His trail was marked by blood dripping from the poker and the partial prints of his blood-stained shoes. Before entering the bedroom, he used his free elbow to flip on the hall sconces. He couldn't risk turning on the bedroom's overhead light and possibly wakening the slumbering addict even though he doubted a solar flare could rouse the boy from his stupor. The light from the hallway was adequate for Bobby to see that Jamie was still dead to the world, figuratively speaking. Once Bobby was finished with him, he'd be dead to the world, literally speaking.

A cocktail of Elaine's pills and whiskey would do the trick. Throw in whatever drug or drugs the boy had taken earlier and the deadly combination would guarantee an end to his drug problems – forever. Bobby quietly set the liquor bottle and empty glass on the bedside table nearest the bedroom door and walked to the other side of the bed where Jamie's head lay. He picked up the boy's limp hand and squeezed it around the handle of the poker making sure the hook was pointed down. He then let the murder weapon drop to the floor. The noise from the poker hitting the wooden bedrail produced no movement from Jamie. Not even a blink. *Maybe he's dead. That would work.* Bobby chuckled to himself. He then looked at his watch. Time was wasting. He silently made his way out of the guest bedroom, down the main hallway, up to the master bedroom and into its adjoining bathroom. He flipped on the light and then searched the medicine cabinet for Elaine's bottle of antidepressants. He knew she was on the medication because she had told him. *She* told him everything. *He* told her nothing. The cabinet looked like a drug store with pills for everything - menopause, migraines, cholesterol, blood pressure, diuretics, weight loss, multi-vitamins, and depression. Bobby found what he wanted and checked the quantity. The bottle was three-quarters filled - more than adequate for his intended purpose.

As he left the bathroom but before leaving the bedroom, he was surprised to see the shattered mirror above Elaine's dresser with its shards everywhere. *Holy shit! She must have been really pissed! Doesn't she know that breaking a mirror brings bad luck?* The thought amused him. He spotted a cell phone laying on the floor in front of the dresser. He instantly recognized it as the special phone he'd given Elaine. To be sure, he checked the directory of names. Only one name appeared: 'Bobby.' He then checked the phone's call history. They all had been to him. *Thank God the bitch hadn't called anybody else, especially Leslie!* Satisfied, he shoved the phone into the leather jacket and headed back downstairs to the guest bedroom.

Bobby stared at Jamie for a few seconds looking for any body movements. There were none. The boy was nearly comatose. Moving quickly, he picked up the empty cocktail glass and headed back to the bathroom where he thoroughly washed the glass with soap and scalding hot water killing off any possible DNA he might have left when he drank from it earlier. He then filled it with cold water and returned to the bedroom where he grabbed the bottle of Jack Daniels and walked over to the side of the bed where Jamie's head lay. He set everything down on the matching bedside table, opened the pill bottle, and poured the entire contents into the glass of water. He gently sat on the side of the bed next to the boy and eased his head up onto his lap where he could see his face. Jamie looked like an unshaven copy of his father, only younger and slimmer. There was no struggle in the young man when Bobby slowly pulled his mouth open. Nor was there any resistance when he began pouring the water and dissolving pills down his throat. In fact, he seemed to crave the water, at times reaching involuntarily for the glass – probably the result of dehydration caused by all the vomiting. Bobby did not rush his efforts so not to cause choking. Once the glass was empty, Bobby rested Jamie's head across his lap. He set the glass down on the table, grabbed the bottle of Jack Daniels by its neck, raised Jamie's head again and began pouring the liquor directly into the young man's open mouth until he started spitting and coughing. He gave him a couple more shots before Jamie began resisting with his hands. During the process, his eyes opened a couple of times and stared at Bobby, and even smiled once. But he closed them just as quickly.

Lastly, before letting Jamie join his parents in the afterlife, he lifted the boy's right hand and squeezed it around the neck of the liquor bottle and then let it drop to the floor. It landed near the bloody poker where the contents of the bottle began to empty onto the floor causing Bobby to wrench with anguish at the waste of good liquor.

He checked the time. He was ahead of schedule. He cautiously stepped over the brass poker and empty liquor bottle and moved around to the wing chair where he'd earlier laid his clothes. He slipped out of Jamie's shoes, stripped off his jeans, and slipped out of the leather jacket letting them all fall randomly to the floor. Wasting little time, he dressed in his own clothes, overcoat, and Jim's borrowed shoes that he had worn instead of his boots. He stuffed Jamie's and Elaine's cell phones into his pocket. Then, realizing he needed Jamie's driver's license, he picked up the boy's jeans from the floor and searched the pockets for his wallet. Finding it, he removed the license, slipped it into his coat pocket, and returned the wallet back to the bloody jeans. Lastly, he slid Jim's Mercedes keys into Jamie's leather jacket. He was finished here. Everything he'd done was instinctive. He didn't need any calculated, unnatural, contrived plan like Wayne's. And more important... *No inconsistencies!*

Before leaving, he looked at Jamie one last time. The boy was hardly breathing. Within thirty to sixty minutes, he would be on the final trip of his life. Bobby flipped off the hall lights and headed to the front door, this time carefully avoiding Elaine's blood trail. As he passed the columned entry to the living room, he hesitated for a brief moment glancing over at Elaine's lifeless body. She no longer posed a threat to his career. Too bad it had to end this way. She was one great fuck.

Jamie's car, surprisingly, started up with no problems. And not surprisingly, it was low on gas. Obviously, he had not used the money he had been given for gas. Bobby slowly backed out of the driveway and onto the street where he then flipped on the headlights. Wayne Peters' townhouse was his next destination.

Bobby had hardly gone a quarter of a mile down the road when the liquor, water, partially dissolved pills, and whatever was left in Jamie's stomach heaved from his mouth and all over the bed and the floor below. Jamie awakened just enough to pull some of the vomit-drenched bedspread over him. While he slept, he dreamed of his mother and father. Some of the dreams were of happy times, some sad. But no dream would compare to the nightmare he was about to face.

Chapter 53

Friday, December 29, 2006, 2:58 a.m. EST

Wayne couldn't sleep. He lay in bed, tossing and turning, his mind running a hundred miles an hour. All he could think about was what Kyle had said. 'There were some inconsistencies.' *What inconsistencies?* When his phone rang, he sat straight up. The time on his alarm clock displayed: '2:58 AM.' Any call that early in the morning was never good news. The caller-ID displayed: 'Bobby Cell'. *What now?*

"So I guess you couldn't sleep either," said Wayne, turning on his bedside lamp.

"No, Wayne, I couldn't. I've decided we need a change of plans. You need to get dressed. Now. I'll be by in about 5 minutes to pick you up. Wear some jeans. And bring Jim's wallet and credit cards."

Wayne was confused. "What'd you mean *a change in plans?*"

"Just what I said. We're going back to the lodge. Now!"

"Oh, I see. Can't sleep. Might as well get Jim buried tonight as well as tomorrow. But we don't have the heaters? How can we dig into that frozen ground without heaters?"

"Forget the heaters. Be ready in five minutes," he snapped and hung up.

Wayne threw back the covers and jumped out of bed. Normally, he would have tried to reason with Bobby. But he seemed so demanding. So insistent. But why? This wasn't going to work. The barn's dirt floor was still frozen. Maybe it was time to let Bobby try his *off the cuff, seat of the pants* kind of logic and when it fails, then maybe he wouldn't be so critical of his (Wayne's) plan. Yes, there had been a few missteps, a few omissions, and modifications. But at least, for the most part, it was a well-thought-out roadmap to get them through this ugly mess.

In less than five minutes, Wayne was fully dressed standing outside his front door. He was wearing his overcoat over his clean and neatly pressed jeans and Nike sweatshirt that still sported the iron creases made by the local cleaners. He wasn't a *jeans* kind of person and he didn't do laundry.

It wasn't long before he saw a car turn into his driveway. It wasn't one that he immediately recognized. At least, not at first. Then he saw Bobby in the driver's seat, motioning with his hands for him to come on, to hurry up. Wayne wasted little time getting to the car that he now realized was Jamie's. Even as he opened the creaking door, Bobby continued to motion for him to hurry up but now with even quicker hand motions.

"Did you bring Jim's wallet and credit cards?" asked Bobby.

"Yes. So why the…"

"Get in," demanded Bobby. Wayne obliged, slamming the door shut. Bobby roared back out of the driveway before Wayne could put on his seat belt.

"What's going on? Why are you driving Jamie's car?"

"Let's say that Jamie and I switched cars. He has Jim's and I have his."

"OK. What the hell's going on?" said Wayne, his voice showing real concern.

"I'm changing your plan. We're moving to plan B for *Bobby's plan*."

"And what plan is that?"

"I had to get rid of a couple of problems, and I decided to do it my way. Your plan had too many loose ends. So I came up with a better one. One where we don't have to keep Jim alive and then have him go missing. One that we don't have to keep doling out money to Jamie. One where Elaine's not a problem. And one that doesn't have *inconsistencies*." Bobby emphasized 'inconsistencies.' "Plus who in the hell would believe that one NAGS employee gets murdered one week and then a week or so later, another goes missing. It reads like a bad novel."

"So what's your plan? And how's it any better than mine?"

"My plan is very simple. Jamie kills his mom and dad, then commits suicide. It's that simple. A *lot better* plan."

"You're not serious," interrupted Wayne, almost laughing.

"I am serious. Serious as a fucking heart attack. That's my plan."

"That's crazy? Jamie's not going to kill anybody, especially his mother."

"It's already happened," said Bobby matter-of-factly as he drove out of the city.

"Wha… what do you mean, 'It's already happened'?" stammered Wayne.

"What do I mean? Just what I said. Elaine is dead, and Jamie committed suicide. It's that simple. Now, of course, I had to help a little, if you know what I mean. But it's so much more believable than that fucked up plan of yours. Now we're going to make it look like Jamie killed his dad."

"I don't understand," said Wayne who was getting a real bad feeling.

"Weren't you listening? Let me repeat. Elaine is dead, Jamie committed suicide, and now we're going to make it look like Jamie killed his dad. That's my plan. And it works!"

"Bobby, tell me that it's not true. Tell me that it's a joke."

Bobby looked at Wayne and smiled

"OH! MY! GOD! You're not kidding!" snapped Wayne, stunned, ready to jump out of the car. He wanted to say something, do something. But he couldn't. Just like when he shot Jim, he did nothing. He couldn't even look at Bobby. He looked straight ahead, unable to think.

"Sorry, Bubba. I felt my way was best," said Bobby calmly, with no emotions, no remorse.

Time passed without a word from either man. Bobby concentrated on his driving and the road conditions while Wayne sat dumbstruck. His mind now wandered aimlessly through the events of the last two days. Nothing he had done or planned could have prepared him for this! All he had ever tried to do was to protect himself, Bobby and NAGS. Sure, he had killed Jim. But that was in self-defense. But Bobby… what Bobby had done was murder. Pure evil. He thought he knew Bobby but he certainly didn't know this man sitting next to him. How could he get out of this? It seemed every door was closed other than turning himself in to the police and spending the rest of his life behind bars. He couldn't do that and Bobby knew it. That was Bobby's plan. As much as he wanted to leave and fend for himself, he couldn't. He was stuck.

Finally, looking at Bobby, Wayne managed one word.

"Why?"

"Why? Wayne, my ultimate goal in life is to become a US Senator, you know that. Elaine and Jamie were roadblocks. I simply removed the roadblocks. I've done it before and will do it again if I have to."

"With NAGS? You did this before with someone at NAGS? I don't know what you're saying."

"No. Not NAGS. What I'm saying is that if something or somebody gets in my way, I remove it. That simple. And I've *had* a few roadblocks in my career," bragged Bobby. "The first was years ago when I was running for the Texas state legislature. My opponent was slightly ahead of me in the polls with about a month to go. The race *could* have gone either way. I just made sure I won. At a party following a debate between me and my opponent, I slipped some drugs in the coat pocket of my opponent's kid and then enough into his drink figuring he'd pass out. An ambulance would be called, and they would find drugs in his system and in his possession. It would be bad press for the kid, and subsequently my opponent. But the kid managed to get in his car and try to drive himself home. He ran off the side of the road, hit a tree and killed himself. At first, I thought it had backfired because everyone was so sympathetic to the kid's father. I was sick to my stomach. But the autopsy results were leaked to the press about two weeks before the elections showing the kid was up to his eyeballs in drugs. The flip-flopping press switched to my corner. I barely won, but I won. And that's all that mattered. Just like with Elaine and Jamie."

"So how were Jamie and Elaine roadblocks to the Senate?" asked Wayne, trying to understand the monster.

"Elaine got mad at me and was going to call my wife, Leslie, and tell her about our affair. That would have ruined everything for me. Elaine was a roadblock so she had to go. I couldn't trust her anymore. And Jamie? He made my plan work. Plus the fucker just got on my nerves." Then mimicking Jamie. *I need money. Where's my money? You got any money?* "A total waste of human life."

"So you were the one screwing Jim's wife!" Now, everything made sense to Wayne. Jim was right! He just had the wrong guy. Until the day he died, he believed it was Wayne. "Bobby, you're sick. We need to stop this. Now! Before it's..."

"Too late?" asked Bobby, completing the sentence. "It's already too late. And anyway, how do you propose we do that? You're an accessory. It would be your word against mine. I can tell you right now that you'd lose. Remember, I wasn't here when Jim and Margie died. I have witnesses. And last night? I was in bed all last night. You can say the same but who'd they believe? What do I have to gain? And, remember the rumors. You were the one they thought was fucking Elaine. Not me. A good lawyer would keep me free, and you would spend the rest of your life trying to protect that tight, little ass of yours from those manly men. So you want to stop. Call the police?" Bobby pulled his cell phone from his coat pocket and tossed it to Wayne. "Here. Go ahead."

Wayne grabbed it and tossed it back, hitting him in the stomach before it fell to the floorboard. As much as he wanted to walk away from all of this, Bobby was right. He was an accessory. He had no way out.

"Am I a roadblock?" asked Wayne, not sure what he would do if he were.

"Do you want to be? You know I can fix that."

"So what do *we* do next?" asked Wayne, knowing Bobby was dead serious and that there was no good alternative other than aiding and abetting the devil incarnate sitting next to him.

"We're heading back up to the lodge to pick up Jim. Drop him off at Jamie's apartment. After that, everything is *business as usual.* That's my plan. Simple, natural and most of all, it works."

"How is any of this natural? And what about Margie? You've completely forgotten about her!"

"OK. Here it is in a nutshell. You, Jim, and Margie are at the office Wednesday. You place Jim on administrative leave. He leaves… leaves mad. You give Margie the rest of the day off. Jamie comes by looking for his dad. He's walked all the way from his house to the office. His car is out of gas, and he's hungry. Margie takes pity on him and since she's leaving anyway, she offers him a ride home. When they arrive at Jamie's house, Jim is there. The two of them get into an argument, probably about money and drugs. Jamie goes berserk, pulls out the gun he stole from his dad's apartment and shoots him. Margie hears the shot, comes running into the house to see what's happened and in a panic, Jamie shoots her. Both Margie and Jim die. He hides Jim somewhere in his house, like a closet, bedroom, bathroom, whatever, because the old man is too big to move. Not sure where I'm going with that part 'til I see Jamie's house. But anyway he takes Margie to the dumpster and leaves the car to be stolen. After a couple of days and lots of drugs, he goes to tell his mother what he's done. She wants him to turn himself in to the cops but he refuses. So she starts to call them instead. That's when he kills her and then commits suicide. End of story. No loose ends. Everything is left to the police's imagination, and you know how stupid they are."

"God. That is so full of holes, I can't believe you think you can get away with it," replied Wayne, trying quickly to find fault. "Like, what about the note from Idella. You forget we made it look like Margie went home with the dirty plate in the sink, the half-empty glass of tea. What about that?"

"No problem. It works. Margie first takes Jamie to her apartment for lunch, probably trying to mother him, get him to join her church. Whatever. Doesn't matter. She feeds him lunch, then takes him home. See? That's the beauty of this whole thing. All we know is that Margie left with Jamie. That's it. That's all we have to tell the police. They'll find Elaine murdered at her home and Jamie dead of a drug overdose. Then they'll find Jim at Jamie's house. The only conclusion that they can come to is a murder-suicide. It happens all the time. Even if they don't associate Margie with Jamie, then the carjacking works. It's perfect."

Again, there was a long period of silence with Wayne still trying to find holes.

"What about the charges we did on Jim's credit card? You forget about them?"

"If they bother to even look at the charges, Jamie made the charges. We're leaving Jim's wallet at Jamie's house so the police can find it. They'll put two and two together."

"What about…"

"What about what? Would you stop with the fucking inquisition? Look. The police are stupid and lazy. With Jamie dead of an apparent overdose, his mother dead and his father dead, they'll simply close the case. If there were any *inconsistencies*, they're gone. Kaput. So drop it. You can relax."

More silence. Then. "How'd you kill them?" asked Wayne, unable to bring himself to use their names. That would bring reality to a surreal situation.

"You don't want to know. And the less you know, the better off *we* are. All I can tell you is it was my version of *shock and awe*," answered Bobby, smiling at his clever response.

Wayne looked out the car window and stared. He saw nothing. Where were they? He didn't know, and he didn't care. He was lost.

Chapter 54

Friday, December 29, 2006, 4:19 a.m. EST

To paraphrase Yogi Berra, the baseball legend and pop philosopher, 'It was like déjà vu all over again.' It was the same long, boring trip from DC to Virginia, the same two commuters and the same dark lodge. Only the car and mission of the trip were different. They were there to pick up Jim's body rather than deposit it. Bobby talked non-stop the entire trip with Wayne only uttering a perfunctory 'yes,' 'no,' 'OK,' 'Uh huh' every now and then. He wasn't listening. Instead, he kept thinking of how foul things had turned, and so quickly. Could Bobby be the modern-day Jekyll and Hyde? Wayne didn't know that Bobby even *had* a mean streak. He had never once seen a glimpse of the demon that now sat next to him. Should he fear for his own life? Did Bobby consider him a 'roadblock'?

As Bobby wheeled Jamie's large Cadillac up the lodge's dark driveway, he began issuing orders: Get the body, get a shovel and get the hell out of Dodge. Zip. Zip. Zip. And the lodge was off-limits. *No one* was to go near the lodge and risk setting off the alarm triggering another visit from the local authorities.

Within twenty minutes, the two men and a body were back on the road.

The trip back to Washington couldn't go fast enough for Wayne. Just like the trip *from* Washington, the conversation on the trip *to* Washington was pretty much one-sided – all Bobby. He particularly got all worked up when talking about the *'If only Margie could have had a gun'* campaign, its importance to NAGS, and how they needed to subtly work that into the press conference. Even if the carjacking angle didn't pan out and Jamie was deemed to have killed Margie, the seed would have been planted. That's all that mattered. The fact that Bobby wasn't the least remorseful, upset or contrite about his horrific deed repulsed Wayne. Did the man not have a conscience?

When the two men arrived at NAGS' office building, they found news media trucks parked and double-parked on the street in front of their building. But there were no reporters or cameramen to be seen.

They were either at home asleep or camped out in their van. Before letting Wayne out, Bobby issued him new orders: Get Jim's gun, get a map of Jamie's address, and get back to the car as fast as you can! No planning; just orders – everything left to luck or fate.

While Bobby waited at a nearby street that gave him a clear view of the building's front door, Wayne headed into the building and up to his office. There was no need to turn on any lights in the building as the main floor parlor always had a couple of porcelain vase lamps turned on and nearly every room and hallway had night lights. Regardless, Wayne could have walked through the building blindfolded having worked there so long.

He quickly unlocked the door to his office and headed straight back to the storage vault. There, he opened its large door, walked over to the secure filing cabinet and from it retrieved the envelope that contained the two guns and spent shells. At his desk, he slipped on a pair of latex gloves and carefully pulled out one of the guns. The gun's serial number showed it belonged to Jim. He placed it on his desk and returned the other gun to the secure filing cabinet, locked it and the storage vault. The sight of the death instrument made his mind flashback to the morning that Jim barged into his office, mad as hell, acting like a crazy person. In retrospect, he should have calmed Jim, defused the situation. Instead, he had pushed him over the edge. In hindsight, he should have never placed him on administrative leave. Everybody knows that means being fired. How could he have been so coldhearted? The man had been with the company for over 30 years. Not only that, he let him die. He lay there pleading for his life, and he let him die. And poor Margie. Would he ever be able to forget the image of her once beautiful face ravaged by a single bullet? *If only Jim __hadn't__ had a gun, Margie would still be alive.* How ironic. He laughed at the thought. Not a ha-ha laugh, but a contemptuous laugh.

The ringing of his cell was a welcome interruption to his melancholy reflections.

"Where the hell are you?" asked Bobby, almost yelling into the phone. "What's taking you so long?"

"Oh… a… uh… printer jam," lied Wayne, very badly, somewhat unnerved.

"Well, hurry up and get your ass out of there before those knuckleheads in the vans wake up."

"OK. I'll…" But Bobby had already hung up.

Wasting little time, he turned on his computer and, with the help of MapQuest and using the address from Jamie's driver's license, printed out the requested directions. He shoved the paper into his coat pocket and shut down his computer. He picked up Jim's gun from the desk, checked the safety, and placed it into a large envelope he'd pulled from his desk. It was Bobby's plan to use the gun as the corroborating evidence for his murder/suicide ruse. As he exited his office and locked the door, a thought occurred to him that an *actual* murder/suicide would put an end to this evil masquerade. He would not discount the implementation of this *new* plan B.

Wayne saw that the old Cadillac was now double-parked in front of the office with the engine running and Bobby slouched down in the driver's seat. He had hardly closed the door to the old clunker when Bobby shoved it into gear and sped off. Their next stop was to Wayne's townhouse to pick up his car. On the way, Bobby issued more orders. Wayne would drive his Jaguar, followed by Bobby, over to Jamie's house where they would: Leave the body, leave the gun, leave the Cadillac, leave no fingerprints, and then leave the house. Very simple and straightforward. Afterward, he smiled. Wayne looked straight ahead and nodded. He couldn't bear to look at his face – the face of evil.

Chapter 55

Friday, December 29, 2006, 5:51 a.m. EST

Jamie's house was located on 4th Street, near Catholic University, approximately 3 miles from NAGS' office. It was an old wooden framed house built in 1929. Jim Barnes had bought the old house as investment property because of its proximity to the University. When Elaine kicked Jamie out of her home, and he needed a place to stay, Jim had the old house somewhat fixed up, and let the boy live there, rent-free. It was nothing fancy, but it sufficed for an out of work, out of school drug addict.

Wayne slowed down in front of several houses on 4th Street, reading each of the house numbers until he found Jamie's. He put on his blinker, drove a few feet past the driveway and motioned for Bobby to turn in behind him. Bobby gave him the thumbs up, turned into the driveway, and parked the Cadillac as close to the house as possible. He quietly exited the vehicle, leaving it running, and the doors locked. He carried with him the envelope containing the gun. Once in the house, he flipped on the lights and looked around trying to get his bearings. By the time Wayne arrived, Bobby had already scoped out the living room and kitchen and was moving to the back of the house to check out the bedrooms. Neither man had to be reminded to wear gloves.

"Did you mean to leave Jamie's car running?" asked Wayne in a softer whisper, following Bobby to the back rooms.

"Yes. I want it to run out of gas. That validates our story."

"Got it. What's next?"

"See if there's a basement in the god-forsaken dump."

"Why? And what if there's not one?"

"Do you have to challenge everything I ask? Do what I tell you. Look around and see if there's a *fucking* basement in the rat hole! And hurry!" yelled Bobby.

The two men spent the next few minutes in total silence frantically opening and closing doors in the house.

"Over here," yelled Wayne from the kitchen, excited over his discovery.

Bobby rushed into the kitchen and gave Wayne a thumbs up. He then found a switch that lit up the stairwell and basement then headed down the steps, still carrying the envelope containing the gun. Wayne followed close behind waiting for further instructions.

"This is perfect. Just what I hoped for!" exclaimed Bobby then laid the sealed envelope on one of the stair steps.

Just what I hoped for? Wayne shook his head in total disbelief. Here they were, two men with a dead body, their lives and jobs on the line, and everything was based on hope? His stomach churned.

The basement was small, only the size of the kitchen above, with crawl space under the rest of the house. Like most basements, it smelled damp and musty. At the very top of the room, on the driveway side of the house were two small 1x3 windows. Both locked. The floor was hardened dirt. And other than a few empty boxes, an old, moldy golf bag containing a dated set of golf clubs, and a fake Christmas tree, the room was empty.

"OK. Let's go get ol' lard ass," ordered Bobby as he headed back up the stairs. Like a lemming, Wayne followed. They were no longer peers. Wayne was now relegated to sidekick, helper, second banana.

Only after a lot of grunts, groans and momentary stops to re-energize were the two men able to transport the late Jim Barnes' body from the trunk of Jamie's car to the kitchen floor. Wayne could only speculate what Bobby planned to do with the body as he watched him silently search through the kitchen drawers. After a brief wait, he turned around holding a pair of scissors and a carving knife.

"Here. We're gonna slice this thing off," he said, referring to the tarp. "You start at that end, and I'll start at the other," instructed Bobby, handing the carving knife to Wayne. "Do not, and I repeat, do not cut anything except the plastic. I don't want any slice marks that might raise questions."

What if I cut your heart out? thought Wayne who obligingly nodded and began methodically slicing open the tarp from his end while Bobby cut away from his. Once the body was free, Bobby stood up and surveyed the kitchen as if trying to figure out his next move.

"Pull the tarp your way while I pull the body off."

"Wouldn't it be easier if we both lifted it off the tarp?" asked Wayne.

"No. I'm gonna do this myself. It's got to look like Jamie did this himself. Alone."

As much as Wayne hated to admit it, Bobby's plan seemed solid. Even though decisions were made on the fly, everything seemed to fall into place. He could sense that Bobby knew what he was doing. As ordered, he bent over and grabbed the tarp and held tight while Bobby pulled the body free of the plastic shroud and onto the linoleum floor. Bobby then positioned it to where the legs lay down the basement steps, and the torso lay on the kitchen floor. With one big shove, he sent the partially frozen corpse sliding down the wooden steps where the torso landed on the dirt floor with the head of the dead man, face up and propped up on the last step.

Bobby turned to see Wayne standing there with his arms folded, waiting for more orders. "Look, I don't mean to be so demanding, but we only have so much time, and I have to think this thing through as we go. Now if you don't mind, can you go get the shovel out of Jamie's car and meet me in the basement? And hurry!"

While Wayne ran his errand, Bobby grabbed a dishtowel and headed down to the basement stepping over Jim's body to get to the dirt floor. Thinking 'what would Jamie do,' he decided to pull the body off the steps, so it lay completely flat on the basement floor. Once the steps were free of the obstruction, Bobby found the envelope containing the gun partially now hidden under the body. He ripped it open, removed the gun, and shoved the envelope deep in his coat pocket along with two bullets he removed from the gun's magazine. With the dishtowel, he began vigorously wiping the gun down to eliminate all fingerprints. When he looked up, Wayne was standing on the bottom step, shovel in hand.

"See if you can dig a hole in the ground. You don't have to do much. I want it to appear as though Jamie tried to bury his dad. Kind of like us up at the lodge. While you do that, I'm gonna look around for a place to hide the gun."

Wayne immediately began punching the dirt floor near the body while Bobby gazed around the basement. His eyes settled on the golf bag. It had four large zippered compartments any of which were ideal for hiding the gun. He unzipped the largest of the four, unwrapped the kitchen towel from around the gun and shoved the weapon into the bag, and zipped it up.

"OK. That's good enough. Leave the shovel. We're done here," barked Bobby. "Give me Jim's wallet."

Back upstairs, Bobby removed the money from the wallet, stuck it in his pocket, and wiped down the wallet and its contents. He then stuck it into the back of the refrigerator's freezer. Before leaving, he searched the house and basement to make sure that everything was in order. Meanwhile, Wayne simply observed, waiting for more orders.

"Well, don't just stand there! Get the tarp and let's get the hell out of here!" commanded Bobby.

Wayne wadded up the tarp into a ball and headed out to the car with Bobby close behind. The house was locked with lights left on in the living room and basement. The old Cadillac was still running and would so for probably another twenty or thirty minutes before running out of gas.

"See how easy that was?" asked Bobby rhetorically, as Wayne backed out of the driveway and drove away. "We're through other than cleaning up the mess we made at Jim's apartment and preparing for the news conference. Unfortunately, you'll have to do most of the cleanup work while I get my talk prepared. It's gonna be my finest hour."

After receiving no comment from Wayne, he continued.

"We… you need to get legal to set up the press conference for, say 11:00 a.m. tomorrow. I mean today. I want to strike while the iron is hot."

"You sure having it today is going to work? You look like hell. I mean those bags under your eyes…"

"See that works, too. More than likely, the press will think that I've been crying. They'll take photos or videos. It shows that we have a heart. Wayne, I'm not trying to belittle your plan and all the work you put into it. You've always been very successful at dotting the i's and crossing the t's. And it works in normal situations. But when you're in the abyss, the dark side, whatever you want to call it, you've got to rely on your gut feelings. Follow your instincts. Do what feels natural. And do whatever it takes, no matter what."

"Like killing Elaine and Jamie?"

"Yes. Like killing Elaine and Jamie."

Chapter 56

Friday, December 29, 2006, 6:47 a.m. EST

The 3rd-floor conference room – 3B – had a '*Reserved -7 AM – 9 AM Lt. Whitehead*' sign posted on the door. Except for the captain's large meeting room, 3B was like every other conference room in the building. The walls were white, the floors were grey, and the furniture consisted of a rectangular table, chairs, and whiteboard. No decorator had been necessary.

There were no stragglers to the meeting with all four participants arriving early, eager to start. Johnny Williams was the second person to arrive just behind Daniel. He brought with him what was left of a dozen-box of glazed Krispy Kreme's. He set them on the table next to the hot pot of Folgers and filled his extra-large coffee-stained mug with the morning nectar. He found a seat directly across from Daniel. Bennie Archer and C. J. Washington from the DFS (Department of Forensic Science) team arrived last. Bennie wasted no time in handing out his meeting notes and a copy of the surveillance DVD while C. J. busied himself setting up his laptop computer.

"Wrinkles. Who brought the doughnuts?" asked Bennie as he poured himself a cup of coffee and grabbed a doughnut leaving C. J. to fend for himself.

"Who do you think?" asked Johnny as he slurped his coffee. "By the way, have you *ever* brought them?"

"Not if I can help it. Too fattening. Unlike some people, I watch my weight," responded Bennie taking a dig at his longtime, portly friend.

Daniel enjoyed the friendly banter between the two police veterans. But he was eager to get on with business.

Meanwhile, C. J. Washington, who was oblivious to everything going on around him, placed a disc in his laptop DVD player and began pushing keys on the computer and the attached video projector until he had an image appear on the blank white wall at the far end of the conference table. After he had the projector focused to his liking he passed the mouse to Bennie who clicked the 'Play' symbol. Once the video reached the frame showing a date/time stamp of 12/27/2006 7:31:36 PM he clicked the 'Pause' symbol. Projected on the far wall was a dark-colored Chevrolet.

"OK. Let's get started," said Bennie. "This is a surveillance video taken from the storage unit diagonally across from the tile warehouse where the victim's body was found. Her identity has been confirmed as being Margaret Irene Hamilton. We know from DMV records that she drove a 2007 Buick LaCrosse. That will be the next car you see immediately after this Chevrolet Impala. I'm sorry everything is in black and white and the quality is so poor, but we did the best we could to enhance and sharpen what we were given." He then clicked on the 'play' symbol.

When the 2007 Buick LaCrosse appeared on the screen, Bennie clicked the 'pause' symbol and then began advancing the video until he got to the frame he wanted.

"This image was taken at 7:31:51 PM. As I said, we believe this to be the victim's car. The surveillance camera was not positioned at an angle to give us an image of the license plate. But it was the only 2007 Buick LaCrosse to pass in front of the surveillance camera from 6 p.m. Wednesday until 8 a.m. the next morning. Sort of."

"What do you mean 'Sort of'? It is, or it isn't," interrupted Johnny.

"Let me finish, and then you'll understand," continued Bennie. "Now where was I? Oh yeah. So let's assume this *is* the victim's car. In the handout you have in front of you, I have some enhanced pictures of the driver of that car. As I said before, they are not very good, not very clear but we can tell that it is not the victim. The person driving the car appears to be a male, Caucasian. Again that's speculation because it could be a female with her hair pulled up under the cap and it could be a light-colored African-American or Latino. And the mustache… it could be fake. Now take notice of the painter's cap and shirt the driver is wear…"

"Wait a minute," interrupted Johnny again. "Go back to the image of the car in front of this one."

"Dammit, Wrinkles! I thought you were sleeping. Don't you go and ruin my surprise," said a smiling Bennie Archer. Daniel looked at Johnny, Bennie and then the image on the wall. Obviously, they had seen something that he hadn't. That's why he was glad to have Johnny as his partner. The elderly detective could see the obvious and, more importantly, the obscure little clues that most detectives missed. Like the missing coat, the wedding ring on the right finger. Overlooked clues that eventually lead to arrests.

Using the mouse, Bennie positioned the video to an earlier frame showing the dark-colored Chevrolet Impala. Daniel looked at the image and immediately saw the same thing that Johnny had seen. The driver in the Chevrolet had on the same type cap and same shirt as the driver of Margie Hamilton's car – or it appeared that way.

"Bennie. This can't be a coincidence. So two people are involved?"

"Yes and I'll show you," replied Bennie. He advanced the video until he reached the frame with a date/time stamp of 12/27/2006 7:36:11 PM. It was the same Buick LaCrosse with the same driver wearing the same cap and shirt. "Look at the time. Now you see what I mean by 'sort of' when I said that there was only one 2007 Buick LaCrosse? This is the same car, just at a later time on the video. Now look at the car in front of the Buick," continued Bennie scanning the frames backwards until the car in front of the Buick appeared. It was the same Chevrolet Impala that had appeared earlier.

"I'll be dammed," Johnny muttered.

"It gets better," smiled Bennie, who clicked the 'Play' symbol and then paused it at the 7:42:12 PM frame. "The Buick LaCrosse a third time." Then reversing the DVD until the image showed the Chevrolet Impala again. Bennie continued. "Based on these images, I can only surmise that the driver in the Chevy, the lead car, was scoping out the alley, making sure no one was around and communicating with the driver in the Buick. I say that because if you look at the last page of the handout, it shows enhanced pictures of both drivers with their hand to their ear, most likely talking to each other on their cell. Now focus on their hands. I would guess that they're wearing gloves. Probably latex. See? Their hand color is way too white when compared to their face color."

"Good observation. Any chance you know what the make and model of the second car they picked up in North Carolina?" asked Daniel, his question directed at Bennie. "If it's a dark Chevrolet Impala, then we might be able to wrap this thing up today."

"I don't have that info yet. We didn't finish working on this DVD until about 3 a.m. this morning and I haven't had a chance to speak to my DFS counterparts in North Carolina. I'll do that once we get back to the office. One last thing. A caveat. Since we don't have an image of the license plate and can't confirm that this is the victim's car, these two guys could be just a couple of painters looking for a job site. Maybe some inside night work."

"Bennie, I don't think so. I've *never* seen a painter driving a new Buick or Chevrolet, for that matter," interjected Johnny. "They usually come to their job sites in vans and old ones at that. I think these are our guys."

"I agree. So that's it. Any questions?"

"No. Not on the DVD, Bennie. But, great job as usual," answered Daniel. "The only other thing is on the victim herself. Anything to add to your earlier report?"

"Besides the identity of the victim, which I've already given, just some info on the residue found on her face and hair. It was from duct tape. It matches samples that we got from Home Depot."

Directing his comments to Bennie, Daniel added, "By the way, in case you didn't already know, the two suspects apprehended in North Carolina don't speak English."

"No. I didn't know that. But I don't think that makes a difference," responded Bennie, standing up as he spoke.

As if on cue, everyone else stood, shook hands, and the two forensic agents left.

"So what do you think?" asked Daniel.

"I dunno," answered Johnny. "Maybe this is the way they do carjackings in Mexico. You know. Kill the victim early in the morning, take a siesta, put on matching caps, overalls, gloves, then drop the body off at night, ignoring the victim's expensive jewelry but taking her winter coat. Then the next day, drive south. Makes perfectly good sense to me."

"So I gather you don't think these guys they caught in North Carolina are the same ones on the video?"

"No, I don't. But you know I've been wrong before," offered Johnny.

"What about the Hamilton boys?" asked Daniel. "They very easily could have been the two men from the surveillance tape. You know we've seen offenders who seemed utterly devastated by the death of a spouse, relative, loved one, friend, whatever, with more tears flowing than a monsoon rainstorm, but guiltier than sin. And you heard what LaShaun said about Aaron. How he walked into the morgue, identified his mother and left. All very business-like displaying no emotions whatsoever. I say we *do not* close our eyes to these two boys. At least, not yet."

"You know me better than that. The only times I close my eyes are when I'm in bed or in church." Johnny laughed at his own humor as did Daniel.

Chapter 57

Friday, December 29, 2006, 10:00 a.m. EST

At precisely 10 o'clock, Daniel Whitehead knocked on Margie Hamilton's apartment door. Johnny Williams stood to the right of Daniel, hat in hand. Both detectives had hoped to have some information back from NCSHP (North Carolina State High Patrol) on the two suspects before the meeting with Kyle and Aaron. But that didn't happen. They wanted to be able to say the case was wrapped up. That the individuals responsible for this senseless killing were behind bars. They couldn't. Not having any good news about a bad situation always made these meetings even more difficult.

The two detectives were surprised when Katie Chandler answered the door. Kyle and Aaron had asked her to come. They wanted her there for support. And she was glad to help. From the horrible experience of having to deal with her own brother's death and funeral, she was well aware of how busy the next few days were going to be. There would be a steady flow of friends and co-workers coming by to offer their sympathies with most bringing meals, casseroles and baked goods. She would help them keep records of who came by and who brought what so that they could later send thank you notes. She also helped answer the ever-ringing phones and provided a much-needed shield from the deluge of reporters who somehow found Margie's unpublished number.

After greeting the two detectives, Katie took their coats and Johnny's hat and showed them to the living room where the two brothers were searching through boxes of pictures of Margie at different times in her life, trying to find the perfect ones to use at her funeral. They seemed to have become very close these last two days, so unlike five days ago – Christmas Day, 2006. Aaron probably didn't remember the day, but Kyle did. Christmas is supposed to be a religious day, a happy day, one to be shared with family and friends. But the Hamilton's Christmases hadn't been the same since their Dad died and this one wasn't any different. As it was, Aaron arrived just in time for dinner. Margie wasn't sure if he'd even show since she hadn't heard from him. But when he did, it made her day. She was determined to keep the family as close as possible. Aaron made it very difficult. He did the perfunctory hugs and kisses then immediately went to the kitchen, made a small plate of the food that his Mom had spent hours cooking, ate a few bites, gave out his 'overly expensive' gifts and left. Margie made excuses for him but it was very clear how unhappy and upset she was. Today, she would be happy to see her two sons sitting side by side, working so closely together, especially under such dire circumstances. Hopefully, something good had come from something so terribly bad.

When Kyle heard the detective's voice, he recognized it immediately. He leaned over to Aaron and whispered, *"Detective Whitehead."* Aaron was not familiar with the name. He had only talked to a Detective Williams on the phone, so he didn't know that two detectives were involved in the case. They immediately left the sofa and walked around the coffee table to greet them. Not wishing to interfere, Katie headed for the kitchen.

"Good morning, gentlemen," said Aaron, extending his hand, first to Johnny and then to Daniel. His handshake was firm and genuine. "I have to apologize for my bad manners and behavior yesterday. You can ask Kyle. I was my *usual* self. But please do forgive me."

His charming behavior took both Daniel and Johnny completely off guard.

"We completely understand. Again let me offer our condolences," said Daniel.

Kyle greeted the detectives then gestured for them to take a seat in the two chairs facing the sofa. He and Aaron returned to the sofa. While Daniel sat comfortably in his chair, Johnny felt wedged in with the sides of his large body sticking out from under the armrests of the tiny chair. He hoped the chair would be able to withstand his size and weight over the course of their visit and would fully recover once he left.

With everyone seated, comfortably (or not), Kyle anxiously asked, "So have you heard anything more? Arrested anybody?"

"All I can tell you is that we do have two suspects in North Carolina in custody. We're now waiting for the extradition papers to be signed. We won't know a whole lot more until we get them back to Washington which could take a while. I know it's not what you want to hear, but that's all we have."

It was obvious that both sons were disappointed. They wanted closure, but not any more so than the two detectives.

"I hope the media hasn't been hounding you too much," spoke Daniel. "But if they are, please keep *everything* we tell you in confidence. Detective Williams and I will give them whatever details we can without compromising the investigation."

Daniel looked at Aaron and then Kyle, saying nothing, letting his request sink in. With the media now knowing that the victim was an employee of NAGS, one of the nation's largest gun rights organizations, the story jumped from the back pages of newspapers to the front; from having no time on national TV news to 'Breaking News.' The media would be relentless in creating stories from the smallest of information. The less they knew, the better.

"Now. Detective Williams and I are going to ask you some questions. Some that may seem offensive or maybe too personal. This is our job. We have the best of intentions. If we can tell you why we're asking a particular question or requesting a particular piece of information, we will," offered Daniel. "We are simply looking for the truth. The motive for this crime. These types of questions will be asked of anyone that we think will help lead to the arrest of the individual or individuals responsible for your mother's death." Daniel had repeated the same dialogue so many times in the past that even Johnny could repeat it verbatim. In almost all cases, everyone who heard his 'preamble' was still surprised at the questions.

"Having said that, do you by any chance have that list of your mother's relatives, co-workers…"

"Yes sir," interrupted Kyle. "We have most of it right here." He picked up the list off the coffee table and handed it to Johnny who was sitting closest to him. "We still don't have a list of Mom's co-workers unless their names were in her address book. I called Mr. Peters, last night. He's Mom's boss. Anyway, he said he'd get it to me this morning but I guess he must have forgotten. If you want me to, I can call him right now."

"That's OK, Kyle," Johnny said in response. "While we don't know Mr. Peters personally, we are *very* familiar with him and his organization. We can call him and request it ourselves. It'll be a *pleasure* to talk to him."

Aaron could sense the sarcasm in Detective Williams' voice and responded immediately.

"I'm aware of the upcoming court appeal regarding the gun ban in DC. It's been all over the news for some time. It's obvious that you and possibly your partner are not big fans of the organization for which our Mom worked. I hope this won't impede this investigation." His words were matter-of-fact, sincere, and without any hostility in his voice.

Daniel responded. "Aaron. Our job is to find out who killed your mother and why. *Nothing* will interfere with this investigation. *Nothing.*"

He then looked at Aaron and then Kyle. No one spoke. After about a minute of awkward silence, Katie entered the room.

"I just brewed some fresh coffee," she offered, lightening the mood. "Can I get either of you a cup and maybe a piece of chocolate cake or cherry pie? A couple of the ladies from Margie's church made them, and they look and smell delicious."

Johnny had already made note of the bounty of food on the dining room table. Just looking at the sweets made his mouth water. If the Pavlovian theory needed any validation, he was proof.

Daniel accepted the offer for the coffee but declined the dessert. Johnny accepted the offer for coffee *and* a slice of pie but politely refused the cake. If Daniel hadn't been there, he might have eaten both.

Johnny quickly devoured the pie and before he had a chance to set the empty plate on the table in front of him, Katie appeared from out of nowhere, took the dish from his hand, asked if he wanted another slice of pie or a piece of cake, to which he begrudgingly refused. *What a sweetheart!* he thought as she left.

Daniel reached for his briefcase, opened it and pulled out a yellow legal pad and pen. Johnny reached in his pocket and pulled out a small notepad.

"OK," he began. "Let's get down to business so we can get out of here."

"We'll be working from a timeline developed by our forensic team who, by the way, is excellent. From their findings, it appears that your mother died this past Wednesday, sometime between 7 a.m. and 1 p.m. Her body was left in an alley around 8 p.m. that night. Keeping those times in mind, I want you both to think back and tell me where you were, what you were doing and with whom. And remember, these are just standard questions. They are not meant to be accusatory. I have to ask them."

Even with this second forewarning, both brothers seemed taken aback. Were they considered suspects? Why are they wasting time questioning them? Weren't the culprits in North Carolina? Their facial expressions showed their surprise. Regardless, Kyle took the lead.

"I was at work at 7:30 a.m. yesterday. Not yesterday, I mean Wednesday, at the GSA Building on 19th Street. Marion Hodges, Maria Jimenez, Eddie Guyton. We were all drinking coffee in the breakroom until about 8 a.m. I'm sure there were others if you need their names."

"No. That's enough."

"After that, I taught an orientation class from 8 until 11:45 A.M. Then around noon, Katie and I walked to the Bread Line and had lunch. We returned to work around 1 p.m."

"And at 8 p.m.?"

"I met Katie again, around 5 p.m. at J Paul's in Georgetown and we stayed until about 11. I have the credit card receipts if you need them."

"I can vouch for him," interjected Katie from the kitchen and who had overheard everything.

"Thank you. You can come in here if you'd like," replied Daniel then looked next to Aaron. Katie quietly made her way into the living room and sat in the chair by the secretary/desk. She turned her chair, so it faced the sofa.

Aaron took the cue. "I was at my home office from 5 a.m. Wednesday until about 2 a.m. Thursday, working on a proposal. I have no one to vouch for me being there. I did order a pizza. That was about 9:30 p.m. And I made a lot of calls throughout the day, but they were all made from my cell phone which meant I could've made them from anywhere. But I didn't. They were all from my apartment."

Daniel nodded then asked, "Do either of you know who might have been the last person to see your mother alive?"

Aaron shook his head. "The last time I saw Mom was here, Christmas, and…." His voice trailed off. He *had* remembered the last, brief time he saw his Mom - alive.

Kyle jumped in. "I'm guessing Mr. Peters, Mom's boss. She had to work on Wednesday. She was supposed to be off all this week but…" Kyle stopped. It was hard for him not to think 'what if.' "Anyway, I called her office that morning, sometimes around 11 but she'd already left."

Both detectives made note of the time that Margie left her office. That narrowed the time of death. Forensics would need to know this.

Kyle continued. "I talked to Mr. Peters instead. He said that he'd given her the rest of the day off. So then I called her phone, here, in this apartment but she didn't answer. Then I tried her cell phone and got voicemail."

"Your mother's apartment phone, does she have voicemail or an answering machine?" asked Daniel.

"Yes. An answering machine. But we, Katie and I, checked it yesterday. The only calls were from me, Mr. Blackwell, Mr. Peters, and some security company. Something to do with an alarm going off somewhere. Would you like to listen to them?" asked Kyle.

"Yes, before we leave."

Daniel paused for a moment before asking the next question. Other than the question regarding one's whereabouts during the time of death, this was the second most offensive one he had to ask.

"Do either of you know who would financially benefit the most from your mother's death?"

Before Kyle could answer, Aaron responded. "I'm the administrator of Mom's estate. When I had my lawyer draw up *my* will, I also had her draw up Mom's. Mom had me appointed the administrator because I was the oldest. As far as her estate goes, she has very little. Most of what Dad left her was used to support us and help send us through college. Because of her generosity, neither one of us have educational loans. That's why Mom went back to work. The money ran out. As far as insurance policies go, if she has any, it would be with her employer, NAGS. You would have to ask them. And as far as beneficiaries, I would assume that any policy would be split between Kyle and me and possibly her church. But to answer your question, based on the will, Kyle and I would inherit her estate."

Johnny continued. "Financially, how sound are you and Kyle?"

"If you mean do we owe a bunch of money, I can only speak for myself," answered Aaron. "I have some money in the bank. I have no debt other than my townhouse. I don't *need* whatever money Mom might have. What I *need* is to find out who did this to her."

"We do, too," Johnny added hearing the frustration in Aaron's voice. He looked to Kyle. "What about you?"

Kyle was not envious nor did he covet his brother's wealth. Aaron worked hard, sometimes non-stop and deserved the fruits of his labor. He knew that if Aaron had wanted, he could have been very boastful about his financial status; but he hadn't. Probably because he didn't want to embarrass his younger brother in front of Katie.

"Well, I have some money in the bank, too; but I also have some debts. I still owe on my car, and I recently bought a new set of Ping irons that I'm still paying off. And I rent. Other than that, I do OK."

"No gambling debts from either of you?" asked Johnny.

"Oh no!" and "Good Lord, no," Kyle and Aaron responded, respectively, both shaking their heads.

Aaron rested his hand on his chin in deep thought then asked, "Based on the questions you are asking us, you have suspicions about this being a carjacking, don't you?"

Daniel responded. "Yes. We do have suspicions, as you say. We could be wrong, but there is some conflicting evidence that we're not at liberty to discuss that gives us pause. Because of this, we are keeping open all possibilities."

"And you're here because the first person or persons investigated is family?" asked Aaron.

"Yes. Probably eighty percent of the time, family is involved; but we're also here to fill in our timeline and to look for evidence and leads," responded Daniel.

"Well, we're not involved. We'll do whatever you ask, answer any questions, show any financial records, give you our cell phones, do whatever. We want whoever did this caught and thrown in the deepest, darkest prison cell you have."

"We understand and appreciate your willingness to help. Now, if we can move on. How well did your mother know her neighbors, say in the apartments to the left and right of her?"

Kyle answered. "She knew them both really well. Mrs. Grant lives on her right as you face the apartment and Mrs. Goldstein lives on her left. Both are on the list I gave you. Mrs. Grant goes to the same church and is the sister of Mr. Blackwell. He's also a friend of Mom's, but I think I told you that already. All are on my list. Why do you ask? Surely they're not suspects."

"No.   We're trying to determine your mother's last known whereabouts and to fill in the time gap from the time she left her office and 1 p.m. If she came by here after work, one of her neighbors might have seen or talked to her."

"She had to come by here!" Katie said excitedly then feeling like she had butted in.

"Katie's right," confirmed Kyle. "We came here yesterday, looking for her and we found that note from work!"

"And don't forget about the dirty dishes," added Katie.

"Hold on. You're going too fast. What note and what dirty dishes?" asked Johnny.

"There was a note from a lady named Idella. Mr. Peters said that he had given the note to my Mom at work Wednesday and we saw it here, on her desk, yesterday. So that means she had to come home," answered Kyle.

"Who's Idella?" asked Daniel.

"Idella works for NAGS. She's their cleaning lady."

"Can I see the note?" asked Daniel.

"Yes, sir." Katie found the note and gave it to the detective who read it, took a picture, and then handed it back to Katie.

"You also mentioned dirty dishes?"

"Yes. Now that was strange. The fact that we found *any* dirty dishes in the sink was not like Mom. She *never* left *anything* dirty in the sink unless the dishwasher was full or in use. And the other strange thing was there was only one plate, a glass, and a knife with mayo on it. The one plate and glass *could* make sense if, for whatever reason, she left them in the sink, dirty. But not the knife with mayo. See, Mom doesn't eat mayo. Can't. She's allergic to it. She only kept it around for me and Aaron and guests. And neither Aaron nor I were here Wednesday. So she must have had company. But why only one plate and glass? That doesn't make sense to me," Kyle said, all excited that he could help with the investigation.

"Are the dishes still in the sink?" Johnny asked.

"No. They're in the dishwasher but they've been washed. I'm sorry," answered Katie.

"That's OK. Don't worry about it," sympathized Johnny. Then looking at Kyle, he continued. "Based on what you've told me, we'll be asking some of our forensic experts to take a look at the apartment sometime later today. They won't take much of your time and won't leave a mess. Maybe they'll be able to ferret out some new evidence. I hate to ask y'all not to disturb anything but…"

"We understand," answered Aaron. "It's probably best if we leave. We can take these pictures with us." He pulled out his keys and removed the key to Margie's apartment and handed it to Johnny.

"One last thing," said Daniel. "The clothes your mother was wearing in the pictures I showed you yesterday, would you consider those her work clothes or do you think she came home and changed into those clothes? Do you need to look at the pictures again?"

"*No!* I don't need to look at them. She always dressed nice wherever she went. I'm certain she wore those to work."

"What coat would she normally wear to work?"

"She has a number of coats, but on cold winter days, she would wear her long brown suede one with a mink collar. That and a wool scarf. Our Dad gave her the coat the Christmas before he died. She loved that coat."

"Why do you ask? Is that important?" asked Aaron.

"Yes. Your mother's coat and handbag were missing when we found her at the crime scene. We're not sure if we're investigating a carjacking or a robbery *and* carjacking. Until we get an inventory of the car's possessions, we won't know," answered Daniel. "On our way out, if you or Kyle could maybe check her coat closet, then maybe we'll know for sure what we're looking for."

With their interview completed, Daniel placed his pad and pen in his briefcase and shut it. He looked at Johnny, nodded, and stood. Using both hands, Johnny pushed his way out of the chair but required some effort to keep it from trying to tag along with his immense torso.

Aaron and Kyle walked the detectives to the secretary/desk where they played the messages on the answering machine then into the foyer where Kyle retrieved the detective's coats and Johnny's hat. A search of the closet showed Margie had two other winter coats, but none like the one Kyle had described. By default, she had to be wearing the brown suede coat with the mink trimmed collar.

Once the detectives were in their car, Johnny turned to Daniel. "You think this case can get any weirder? Jeez. Talk about disjointed facts! But two crimes? You don't really think there were two crimes, do you?"

"Well, *you* said it was weird. I don't think we should rule out anything. The poor woman might have given her coat to a homeless person and then got carjacked as she was getting back in her car, or at a gas station, or a parking lot. Or this whole thing could be gang-related. But two crimes? I doubt that very seriously. Still, it's probably something we should consider. But who knows?"

"Yeah. Who knows?"

Chapter 58

Friday, December 29, 2006, 11:00 a.m. EST

The Washington Post, Washington Times, CNN, FOX, ABC, NBC, CBS, plus every local radio and TV stations in the Washington D.C. metro area had been given notice by NAGS of the 11 o'clock news conference to be held at the front of the NAGS Washington D.C. Headquarters regarding the death of Margaret Hamilton, an employee of NAGS. The notice was hardly necessary as most of them had been camped out in front of the building ever since the discovered body had been identified as an employee of NAGS *and* had been shot. The media didn't care that it was a woman, a widow, a mother of two, a hard worker, and a devout Christian. All that mattered was that she worked for NAGS and had been shot. Prior to the news conference, a history of Margaret Irene Hamilton's employment at NAGS, composed by one of NAGS' top lawyers, had been emailed or faxed to each of the media's News Directors. The document contained many company photos of her, mostly taken at their Virginia hunting lodge. The majority of the pictures had Margie holding a rifle. NAGS had its agenda. But so did each of the reporters – either pro or anti-gun control. Very few of the reporters were at the conference for the newsworthiness of Margie's death.

Dark snow clouds ruled the sky with its flakes littering the air when at precisely 11 a.m., Wayne Peters and Bobby Armstrong, dressed in similar dark blue suits, heavy starched white shirts, conservative ties and each wearing a black wool overcoat complete with an American Flag pin in its lapel, walked slowly out of the NAGS headquarters' front door and down the steps to the bouquet of microphones. News reporters and their photographers and cameramen were everywhere with each one searching for the best photographic angle. Once the dark mahogany door opened, the incessant chatter of the attendees abruptly stopped. Out of respect, Bobby had chosen not to wear his 'LBJ.' The expression on the two men's faces was somber. And their eyes, all red and puffy from their all-nighter, easily caught the attention of the media. As hoped, everyone assumed it was due to their grief and sorrow. As decided earlier, Bobby would address the press with Wayne at his side but two steps back. Then after Bobby spoke, both men would take questions from the press. They knew who their friends were among the media. They also knew their enemies. The enemies rarely got to ask their questions.

Bobby addressed the crowd and, with no notes in hand, began to speak.

"Good Morning, Ladies and Gentlemen. My name is Nelson Robert Armstrong. I'm president of the North American Gun Society. To my right is Wayne Jordan Peters, the executive vice-president of our organization. It is with deep pain and great sorrow that we have called this news conference. As you probably know, we learned just yesterday that we lost one of our most valued associates... No. One of our most valued family members. Mrs. Margaret Irene Hamilton. Margie was with our family for over ten years coming to us after her husband of 26 years died. She loved working here. She was a great asset to our organization. But more than that, everyone here loved her. She was an all-American worker, mother, and friend. She will be sorely missed by everyone. I..." Bobby's voice quivered. "I will miss her." Bobby paused as real tears began to flow. He looked down for a second, as if trying to gain control of his emotions, pulled out a handkerchief, and then looked out into the media making sure the cameras caught his angst and sorrow before wiping his eyes. In reality, Bobby could hardly remember Margie's name, so his tears weren't for her. Years ago, while taking a drama class in college, he learned how to cry on cue. The trick was to think about something extremely sad. So whenever tears were needed, he always thought about his old English bulldog, Sir Isaac Newton, Newt for short, who was run over right in front of his eyes by his drunk Uncle Travis. Bobby was only ten at the time. The dog died in Bobby's arms. He never forgave his uncle, even refusing to go to his funeral when he died of liver cancer years later.

After composing himself, Bobby continued.

"Margie leaves behind two wonderful sons, Aaron and Kyle. They are devastated by the loss of their mother, and I would ask that you *please*, out of common courtesy, give them time to grieve, to give them time to find solace with their friends and family without outside interference from those who did not know Margie."

"From what we've been told and what we've heard on news reports, Margie's death was the result of a carjacking. Her life was taken… No. Stolen by thugs who have no respect for human life. They only wanted her car and didn't care if they had to kill a sweet elderly woman to get it. I'm sure many of you find it ironic that one of our family members was shot down in cold blood by a gun." Bobby paused to let the last sentence sink in. "Well, we don't. We think this vicious and heinous crime could have been prevented. If only Margie could have legally carried her handgun with her, in her car, in her office, anywhere, she, most likely, would not be dead today."

While Bobby continued with his *'If only Margie'* campaign, citing the District's crime statistic, bringing up similar shootings, telling success stories in other states where citizens are allowed to carry guns into restaurants, churches, and schools, Wayne couldn't help but think of how just two days ago Margie lay dead, upstairs, with her one eye open, staring at the ceiling. And how atrociously they had treated her – throwing her lifeless body next to a trash dump in the cold and snow. Heinous? That was heinous. Tears began to well up in Wayne's eyes. Unlike Bobby's, they were real. A number of the reporters also took note of this - the human side of Wayne Peters as he silently wept for a lost co-worker. He truly did miss her.

No one said a thing as Bobby continued his sermon-like oration. Those for gun control discounted everything he said. Those against gun control nodded in total agreement, captivated by the story Bobby told.

Bobby continued.

"We can go over case after case in this city of the victims who could have possibly warded off threats or could have provided protection for themselves and their families had they been able to arm themselves to defend themselves. But no. For over 30 years, the officials running the District of Columbia, including the current and retiring mayor as well as their hand-picked Chiefs of Police, have continually supported the law banning honest, law-abiding citizens from owning and possessing firearms. Since then, we have gone unprotected while the criminal element shoots at will. It is time for us to change that law. We *now* have that opportunity. The U.S. Court of Appeals for the District of Columbia will soon be making that decision. We have worked day and night making sure that everyone involved, including our many members, have the correct, factual information."

"Margie Hamilton was a strong supporter of the 2nd amendment. She worked tirelessly with us in trying to overturn this incursion into our individual rights and liberty. If only Margie could have had her personal handgun, we might not be here today, on the steps of our Headquarters Building, grieving over her loss. Let her death not be in vain. Let's hope the judges who are about to make this decision remember the Margie Hamilton's of the world and will overturn the restriction of our individual freedoms."

Bobby paused a few seconds to make sure that what he was about to say next had the proper dramatic effect. Once he felt the timing was right, in his most determined and forceful voice, he continued.

"We want to find those thugs. Those hoodlums. Those cowards who murdered our friend and colleague and we want this done as fast as possible. Having said that, NAGS will use all of its powers as the United States' largest gun rights organization to bring justice to Margie and her family. We are prepared to offer a $50,000 reward for any information that leads to the arrest and conviction of the person or persons who took our Margie's life. We want those lowlifes, those *bastards* caught, tried and convicted. That's the least we can do for our dear Margie. I want to thank you for your continued support. We need it in times like these. God bless America and God bless people like Margie Hamilton. Please keep her and her family in your prayers."

Chapter 59

Friday, December 29, 2006, 11:24 a.m. EST

"Well, what do you think? You think it went over well?" Bobby asked after the two men had retreated to the safety of their office building. Even though he asked, Bobby didn't care what Wayne thought. As far as he was concerned, it went great.

"It was perfect. But I expected that," replied Wayne. "And I loved the way you slipped in the '*If only Margie*' part. But don't you think you should have at least consulted me about the reward? $50,000? My God! That's a lot of money. What was wrong with $25,000? $25,000 would have had the same effect." But that was Bobby. More often than not, his mouth moved without his brain fully engaging.

"Don't be so fucking tight. We've got the money. Look at all the publicity! Look at all the new members we'll get!"

"You're right," responded Wayne. "Now all we have to do is to get the Hamilton's buy-in. Oh God! I was supposed to call Kyle with the list of Margie's co-workers. I can't believe I forgot it." But Wayne could believe he had forgotten it. With his well-conceived and thought-out plan out the window, Bobby was in charge. Forget about pre-planning, working out small details or dependencies, timelines. Just act and react.

"That's OK," said Bobby calmly. "Gives us a reason to call him. See if we can come over, or if we can take him to lunch. And remember to tell him we'd like to pick up the tab for the funeral. That's the least we can do. We need him and his brother on our side. Oh. And one last thing. Call the mayor. Read him the riot act. Jerk him around a little bit. Ask him why it's taking so long finding Margie's killers. While you do that, I'm going to take a nap. "

Wayne took the elevator up to his 2nd-floor office while Bobby headed to the sofa in the parlor. Wayne had had enough of him. Just looking at him and hearing him talk, nauseated and disgusted him. Normally he would have walked the eighteen steps, but today he was tired. Last night was exhausting and eye-opening. You would think that after all of the years of working together, you would know someone. Only last night did he come to know the real Bobby Armstrong. From now on he'd be watching the monster's every move or else *he* might be thrown under the bus. Bobby didn't care about the 2nd Amendment. Bobby cared about Bobby. End of story. NAGS and anybody else just happened to be rungs in his ladder to the top.

Wayne sat down in his leather chair and closed his eyes. He hated his office and dreaded being there. Even though he didn't see the bloodstains or the bullet holes, they were there, and he knew it. Would others feel the death that permeated the room? Would they sense his anxiety and trepidation?

Wayne shook his head vigorously as if to clear his mind. He needed to be composed and business-like when he talked to the mayor. Not being one of His Honor's insiders, it took Wayne well over ten minutes to track him down for a five-minute phone call. The mayor and NAGS were at odds over the District's gun control laws, yet, he always welcomed Wayne, either in person or by phone. After the obligatory personal interactions, Wayne moved right into the purpose of the call: Find Margie Hamilton's murderers. The mayor completely understood Wayne's concern and assured him that the police were doing everything possible. The call ended cordially with the Mayor assuring Wayne that he would personally contact the chief of police and impress upon him the urgency of the matter.

Wayne checked the time. It was close to noon. Too late to ask Kyle to lunch, as Bobby had suggested. He quickly scanned his cell phone's incoming call log for Kyle's number and after finding it, dialed it on his landline. Kyle picked up after a couple of rings.

"Kyle, this is Wayne Peters. I am so, so sorry that I didn't get back to you with that list you asked for. With all that's been going on, I completely forgot."

"That's OK. I understand, Mr. Peters. It was the detectives who wanted it, but they've already left. They said they'd call you."

"Did they ever say *why* they wanted the list?"

"No, sir. They didn't give us any reason. I mean, they've already arrested a couple of guys in North Carolina, caught red-handed driving Mom's car, so I'm surprised that they needed anything else. They did say they had suspicions that it wasn't a carjacking. Something about conflicting evidence. But then they said it could be a robbery, a carjacking or both. It was very confusing. If you can keep that to yourself, I'd appreciate it. They asked me not to tell anybody what I just told you. But I trust you."

"Believe me. My lips are sealed."

After a brief silence on the phone by both parties, Wayne continued.

"Kyle, again I can't express how saddened we are about your mother's death. She meant so much to us. To me. Especially me. Please forgive me if I'm out of line but would you and your brother consider letting us, NAGS, pay for Margie's funeral. We would consider it an honor and a privilege. It would be our way of paying homage to her."

"I appreciate the offer but Aaron and I will take care of it. And as far as you being out of line, you could never do that. My Mom had the utmost respect for you. That was one of the main reasons why she worked for NAGS."

"Those are very kind words. They mean a lot to me. We're going to miss her." Wayne paused a few moments then continued. "Would you mind if I came by for a brief visit and possibly bring my boss, Robert Armstrong? He wants to meet you and to express his condolences,"

Kyle thought for a moment. "Any time today after 6 p.m. would be fine but call before you come. Aaron and I have to be at the funeral home at three to finalize everything. We should be back at Mom's apartment by then. Do you have her address?"

"Yes, Kyle. I know where your mother lives." *I've been there before!*

Chapter 60

Friday, December 29, 2006, 12:06 p.m. EST

When Daniel and Johnny got back to their office, Daniel found a hand-written note on his desk from 'VM' (Vernon Martin) for him to stop by his office. Everybody who worked for the captain liked him. He was fair and very supportive of his people. The note didn't say what he wanted, but Daniel knew.

He crushed the note and tossed it in the trash, catching Johnny's attention.

"What's wrong?"

"The captain wants an update. So what do I tell him? We've got nothing! Absolutely nothing! The guys in Carolina (NCSHP) haven't called back so I'd be speculating what they've found. We just put in the paperwork to get court orders for Margie's phone and bank records, so we don't have anything there. Talking to the Hamilton boys didn't add anything and we haven't had a chance to even *look* at their list. We still need to talk with Wayne Peters to know when Margie left work, who she left with, if anybody, or if she was to meet up with anyone. To make matters worse, neither you nor I are convinced this was even a carjacking. I've got nothing to tell him. Nothing. And you know he's got to be getting some real heat from the top. I think I'm just going to avoid him. Wait until I've actually got something to tell him."

"You through? Well, if you want my opinion, and you know I'm gonna give it to you anyway, I'd go see him right now. *Before* we hear from the Carolina guys. That way, you can tell him we've got a couple of suspects in custody in North Carolina that were caught driving the stolen car. If he wants to think this thing is close to being wrapped up, then let him. That should get him off our ass for a couple of days. Plus if you go *now*, he's probably at lunch. That way you can leave him a voicemail or a note."

Daniel immediately headed to VM's office. As Johnny predicted, the captain had gone to lunch.

As he was leaving a message for the captain, Johnny stuck his head in the office and mouthed *North Carolina called*, then left. Daniel finished his voicemail and returned to his desk.

"What did they say?" asked Daniel.

"I told them we'd call them back. Do a conference call. You and me. I've reserved 3A."

The sergeant from NCSHP was very succinct in delivering the facts, valuing everyone's time. He reported that the Buick had been impounded and was positively identified as Margie Hamilton's. It was clean except the prints of the arrested driver. There were no traces of blood, no bullet holes, no guns, no drugs, and no large amounts of cash. The Buick had a 'Temporary' license plate like those used on recently purchased vehicles. The second car, a 2001 Toyota Camry, was also confiscated and its driver arrested. The prints taken from the second car were those of the driver, the driver of the stolen Buick, and numerous unidentified ones. The Toyota's interior was fairly clean other than a couple of McDonald's bags filled with fast food wrappers and beverage cups. The trunk contained work boots, leather gloves, and a fishing tackle box. And just like the Buick, the Toyota had been reported stolen from the DC metro area, but about ten months earlier.

To the dismay of Daniel and Johnny, it was not a dark-colored Chevrolet Impala, the make and model of the second car in the DFS surveillance tape.

The sergeant reported that both suspects were illegals who lived in North Carolina and worked for a small landscaping company. According to their confessions, which were taken separately via translators, neither knew the cars they were driving were stolen. They said they had paid cash to a guy known as 'Otto Max.' They had gotten Otto's name from the night clerk who worked at their extended-stay motel in Durham, NC. They said that they met up with Otto around 1 p.m. Thursday, December 28th at the I-85 South Carson Rest Stop where they exchanged money and car. The buyer was given a 'notarized' bill of sale on Otto Max's letterhead and a 'Used Car Limited Warranty' document. The illegals said they were told that the car came from a Virginia Auto Auction and the reason for its extremely low price was hail damage which had been repaired.

The N.C. sergeant cleared his throat, then continues. "We checked for prints on the sale documents, and the 'Temporary' license plate but the only ones found were from the illegal buying the car. The 'notary' seal was a fake. But surprisingly, the address on the documents was legit, but not to an Otto Max Used Car lot. You *might* recognize the location."

The NC detective could hardly finish reading the 1600 Pennsylvania Avenue address before he broke out in laughter. Johnny and Daniel failed to see the humor.

"Great. A crook with a sense of humor," said Johnny.

After the sergeant's laughter subsided, he told the two DC detectives that they hoped to have their initial report completed and faxed to them that afternoon. It would include a report from the State Crime Lab, photos of the suspects, description, and inventory of the two cars, and a description and sketch of Otto Max. They would also fax any information regarding the night clerk once he was located and questioned by the North Carolina Bureau of Investigation (NCBI).

Daniel thanked the sergeant and clicked off the speakerphone.

"1600 Pennsylvania Avenue. You have to admit that's pretty funny. So you think this Otto Max is our carjacker?" asked Daniel.

Johnny looked at his watch before answering. Daniel knew what that meant.

Chapter 61

Friday, December 29, 2006, 12:08 p.m. EST

Where was he? The scene was all too familiar for Jamie. After a night of drugs, he never knew where he might find himself the next day. As he opened his bleary, bloodshot eyes, everything was fuzzy, totally out of focus. To his credit, at least he had somehow found a bed. Then the smell hit him. The rancid smell of vomit. A familiar consequence of his overindulgence. He also caught a whiff of liquor. Not an unpleasant smell on its own. But the blend of liquor and vomit made him nauseous. But why *was* there a liquor smell? He didn't remember buying any. He certainly didn't remember drinking any. He liked liquor, but he never mixed it with drugs. Too dangerous and too costly. If he hadn't needed more sleep, he would have gotten up, dressed, and gotten out of there. That didn't happen. Instead, he shoved the vomit-laden bedspread aside, turned away from the foul odor, and blindly grabbed the duvet cover from the foot of the bed. He pulled it over his naked body and immediately fell back asleep.

Forty minutes later, the ache in his stomach and the pain in his bladder were greater than the need for sleep. He needed food. He needed water. And he needed to pee. Badly. Slowly he opened his eyes. To his surprise, he was at home. Not his bedroom at the house on 4th Street, but the guest bedroom in his real home. Why? Why was he still at his mother's house and not his? His mother never let him stay over. Especially when he'd been using drugs. Maybe this time she'd taken pity on him. Then the sour smell of vomit mixed with liquor hit him. *Oh God! This is not good!* He slowly slid over to the side of the bed closest to the bathroom and sat up. His head hung down almost to his lap. His eyes were mostly closed and his feet dangling just above the floor. God, he felt bad. Why did he do these things? Remorse. Always remorse after a night of heavy drug use. But remorse wouldn't stop him from getting stoned again. That's why it's called an addiction. As he looked to the floor before stepping out of bed, he saw the vomit. He jerked his feet up and turned his head away. That's when he saw the discolored, rank-smelling sheets and bedspread. *Oh no! She's gonna kill me when she sees this!* He needed to get out of there and fast. He eased his way down to the foot of the bed where the floor was clean. Using the bedpost to stabilize himself, he slid out of the bed and wobbled to the bathroom. His head was pounding. Once he made it to the toilet, he leaned forward, placed both hands on the wall in front of him for balance, and let loose a steady stream of poisons from his body.

Jamie felt like an eighteen-wheeler had run over him. When he glanced at himself in the bathroom mirror, he looked just like he felt. Why did he do this to himself? He had no answer because he didn't want one. Two white terry cloth bathrobes hung on the back of the bathroom door. He slipped on the larger of the two. His mother kept them there for guests. Wasn't he a guest? At least she made him feel that way. He headed to the kitchen using the back hallway yelling for his mother as he did. There was no answer. *Good. There is a God!* More than likely she was out with one of her fancy country club friends or with that nosy next-door neighbor. At least he hoped so. That might give him enough time to get showered, dressed and get the hell out of there before she returned.

Hangovers, whether drug or alcohol induced, made you hungry and thirsty. Jamie poured out the stale coffee that had been left in the pot by his mother and started a fresh pot. Before he left the kitchen, he had downed two bottled waters, two mugs of coffee and a large bowl of cereal. It felt great to be back home. This is where he belonged, but with *both* parents. If he could get them back together, maybe he could quit drugs. Well, maybe. He placed everything in the dishwasher and wiped the table and counters clean, and then headed back to the guest bedroom where he showered and shaved. The hot twenty-minute shower was therapeutic - just what the doctor ordered. And his mother was the perfect host – travel-size shaving cream, toothpaste, hairbrush, comb, Bic throwaway razors, and toothbrushes - everything a guest would need - neatly placed in the bathroom drawers.

The bathroom looked like a steam room after his lengthy shower. The mirror was covered with condensation that required two or three wipe downs before he could see good enough to shave, comb his hair and brush his teeth. Once he finished, he slipped on the bathrobe, neatly hung the used towels, and returned to the bedroom to dress.

Jamie saw his clothes in a pile on the floor. They were a disgusting mess, all covered in vomit and… *What the hell is that?* There were dark splattered stains on his jeans, his favorite leather jacket, and his shoes. For the life of him, he couldn't remember why they were there or where they came from. Mud? Chili? Motor oil? *Oh no. Don't tell me I've got a problem with that pile of shit I drive.* That's the problem with doing drugs – you have no recollection as to where you've been, who you've been with, or what you did. So there was no telling what it was. Jamie retreated to the kitchen, grabbed a trash bag then returned to the bedroom where he picked up his clothes and shoes as though they were radioactive and dropped them into the bag. Fortunately, his mother kept some 'emergency' clothes in his old bedroom. He would have to borrow them.

Without wasting time, he made his way down the hall leading to the foyer and the second-floor stairwell, never once noticing the trail of blood. Then it hit him. *Oh, God. What if she's still here, in bed with a migraine, and didn't hear me? I'm toast!*

Jamie tip-toed up the steps then peeked into his mother's bedroom. The curtains were drawn, but the lights were on. He called out to his mother, but there was no answer. What struck him as odd was the bed. It was unmade. She never left the house with the bed unmade. Both parents were anal that way. Then he saw the shattered dresser mirror. What the hell was that all about? Maybe she got mad at him over his untimely visit or the mess he'd made and flipped out. Or maybe she got mad because his Dad didn't come and get him. Or maybe his Dad did come and they got into one of their heated arguments over how they should have raised their lost son and she went apeshit. Regardless of what happened, it was obvious that her anti-depressants weren't working. But they would work on him. Jamie checked both the bathroom and the bedroom for his mother's pills. Nothing. Disappointed, he headed to his old bedroom.

The 'emergency' clothes weren't his normal, everyday attire. Besides the basic necessities including clean underwear, black socks, and t-shirts, she kept a dark blue suit still in its dry cleaning bag, a blue blazer, dress khaki pants, oxford cloth shirts, dress shoes, penny loafers, and a couple of matching ties. He never questioned why she kept the clothes. But more than likely, it was so she would have something nice to bury him in case he OD'd.

Jamie opted for the khakis, oxford shirt, blazer, and penny loafers, dressing as fast as he could. After slipping on the highly polished loafers, he glanced at himself in the mirror. It was an amazing transformation. He looked nice. He wished his mother could see him now. Well, not really. She would kill him if she saw him in his 'emergency' clothes without getting her permission. Without warning, a wave of nausea hit him. He might look good, but he felt bad, the side effects of drugs. He needed to go. He needed some grease in his stomach – maybe a couple of Big Mac's and some fries – something more substantial than cereal. He grabbed the terry cloth bathrobe and hurried back to the steps leading downstairs.

Once he reached the bottom landing and turned to take the last two steps, he saw her. Lying on the living room floor. He stood motionless for a few seconds until the reality of what he was seeing sunk in. He dropped the robe and ran to his mother yelling, "MOM! MOM! WHAT HAPPENED? ARE YOU ALL RIGHT?"

Before he reached her, he could see the blood on the rug surrounding her head. His first thought was that she must have fallen, hit her head on the pointed edge of a nearby table and was knocked unconscious. Then he saw the horror of her face and head or what was left of it. His mother was dead!

"OH MY GOD. MAMA! OH MY GOD! MAMA! WHAT HAVE I DONE?"

He kneeled down next to her body with tears pouring down his face. He collected himself enough to check her pulse, but he knew there would be none, and there wasn't. His mind swirled with a multitude of thoughts, but they all centered on what he had seen on his jeans and jacket. It wasn't mud, chili or oil. It was blood! His mother's blood! He had killed his own mother! The evidence was all there. The broken dresser mirror. Blood on his jacket. Maybe they had an argument. Maybe he was trying to steal some of her medicine, and she caught him. Could that have been it? Was that why he killed her? Drugs? Jamie shook his head in disbelief. He did drugs, but he'd never been violent. If anything, when he got stoned, he got maudlin, lovey-dovey, weepy-eyed and sometimes just plain goofy.

Fear and panic began to overtake him causing him to shake uncontrollably. He had to get out of there. He needed his Dad. His Dad would help him. His Dad had always helped him. As he backed away from his mother, he stepped on a serving tray. Coffee mugs lay near the tray. Something else he didn't remember. Frantically, he ran toward the front door, then stopped in mid tracks realizing he had left the keys to his car. He ran as fast he could back to the guest room where he grabbed up his bloodstained jacket and started back to the front door searching the pockets of the jacket for the keys. Once his hand felt their jagged edges, he jerked them out of the pocket and threw the jacket to the floor.

The wind was blowing, and the air was frigid as he stepped outside. Gone was the yellow vomit, replaced by pure white December snow. Gone, too, was his car. In its place was his Dad's Mercedes. This was all too bizarre. He couldn't have hallucinated anything like this. Not even with the worst of drugs. Why was his Dad's car here? Jamie glanced at the keys in his hand. They weren't his. They were his Dad's. Another horrible thought came to him. Maybe he killed his Dad, too! Just as quickly as he left, he returned to the house and started a frenzied search for his Dad, going from room to room, hoping not to find another body.

"Please God. Don't let my Dad be dead too," he prayed over and over as he conducted his brief, albeit thorough, search. Not finding his Dad brought him a small sense of relief. He hated to leave his mother, but there was nothing he could do for her. After all, hadn't he done enough already?

On the way out of the house, he paused momentarily to look one more time at his mother, lying dead on the living room floor. How could he have done such a thing? Why didn't he have any memory of this horrible deed? He had no answers.

Then he left, running as fast as he could, out the door and down the front porch steps to his Dad's unlocked Mercedes. It started up so much easier than his old Cadillac. Without putting on his seatbelt, he backed out of the driveway and headed toward the city. Automatically, he searched his coat pocket for his cell phone. He had to call his Dad. He needed to check on him and make sure he was all right. But what the hell was he thinking? He didn't have his phone. He'd left it. He'd left his fucking phone! Jamie slammed his hand onto the steering wheel. It hurt, but he didn't care. Nothing mattered anymore.

He turned on to Wisconsin Avenue and headed to the Watergate Apartments. His Dad would help him. He had to. He always had.

Chapter 62

Friday, December 29, 2006, 1:05 p.m. EST

Since the news conference, NAGS' answering service had been flooded with calls from board members, friends and colleagues of Margie's and supporters of NAGS. Those who could not talk personally to Wayne or Bobby left messages offering their condolences and their unwavering support for the cause. The calls had gotten so numerous that they considered bringing in a skeleton crew to help with the donations and new memberships but decided against it so not to be accused of profiting at the expense of Margie's horrible death. However, an idea that was now being bantered about by many of NAGS' supporters was the establishment of a fund in the memory of Margie to provide aid for the families of gun-related deaths in the DC metro area. It was an idea that Wayne and Bobby liked, but both felt they needed the two sons' approval before pushing forward.

Even during lunch, which they chose to have delivered to the office, Wayne and Bobby continued to take calls, leaving hardly any time to eat. The most important calls were from their staunch supporters in the House and Senate, all reaffirming their continued support. A couple of calls came from representatives who had heretofore been their opposition. Their *'If only Margie'* campaign was going better than they had ever imagined. Bobby could hardly contain himself with all of the positive feedback and publicity hype. Wayne knew what the monster was thinking. Was he underestimating himself by running for the Senate? Should he be aiming higher? But Wayne was thinking, *Should I have shot him when I had the chance?*

While Bobby was in the midst of applauding himself, which he frequently did, the answering service called. They had a Detective Whitehead on the phone and wanted to know if they should patch him through. It was a call that Wayne had expected but dreaded. How would he come across? Would he be convincing? Should he put this off until he felt more comfortable with Bobby's plan, such as it was?

"Who is it?" asked Bobby seeing the concerned look on Wayne's face.

"It's a detective. You think I should take his call now or wait?"

"Now. Take it now. Let's get the ball rolling."

"OK. But I'm gonna put us on speakerphone, so you can hear what they're asking me. I think I know what I'm supposed to say but if I goof up… Here. Use this." Wayne handed Bobby a legal pad and a pen. "Write down anything I should say that I might have forgotten or anything I need to change, correct or whatever. You're guiding this ship now."

"All you got to do is work him like you do the directors at our board meetings. You'll do great. Remember. He's only a detective. Not a rocket scientist."

The phone rang once, and Wayne answered. Greetings were exchanged, and both parties asked if the other minded being placed on speakerphone. Detective Whitehead introduced Detective Williams, and Wayne introduced Robert Armstrong, president of NAGS. The conversation started very cordially with Daniel going over the facts of the case. It was nothing more than a rehash of what the media had already reported.

"Detectives, we want to help any way we can. I'm sorry we didn't get that list of employees to Kyle but so much has gone on the last few days that it completely slipped my mind. We're seeing the Hamilton's tonight, I could bring it to him then. Or if you want, I can fax it over to you right after we hang up."

The lieutenant gave them their fax number and Peters continued.

"You know Margie meant the world to us. We were all very close to her. I really can't imagine this office without her. I know her sons are devastated. We want whoever did this heinous crime to be caught, so if you need *any* help, we are very willing to pay for some private investigators."

Bobby gave Wayne the thumbs up at the intended dig. Bobby figured it went right over the detective's head.

Daniel let it pass, but he could see Johnny starting to puff up like a blowfish. Johnny was pretty much apolitical, but NAGS was one of his hot buttons.

"We'll let you know if we run aground and need some assistance. My partner and I talked with the Hamilton brothers this morning. They were extremely helpful but left some questions unanswered. I'm hoping you can fill in some of the blanks."

"We'll do our best. Fire away." Bobby grinned ear to ear at Wayne's unintended pun.

"From what I understand, Margie Hamilton came to work Wednesday morning. Is that correct?"

After each question, Daniel wrote down the answer on his legal pad. Johnny used his pocket pad.

"Yes, Detective Whitehead. Margie came to work at 7 a.m. and left sometime around 10:30 or 11. I would have to check her timesheet."

"Why did she leave so early? Is that her normal workday? Is she part-time?"

"No. She's not part-time. But we had wrapped up as much work as we could without Mr. Armstrong being here, and he wasn't going to arrive until late Wednesday afternoon so I told Margie that she could leave. Of course, we planned to pay her for a full day. That's company policy."

"So once she left your office, do you know where Ms. Hamilton went?"

"Margie left the office with Jamie Barnes. Jamie is the son of one of our employees, Jim Barnes, our special events coordinator. Anyway, Jamie came by looking for his father needing some gas money and a ride home. His father wasn't here, so I gave him a twenty and Margie offered him a ride home. Detective, do you think that Margie was carjacked somewhere near Jamie's house?"

The lieutenant ignored the question. "Do you happen to know where Jamie Barnes lives or his phone number?"

"I think he lives somewhere near the Catholic University in a house that his father owns. And I think our answering service might have Jamie's phone number. If they do, I'll add it to the fax."

Johnny immediately began a search on his computer for the address.

"Is Jim Barnes there? If so, could you put him on speakerphone? We'd like to talk to him."

"He's not at work today. But if you'll wait a second, I'll get you his apartment and cell numbers."

Wayne searched his cell phone and relayed Jim's phone numbers and the Watergate apartment address to the lieutenant. As Daniel wrote down the information, Johnny mouthed *I got it* regarding Jamie's address.

"Why didn't Jamie call his father and ask *him* to come get him?"

"I don't know. I would assume that he *tried*. Your guess is good as mine regarding what Jamie would or wouldn't do. You see, Jamie has issues. And off the record, we don't like him hanging around our office. He's always dirty looking. His clothes look like he's slept in them which he probably has. And sometimes he smells. The rumors are that he's heavily into drugs which I believe to be true. And we also suspect that he broke into our lodge and stole some things. I know I shouldn't say that since we don't have any proof. But I've said it and I also believe that to be true. Anyway, Margie knew how we felt about Jamie and I think that's why she gave him a ride home. Just to get him out of our office and because that's the kind of person she is... or was. She was kind and sweet to everyone."

"The son sounds like a real gem. So when Ms. Hamilton left with Jamie Barnes, was that the last time you saw her or heard from her?"

"Yes. Detective."

"Do you know a person by the name of Idella?"

"Idella? Yes. She's our cleaning lady. She and her husband Jerome clean our offices two or three times a week."

"Do you have their telephone number?"

"Yes. I'll add that to my fax."

"By any chance do you know a Winston Blackwell?"

"Not in person, but Margie did speak of him. I think they might have been dating."

"Did you see Ms. Hamilton and Jamie Barnes get in her car?"

"No, sir."

"Do you know where she would have parked her car?"

"In our private parking lot adjacent to our office building. All employees, who work here at the administrative office, park in that lot."

"I think that's all for now. I appreciate your time and help. If you think of anything else, please call me or my partner immediately." Daniel gave Wayne, his and Johnny's office and cell numbers, and then hung up.

Before the telephone call to Peters and Armstrong had ended, Johnny had a printout of Jamie Barnes' address, criminal record, his arrest picture, and driver's license picture. The troubled boy had no felonies but based on the number of misdemeanors for simple drug possession, it was only a matter of time before that would change. It was a pattern the detectives had seen so many times.

While Daniel called Jim Barnes' cell and apartment numbers, Johnny waited by the fax machine. Before long, the machine cranked out a couple of pages. On the last page was Jamie's phone number. All calls to Jim Barnes and his son went unanswered. With the younger Barnes being the last known person to have seen Margie Hamilton alive, the detectives decided they should pay him a visit. Maybe he could provide some clues as to what happened to Margie. Maybe one of his drug dealers had something to do with her murder. Just possibly Jamie might know Otto Max. Maybe Otto Max had branched out from stealing cars to murder. Or maybe this Winston Blackwell III preyed on older women. Maybe he had a connection with Otto Max.

So many possibilities.

Chapter 63

Friday, December 29, 2006, 1:36 p.m. EST

Wayne looked at Bobby who was smiling. "From the look on your face, I guess I did OK. You approved of my performance."

"It was perfect. Not too much information but just enough to put them on the right track. And I loved your *private investigators* putdown. I doubt those two boneheads even noticed the slight. I'm telling you, they're dumber than a stump. Probably don't know enough to come in out of the rain."

Wayne didn't know about the detectives in Bobby's home state of Texas but, in Washington, they weren't to be taken lightly. They weren't just a bunch of good ol' boys wearing a badge. Most were college graduates, highly trained and motivated.

"What about Jim?" asked Wayne. "You think I should have mentioned anything about him being put on administrative leave?"

"No. I'm sure they'll call back when they find his body. That's when you tell them about Jim coming back to the office and finds out that Jamie had come by earlier. That you had given his boy some money and he had left with Margie. You then tell the bozos that Jim got really mad at you and his son, *especially his son*. Then you say he left yelling and cussing. And if it makes sense, you can tell them about him being shit-canned."

Wayne's cell phone rang before he could correct Bobby for the millionth time about Jim's departure. The call was from Congressman John Richards. Being the chairman of the House Judiciary Committee and a major supporter of NAGS, Richards couldn't be ignored.

"Wayne, this is John. Sorry to hear about the woman. Tell Bobby he was great. No, don't do that. He'll get a bigger head than he already has," laughed Richards. "I've got an idea I'd like to talk to you about. How about I swing by say around 2:30? Will that be OK?"

Bobby could hear Richards' loud, booming voice coming from Wayne's cell even though it wasn't on speaker. He started shaking his head and mouthing, *No can do.*

Why, Wayne mouthed back then covered the mouthpiece of his cell.

"FedEx at Jim's apartment. I gotta go," answered Bobby.

"Wait one second," whispered Wayne.

"You still there?" asked Richards, waiting impatiently for a response, not used to being put on hold.

"Sorry, John. Bobby's not here. But he should be back around four. Is it something you and I can do alone or should we wait for him?"

"Me? Wait for Armstrong? Hell no. We don't need him anyway. I'll see you at 2:30."

Wayne turned to Bobby as he slammed his cell shut.

"Why in the hell do you have to go to Jim's apartment right now? The concierge will keep the letter if you're not there to get it. You know I don't like being alone with that jerk. You know how he is."

"Because once the police find Jim's body, they'll be all over his apartment like white on rice. If we're going to get into that safe, we need to do it *now.* You can handle Richards. If he starts making any overtures, remember, we need him. So humor him."

Wayne knew that Bobby was right. If they didn't get those folders now, they wouldn't get them at all, not once the police showed up. He would just have to deal with Richards. After all, he wasn't that much worse than Bobby, with both wanting to tell you how great they are. And a break from Bobby *would* be a relief.

Chapter 64

Friday, December 29, 2006, 1:47 p.m. EST

"Please God. Let him be there. Please, God! Please!" Jamie prayed aloud and often as he drove his Dad's Mercedes over to the Watergate apartment. He tried not to think of his mother, but the image of her dead body with her crushed in face kept appearing in his mind. As hard as he tried, the vision wouldn't go away. He tried shaking his head, at times most violently, trying to block out the image. When that didn't work, he tried banging his hands on the steering wheel hoping the pain of his mother's death would be replaced by the pain in his hands. That only compounded his suffering. Tears started and stopped indiscriminately. He tried to think about last night, to remember what had happened, but his muddled brain wasn't functioning. How could he have done something so vile, so monstrous, and not remember a thing other than standing out in the snow, yelling to his mother? Did Nate sell him something that caused him to become violent? And why would he kill… No! He couldn't say or even think that *word*. Then, suddenly, without warning, he remembered the eyes. Those evil, sinister-looking eyes staring at him. The eyes of Satan. That he remembered. But were they real or just part of a drug-induced dream? Were they there to confirm his horrific behavior? With the image of his disfigured mother and the specter of the hideous, red-veined orbs occupying his mind, he was completely unaware of the drive over to the apartment complex until he was there. He never remembered making any turns, stopping at any red lights, or passing any cars. He did realize once he reached the Watergate garage, he'd not only left his cell phone, but also his wallet which had the garage card. So he parked on 25th Street and did a fast walk over to the complex.

With his preppy new look, no one stared at him contemptuously as they normally did as he rushed over to the elevators and began impatiently pushing the 'up' button waiting for one of the bank of doors to open. He needed to see his Dad. He didn't care how many sermons he had to listen to. He didn't care that his Dad would find out that he had a key to the apartment or that he had been taking money from the safe. He just needed to see him. His *Dad* would make things right. He fought back the tears as he ran to the apartment door.

The knock was gentle at first. But when no one answered, Jamie resorted to more violent and hurried raps. Unwilling to wait any longer, he used his Dad's keys to unlock the door. He silently prayed that his father would be there, waiting for him as he pushed the door open. No one was there. An uneasy feeling came over him. Then fear. Then the same terrifying thought he had at his mother's house. Could he have killed his Dad, too? Anxious as to what he might or might not find, he rushed through the apartment, searching every room. He desperately needed to see him – alive. But he found no one.

It wasn't until he walked back through the living room, the foyer and into the office that he realized something was different. The mess. It was gone. The dinged area on the living room wall now had a picture covering the damage. The entire apartment was spotless just as his Dad normally kept it – a fact that lifted Jamie's spirits. Yet, at the same time, it was very depressing.   There was no indication that anyone lived there. It was almost like visiting a model apartment. Everything staged. No hint of family. No family pictures. No travel souvenirs. No keepsakes. Nothing. It wasn't a home. It was just a place to sleep, not unlike the house he lived in. Guilt began to creep back into his mind. He felt responsible for this too. His drug use was the reason for their break-up, not the rumored infidelities of his mother. Yet... if he could get his hands on the right drugs, he could make all of this go away, at least for a while.

He walked over to the desk and picked up the phone. But instead of calling Nate, he dialed his Dad's cell. The phone went immediately to voicemail. He left a message asking him to *please, please, please* call him back on his *apartment* phone, emphasizing apartment phone. That it was very important... most urgent.

Jamie hung up the phone and sat down on the leather couch with his arms folded. He wasn't leaving until his Dad returned. He would know what to do. He tried not to think of his mother but that was impossible. Especially with the apartment so quiet. There wasn't a sound anywhere except the faint rhythmic tick-tock from a grandfather's clock in the living room and the occasional rumbling noise from his stomach, the latter of which was becoming harder and harder to ignore. He couldn't remember the last time he'd eaten, what he'd eaten, or where he'd eaten, and he was famished. He would have stopped at a

McDonald's on the way over, but given he had no money, that didn't happen.

Yielding to his hunger pangs, he headed to the kitchen in search of food. The room was just like the rest of the apartment - pristine. A search of the fridge proved fruitless. Nothing but bottled water, soda water, and Cokes. The pantry was just as bare save for a half-empty can of nuts. The limited supplies made his choice easy. He grabbed a Coke, the can of nuts and returned to his Dad's office where he plopped back down on the sofa. He felt comfortable sitting on the leather couch. He had heard numerous sermons there - a prerequisite for getting that extra cash. The memory made him smile.

Jamie grabbed a handful of nuts and chased them down with a swig of his Coke. He then found the TV controller sitting on the armrest of the sofa and flipped on the large Panasonic plasma flat-screen TV that hung on the opposite wall. To no surprise, Fox News came on. It was the only channel his Dad ever watched. Immediately catching his eye, causing him to sit up and turn up the volume, was a news conference with Mr. Armstrong talking and Mr. Peters by his side. At the bottom of the TV screen was a running message board letting the viewers know that they were watching a tape replay of an 11 a.m. news conference. As he watched and listened more closely to Armstrong, he heard Margie Hamilton's name mentioned multiple times. Then he saw the scrolling message board:

NAGS EMPLOYEE KILLED IN CARJACKING!

How could this be true! His mother and now Mrs. Hamilton! It was like a bad drug experience, only worse. Tears began to well up in his eyes. He tried not to think of his mother and what horrible things he had done to her. But he couldn't. Then almost like a slide show, the image of his disfigured Mom's head switched to the smiling face of Mrs. Hamilton. That's the way he remembered her. She had always been kind to him. She was the only one at NAGS who didn't treat him like a leper. Then suddenly another thought. His Dad. He wasn't answering his cell or returning his call because of Mrs. Hamilton's death! That had to be it! He was probably at the funeral home, or maybe at a board meeting, discussing her death. His phone would have to be turned off. Jamie's spirits, as low as they were, were lifted.

At least he still had his Dad.

Chapter 65

Friday, December 29, 2006, 2:18 p.m. EST

The apartment was clean when Jamie got there. It would be clean when he left. He finished the last of the peanuts, drained his Coke, and dumped the remains into the kitchen trash can. Cleanliness had always been a part of his life. He grew up in a very clean house. Somebody was always cleaning. His mother, his father, the maid. Everybody but Jamie. It was a trait that didn't get passed down to him. Now that he lived by himself, his house stayed a mess unless he knew his Dad was coming over. His mother never once stepped foot in his house. She would have been appalled even at its cleanest.

But she was pretty much appalled at everything he did, stoned or otherwise. She wouldn't have let him stay over at her house if she weren't dead. It was she who had him thrown out of the house and living on the streets until his Dad rescued him. What kind of person does that to a child? She had treated him like a dog. No, worse than a dog. And she never gave him any money. Why couldn't she love him? Weren't parents supposed to have unconditional love for their children? It had been over five years since he had a real hug from her much less a motherly kiss. Anybody would have cracked under those conditions whether under the influence of drugs or not. It was not all his fault. At least, that's how Jamie rationalized his irrational behavior.

Self-inflicted grief has many phases. Not everyone goes through the same ones. Jamie had gone through the remorseful phase, the denial phase, and now was moving to the self-preservation phase.

He knew what would happen when he told his Dad what he'd done. He'd want to help. But he would want to do what was right. He would want him (Jamie) to take responsibility and call the police. Then he'd get the best lawyer possible. But not even O.J. Simpson's lawyers could keep him from going to prison. He'd spend the rest of his life in some hell hole. That wasn't going to happen. He'd already done jail time – twice. Both times as a juvenile. And both times for drug possession. The first arrest had been expunged as a first-time, youthful offender. A slap on the wrist. The second arrest took a good lawyer and a pretrial rehabilitation status to make it go away but not expunged. Again, a slap on the wrist. But the two days in jail lockup was enough for him to know that he *couldn't* and *wouldn't* go back. Anything but prison time, regardless of how long.

He began pacing back and forth, racking his brain trying to think of a solution. It didn't take long to realize there was only one: Leave the country. It fixed everything. He wouldn't need his Dad and he wouldn't go to jail. To do that, he was going to need a new identity. Nate was his man. He could make that happen. But it would cost. A lot. And the move out of the country? That, too, was going to cost. After moving, he had to live. He had no job skills. And he would have to find a new supplier. That would all take money. Nothing was free.

When you need money, you go to the source. Jamie headed straight for the safe. In less than a minute, the bank was open for business. As with his last two 'withdrawals,' he had to contend with the brown folders. This time, there was no need to keep them in order since he was taking *all* the money. His Dad could replace it with his (Jamie's) inheritance from his grandfather. So it wasn't really stealing. It was borrowing. He grabbed the first few folders and stacked them on top of the safe. He repeated the process until he saw the money stacked behind the remaining folders.

As he reached to remove the remaining folders, he heard the front door slam. It was his Dad! *Thank God!* Without thinking, he quietly closed the door to the safe which automatically locked. *Oh no! The folders!* He knew he didn't have time to re-open the safe, so he gathered them up, tip-toed back into the office and quietly slid them under the leather couch. He had just begun to think of an explanation of how and why he was in the apartment when he heard a voice, but it wasn't his Dad's! It was Mr. Armstrong's.

"……hold on a second, and I'll tell you." Armstrong placed his cell phone on the credenza, removed his leather gloves, opened the FedEx envelope and reviewed the contents. Picking up his cell, he replied. "OK. It's here - just like I told you."

"Don't forget to wear gloves! And hurry!" Wayne countered.

"You worry too much."

"Call me back as soon as you know something."

"You just take care of Richards."

Jamie waited for his Dad to say something. But all he heard was the one-sided cell phone conversation between Armstrong and whomever he was talking to. Armstrong seemed to be alone which was puzzling. Where was his Dad? Why was Armstrong in his Dad's apartment again without his Dad? This was not good. Jamie looked for a place to hide. His choice was simple. The adjoining bathroom. He quickly and quietly stepped into the bathroom, slipping behind the door.

Through the one-half inch opening between the door and the door casing, he could see Armstrong entering the office while pulling on a pair of latex gloves. This was even more puzzling. He seemed to be in a big hurry as he headed straight to the walk-in closet containing the safe. And the money! Even though the closet was out of Jamie's sight, he could hear Armstrong's every move. He prayed that Armstrong couldn't hear him as he took short silent breaths. His legs quivered as he tried to remain still behind the door.

Inside the closet, Bobby removed his LBJ hat and placed it on top of the safe along with his cell phone. In less than a minute, he had the safe open.

The next thing Jamie saw was Armstrong carrying the folders and setting them on the desk. Not the money. The folders! He then headed back to the walk-in closet and returned with his hat and cell phone, dialing as he did. He had left the money!

"Well, I got 'em," bragged Bobby.

"Make sure you got them all."

"I got all that was in the safe which was about a half-dozen. Is that what we're missing?"

"No! No! No! There should be at least twenty. Check your count."

"You think I'm a fucking moron? You don't think I can tell the difference between a half dozen and twenty?"

"There's got to be more. Can you *please* check the safe again?"

"Yeah. Yeah." Bobby knew the importance of finding all of the folders. He set his cell phone down and returned to the closet where he checked the safe, this time more closely. There weren't any more folders. He returned to the office and picked up his cell.

"None in the safe. And I have exactly five folders. Five," confirmed Bobby.

"Unbelievable," said Wayne, dejectedly. "See if you find one with Richards' name on it? That's probably the most important one."

Bobby set his phone down again, checked the names on the outside of the folders then picked up his phone.

"Nope. You should've kept 'em safer. Barnes should've never been able to get his hands on them. This is on *you.* I'll check the apartment one more time, and you check the entire office. You better pray that Richards never finds out or he'll kill us all."

Bobby slammed his phone shut. Jamie could see him furiously rummaging through his Dad's desk and then heard him rifling through the closet. After that, he saw him rush out of the office and turn toward the living room. The next sounds he heard were the opening and closing of doors, cabinets, and drawers throughout the apartment. After about ten minutes or so, he marched into the office, picked up the folders, his hat, and left, slamming the front door behind him.

Jamie was totally confused by what he had just seen and heard. His mind was filled with questions. Who was Mr. Armstrong talking to? His Dad? Peters? Why was he wearing latex gloves? Where was his Dad? Why was Mr. Armstrong in the apartment without his Dad? How did he know the combination to his Dad's safe? Why did he take the folders and not the money? And who was this Richards guy?

There was no time for Jamie to consider any of these troubling questions. He had to leave. And now! With the money! Looking around the office, he saw a large leather computer satchel next to the desk. He grabbed it and headed to the closet where he filled it with all the money. He then used a Trader Joe's canvas tote he'd found in the kitchen for the folders. He wasn't leaving them. If the folders were in his Dad's safe, they were there for a reason, and *his Dad* would get them. Not Armstrong!

Before leaving, he checked the foyer closet for a coat. It was freezing cold outside and walking around in just a summer blazer would only attract unneeded attention. He found two - his Dad's hunting jacket and his London Fog raincoat. He pulled out the raincoat and slipped it on. It was big on him, but his Dad was a big man. It reminded him of the times when, as a child, he would put on his Dad's shoes, coat, and hat and walk around pretending to be him. The spectacle made everyone laugh. His mother, Dad, and himself. Those were good times. He'd hoped that he would grow up to be just like his old man. But he hadn't. He'd never grown up. Period. But the time had come. He had to start making his own decisions. He couldn't depend on his Dad anymore. In fact, if he left the country, he'd probably never get to see him again. That thought made him question his decision. Was leaving the country his best option? He needed time to think things through – clearly and not under the influence of drugs. He needed a quiet and peaceful place. As he left the apartment and made his way down the hallway, he thought of such a place.

Chapter 66

Friday, December 29, 2006, 2:23 p.m. EST

Jamie Barnes' house was less than three miles away from the Metropolitan Police Department, 5th District Station. With Daniel driving, he and Johnny were standing at Barnes' front door in under 8 minutes. For an older house, it appeared to be in decent condition. The exterior siding was painted a bright white with green shutters framing each window. An old boat-sized Cadillac registered in the name of James H. Barnes III sat at the end of the driveway.

Daniel waited by Johnny's side as he repeatedly knocked on the door. That no one answered was no surprise, especially with Johnny yelling, 'Police. Open up!' They had no search warrant issued against the Barnes boy so if he chose not to answer, that was his right. The detectives were there only to ask him a few questions. With a car parked in the driveway, a typical indicator of someone being home, they decided to stay a little longer hoping that the constant rapping on the door might irritate any occupant enough to answer. While Johnny continued to knock, Daniel circled around to the rear of the house to check the back door. It, too, was locked and had no response to Daniel's banging. A visual check through its window showed no activity, so he left. On his way back to the front of the house, he spotted a couple of 1x3 basement-type windows just above ground level. One glance into the window sent him racing back to the front of the house as fast as he could go.

"Johnny! Break it down!"

"What?"

"A body! There's a body in the basement!" he yelled as he rounded the house, gun in hand.

Instinctively, Johnny pulled his gun and yelled one more time. "Police. Open up!" He waited about two seconds then tried his best to bash in the door with his right shoulder using the entire weight of his body. Even with his size, the door didn't budge. He moved aside making room for Daniel who executed a swift side kick striking the door just beneath the keyhole. The wooden door frame broke apart as the door swung open.

Daniel scanned the front room using his weapon as a pointer moving from left to right making sure they weren't being baited. Satisfied, he quickly entered the room. Johnny stayed behind long enough to call for backup, then entered the front room moving to Daniel's side. Like most of the early WWII homes, the front door entered directly into the living room. Having found nothing, Daniel motioned for Johnny to head to the kitchen while he moved to the back of the house and began checking out the two bedrooms, closets and the bathroom. The connecting hallway had a small 2x2 square door in the ceiling leading to the attic. It was reachable only by ladder and did not appear to have been used recently. Even so, he'd still have the backups check it out. Until then, he'd keep a sharp ear out for any sounds coming from above.

On the way into the kitchen, he saw Johnny pointing to the light coming from the opening beneath a door. "Basement?" he whispered then moved into a crouched position and slowly opened the door. With light coming from the room below, he saw a body, lying at the bottom of the steps, face up. With his gun pointing the way, he slowly made his way down the wooden stairs. All the while, Daniel remained in the kitchen as a backup, his gun also drawn. Johnny was relieved to find no one else in the basement. He wasn't sure how much longer he could do this – putting himself in harm's way – never knowing when a bullet had his name on it. But he couldn't very well ask Daniel to always lead the way just because he was younger and in better shape. He had to hold his own or hang it up.

Johnny did a quick survey of the smallish basement and then using his flashlight checked out the much larger, but empty, crawl space. With the basement inspection complete and secure, Johnny holstered his gun and hollered up to Daniel, "All clear." Daniel hurried down the steps with his gun pointing the way, just in case.

"Footprints!" yelled Johnny, pointing his flashlight to the partial prints near the body. Daniel acknowledged his partner's warning and paused on the bottom step. He holstered his gun and like Johnny had done, slipped on a pair of latex gloves and shoe booties. Out of habit, Johnny checked the body for a pulse, but it was quite obvious the person had been dead for quite some time. Johnny looked at Daniel and shook his head.

"Deader than a doornail. If I'm not mistaken, I think that's blood and a bullet hole in his coat. It could be that the guy was heading down to the basement with a loaded gun in hand, slipped, hit the rail, the gun went off, and now, like I said, deader than a doornail," observed Johnny.

"You don't *really* believe that?"

"Not for one second."

Daniel stepped gingerly towards the body, careful not to disturb anything, and began taking pictures while Johnny called DFS. The faint sounds of sirens of the backup units could be heard in the distance and would be there shortly. Before heading back up the stairs to wait for their counterparts, both men studied the face of the deceased.

"I can tell you unequivocally that this isn't Jamie Barnes. Not unless he's picked up about seventy-five pounds since he had his driver's license picture made," observed Johnny. "I think it's the boy's father. He looks just like the boy only fatter, older, and deader."

"Yeah. I agree," nodded Daniel. "I'll put out a BOLO (Be On the Look Out) for Jamie Barnes. I'll also see if I can get the elder Barnes' photo downloaded from the DMV."

"Sounds good. I'll do the same for the old man's car."

Both men returned to the kitchen and made their calls. The BOLO for Jamie Barnes was ordered as well as a request for the driver's license photo for the elder Barnes. However, there were no vehicle registrations found for a Jim, James or J Barnes at the Watergate address given to them earlier by Wayne Peters. So the BOLO for the elder Barnes' car would have to wait.

"So what do you think's going on here?" asked Daniel gleaning his partner's intuitive thoughts.

"What we have here makes a hell of a lot more sense than a carjacking. But I'm not sure I understand what we *do* have. Margie Hamilton is dead. And now Jim Barnes is dead, assuming the victim *is* Jim Barnes. Both victims were shot, and both worked for NAGS. Unless we find otherwise, Jamie Barnes was the last person known to have been with Margie. So the logical connection is Jamie. But what's the motive? And where does the father fit into the picture? Certainly not robbery. The only common denominator we know for sure is NAGS. So I say we call Wayne Peters. Maybe he can shed some light on all of this."

Once their backups arrived, Johnny directed one team of patrolmen to guard the front and rear entrances of the house. He had the other team begin cordoning off the perimeter of the house with crime scene tape and then to check out the attic. He ordered the third team to begin a house to house canvas in hopes of finding possible witnesses to the crime. While Johnny was giving out instructions, Daniel retrieved his briefcase from the car.

On the way back to the house, Daniel saw Bennie Archer pulling into the driveway followed by the DFS truck. He waited at the front door until the entire forensic team had assembled then did a quick debriefing of their initial findings. Then the teams began their search for clues and evidence, scouring the house and the old Cadillac. He and Bennie headed into the kitchen where they found Johnny sitting in one of the kitchen chairs, making notes.

"So what's going on here?" asked Bennie, closely examining the body.

Daniel answered. "We're not sure, but we believe the victim is Jim Barnes, father of Jamie Barnes who lives in this house. Assuming this is the elder Barnes, he works for NAGS, just like Margie Hamilton. And it appears that the victim was shot, just like Hamilton. So we think the two cases are related. Jamie Barnes was the last known person to be with Mrs. Hamilton, so we've put out a BOLO on him."

"So you don't think the Hamilton lady was carjacked?"

"No, we don't. But we can't close that door. Not just yet."

"So where do think the two guys from North Carolina fit in?"

"Most likely just a couple of illegals who bought a car from a guy in DC named Otto Max. What we don't know is how the Barnes kid and this Otto Max link up. It could be some kinda underground network of buying and selling stolen cars. We won't know until we do some more digging. Needless to say, we need the information on this one ASAP."

"That's understood. I'm getting the same heat from VM as you two guys are."

Bennie headed down to the basement while Daniel sat down at an old Formica kitchenette table across from Johnny to prepare for their call to Wayne Peters. Daniel pulled his legal pad from his briefcase and jotted down the questions both detectives could think to ask. Then Daniel made the call. As expected, the call was picked up by NAGS answering service who put Daniel on hold. Learning to wait was a fundamental part of a detective's job.

Chapter 67

Friday, December 29, 2006, 2:48 p.m. EST

The last thing that Wayne Peters wanted to do was to follow up a phone call from John Richards with a phone call from Detective Whitehead. Richards was an ass and Whitehead, an adversary. But Bobby had predicted the police would call and he was right. Before taking the call, Daniel spent a few minutes reviewing his 'Bobby' notes that had been logged in his computer.

"Hello, Mr. Peters," answered Daniel. "Thank you for taking my call."

"I'm sorry you had to wait. I was finishing up a call with Congressman John Richards. I hope you understand. So how can I help you?" asked Peters.

"I have a few more questions. If it's OK, I'm gonna put you on speaker so my partner, Detective Williams, can participate." Daniel pressed the speaker button on his phone and set it on the table where both he and Johnny could hear and talk. He pulled his legal pad close so he could see their new questions and, if necessary, refer back to his notes from the previous call to Peters.

"Not a problem. Anything I can do to help."

"I just want to make sure I have everything right. You did say that Jamie Barnes left with Margie Hamilton this past Wednesday. That she was taking him home. Is that correct?"

"Yes."

"And James Barnes. I think you called him Jim Barnes. He works for NAGS and is the father of Jamie Barnes. Is that also correct?"

"Yes."

"Can I speak to Mr. Barnes?"

"He's not at work today. Have you tried calling him? I believe I gave you his number."

"When was the last time you saw Jim Barnes?"

"Wednesday. He came back to the office right after Jamie left with Margie. Why are you asking so many questions about Jim?"

Daniel ignored Peter's question.

"According to *my* notes, you said that Mr. Barnes *wasn't* at work Wednesday."

"Technically, he *wasn't* at work Wednesday, but he did come by to pick up some of his things. Just so you know, and this is not to go beyond this phone conversation, Jim Barnes is on administrative leave." Wayne made sure to reference Jim in the present tense. "We felt he needed time off from work. His mother had just recently passed away and he and his wife got a divorce. We felt he was too stressed to work effectively. He was *very* impatient with our members and supporters. And he got easily angered at the most trivial things. For instance, when he came by Wednesday, he found out that I had given Jamie some money for gas. Instead of being grateful, he blew up, cursed me, told me to stay away from his family and left in a huff. I'd never seen him act that way."

Peters was amazed at how easy it was to adlib an answer. He quickly added his reply to his notes so he wouldn't forget what he had told the detective in case he had to tell his story again. His 'shoot from the hip' answer would probably make Bobby proud.

"Just to confirm our earlier phone conversation, you did say that Jim Barnes lives at the Watergate apartments."

"Yes. I can give you that address *again* if you need it. But just so you know, the apartment is actually owned by NAGS. Jim is staying there until he can find his own place. Because of his position with the company we haven't given him any deadline to move out. But what does any of this have to do with Margie's death? I don't see…"

"I would appreciate it if you would let me ask the questions, Mr. Peters."

There was no response from Peters. He didn't need to. Everything was going fine, just as Bobby had said.

Daniel continued. "You said Jim Barnes and his wife had recently divorced. What is his wife's name and where does she live?"

"Ex-wife, Elaine Barnes," replied Peters, correcting the detective. He then proceeded to give Daniel, the ex-wife's Georgetown address. Almost immediately, Johnny left the kitchen but not before mouthing *I'm on it.* To which, Daniel gave a thumbs up.

"Detective Whitehead, would you mind telling me what Jim Barnes or Jamie Barnes has to do with Margie's carjacking? I've been very patient. If you're not willing to tell me, I do have *other ways* of finding out."

Although Daniel had never met Wayne Peters and had never had a conversation with the man until earlier today which had been cordial, Peters' reputation was not that of an arrogant man, not one to abuse his power as the executive vice-president of one of the country's most powerful organization with massive political ties. But that was hard to tell with the way the conversation had preceded thus far. The fact that Daniel personally opposed Peters' organization's stance on many gun-related issues added to the difficulty of the conversation. While he agreed with NAGS that homeowners in the Washington D.C. area should have the right to own guns for hunting and the protection of their families, he opposed the quantity and types of guns that NAGS so vigorously advocated. Daniel felt there was no need for anyone to own more than a couple of small caliber guns or hunting rifles. And certainly not AK-47s or extended clips and magazines. Daniel feared that once the gates of controlled gun ownership were open, the criminal and terrorist elements would legally abuse the system. Regardless of his feelings toward NAGS or Wayne Peters, he needed to make certain that he was fair and open-minded in his investigation of Margie Hamilton's death.

"You've been very helpful, Mr. Peters. And I don't mean to be so evasive about this case. But, because Margie Hamilton worked for NAGS, this homicide has attracted a lot of attention from my boss, his boss, the chief, the mayor, local and national media. You name it. My partner and I are under a lot of pressure to bring this case to a speedy conclusion. Having said that, we want to make absolutely sure that we find the person or persons responsible. We cannot afford to make mistakes. And we certainly don't want the media running off half-cocked, making false accusations or harmful innuendos based on hearsay. By keeping facts close to the vest, we feel like *we* are in control and can conduct our investigation unimpeded. Now. Jamie Barnes. As far as we know, he was the last person to see Margie Hamilton alive. His father, Jim Barnes..." Daniel stopped to think about what he should tell Peters. After a few moments of deliberation, Daniel felt it best if Peters was on his side. The last thing he needed was more heat from above. "What I tell you next must remain in the strictest of confidence because it involves your organization. I ask you to tell *no one.*" Daniel paused to let the words sink in. Then. "Jim Barnes, or at least we believe it to be Jim Barnes, was found shot in the chest. He's dead. We found his body in Jamie Barnes' basement."

Wayne Peters gasped. He, too, paused. But for effect.

"Jim? Dead? That can't be. He was just here, Wednesday. But you did say you *think* it's Jim. So there's a chance you could be wrong?"

"Like I said, we're not a hundred percent certain since we don't have a positive ID," responded Daniel. "That's why I hesitate to give out unconfirmed information."

"Oh, God. I hope you're wrong! Let's pray you're mistaken. We've been so devastated around here with Margie's death. Now Jim's? I can't believe it. This is unreal. Detective Whitehead, I appreciate your confidence, and now I understand why you were so elusive. Forgive me for my, shall we say, less than gentlemanly behavior. If there's anything, and I mean anything, that I, or our organization, can do, please call me."

Just as the call was ending, Johnny returned. Peters gave Daniel his office, home, and cell phone numbers then hung up. After a shaky start, the call ended on a positive note.

"So what'd you find out?" asked Daniel.

"No answer at the ex-wife's house or the Watergate apartment. I think we need to send a couple of our guys over to check them both out, just in case. Jamie could be at either."

"Agreed," replied Daniel.

"And for what it's worth, I thought it odd that Peters never asked about Jamie. Didn't ask if we had him in custody, if he was involved, or if he did any of the killings. Nothing."

"No. But I wouldn't read anything into it. After all, he's not a detective."

"So you two are buddies now?"

Daniel ignored the comment and, instead, called in a request for the on-duty judge to issue search warrants for the residences of James H. Barnes III, James H. Barnes and his ex-wife, Elaine. At the same time, Johnny called dispatch and requested police squads be sent to both residences once the warrants had been issued. A search of the DMV records showed a 2006 BMW, model 745 registered to a James H.

Barnes at his ex-wife's Georgetown address. Daniel added the BMW to the BOLO.

Like maggots seeking out manure, the media arrived in full force requesting a statement from the police. Satisfying them was always one of the hardest aspects of any case. You wanted to tell them enough but not too much. Johnny always volunteered as he was a master at handling their voracious appetite for the macabre. After letting the herd stew a bit, Johnny appeared at the end of the driveway, not too far from Jamie's old Cadillac and gave them as many facts as possible but would not ID the victim since the identification was not official. Neither did he make any connection between this shooting and Margie Hamilton's. He would only say that Jamie Barnes who lived at the residence was considered a 'person of interest.'

While Johnny was out fending off the media, Daniel walked back down to the basement to find Bennie Archer examining the hardpan floor around the body.

"Looks like someone tried digging a grave," Bennie offered as he saw Daniel at the foot of the steps.

"Yeah. That's what it seems. Any chance of us getting together tomorrow morning, say 7 a.m., with your preliminary findings? I'd like to get on a whiteboard, map this out, and see if anything jumps at us. "

"That'll work. Tell Wrinkles, this time I'll bring the breakfast snacks."

As Daniel headed up the steps, two men with a stretcher headed down the steps to meet Bennie. Their job was to transport the body to the morgue where DFS would continue their investigation and conduct an autopsy. Daniel went outside where he found Johnny… antsy.

"You ready to get back to the office?" asked Daniel. "I need to make a few calls."

"If you're waiting for me, you're backing up, Danny boy."

"By the way, we got a meeting with Bennie tomorrow at 7 a.m. Says he's gonna bring the breakfast snacks."

"Oh Jeez, you know what that means. Lox and day-old bagels. You know that old fart still has his first nickel? You ever see the car he drives when off duty? Makes that old Cadillac over there look like something right out of the showroom."

Daniel and Johnny were silent in thought as they headed back to their office. Both men were mentally working the case. Questions occupied their thoughts. Did Jamie kill Margie or was she carjacked? If he did kill her, why? And did he kill his father? And if so, why? And where *was* he?   If he was the guilty party, did he have an accomplice? Maybe the second driver in the video surveillance tape? And where did Otto Max fit into the picture?   And then there was Margie's coat. Where was it?   So many unanswered questions and all seem to be pointing to Jamie Barnes. But was he another victim, yet to be found?

Chapter 68

Friday, December 29, 2006, 3:05 p.m. EST

Wayne sat back in his office chair staring at the ceiling thinking about his last phone call. By Bobby's standards, he'd done good, as they say. The way he handled the detective and his questions couldn't have gone better. He never thought himself much of a good liar, but even he believed what he had said. And the way he said it? He probably could have passed a polygraph test. Even so, it bothered him that he had pulled it off with such ease. Was he becoming another Bobby? Do whatever it takes to protect one's job, career, and reputation?

Knowing the devil would be returning soon, he leaned forward and began keying into his laptop all the notes he had made during the phone call with the detective. The lies, half-truths, and truths. He and Bobby had to make sure they were consistent in whatever they said.

He had just finished his update to his 'Bobby' notes when he heard the sound of heavy footsteps making their way up the stairs. It was Bobby.

"This is all I could find," he said, laying the red-roped, brown fan folders on Wayne's desk. He took off his overcoat, threw it on one of the two wing chairs facing the desk and sat down in the other.

Without saying a word, Wayne pulled the folders over to him and did an inventory of the names printed on the outside. 'Not good' was all he said as he carried the folders into the security vault and locked them in one of their secure filing cabinets.

"Not even a *thank you* or a *kiss my ass*?" asked Bobby.

"Sorry. Just disappointed."

"Besides Richards, which other ones can hurt us?"

"All of them. But, if I had to guess," mulled Wayne, "probably Judge Stewart. But, it doesn't matter. Like I said, if any of them fall into the wrong hands, we're toast. For the life of me, I can't think of why Jim would take some of them and leave the rest in the safe. That doesn't make any sense. But given his state of mind…"

"You think he could have mailed them to a board member, to get back at us? Or worse, to the perverts named on the folders?"

"I don't think so. That doesn't make any sense. He would've lost his leverage with us. Plus *his* job would have been in more jeopardy than ours since he was the 'Special Events' coordinator. It was at those events and mainly at the lodge where most of the pictures were taken. They would think he took them. No, I don't think he had enough time to do anything with them. And if he had, we would've already heard from at least one of those *perverts*, as you call them."

"Good point. So what about Jim's car? You think he could have brought them to the office the day you shot him?" asked Bobby, continuing to offer solutions.

"Yes! Yes! That's gotta be it! I don't know why I didn't think of that. It's the only thing that makes sense. We've got time to go back to the apartment…"

Bobby began shaking his head and waving his hand back and forth stopping Wayne in mid-sentence.

"Not gonna happen. I left the car at Elaine's. Part of my plan. So there's no way we can be seen anywhere near that car or that house."

"So unless we can figure a way of getting the car back, we're screwed," said Wayne, racking his brain for other options.

"I say we start preparing ourselves for the fallout. We're going to have to make it appear as though Jim was doing this on his own, without our knowledge. Then, get our lawyers on board," responded Bobby, already thinking of ways to distance himself from Wayne, Jim and NAGS.

"Lawyers! That's it! Jim's car, my car, your truck. They're all leased. That means they are *our* property. *NAGS'* property. Our lawyers should be able to get Jim's car back without a whole lot of effort since it wasn't used in the commission of a crime."

"If anyone can get that *damn* car back, it's our lawyers. They're the best. Glad I thought of it," gloated Bobby. "I say we let them do their job, we do ours and quit worrying."

"I'm glad we've got that solved," said Wayne, not believing for one moment the folder issue was over. "By the way, you were also right about the police. That Detective Whitehead called just before you got here and asked about Jim. Asked me the last time I saw him. I told him everything we discussed. It seemed to satisfy him. I worked into the conversation that Jim came looking for Jamie and left here upset, mad, even cursing. After that, he confided in me that Jim was dead. I acted shocked and upset. I think I was pretty convincing if I must say so myself."

"See. I told you. Don't complicate things. Keep it simple and real. Everything will work out," commented Bobby. Then, suddenly. "Wait a minute. I thought you were seeing Richards. You didn't talk to the cops while he was here, did you?"

"No. He was a no-show. He called, instead."

"So what'd he want? More Super Bowl tickets? Masters tickets? Final Four tickets? A blow job?"

"Do you always have to be so crass? He was actually very pleasant. He immediately jumped on board with our *'If only Margie'* campaign. And then talked about setting up a victim's family fund in Margie Hamilton's name. He said he'd just thought of it. Can you believe that?"

"What an ass! That fucker's never had an original thought in his life. So, what'd you tell him?"

"I acted as if I had never heard of it before. Told him it was a great idea. Then I told him that I would bring it up when we went over to the Hamilton's tonight. Then he asked if he could tag along. He wanted to *personally* talk to the family about the Margie Hamilton Victim's Trust Fund. So I put him on hold and called Kyle who said OK. So, now the three of us are going. We gotta pick him up at 6:15."

"Great. One big kumbaya."

"One last thing. He also wanted to talk about Jim. He said he got an email from one of the board members who was pretty upset that we had placed Jim on administrative leave. Richards wanted to make sure that Jim knew that *he* wasn't the one responsible. He wanted me to assure him that I wouldn't fire him. So I told him that wasn't even a consideration. That we were giving him some time off to get over his grief and his divorce. That he would be back sometime in January."

"Wayne, you're getting good at this. I know I'm repeating myself but see how easy this is? Not like all that bullshit you were planning. Now once the police get to Elaine's house and find her and the boy, it's over. Finished. Kaput," replied Bobby with a smile growing on his face that was only exceeded in size by his ego.

At five o'clock, they turned on the local FOX channel. The lead story began with a grim-faced, local reporter, wearing a black trench coat, black fedora, and black gloves, standing behind an old car with a white clapboard house in the far background. Everything in sight was cordoned off with yellow crime scene tape. He reported that an unidentified dead body had been found in its basement. The TV camera zoomed in on the house showing the police and the DFS agents, all scurrying about. While the reporter continued to talk, a video began to play showing a body being transported from the house to an ambulance. Next, an interview with one of the lead detectives at the scene was played. The detective was mostly non-committal but did say the cause of death appeared to be a gunshot. The reporter identified Jamie Barnes, an occupant of the house, as a person of interest.

Bobby and Wayne listened to the entire newscast including a replay of their earlier news conference. There was no mention of a link between this murder, Margie or NAGS. But they knew it was inevitable. The news ended with no mention of the two dead bodies in Georgetown. They knew that too was inevitable.

Bobby smiled at Wayne. Everything was going perfect.

Chapter 69

Friday, December 29, 2006, 3:20 p.m. EST

Before leaving Washington, Jamie decided to swing by his house to pick up a suitcase and a few clothes. There was even a slim possibility that his Dad might be there, waiting for him before he called the police. He wouldn't mind seeing his old man one more time. Getting one more hug. One more sermon. But he didn't need his help. Maybe leaving the country was his best option. Maybe not. Regardless, he was certain he wasn't going to spend the rest of his life behind bars. His Dad would want him to face the punishment. Do the time. It was the right thing. But knowing that for the rest of their lives, they would only be able to see each other through a scratched-up, smudged Plexiglas window while talking on a rank-smelling jail phone wasn't going to happen.

As he approached his house, the traffic slowed to a snail's pace. Only when he saw the TV vans, police cars and trucks parked in *his* driveway and double-parked on the street in front of *his* house did panic set in. Had his Dad called the police? Or had someone else discovered his mother's body, found his bloodstained clothes in the house and had called them. Were they there to arrest him? If so, why the yellow crime scene tape? Were they there looking for the murder weapon? Then he realized he didn't even know what the murder weapon was. Surely he should have remembered how he killed his own mother. As he inched closer to the front of his house, he could see his old Cadillac in the driveway with doors and trunk open with cops bagging everything in sight. Knowing that his Dad had switched cars, maybe he was there. But why? And why had he switched cars? Nothing made sense to him. But one thing was certain, he had no plans to pull into the driveway and turn himself in. Not before he had time to think things through with a clear mind which meant no more drugs… at least temporarily.

Once he reached the front of his house, he came to a complete stop just like all the other rubberneckers had done before him. With the house surrounded by yellow crime scene tape, it was like watching a TV police show but for real. He didn't know how long he had stopped but it must have been longer than the driver in the back of him could tolerate.

The next thing he heard was the blaring of the guy's horn. As he slowly moved forward, he saw a police officer in the middle of the road, directing traffic. Unnerved but calm, Jamie rolled his window down and stopped alongside the patrolman.

"Officer, what's going on?" He hoped to learn something. Anything. Instead, the officer barked at him to move on, motioning even faster with his hands.

Jamie slowly picked up speed. He peered at the rearview mirror to get one last glimpse of his house. It was old and dated but it was his. He felt violated with all those strangers rummaging through his house. And the things they would find! His assortment of pipes, bongs, rubber hoses, drug magazines. The press would make him out to be a drug-crazed murderer, which, evidently, he was. But he didn't care what they wrote about him. What he hated the most was the negative impact it might have on his Dad. He was already depressed enough with his divorce and the loss of Grammy. He prayed this wouldn't crush him or destroy the unconditional love he had for his murderous son.

Jamie shook his head. What a failure he was. A total loser. It couldn't possibly get any worse than this.

Chapter 70

Friday, December 29, 2006, 4:39 p.m. EST

It was times like these that Daniel wished he had gone to law school. He had chosen homicide as a career. It had not chosen him. Reeling in gang members, thugs, and career criminals, people worse than animals who killed just to be killing with no remorse or guilt… that was his calling. Putting them behind bars for the rest of their lives is what motivated him. But more often than not, most murders were committed by someone the victim(s) knew – family, friend, co-worker, neighbor. The worst kind to investigate. And the Hamilton / Barnes' murders appeared to fall into that category with Jamie Barnes being both friend *and* relative.

Daniel was busy studying his notes on the two cases when Johnny walked up to his desk with a cup of coffee in one hand and a Mr. Goodbar in the other. Johnny did his best thinking in his walks to and from the breakroom.

"What? No Snickers?" asked Daniel.

"Nah. Decided to venture out in my old age. Hey, you want a bite? This one has sections. You want me to break you off one?"

"Just one? No. I'm good. So, Wrinkles. I was thinking we should call the Hamilton's. Let them know about Jamie Barnes before they hear it on the news. You know it won't be long before the reporters connect the two killings if they haven't already. What do you think?"

Johnny nodded as he took a chomp out of two sections of his candy bar.

Daniel dialed and Kyle Hamilton answered the call in a whispered, "*hello.*"

"I'm sorry to bother you, Kyle. This is Detective Whitehead. Is this a bad time?" He set his cell on speakerphone and laid it on his desk in front of him. Johnny stood close by.

"Yes… No… We're at the funeral home picking out a casket," Kyle responded with his words moving from a whisper to his normal voice. "OK. I can talk now. I'm out in the hallway. So have you found out anything?"

"I'll make it brief. We have a suspect. Actually, more of a person of interest. Unfortunately, he's not in custody yet, but we wanted you to know before you heard it on the news or some reporter called you."

"I'm listening," answered Kyle then mouthed *Detective Whitehead* to Aaron and Katie who had joined him.

"After talking to you, we called Wayne Peters and found out that the last person that might have seen your mother alive was the son of a NAGS' employee. His full name is James H. Barnes III, known as Jamie Barnes. While we aren't certain...."

"Jamie Barnes?" gasped Kyle, interrupting the detective. "No way. No way! Jamie has problems, but he's not a killer. You're moving in the wrong direction!"

"*You* know Jamie Barnes?" asked Daniel Whitehead, having been taken by complete surprise. Johnny almost dropped his coffee by Kyle's response.

"Of course I know him. At one time, he was my best friend."

Daniel's cell phone rang. He didn't answer. He was trying to listen to Kyle. Then Johnny's cell phone rang. He answered it, listened and then interrupted Daniel.

"Daniel, we gotta go. Now! They've found another body."

"Kyle, I'm sorry I'm gotta cut you off. Something's come up."

"Why do you think Jamie…"

"I'm sorry, but I've *got* to go! I'll call you back." He picked up his phone and pressed the 'OFF' key.

"What's going on?" Daniel asked as he grabbed his overcoat.

"They found a woman's body at Elaine Barnes' Georgetown address. They've already called Bennie. He's supposed to meet us there." Within minutes, the two detectives were heading out of the building.

"Did you hear Kyle?" asked Daniel.

"You mean about Jamie being his best friend? Yeah. Talk about being blindsided. I didn't see that coming at all. This case has had more twists and turns than a square dance."

Within minutes the two detectives pulled out of the police parking lot with the siren blaring and the emergency warning lights flashing. The case seemed to be taking on a life of its own. It was running and they were walking. They needed to close the gap. And soon.

Chapter 71

Friday, December 29, 2006, 5:12 p.m. EST

Yellow crime scene tape always brought out the crowd, regardless of the neighborhood, regardless of the weather. By the time Johnny and Daniel arrived at Elaine Barnes' house, curious neighbors who rarely spoke to one another were huddled in the street and on the sidewalks talking to each other like they were the best of friends, asking if they knew what happened. Rumors were cropping up faster than zits on a teenager. It was exciting yet disturbing as crime scenes were virtually non-existent in high-end neighborhoods such as this.

Daniel pulled his government-issued Ford past the patrolman directing traffic and double-parked on the street next to one of the three police cars already at the scene. Normally, crimes committed in Georgetown were handled by the 2nd District. But because this crime appeared to be related to the Hamilton / Barnes murders, the case was handed off to Daniel and Johnny from the 5th District. Both men quickly exited the vehicle and surveyed the crowd, looking for Jamie or anyone suspicious who might have stayed around to view the excitement of their deadly handiwork. This was rare, but the two detectives always made it a habit to check out the onlookers. Not seeing anything out of the ordinary, they made their way into the house and to the murder victim. Bennie Archer arrived minutes later along with two DFS vans. Bennie parked behind Daniel's car and the two vans parked in the driveway. Johnny met him at the front door.

"Sorry, I'm late. I got here as fast as I could. Five o'clock traffic, you know," said Bennie as he grabbed a pair of booties and latex gloves from his pocket and slipped them on and walked in with Johnny.

On the way into the living room, the detective pointed out the dark-stained leather coat on the floor near the front door and the white terry cloth robe on the stairs leading into the foyer. Bennie took it all in. "This one's ugly," he continued as they entered the living room where Elaine Barnes' lifeless body lay. Daniel saw Bennie, gave him the high sign, then continued taking photos of the body and the area surrounding the body. "Looks like we've got one sick dude on our hands," added Johnny.

"You would think that after all these years we'd get used to this. But I can't. Why do people do this? It makes no sense. This wasn't something done in a fit of passion," Bennie observed as he looked at Elaine's disfigured face. "This was premeditated. Whoever did this wanted to make sure the victim wouldn't see another sunrise, drink another cup of coffee, have a..."

"OK. Ok. We got it!" interrupted Johnny knowing Bennie was about to start orating on the imperfections of mankind. "Hey! Speaking of coffee, Daniel tells me you're bringing munchies tomorrow morning. You win the lottery?"

Bennie ignored Johnny's comment. Instead, he knelt down by the body to get a closer look at the smashed-in face of the victim.

"You're right, Johnny. Whoever did this had to be one sick bastard. I'm not sure I've ever seen such viciousness. Fortunately, I don't think she ever saw it coming," Bennie commented without looking up. He then began smelling the Oriental rug. "Coffee," he confirmed. "Looks like she was carrying that tray of coffee mugs when she got whacked." He then pointed his camera at the area of the rug where the tray, mugs, sugar bowl, and creamer lay scattered.

"That must have been some really bad coffee," mused Johnny.

"Don't make light of this, Johnny," Bennie barked. "This is... was a human being we're talking about."

"Sorry, Bennie. I'm trying to get through this thing just like you."

"So you and Daniel think the Barnes' kid did this? Killed his father *and* mother?" asked Bennie.

"It appears that way. But we need to do our homework before we start pointing fingers. Two different murder weapons and two different degrees of violence. One a single gunshot to the chest and the other a brutal, vicious attack to the head and face with God knows what. Could one person be capable of doing both?"

"Well, speaking of guns, we found a 9mm pistol hidden in a golf bag down in the basement at the young Barnes' house," said Bennie. "There's a real good chance it's the same weapon used in the Hamilton case."

"So I guess he forgot to bring it here and brought a golf club instead," interjected Daniel extemporaneously.

Johnny laughed first. Then Daniel, realizing the insensitivity of his comment. Then, even Bennie laughed. A needed respite for all three.

"Bennie," continued Daniel, somewhat red-faced. "Johnny and I are going to take a quick look around before your guys bag everything. We'll be careful."

Bennie nodded, and the two detectives left the meticulous ME to do his work.

They started in the dining room. It looked like something out of an Architectural Digest magazine. A large banded inlay mahogany antique table was its centerpiece with an impressive antique 18 light Baccarat crystal chandelier centered above. Surrounding the table were twelve matching ball and claw chairs. On one wall was a large antique china cabinet and an equally beautiful antique sideboard on the opposite wall. The hardwood floor was covered with a 10x14 silk Persian rug. Other than the fact that the victim's last few steps were through this room, it held no clues nor produced any evidence for the case.

The kitchen would have made a chef proud with its Viking appliances, pristine white cabinets, and newly installed dark granite countertops. It was neat and orderly with everything in its place. The only evidence that it was an actual working kitchen was the grounds left in the Cuisinart coffee maker.

As they moved down the back hall to the first-floor bedroom, a distinct odor of old vomit caught their attention even before they entered the room. Unlike the rest of the house, this room was a mess. They found a bag of dirty clothes on the floor next to the bed and a pool of dry vomit on the bed. On the floor of the far side of the bed lay an empty liquor bottle in another pool of nearly dried vomit. Lying close by was a fire poker, the probable murder weapon. Upon careful inspection, Daniel noticed what appeared to be fragments of skull and brain matter stuck to the end. On the far right night table was an empty prescription bottle of a well-known anti-depression medicine.

In the adjoining bathroom, they found small amounts of water on the shower floor. A balled up, damp washcloth lay on top of a soap bar in the shower's soap dish and a damp towel hung neatly on a towel rod next to the shower door. The sink contained small amounts of dried shaving cream and remnants of a two or three-day-old beard. A comb lay on the counter, and a used razor and a string of dental floss were found in a wastebasket next to the bathroom counter.

After making numerous photos and taking several pages of notes, the two detectives moved to the second floor. The only room of significance was the master bedroom. Other than an unmade bed and a broken mirror in that room, the upstairs was immaculate, just like most of the rest of the house.

"So, you got any ideas?" inquired Daniel as he and Johnny walked down the stairs to the first floor and then into the living room where one of the forensic techs was videotaping everything.

"I don't know, Daniel. I should probably pass until we see what Bennie has to offer."

"Well, just give me your gut feeling."

"On the surface, it appears that Jamie is responsible for all three killings. As far as we know, he was the last person to see Margie Hamilton alive. Then we find his father dead in his basement. And now we find his mother dead with presumably the boy's clothes on the first floor. I say case closed. Everyone is happy. VM, the commander, chief, mayor. Everybody except the victims and Jamie. But why? Drugs? Money? Assuming he sold Margie's car to Otto, he would have money for drugs. Let's say he was paying off a drug debt. You and I both know that dealers don't let addicts carry that much drug debt. Not a brand new car's worth. And then we have the coffee mugs and stains near the body. If they were in the midst of some kind of heated argument over money or drugs, why would she stop to go make coffee? If Jamie did this, he must be one callous, heartless son-of-a-bitch. But you asked me my gut feeling and my gut feeling says that something's not right here."

Daniel could see the look in Johnny's eyes. He'd seen it before. He was mad. Ready to wreak havoc on the butcher responsible for the evil, malicious hack job done to the defenseless woman sprawled on the floor. But he wasn't ready to blame Jamie Barnes even though everything seemed to point to him.

Having seen enough, the two detectives headed toward the front door. Before Johnny could reach for the knob, the door swung open. A patrolman, who was obviously on a mission, stood at the entrance. He quickly introduced himself and said he'd found a possible witness – a next-door neighbor. He also asked if someone could please talk to the press. That they were hounding everyone, looking for information.

Almost simultaneously, both detectives removed their latex gloves and booties and pulled on their leather gloves.

Johnny headed down to the street to give a statement to the ever-growing media. With the press and a number of nearby neighbors listening, Johnny informed them that James H. Barnes III, aka Jamie Barnes, was a 'person of interest' in this case and the 4th Street case. That he was the son of Jim and Elaine Barnes, recently divorced. He then took questions, most of which got the 'It's an ongoing investigation' or 'No comment' response, especially if the questions pertained to NAGS or Margie Hamilton. Then he left. The media continued to shout out questions knowing there would be no answers.

Meanwhile, Daniel followed the patrolman down the walkway to the sidewalk where a heavy-set middle-aged woman was waiting just outside the crime scene tape. She was wearing a full-length mink coat with matching hat. In her arms, she held a small fluffy white dog. The woman who was almost as wide as she was tall looked more like a brown bear than a Georgetown housewife. Her breath wreaked of alcohol and cigarettes. After quick introductions, the patrolman excused himself and rejoined his fellow officers. Daniel wrote down the lady's name – Chloe Wilson - her address and telephone numbers and automatically gave the lady his business card.

"What's going on over there? Did Jamie OD?" asked the lady.

Daniel ignored the question. "The officer said you were witness to some type of disturbance last night. Is that correct?"

"Yes, sir. Do you mind if we go inside? It's really cold out here." The Wilson lady then lifted up the yellow tape and began to walk under it until Daniel halted her.

"Ma'am. I appreciate you coming forward to help in our investigation, but we can't go into that house. It's a crime scene. We might contaminate the evidence. We can either go inside *your* house, get in my car, or we can stay right here and talk," he replied trying to be polite to the nosy woman.

The lady said nothing but moved back outside the crime scene tape not hiding the fact that she wasn't happy she hadn't gotten her way.

Daniel continued. "Can you tell me exactly what you saw, heard and when?"

"Well, I didn't see anything. But I heard Jamie. Jamie Barnes. Elaine's son. He was outside yelling. At 1 a.m. in the morning!"

Is there another 1 a.m. beside in the morning? thought Daniel. "How'd you know it was Jamie Barnes if you didn't see him?"

"I recognized his voice. He was yelling so loud that he woke me and Pookie up."

"Pookie's your husband?"

"No. He's much better than a husband. He's my baby. My Maltese," cooed the woman as she gave her little white companion a kiss on the mouth.

"So you know Jamie Barnes?"

"No. Not really. I've only lived here for about three years. Jamie had already moved out... well... more like kicked out before I got here."

"So how'd you know it was Jamie's voice?"

"Well, this isn't the first time he's done this. If Elaine hadn't already told you, Jamie's into drugs, big time. Elaine and I have talked about it many times. She's been much nicer and closer to me since she got divorced. Jim was such an ass, like most men... er... husbands."

"So why was he yelling? What was he yelling about? Was he yelling threats to Ms. Barnes?"

"Oh God no. He sounded like a lovesick puppy. Yelling things like *'he loved her'* and *'please don't be angry.'* Things like that. Anyway, according to Elaine, Jamie wanted her and Jim, that's Elaine's ex-husband, to get back together. That Jamie felt responsible for their divorce. She told me that the boy *never* came over or even talked to her unless he was stoned. I'm sure that's what happened last night. Like I said, he's done this before." The lady caressed the head of her dog then gave him another kiss on his mouth. The second kiss was too much for Daniel who chose to look down at his notepad, instead. *I wonder if that dog knows where **that** mouth's been.*

"Did you see Jamie or Elaine this morning?"

"No. After episodes like last night with Jamie, I would always give her time to get some extra sleep the next morning. You know, to let her get over the ordeal. So I never called her until after lunch, you know, to see what happened. To see if there's anything I could do to help. Now here's what's strange. When I took Pookie out for his morning walk, *Jim's* car was in the driveway. Not that old beat up piece of crap of Jamie's. See, Elaine always made Jim come to get Jamie. To get him out of her house. And believe me, she didn't care what time it was. She *did not* want him at her house, especially in that condition. So *Jamie's* car would always be out in front of her house the next day or until he came back to get it which sometime could be days. But this morning, Jim's car was there when I walked Pookie. Not Jamie's. And now, nobody's car's there. But I guess you can see that."

"So you didn't see Jim, Elaine or Jamie last night or this morning?"

"No. That's what I told you."

"What kind of car does Jim drive?"

"He has a Silver Mercedes. But I don't know what model or anything. I'm not a car person."

"How'd you know it was Jim's car?"

"The license plate. NAGS 2. When I moved here, I asked Elaine if that was supposed to be funny. You know that he nags, too. But she told me that's where Jim works. I'd never heard of NAGS until I met the Barnes. I'm not a gun person either." The dog started squirming, so the lady put him down on the sidewalk where he squatted like a girl dog and peed right where she sat him. When the dog finished, he gave Daniel a look that could only be described as condescending. The lady grunted as she bent over to pick up her dog.

"Did you see who left in the Mercedes?"

"No. I called Elaine around 1 o'clock this afternoon, but no one answered. Then around three. Again, no answer. I was about to call again when all the police cars came driving up. I figured they were looking for Jamie?"

"Why do you say that?"

"You know. His drug problem and all. There's no telling what these addicts do when they need drugs, and I *know* Elaine doesn't give him any money."

Daniel closed his notebook. "Thank you, Mrs. Wilson. You've been very helpful. If you can think of anything else, please call me, anytime, day or night. My number's on the card."

"It's Miss... Miss Wilson. Detective, you never told me what happened next door."

"I'm sorry, Miss Wilson. I can't comment on an ongoing investigation. But I'm sure you'll probably know *everything* by the time our investigators leave."

Daniel turned from the plump woman and her dog and headed up the sidewalk where he saw Johnny, waiting by their squad car. On his way to the car, he pulled out his cell phone and called Kyle. Before the call was finished, all the nearby neighbors had descended on the Wilson lady. Her mouth was working in overdrive.

"I hope you don't have any plans tonight," said Daniel as he and Johnny were fastening their seatbelts.

"Just my usual Friday night date with my recliner and a beer. Why?"

"We're meeting the Hamilton's around seven. He has questions and I have questions. We both need answers. Oh, I did find out that Jim Barnes drives a silver Mercedes with a *NAGS 2* license plate. Obviously a company car. I put out a BOLO. We have to assume that Jamie is driving it."

"What about the witness. Was she any help?"

"Yes. I'll fill you in on the way back to the office. Oh. And remind me to renew my PETA membership."

Chapter 72

Friday, December 29, 2006, 6:12 p.m. EST

The motion-sensitive spotlights dutifully awakened as the silver Mercedes, licensed plate *NAGS 2*, breached the lights' surveillance perimeter, highlighting the curving driveway leading up to the NAGS hunting lodge. Tire tracks left by the large sedan were quickly being erased by the heavy snow falling over the mountainous region of Virginia. The car's wipers worked furiously sweeping the large snowflakes from the car's windshield providing an unobstructed view of the lodge.

It was ironic that Jamie had chosen the NAGS lodge as his safe haven as he was no longer welcome there – at least not since the break-in. He had never been formally charged with the crime, but that didn't matter. And the fact that he didn't do it didn't matter either. What mattered was that everyone, including his Dad, believed he was guilty. No investigation, no trial, no discussion.

Regardless, seeing the lodge brought comfort to Jamie, bringing back wonderful memories of the many times he and his Dad had spent together there. Hiking, camping, communing with nature. Just the two of them, having fun being together. Even though it was a hunting lodge, Jamie wasn't a hunter. The truth be known, he was afraid of any kind of firearm, especially handguns. Jim Barnes recognized his son's fear but never exerted any undue pressure for him to overcome his phobia. Of course, no trip was complete without one of his Dad's famous sermons. As a youngster, his Dad "preached" about getting a good education, not worrying about always being one of the guys, always doing your best, always telling the truth, and being a gentleman. But as Jamie slid into the black hole of drugs, the sermons changed. Now they dealt primarily with his addiction to drugs and putting his life back together.

His last trip to the lodge was a little over a year ago. That's when his Dad told him about his and Elaine's decision to end their thirty-year marriage. Even with the love/hate relationship Jamie had with his mother, he didn't want his parents to divorce. Irreconcilable differences were the only reason Jim gave for the divorce, never mentioning their constant bickering over Jamie's lifestyle of drugs nor Elaine's possible infidelities as the real main reasons. Jamie begged, pleaded then broke down in tears in an effort to change his Dad's mind. When his Dad refused to even consider reconciliation, Jamie ran out the front door kicking and bashing anything in his way. He ran down to the highway where he hitch-hiked back to Washington and proceeded to get wasted. He stayed that way for a week.

There was no plan to get wasted this trip. No time. No Drugs. He parked the car in the barn, grabbed the bag of groceries that he'd bought earlier at a K-Mart in Chantilly, Virginia, and closed the two large doors behind him. He made his way to the lighted porch where he began working through his Dad's keys in search of the one that unlocked the front door. Had none of the keys worked, he was prepared to break into the lodge. After all, he had already been accused and convicted in everybody's mind of the earlier break-in, so he figured he was owed the benefits.

As he opened the door, the loud shrill that normally filled the air was silent. A frightening thought occurred to him. What if someone was staying there for the holidays? He flipped on a couple of lights and began a quick search of the bedrooms and closets for clothes and luggage. He was relieved to find none since he had no other place to stay.

The lodge was frigid and smelled of chimney smoke. He cranked up the thermostat to 72 degrees and headed to the fireplace where he added three logs he found in the log holder to the remnants of previously burned logs in the open hearth. Thanks to the gas starter, it wasn't long before they were blazing. Jamie removed his Dad's raincoat and tossed it over one of the two large leather chairs that faced the fireplace. Using the nearby poker iron, he began stoking the remains of the previously burned logs causing them to blaze up and their hot cinders to fall through the grate. The warmth of the fire was soothing to his body but not to his ever racing mind.

Jamie turned off the lights, plopped down in one of the big leather chairs and began to think about his past and his future. His past was easy. It consisted of drugs and more drugs. Everything else was a blur except the friction, disappointment, hurt, anger, heartbreak and emotional bankruptcy he had caused his parents. And the lies! Everything about his past was a bunch of lies – where he was going, who he hung out with, why he skipped school, why he couldn't stay employed. The lies came so quickly and easily that at times he couldn't tell them from the truth. And the stealing! How could he have stooped so low to steal from his own parents – their money, their valuables, even their prescription drugs! Only God knows why he never stole from anyone else. Probably fear. Regardless, he always told himself that he could quit drugs anytime. Yet, even now, he wanted something, anything – crack, weed, cocaine, meth – anything to help him forget the horror and images that filled his mind - those of his dead mother's face and the evil eyes of the devil who, no doubt, was eagerly waiting for him in hell.

Jamie's thoughts turned to his Dad. While outwardly, his Dad expressed anger and bitterness towards his now ex-wife, he knew that deep down, he still loved her. Jamie could never, ever expect his Dad to forgive him. The question that seemed to have taken up residence in his mind was how could he have committed such a horrible deed? How could he have ever crossed that line? To murder his *own mother*? What could have provoked him to the point of becoming that violent? He wasn't that kind of person, not even when he was high. At least that's what everyone said. He and his mother had their differences but he never felt the need to harm her, to kill her. But he did. He had to. She was dead! Tears began to fall. The reality of her death was now sinking in replacing the horror and panic that had consumed him. He loved his mother. She had been hard on him, never believed the lies he told, never gave him any money. But she was right. She knew he would just spend it on drugs. She was ashamed of him, but she should have been ashamed of him. He was ashamed of himself. He was worthless. He had never done anything in his life but go from one high to the next. He couldn't stop the tears and didn't want to. He would never see his mother again. He could never hug her again, hear her voice, see her smile, see her frown - ever again. He was responsible. He had killed her, and by God, it became crystal clear what he had to do. Crystal clear.

The warmth of the fire was anesthetizing. Jamie closed his eyes. Resolution helped his sleep come quickly. For Jamie Barnes, it was the end of what had been a hellish day.

Chapter 73

Friday, December 29, 2006, 6:15 p.m. EST

Wayne and Bobby arrived promptly at 6:15 p.m. at Congressman John Richards' townhouse. The congressman greeted his guests, walked them to the living room, and returned to his bathroom where he spent the next ten minutes working on his comb-over. While the congressman had no patience for people who made *him* late, he had no problem in making others wait on him. When he re-entered the living room, he looked immaculate wearing his neatly pressed H. Huntsman suit, heavily starched white shirt, and solid red tie. Not one strand of his lacquered hair was out of place and would stay that way even in the strongest of winds. Tornadoes from Kansas would have a hard time dislodging a single strand from its designated place. Richards did not apologize for his tardiness but only clapped his hands as a signal to go.

On the way over to Margie Hamilton's apartment, Wayne coached the congressman repeatedly with the names of the Hamilton brothers. Richards was good at many things, but remembering unimportant people's names wasn't one of them. The main purpose of his visit was to initiate the conversation about the Margie Hamilton Victim's Trust Fund and get the brother's approval. Wayne and Bobby were there mainly for support and, if necessary, to provide any details. The trip over was interrupted by a quick stop at Cake Love on U Street where Wayne picked up one of their famous gourmet pound cakes. One never went to a wake without food.

Katie answered the door for the earlier than expected guests and graciously accepted the boxed pound cake from Richards who immediately took full credit for the gift. After introductions were exchanged, the three men shed their coats and laid them across a chair in the foyer with Bobby's LBJ sitting on top. Katie then led the men to the living room and then exited to the kitchen. Kyle and Aaron, who were busy putting together a computerized slide show of Margie's life, immediately stood to meet their guest.

Wayne took the lead and introduced Bobby and the congressman to the two brothers with each guest offering their deepest sympathies and the all too familiar 'if there's anything I can do for you' addendum. Richards' introductions always included direct eye contact and his most sincere handshake which meant adding his left hand to the shake. Neither Kyle nor Aaron had any idea why Peters had invited the congressman but were somewhat awestruck by his presence.

Congressman Richards then offered a prayer. Everyone joined hands as the congressman prayed for hope, courage, and comfort. He ended with the 'Lord's Prayer' with everyone joining in. Wayne was not surprised at how convincingly sincere Richards was with his prayer as he was a better actor than he was a public servant.

After everyone had taken a seat, Katie appeared from the kitchen. "Can I get anyone something to drink or eat? Maybe some coffee and a slice of the delicious smelling pound cake that Congressman Richards was so kind to bring?" Wayne chose not to correct her. Richards was far more important to NAGS than who got credit for bringing a pound cake. Each guest responded with a polite 'No thank you.'

Without hesitation, the congressman began his mission. "Kyle, Aaron. Mr. Peters and Mr. Armstrong have told me a great deal about your mother and what a wonderful person and co-worker she was. Again, I am deeply sorry for your loss. I only wish that I could have had the privilege of meeting her." As Richards spoke those last words, Wayne's head dropped, and he stared at the floor. He couldn't bring himself to look at Kyle, Aaron or Richards, especially Richards. The congressman had to pass by Margie's desk every time he came to Wayne's office. Yet, he barely acknowledged her presence or her greetings when he did. He was far too important to spend any time with anyone like Margie – a mere secretary.

Richards continued. "I can't even begin to imagine how you feel or the pain and suffering that you have endured. And nothing I can say can ease that hurt. I do think of *my* mother and how devastated I would be if something like this happened to her. I have been moved by your loss and would like to somehow, honor your mother. That's why I asked Mr. Peters and Mr. Armstrong to include me in their visit. I hope I haven't overstepped my bounds."

Congressman Richards looked at Kyle then Aaron with his most practiced heartfelt look.

"Absolutely not!" responded Aaron, wondering where this was heading.

"Well, if I may continue," responded Richards smiling very sincerely at the two brothers then to Wayne and Bobby. "Washington has become a very dangerous place to live and work. The number of murders, carjackings, and robberies that occur in this city are a national embarrassment. The majority of these crimes involve illegally obtained handguns, and we as residents and workers of this lovely city have no way to defend ourselves. We are at the mercy of these hoodlums, these lowlifes. But thanks to these two gentlemen," Richards stopped his oration long enough to motion with his hand toward Bobby and Wayne, "we may one day correct that injustice." Seeing that he was confusing his audience, Richards regrouped. "I'm sorry for getting sidetracked, but I get very emotional when I talk about 2nd amendment rights. My *purpose* in coming today is to extend an offer to create a Margie Hamilton Victim's Trust Fund. A fund that helps the families of victims of gun-related deaths here in the District of Columbia. A fund that would offer assistance with funeral expenses, create college scholarships for the orphaned children and offer defensive training courses for the unarmed population. I've discussed this with Mr. Armstrong and Mr. Peters, and they are ready to immediately direct NAGS to place *one million dollars* into the fund, assuming we have your approval."

Neither Kyle nor Aaron responded immediately both trying to take in all that the congressman had just said. Finally, Aaron spoke. "I'm not sure what to say. Your offer is most kind and generous and certainly unexpected. Kyle, unless you believe otherwise, I think it's a wonderful idea. She... she... was a wonderful Mom," stammered Aaron, becoming choked up and teary-eyed. "If there's anything we can do in her memory to ease the pain of other victims' families, I'm all for it. Kyle, how 'bout you?"

"I think it sounds great!" he quickly responded, reining in his emotions.

"Congressman Richards? Do you mind if I ask a couple of questions," asked Aaron, brushing away his emotions, his skeptical side of his demeanor kicking in.

While Aaron was most appreciative of the offer, he was not naïve. He had been around enough politicians to know "buyer beware." They were very generous with other people's money and never offered anything without themselves benefitting somewhere along the way. And NAGS and Congressman Richards were no different. Even though his Mom worked for the organization, he was wary of their motives.

"Oh. Absolutely," responded the congressman, wholeheartedly.

"I don't know if the details have been worked out, but who would administer the fund? Certainly not Kyle or me. It seems like this could be a lot of work, and neither of us has the time, money or resources to do so."

Wayne took the queue from Richards' uncertain look to jump in. "NAGS would administer the fund. We do have the resources to commit to this project. And we have the expertise."

The word 'project' did not sit well with Aaron. A trust fund should be a mission, a calling, not just another work assignment for some underling at NAGS.

"Would Kyle or I have any say as to how any donated monies were spent?"

"Absolutely. We would hope that both of you would take a seat on the trust fund's board," answered Wayne.

"We would like that but would Kyle or I have any authoritative powers? Would we have any veto power on how or which victim's families or recipients, for a better word, were nominated?"

This was NOT what Wayne and Bobby had expected. This was supposed to be a slam dunk. We present, they agree.

"Anyone could suggest or nominate a victim's family, but the board would have the final say as to which families would benefit from the fund and how much money they would receive."

"And what about the veto power? Would Kyle or I have any? And who else would make up the board beside Kyle and me?"

"You and Kyle and the current NAGS board of directors would run the trust and make *all* decisions," replied Wayne, emphasizing 'all.' "Your opinions… yours and Kyle's would carry as much weight as any other board member. We would *not* do anything that would tarnish your mother's good name. You have my promise on that."

Wayne looked at Bobby who nodded his head in approval. Wayne felt he had successfully avoided answering the 'veto power' question because Aaron didn't bring it up again. But Aaron got the message. He and Kyle had *no* veto power. They were only window dressing.

"Earlier, you mentioned only victims of *gun-related* deaths. What about families of victims that were killed by other means? If there was enough money in the trust, could we possibly consider them? After all, if Mom had been killed with a knife, would you three gentlemen be sitting here with this offer? Neither Kyle nor I want this fund to seem political or agenda driven."

That wasn't going to happen. The fund's primary purpose was to serve as an alternate way to educate people on their 2nd amendment rights but in a subliminal way.   Funeral expenses and college scholarships were secondary and of no real importance other than to publicize the fund's existence *and* NAGS.

"I don't think we would have the resources, money or people, to take on that large of a project. I think we would have to limit ourselves to something more manageable and an area that we are most familiar," countered Wayne, adding "at least in the beginning" in an effort to appease Aaron.

No one spoke for what seemed forever. Then as Aaron started to speak the doorbell rang. Katie immediately excused herself from the room. She welcomed the opportunity to leave. At the door were Detectives Whitehead and Williams.

Aaron waited until Katie had left the room to continue. "Congressman Richards, we appreciate you, Mr. Armstrong and Mr. Peters coming over, paying your respects, and making this generous offer. But I think Kyle and I will need to see the details of the plan in writing before we commit our mother's name. What we don't want to see happen is NAGS or anybody else using our mother and her untimely death to further their own agenda. Should we agree to support the trust fund, only the families of the victims should benefit from the fund."

Richards had had enough. "Aaron. Kyle. I see that you have company so we should take our leave. We'll get you a detailed plan of the Victim's fund and will certainly take into consideration every one of your concerns. I can assure you that our intentions are honorable. We appreciate your time, and again we offer our condolences." With that, the three visitors stood, as did Kyle and Aaron, shook hands, and headed to the foyer to retrieve their coats.

None of the three guests were smiling.

Chapter 74

Friday, December 29, 2006, 6:57 p.m. EST

Johnny and Daniel were in the foyer having just removed their coats and Johnny's hat when the three earlier visitors appeared. While the detectives had never met Richards, Armstrong or Peters, they instantly recognized them from their numerous times on TV, especially most recently as they discussed the upcoming Appeals Court case. At the same time, Wayne recognized Johnny Williams as he, too, had appeared on TV many times giving statements and answering questions from the press about ongoing investigations. The two detectives stood aside as the earlier guest donned their coats, exchanged good-byes with the Hamilton's, and then left. They barely acknowledged the two detectives on their way out which suited the two new guests just fine.

Once everyone was seated in the living room, with Johnny, to his delight, given the right half of the sofa, Kyle immediately began his third degree of the detectives – a reversal of roles.

"I saw the news. Everybody's calling Jamie a person of interest. Why do you think *he* killed our Mom? And what about the two carjackers? I thought they were the ones who killed Mom. And that dead man in the house near Catholic University, who was he? And what about the discrepancies you talked about? What…"

"Whoa. Time out," interrupted Daniel cross waving both hands. "Take a breath. I thought *we* were the detectives here."

"I'm sorry. I'm just trying to understand all of this. Especially, after you said Jamie killed our Mom. I'm telling you, that didn't happen. No way."

"We understand your frustration. And just so you know, we only said that Jamie Barnes was a *person of interest*, not that he killed your mother. That's still under investigation," answered Johnny.

"Well. I know Jamie. Aaron knows Jamie. He's not your killer."

"Tell us what you know about him," requested Daniel.

"If it's OK, I'm gonna go way back." Kyle did not wait for a response. "Jamie and I were once best friends. We grew up together. If I wasn't at his house, he was at mine. Mostly mine. He *loved* my Mom, probably more than his own mother. His mom was really tough on him. Always on his case about the way he looked, dressed, acted. Everything. And when I was there, she was always bitching about us making too much noise or coming in the house with dirt on our shoes or eating where we shouldn't. I could go on, but that's beside the point. Jamie and I did everything together, good and bad. In fact, I feel like I'm the one who got him hooked on drugs. I still remember to this day what happened. Jamie and I were thirteen, no… fourteen. We were freshmen in high school. One day, he came over to the house after school. Mom wasn't there. I had found these two joints in a plastic baggie in my bookbag while I was putting away my books. I don't know how they got there unless somebody at school got my bag and theirs confused. Anyway, I told him I wanted us to try them. He looked at me like I was crazy. I told him that everybody was doing it and dared him to smoke one. I told him nothing bad could happen. He refused. He didn't want to do it. I kept on badgering him, telling him that he was a sissy and a pansy if he didn't do it. He finally gave in and…"

"Kyle," interrupted Aaron. "This wasn't all your fault. Those were *my* joints. I'm the one who stuck them in your bag. I had tried smoking weed a couple of times, but it never clicked with me. Made me feel out of control which is not my persona, so I never did it again. I had just gotten them down from the back of the closet and was planning on flushing them down the hall toilet when Mom knocked on our bedroom door. I panicked and hid them in your bag. I meant to get them out and get rid of them, but I somehow got distracted and totally forgot. Anyway, the next day when I came home from school, after baseball practice, I smelled that skunky aroma coming from the back of the house. I found you and Jamie acting like idiots… more so than usual… you know… laughing, thinking everything was funny, falling down stupid, eating everything you could get your hands on. I made some coffee, made you and Jamie drink it, and then made y'all walk around the block with me until I thought you were acting somewhat normal. So I've also felt partly responsible for Jamie's problems. But neither you nor I forced him to continue. That was *his* choice."

Kyle was surprised by Aaron's admission. He never thought his brother ever did anything wrong. He was always the perfect child.

Honor student. Athlete. Eagle Scout. Student Council. Yet, there he was, taking the blame. Protecting his younger brother.

"You asked us to tell you about Jamie. Is this what you want?" asked Kyle.

"Yes. Go on," confirmed Daniel, both he and Johnny nodding.

Kyle continued. "After that, whenever Jamie came over to the house, he would ask me if I had any more weed. I always thought he was just kidding. But he wasn't. I told him that was my one and only time. That I didn't want to do it anymore. Eventually, Jamie quit coming over. Instead, he began hanging out with some older guys, some potheads. Every now and then he would call me up, ask me if I wanted to smoke some weed with him, then laugh and hang up. I knew he was high. His Dad and Mom put him in a number of rehabs, but he always ran away. When Jamie's Dad got a big promotion, they moved into a nicer neighborhood, somewhere in Georgetown. They sent Jamie to a private school, somewhere out of state, so I never got to see him much after they moved. Then when Mom went to work for NAGS, she kinda kept me up to date on how he was doing so I know he wasn't doing well. The last time I actually saw him was a couple of years ago. We had a quick lunch and exchanged cell numbers. We promised to get together again. But the next time I called, somebody else had his phone number."

"I haven't seen him since high school," added Aaron.

"From what we saw in Jamie's house, it was quite evident that *someone* was using drugs," replied Daniel. "And from what you've just told us and from other sources, that *someone* is probably Jamie Barnes. And evidently, he's been using drugs for quite some time. From our experience, people who have been on drugs do change, especially those who have been on them for an extended period of time. They are apt to do anything to get money for their drugs. So we still consider Jamie Barnes, a person of interest in this case. Nothing you've told us makes us think otherwise," said Daniel.

"But you said Mom was *shot!* Jamie couldn't have done that. He hated guns. Matter-of-fact, he was deathly afraid of them. Whenever our Dads went hunting, only Aaron would go. Jamie and I stayed home and played golf or Nintendo. Anything but hunting or camping! Aaron was the Eagle Scout. Jamie and I never made it past Tenderfoot. Unless Jamie did a complete about-face since the last time I saw him, there is *no way* he would get near a gun. No way." Kyle shook his head as he finished his last sentence.

"What about the two people you arrested in North Carolina, the ones that were caught driving Mom's car? What about them?" asked Aaron.

"We haven't ruled them out, either. We'll interrogate them when we get them back to Washington. But, truthfully, Jamie is our prime suspect. *And* he could have had an accomplice. So maybe what you say about Jamie and his dislike for guns is true, but that doesn't rule out a partner. Do you know if Jamie kept in touch with any of his old friends from high school?"

"If you mean the older guys he used to do drugs with? I don't know. I had nothing to do with those guys. I didn't even know their names. But he might have stayed in touch with Ziggy."

"Ziggy?" Johnny asked.

"I'm sorry. He was one of my golfing buddies, growing up. We each had nicknames for the way we played golf. You know, like we had Ziggy, Sandy, Lefty, and Woody. I was Woody because I had a tendency to hit my drives in the woods. Ziggy, that was Billy Saperstein. He would zigzag his way to the green, army style. Left, right, left, right. Ziggy... I mean Billy Saperstein... he got caught with Jamie smoking pot in the school parking lot. Both got suspended. Billy's folks put him in private school after that. But I heard he got into trouble again. I heard he tried to sell a joint to an undercover cop and got busted. He's the only one I can think of, but I don't know his address or telephone number."

"We'll come back to that later," replied Daniel. "I meant to say this earlier, but Detective Williams and I want to apologize for having to conduct business at a time when you and your brother are mourning the loss of your mother. I'm afraid it's the nature of the job."

"There's no need to apologize. We want you to get whoever killed our Mom as quickly as possible. We're willing to do *anything* that will help. So we do understand," answered Aaron with Kyle nodding his head in agreement.

Daniel looked at his notes and continued. "Right now, I want to go back to something you said earlier about Jamie's mother, Elaine Barnes. You said that Jamie's mother was always on his case. That's not unusual. I thought every mother did that. I know mine did. But did she ever physically or verbally abuse Jamie or vice versa?"

"Ohhhh no!" quickly countered Kyle wondering why the reason for this line of questioning. "They had their spats, just like Aaron and I did with our Mom. And Mrs. Barnes was harder on Jamie than our Mom was on us but there was never any abuse or Jamie would have told me."

"Do you know why Jim and Elaine Barnes divorced?"

"No, sir. Not really. Mom mentioned they were divorcing, but she wasn't into gossip. Why do you ask?"

"What about Jamie's relationship with his father? Good or bad?"

"Jamie *loved* his Dad. Adored him. But like I said earlier, I haven't kept in touch with him. Just the lunch about two years ago. Even then, we didn't talk much. I think he was embarrassed the way things turned out for him."

Aaron silently stood by as Kyle answered the questions about Jamie. Jamie was more Kyle's friend than Aaron's and knew him better. But he, too, was confused by the line of questions the detective was asking. Finally, Aaron spoke. "Detective Whitehead? Why are you asking us so many questions about Jamie's mother and father? Why don't you just ask them?"

Daniel looked at Johnny who nodded his head in agreement knowing what Daniel was thinking.

"Regardless of your defense of Jamie Barnes, he's our prime suspect. Everything we have seen and heard points to him." Detective Whitehead paused. "What I haven't told you is that Jamie Barnes is also a suspect in *two* other killings."

Kyle gasped, shaking his head. "No way! No way!"

"What I'm about to tell you is strictly confidential, so please do *not* say anything until you've heard the details on the news. They found a body at a house on 4th Street, Jamie Barnes' residence. We believe the body to be Jamie's father, Jim Barnes…"

"Oh no no no no!" blurted out Kyle whose face turned ashen. "I don't care how many drugs Jamie took, that could *never* happen. Never!"

Aaron didn't feel the same about Jamie as Kyle did. If the detectives thought Jamie had killed his Dad, then they had their reasons. But Kyle's loyalty to Jamie was so fervent that Aaron kept his feelings to himself. Kyle might not think Jamie couldn't change. But he could. Just like Aaron knew he'd changed. And he didn't do drugs or alcohol.

"You mentioned he was a suspect in two more killings. Who else besides his father?" asked Aaron.

"Again. This is confidential. Elaine Barnes appears to be the other victim."

Kyle tried to say something but was too stunned to talk. He just shook his head in disbelief.

"So you think Jamie killed our Mom, his mother, and his father?" asked Aaron.

"No! No! You've got this all wrong! You've got the wrong guy. I'm telling you. You've got the wrong guy. There's no way, none, nada that Jamie could do that. By himself or with somebody. I don't care how many drugs he took, he could never, never do that. Jamie's the kindest, most gentle guy you'll ever meet," cried Kyle who then leaned back on the sofa.

The visit had not been as fruitful for the two detectives as they'd hoped. They did not come away with more ammunition to nail down their 'person of interest.' Instead, what they got was a story about a good kid who got hooked on drugs at an early age. But there was no mention of the suspect having a history of violent, abusive, or aggressive tendencies. No talk of bullying, stealing, anger or rage. And he hated guns. Unless Jamie's life had done a one-eighty, the case was back to square one.

Chapter 75

Friday, December 29, 2006, 7:01 p.m. EST

"That went *really* well," Richards said sarcastically as the elevator doors closed. "I did *my* job. It was obvious that you two weren't prepared. You certainly underestimated that Allan boy."

"Aaron," responded Wayne.

"What?"

"His name was Aaron," repeated Wayne wishing he could add 'you stupid twit.'

"Well, *Aaron* sure made you two clowns look like a couple of amateurs!"

Richards' condescending remarks didn't make things easier for Bobby or Wayne. They *had* done their homework. Margie Hamilton worked for NAGS. Her son, Aaron, was a member of NAGS – had been one for over ten years. The victim's trust fund, as they had envisioned and explained to Richards, should have been readily accepted by the Hamilton's. There was no reason to expect Aaron's hostile response. It was a win-win situation. The Hamilton's got a memorial to their mother and NAGS got the publicity.

"As far as I'm concerned, the whole damn thing is off!" continued Richards. "I need some sort of diversion tonight. Something to take my mind off the complete mess you two made of something that should have been so simple. The embarrassment you've caused me. I don't need stress like this."

Nobody spoke as the elevator descended to the first floor. Wayne and Bobby stared at the changing floor numbers while Richards eyed each of the two men.

"OK. Here's what I need to cheer me up. *Citronelle.* Yes. *Citronelle.* I want to go to *Citronelle.* If you've never been, it's a great restaurant on M Street. The food is absolutely divine, the wine selection is one of the best in Washington, and the service is spectacular! Plus I'm friends with one of the waiters. I'm sure he'll get us a great table!"

Richards didn't look for approval from either Wayne or Bobby. They needed him, he knew it, and he took advantage of it, just like any good politician would do.

Richards continued. "Then after that, I want to go to that "titty" bar that's near your office. Yes! That's what I want to do. That's what I need to cheer me up."

Wayne was all too familiar with Richards' 'diversions' with the last one costing NAGS nearly two thousand dollars. Tonight would be no exception. Wayne had dined once at *Citronelle* with his now ex-wife, but it had been a special occasion. As Richards said, it's a great restaurant but also an expensive restaurant. The "titty" bar that Richards referred to was the *Camelot Show-Bar,* an adult nightclub, just a couple of blocks from NAGS headquarters. Bobby was most familiar with Camelot having frequented it many times. Sometimes with contributors, supporters and local politicians. And sometimes by himself.

Wayne completely understood *Citronelle* as Richards considered himself a wine and food connoisseur. But given Richards' proclivity for men, the "titty" bar was totally out of character unless it was his way of squelching the rumors about him being gay. Regardless, this was going to be a long, long night.

Chapter 76

Friday, December 29, 2006, 8:36 p.m. EST

Daniel's cell rang just as he pushed a handful of McDonald's fries into his mouth. He knew better than to eat and drive, but it was late. His stomach was growling, and he wanted to get home. Normally, fast food wasn't high on his list, but tonight for some reason, he craved a Big Mac and a large order of fries. Daniel chewed as fast as he could as he grabbed his cell phone out of the empty cup holder. He didn't recognize the number but since it was from the DC area, he answered it.

"Detective Whitehead," he garbled, choking down the rest of the food still in his mouth.

"Good evening, Detective Whitehead. This is Chloe Wilson. I am the lady who lives next to Elaine Barnes. We talked this afternoon."

"Oh yes. I *remember.*"

"I would've called earlier, but I was too upset. Everybody was saying that it was Elaine. That she was murdered. Is that true? Was she murdered?"

Daniel's Big Mac and fries were getting cold, he was tired, both mentally and physically, and now this nosy neighbor was calling him just to satisfy her morbid curiosity. It took every ounce of willpower to keep civil.

"Miss Wilson, I really can't discuss this case with you. If you don't have anything to add to what you've already told me, I'm afraid you've wasted your time."

"I know it's Elaine. It can't be Jamie, and Jim did it. He killed her."

"I'm sorry, Miss Wilson ..."

But Chloe Wilson continued to talk, ignoring Daniel. "Jim must have found out about Elaine's boyfriend. That's why he killed her. Jealousy. Pure and simple. That's what men do when they can't have what they want. Men are such ..."

"Miss Wilson," interrupted Daniel. "The Barnes were divorced. She could have boyfriends. Jim Barnes could have girlfriends. What makes you think Jim killed Elaine?" As soon as the words had left Daniel's mouth, he knew he had been snookered! And by a nosy old woman!

"I was right. I knew it was her. I knew it. And I know Jim did it. See. Elaine had a boyfriend *before* she was divorced," said the most elated Chloe Wilson with an emphasis on the word 'before.' She continued, hardly stopping to take a breath. "Like I said earlier, Elaine was a lot friendlier to me after her divorce. Matter-of-fact, she was *never* friendly to me *before* the divorce. Totally ignored me, like I didn't exist. At least until she and Jim divorced. Then one day out of the blue, she called me. She was very lonely and needed someone to talk to. I don't know why she called *me* instead of one of her snooty country club friends. But that doesn't matter. I came over, and she unloaded on me. After that, we had coffee together almost every morning. But not this morning. Not after her late-night visit from that good-for-nothing son of hers and Jim. Remember, I *saw* his car. You know, NAGS 2, Mercedes. Anyway, I know for a fact that she had an affair *before* her divorce, while Jim still lived at the house. And it was someone at work! She wouldn't tell me who it was, but she told me that they couldn't go public with their relationship even after the divorce because of the friction it would cause at work. In fact, she said that he couldn't even take her out in public because *he* might be recognized. I told her to dump the son-of-a-bitch. She was too pretty of a woman, too much to offer to limit herself to a guy that wouldn't even take her out. She told me the *asshole* even squelched their New Year's Eve plans, even after she went out and bought an expensive new dress. If I were her…"

Finally, Daniel had had enough and interrupted, "But why do you think Jim killed his wife. Why wouldn't he have just killed her lover?"

"Well, maybe he has! Maybe he's killed both. I bet Jim found out who it was, probably went berserk and killed her and maybe him. That's what I think."

Daniel let Miss Wilson ramble on while his Big Mac and fries got colder and colder. He listened but found nothing she said of value. After all, Jim couldn't have done it. But he wasn't about to be duped again by the old biddy. When she began repeating herself, Daniel had heard enough and stopped her in mid-sentence.

"I'll keep what you said in mind, Miss Wilson. I appreciate all your help." Most of what he'd just heard was no more than gossip from a meddlesome busybody. He would file this conversation away as conjecture. But not irrelevant. In his line of work, nothing was irrelevant.

"Well, I'm just trying to do my civic duty. I'll call you again if I think of anything else."

"Please do," said Daniel, begrudgingly. "One other thing. Please keep what we've said confidential. I do not, and I repeat, do not want you talking to other neighbors, reporters, or anyone about this case. By doing so, you could harm our investigation, and if that happens, you could possibly be charged with obstruction of justice."

"Oh, no sir. My lips are sealed. Zipped. You can trust me."

Daniel flipped his cell phone shut. Daniel's dinner, for what it was, was ruined. But at least he'd shut up the old busybody. He'd eat a bowl of cereal when he got home and then call Johnny… the highlight of his evening. Maybe he needed a girlfriend. Or… maybe not.

Chapter 77

Friday, December 29, 2006, 10:25 p.m. EST

Johnny Williams was waiting for Daniel's call. He answered on the first ring.

"You watching the local news?" asked Daniel.

"Yeah. I looked pretty good, didn't I? Maybe a little overweight but you know what they say, TV adds what? 10… 20 pounds to your figure."

"I wasn't talking about you, but yes, you looked wonderful and sounded very professional. What I was really talking about was the replay of the press conference at NAGS just before lunch."

"Yeah. I saw that too. Makes you wanna puke. Armstrong was milking Margie Hamilton's death for all it's worth. You'd thought they planned the whole damn thing."

"Yeah, and did you notice, Armstrong's got a mustache. So that's it. Case solved," replied Daniel, referring to the mustachioed man driving Margie's car caught on surveillance tape near the dumpster where Margie's body was found. Johnny understood what he meant.

Both Johnny and Daniel laughed at the absurdity of what was just said.

"And guess what else I found out?" asked Daniel, rhetorically. "Jim Barnes killed his wife… well, ex-wife. At least that's what that old busybody who lives next door to Elaine Barnes told me. She just called me. Told me that Elaine was having an affair with someone at NAGS. That Jim found out and killed her."

"Wait a minute! You're on to something here. Check this out. Elaine was having an affair with *Margie!* So Jim kills them both. He kills Margie with a gun and dumps her body in the alley. He then sells her car to the two illegals. But with his old lady, he's not so kind. He beats her senseless with a poker iron after deciding a gun would be too civil. After his son wakes up at his mother's house and finds her dead, he becomes enraged. He tricks his old man into coming over to his house where he kills him and dumps his body in the basement. To make it look like a suicide but hung out on drugs, he shoots him in the chest. You and I both know that any good detective worth their salt would immediately know that if they found a victim with a bullet hole in their chest, it must be suicide. Then the boy hides the gun in the golf bag where *no one* would *ever* look, steals the money, the Mercedes, and then leaves. Heads off to Mexico. *So I say we're done!* Shall I call Bennie and tell him the meeting's off? Not to bring the day-old bagels?" said Johnny, laughing.

"Wrinkles, if I didn't know any better, I'd swear you talked to the old busybody before she called me. If not, I could fix you two up."

"Good night, Danny boy."

"Good night, Wrinkles. See you at 7."

Chapter 78

Saturday, December 30, 2006, 6:50 a.m. EST

Johnny Williams had a lively bounce to his step as he waltzed into Conference Room 3A, carrying his large mug of hot coffee. He found Daniel methodically laying out the three cases in columnar format on the much used and misused whiteboard. Even with the big 'DO NOT USE PERMANENT MARKERS' sign permanently written at the top of the board, remnants of previous cases remained from those who failed to heed the instructions. At the top of each of Daniel's columns were the names of the victims: M. HAMILTON, J. BARNES (T), E. BARNES (T). While Margie Hamilton had been positively identified, the other two victims' identities were given tentative status pending verification. Rows, spaced about two inches apart, were drawn under the column headings all the way down to the bottom of the board. A number of them were already filled in with standard homicide labels such as *Date, Time of Death, Cause of Death, Weapon Used, Suspects, and Motive.* Other row headers were left vacant pending new information from Bennie Archer's Medical Examiner's (ME) report. In the *Suspects* row, Jamie Barnes' name appeared under each of the three victim's column. Otto Max's name appeared under Margie Hamilton's name. Jamie Barnes was the only common denominator in all three cases.

The whiteboard, where all known facts could be seen, was one of the most important tools in solving homicides. This time Daniel wondered if the board exercise was just a waste of time. After all, everything they had seen and heard pointed to Jamie Barnes. Pressure from the higher-ups and the district attorney's office had reached a boiling point and they wanted closure. Even Vernon Martin who normally stayed out of the fray had called a 9 a.m. mandatory meeting with Daniel, Johnny and Bennie. And the commander had been invited. Not a good sign.

Bennie looked frazzled as he rushed in the conference room wheeling two large brown briefcases behind him, one on top of the other. A white stubble graced his face, and his clothes looked disheveled. Without saying a word, he grabbed a cup of coffee and took a seat.

"So where are the breakfast snacks?" asked Johnny, finger quoting 'breakfast snacks.'

Johnny's mouth dropped when Bennie pulled out the familiar green and white Krispy Kreme box from the top briefcase. Bennie was smiling from ear to ear with almost every tooth in his mouth visible.

"Well, I'll be damned," blurted out the astonished Williams. "This *is* a red-letter day. Daniel, mark our calendar. We'll be celebrating this day from now on 'cause I know, sure as hell, Bennie won't let us forget it."

"So where's your partner in crime?" asked Daniel.

"If you mean C. J. (referring to C. J. Washington, Bennie's PC and video expert), he's back at the office finishing up a few things. He won't be at this meeting. I don't have to tell you we're under the gun on this one, no pun intended. VM called yesterday. He told me about the 9 a.m. meeting and said to burn the midnight oil if I had to. We pulled an all-nighter. So, Wrinkles, *don't* piss me off this morning 'cause I'm not in a good mood."

"But you're never in a good mood! I'm guessing that buying these doughnuts probably sent you right over the edge. I hope you're not carrying anything dangerous in one of those briefcases," retorted Johnny. As usual, Bennie ignored the comment.

"So Bennie. Don't leave us hanging. What'd you find?" asked Daniel who then uncapped the black dry-erase marker, prepared to begin filling in the blank cells.

"A lot considering how little time we were given… at least for the two new homicides. With Margie Hamilton, there's not much more to add, but I will review what we know as a refresher." He then handed to the two detectives a copy of the ME report on Margaret Irene Hamilton.

"Wait one second. Let me get my new tape recorder out," asked Johnny digging into his coat pocket and pulling out a silver micro-recorder.

"And you couldn't have done this earlier?" asked Bennie, clearly agitated.

He then adjusted his drugstore-bought reading glasses as he scanned his notes. The thick lenses of the rectangular-shaped frames magnified the red in his tired, blood-shot eyes. Without fanfare, he began and, as usual, was all business.

"OK. Margie Hamilton. Location of death is still unknown. You already have an approximate date, time, cause of death, and type of weapon used. Weapon Found? Like I told you yesterday, we did find a 9mm pistol at Jamie Barnes' house. But the real question remains, is it the murder weapon? That we can't tell. The wound in the victim *could* have been caused by a 9mm or not. So far we've been unable to find a single bullet or empty shell casing at any of the crime locations. And I mean our guys checked. Nothing found in the alley or dumpster, nothing in Margie Hamilton's house or the house on 4th Street and, from our Carolina associates, nothing in Margie Hamilton's car. So, the only thing we can add to the Hamilton case is that we may or may not have the weapon that was used."

"Bennie, I hope to hell it gets better than this or we're wasting our time… other than the doughnuts," Johnny responded.

"It does. Trust me." He then handed each detective a copy of the Medical Examiner's report on James H. Barnes Jr., including photos of the victim, and details of the DFS (Department of Forensic Science) findings.

Bennie gave the two detectives a few minutes to scan through the document. Once he was satisfied that he, and not the document, had their full attention, he continued.

"OK. James H. Barnes Jr., aka Jim Barnes," said Bennie peering over the top of his glasses, looking more like a professor than a forensic investigator. "The victim has been positively identified as James Howard Barnes Jr. by matching the deceased's fingerprints to those stored on the FBI's national database. Photos obtained from the victim's DMV records and a driver's license found in a wallet discovered in the freezer section of a refrigerator in the house on 4th Street confirm the ID. That house where the victim was found is owned by the victim and, according to nearby neighbors, occupied by James H. Barnes III, aka Jamie Barnes. We haven't found a rental agreement to confirm this, but other evidence found at the house does corroborate it. Back to the victim. Under *Location of Death,* a big question mark. The date and time of death, Wednesday, December 27, between 7 a.m. and 1 p.m. Same as Margie Hamilton. Under cause of death, a gunshot to the victim's chest striking the superior vena cava. Wrinkles, that's a big vein that lets blood flow into the heart." Johnny ignored Bennie's attempt at humor and grabbed another doughnut instead. "There were lacerations and abrasions to the back of the head, neck, hand and facial areas. Most of the wounds contained wood particles that originated from the basement steps indicating that the body was either dragged or pushed down the steps. What's interesting is these wounds had little or no blood residue indicating the victim was dead for some period of time prior to being pulled or shoved down the basement steps. Questions?"

Johnny shook his head and took a swig of coffee. Daniel erased the *(T)* next to J. Barnes' name on the whiteboard.

"OK, so continuing with Jim Barnes. An analysis of the victim's blood and urine indicates he had consumed a great deal of alcohol in the 24 hours prior to his death. Nothing was found under the victim's fingernails to indicate a struggle. The victim was wearing a wool overcoat, and on it, we found an adhesive residue, just as we found on Margie Hamilton's body. The two residue samples had the same characteristics, so more than likely the same roll of tape was used on both victims. We found some ice crystals still formed in the victim's body indicating the body was either refrigerated or left out in the cold for a period of time. Again, similar to the Hamilton case. Lastly and most interesting, the victim had small traces of gun powder on his right hand that matched the gun powder residue found on the 9mm pistol we discovered at 4th Street address."

"What!" Johnny blurted out, almost knocking over his coffee as he did. "Talk about a curveball. I never saw that one coming." Johnny double-circled that part of his ME report.

"OK. Getting back to the 9mm pistol we found at the 4th Street address. The weapon had been recently fired, and at least three bullets were missing from the clip. No prints were found on the gun and, like I told you yesterday, it was found in a golf bag in the basement. Pages 10 and 11 show the pistol as it was found and retrieved. We also have pictures of the clips and the bullets from the clip. The bullets are round nose and *could* have been the type used to kill both James H. Barnes Jr. and Margie Hamilton."

Daniel and Johnny carefully studied the photos then turned the page.

Bennie continued. "We ran the serial number on the gun, and it's registered in Virginia, Loudoun County, to James H. Barnes Jr, the victim. It's an old Smith & Weston Model 59. I believe they stopped making this model in 1980. While legal in Virginia, not so in DC."

"In the basement of the house on 4th Street, we found what appeared to be the start of a grave near the victim. And near the diggings, we found the shovel that was used. There were no prints." Bennie paused and readjusted his glasses. "Regarding prints, we checked the entire house. All of the prints in the house belonged to James H. Barnes III, aka Jamie Barnes. We matched them to prints obtained from a 1992 juvenile arrest. With no other prints, it's obvious he was a loner. We also found hair in the bathroom's sink and tub. That should give us a good DNA sample. There were no indications of forced entry other than the front door which I presumed was done by you two."

Both detectives nodded.

"We found drug paraphernalia in almost every room including pipes, bongs, modified gas masks, rolling machines and paper, pipes, spoons. You name it. Everything but needles. The guy loved his drugs. All of the aforementioned items should be able to provide us with additional DNA samples should we need them. We used the forensic vacuum over the entire house and basement. I'll let you guys know if we find anything significant. There just wasn't enough time to get it all analyzed. Moving outside, we checked the porch but found nothing but snow. The car parked in the driveway, a 1992 Cadillac Deville, is registered to a James H. Barnes III. We did find some prints in the car. All but one set belonged to the owner. The other partial set belonged to Nathaniel J. Freeman, aka 'Skinny,' aka 'Nate Freeman.' He's a small-time drug…"

"Yeah. We know Skinny," interrupted Johnny. "I thought we had him off the streets… at least for a while. But I guess that's our great legal system for you."

"Johnny! Maybe that's him!" exclaimed Daniel. "Maybe Nate's the second man in the surveillance tape. That would make sense! Maybe he's Otto Max!" He excitedly wrote Nate Freeman's name with a question mark next to it on the whiteboard under Margie's column in the *Other* row.

"I thought the surveillance tape showed two white dudes," replied Johnny.

"Yeah, but Skinny's light-skinned, has a mustache or did have a mustache and besides, the tapes aren't that clear," said Daniel, reviewing his notes. "I say it's worth a shot."

"I'll put out a BOLO for him after the meeting. We probably need to jerk ol' Nate around anyway. Looks like he's back to his old tricks."

Bennie returned the 'James H. Barnes Jr.' folder to his briefcase and pulled out his 'Elaine M. Barnes' folder and handed out the ME report to Johnny and Daniel.

Bennie continued. "You can study the entire James Barnes' report at your leisure. You guys have any questions? Need a bio break?"

"No. Not me. What about you, Johnny?" asked Daniel. Johnny shook his head.

"OK then. Don't say I didn't ask. Now, moving on to our last victim. Based on a match of the deceased fingerprints to those in the FBI's national database, we have positively identified the victim as Elaine Morgan Barnes. We estimate the date and time of death to be between Thursday, December 28th, 10 p.m. and Friday, December 29th, 4 a.m. The cause of death was a penetrating trauma to the head caused by multiple blows from a fireplace poker iron." Both detectives studied the close-up pictures of the left side of Elaine Barnes' head.

"It appears that the victim was struck twice with the poker. One blow shattered the skull with the weapon becoming lodged in the brain. A second blow passed through the left eye socket completely destroying the left eye and surrounding bone structure. The angle of entry from the two blows to the victim's head indicates the assailant used his right hand. We found the murder weapon on the floor in the bedroom on the main floor. Turn to page 12, and you'll see a photo of the weapon. Blood and brain matter found on the poker matched that of the victim. The victim was struck by the assailant as she entered the living room from the dining room." Bennie paused as Daniel and Johnny looked at the diagrams and photos of the living room and dining room taken from different angles. "We found the victim's blood on her clothes and in her hair. There was no indication that the body had been moved either by lifting or dragging. We also found the victim's blood on the carpet, wood floor, couch, and walls. We also found coffee, cream, and sugar on the carpet in the same area as the body and on the victim's robe but nowhere else. Also, near the victim's body, we found a tray and three coffee cups. It appears that she had come from the kitchen through the dining room and..."

"Wait! Did you say three? Don't you mean two?" interrupted Johnny.

"No. Three. Two near the body and the third found underneath the Christmas tree."

"How did we miss that?" asked Daniel. "Talk about sloppy detective work!"

"If I wasn't confused before, I'm damn sure confused now." Johnny wrote down three cups and circled it a couple of times adding a bunch of question marks next to it. Daniel did the same on the whiteboard.

Not waiting for questions, Bennie continued. "The victim was not sexually assaulted, and there was no evidence of a struggle of any kind. We checked under her fingernails and found nothing. As far as fingerprints are concerned, besides finding the victim's throughout the house, we found a perfect right thumb and portions of four right fingers on the fore-mentioned poker iron which matched up perfectly with a set of prints of James H Barnes III, aka Jamie Barnes, *son* of Elaine Barnes. Again, these prints matched his prints from his juvenile arrest. His prints were also left on an empty liquor bottle and water glass found in the main floor bedroom. In the adjoining bathroom, we found his prints on the lavatory handles, the wall above the toilet, and shower door. In the kitchen, and more specifically in the dishwasher, we found his prints on a coffee mug, small bowl, and eating utensils. Last, we found them on a closet doorknob and wooden coat hangers in an upstairs bedroom. There..."

"Sorry to interrupt. What about the coffee cups found in the living room? Any prints" asked Johnny.

"Only Elaine Barnes'," Bennie quickly replied as he checked the time on the large wall clock.

Bennie continued. "There was a trail of blood that started at the victim's body, traveled through the living room on the Oriental rug, continued down the hallway, and into the first-floor bedroom. Additionally, there were partial bloody shoe prints found on the Oriental rug near the victim's body and alongside the trail of blood leading into the first-floor bedroom. The shoe prints matched the right shoe found in the plastic sack that was found on the first-floor bedroom. That same shoe had traces of blood on its sole. You have photos on pages 19 and 20 showing the trail of blood, shoe prints, and right shoe. A diagram of the entire house can be found on the preceding pages. The blood on the carpet, hall, and shoe matched the victim's. We also have excellent DNA samples from the vomit found on the bed cover and floor in the main level bedroom. As to the composition of the vomit, a large amount of benzodiazepine, a tranquilizer commonly known as diazepam or valium, cocaine, heroin, and a small quantity of liquor were present, among other things. An empty bottle of valium prescribed for the victim was found on a bedside table in the first-floor bedroom. Interestingly, only smudges of the *victim's* prints were found on the bottle, no one else's. Based on the amount of benzodiazepine found in the vomit, a possible suicide attempt was made."

Bennie paused again, looking at Daniel and then the clock keeping in mind the 9 o'clock meeting. He wanted to make sure everyone was up to date with all known and relevant facts before the meeting.

He continued. "We found a leather coat near the front door and a bag of clothes in the first-floor bedroom. The bag contained a pair of jeans, flannel shirt, socks, underwear, and a pair of size 11 tennis shoes, the right one having evidence of the victim's blood that I mentioned earlier. The clothes would fit a person, most likely a male, weighing between 180 and 200 pounds, and six foot one to six foot three in height. Interestingly enough, we found two different hair types in the pants and jacket indicating that two people wore them, but *obviously* not at the same time, Wrinkles," jabbed Bennie. Johnny could only smile at Bennie's lame effort at humor as he drained his coffee mug.

Bennie continued. "We also found a wallet in the leather jacket that contained three dollars, a parking card for the Watergate apartments, a Blue Cross health insurance card and Blockbuster card, both issued to James H. Barnes III."

Bennie looked at Johnny and Daniel. "Any questions?"

"Yeah, but I can wait 'til you finish," responded Johnny.

"Same here. Keep going, Bennie," replied Daniel.

"OK. Moving to the adjoining bathroom. A few water puddles were still on the shower floor when we got there, and the bath towels and face cloth were still damp. Based on that evidence, we feel quite confident that a shower was taken yesterday, sometime between noon and 4 p.m. and, obviously, not by the victim." Bennie looked up and at Johnny. "Hair was found in the shower, sink, and countertop. They were all a match. However, none of the samples collected matched the *victim's* hair. They do, however, match the hair samples collected in the house on 4th Street. We also found a comb with hair strands by the sink and a used toothbrush and dental floss in the nearby wastebasket. Without saying, everything will be tested for DNA and we'll let you know the results as soon as we get them."

Bennie turned the page of the report and continued.

"Moving upstairs, we found very little. In the master bedroom, we found a king-size bed that had been slept in by the victim. The way the bed was partially unmade, it appears that only one person was in the bed. The victim. We did find hair that microscopically matched the victim's. There was nothing to indicate any kind of struggle to remove the victim forcefully from her bed. The only disturbance we found was a broken dresser mirror. It appeared to have been smashed by some kind of blunt instrument. We can't be certain what blunt instrument caused the damage as there was nothing found behind, under, on, or in front of the dresser other than shards of the broken mirror. We ruled out the poker iron based on the absence of any glass residue. My guess is that someone threw something like a shoe, book, maybe a phone then retrieved it. So far, we've found nothing in the house with any mirror dust or residue. If you feel that's something we should investigate further, let me know, and I will send a team back over there to do a hardcore search."

"We'll let you know. I like the phone idea," answered Daniel. At this time, he had not completely mapped out what had happened at Elaine Barnes' house and did not want to add any more work to Bennie's teams.

"In a smaller bedroom upstairs and down the hall from the master bedroom, we found three coat hangers on the closet floor. Hanging in the closet was a man's dress suit, size 46 long, along with a white dress shirt, size 16 ½ - 17 by 35. These matched the size of clothes found in the plastic sack in the first-floor bedroom. And that pretty much covers the inside of the house. On the outside, we did find evidence of vomit on one of the columns. It was consistent with the vomit found on the clothing inside the house but without the benzodiazepine or liquor. We'll check the DNA to see if the two match. Because of the snow, we didn't find any usable footprints or tire marks. There was one car in the detached garage. A 2006 745 BMW registered to Jim Barnes. The only distinguishable fingerprints in the car belonged to Elaine Barnes. There were print smudges on the door handle of the passenger side but couldn't find a match for them in our database. So, that's it. Any questions?" asked Bennie who once again looked up at the clock on the wall.

"Great job, as usual, Very thorough and organized. Thank you," answered Daniel. Johnny nodded in agreement and pushed the doughnut box over to Daniel who pushed it over to Bennie.

"I do have a couple of questions," replied Johnny. "The ice crystals found in Jim Barnes' body. Could that have happened in the basement?"

"Only if the basement were 28 degrees or colder. That's when ice crystals begin to form in the tissue. But the basement wasn't that cold. It was probably only 55 degrees so, no, that's not possible," answered Bennie.

"And you found no prints of *Jim* Barnes in the house on 4th Street?" asked Daniel, emphasizing 'Jim.'

"No."

"What about Nate Freeman? Any of his prints in the house on 4th Street or the Georgetown house?" asked Daniel.

"No."

"The coffee cup found under the tree. Did it match the others found near the body?" asked Johnny.

"Yes," replied Bennie, again nervously looking at the clock on the wall.

"Giving the evidence we have, do you think anyone could have done this other than Jamie Barnes?" asked Daniel.

"You're the detectives. I'm not. But it certainly looks that way."

"What about you, Johnny? You think we should lead with Jamie Barnes?" asked Daniel as he stood and took a couple of pictures of the whiteboard.

"I don't think we have any choice. The DA will be thrilled with the case, but I'm certainly not. Too many loose ends." Johnny then pushed himself back from the table, got up and walked over to the whiteboard where he grabbed a red dry erase marker and began furiously circling areas on the board. Daniel took a seat on the edge of the conference table, and Bennie sat down in a chair next to Johnny's vacated one.

"Here's what I'm talking about. We've got two bodies with bullet holes in them, and no one knows *where* they were shot. We've found a 9mm that could be the murder weapon in two of our cases, or not. But no casings or fingerprints were found. We have a surveillance tape with two cars and two drivers that are circling the area where Margie Hamilton was found but have not confirmed the identity of the drivers of either car nor the whereabouts of that second car. Then we got Jim Barnes. His dead body, found in Jamie Barnes' house, was either left out in the cold or put in a freezer and if that's not enough, he had gun residue on his right hand. Then we've got the three coffee cups in Elaine Barnes' house that only have her prints. We've got prints of Jamie Barnes all over Elaine Barnes' house including the murder weapon but not on a pill bottle whose contents were found in the vomit, assuming it's Jamie's. And what about the broken mirror? Why was it broken? And what was used to break it? Possibly a phone? If so, where is it? Finally, we've got Jamie Barnes who murders his mother, then goes to bed, maybe tries to commit suicide, wakes up the next morning still alive, eats breakfast, takes a shower, shaves, dresses in nice, clean clothes, picks up his *bloody* clothes, puts them in a garbage bag, then leaves but not before dropping his bloodstained leather coat and bathrobe in the hallway on the way out. And to make our job easier in making an identity, he leaves his wallet containing his Blockbuster and insurance cards. None of this makes any sense to me. And what about motive? What the hell's the motive for all this? And last, but not least, where's Margie's coat? Where's the damn coat?" Johnny paused a moment to catch his breath. "Other than that, I think everything points to Jamie." Johnny capped the red marker, half slammed it on the white board's tray, then returned to his seat.

"Well, based on everything you say, looks like we've got ourselves an air-tight case," Daniel quipped then swallowed a gulp of cold coffee. "You're right about the DA. He's got Jamie's fingerprints on that poker iron, and that's all he needs. Everything else is gravy. Look, we've got to tell Vernon and the commander *something*. I say we go with Jamie." He then looked to Johnny for his response.

"Yeah, I agree. He's *probably* our guy, but he sure isn't making things easy."

Chapter 79

Saturday, December 30, 2006, 9:02 a.m. EST

Wayne could smell the coffee's aroma as he made his way to the kitchen. He could hardly wait to pour himself a cup of the delicious brew. He wanted it strong, he wanted it black, and he wanted it now. His head was still pounding from last night's festivities. What had started out Friday night to be a diversion for Congressman Richards had morphed into a late night, early Saturday morning party of self-indulgence and ribaldry by Bobby *and* Richards. The evening had begun tame enough with a relaxed dinner at *Citronelle's*. The food was unbelievable, but so was the tab. Price was no object for Richards. He ordered the most expensive meal on the menu and an even more expensive bottle of French burgundy wine. Wayne tried to be reasonable with his order, but Bobby followed Richards' lead. The one bottle of the French burgundy barely made it through the appetizers, so two more were ordered to accompany the meal. When the waiter brought the bill, without looking, Richards figured his portion to be $100 which he charged to his congressional expense account. This would keep him under the ethics watchdog's radar. Wayne and Bobby split the remaining $1575. Nothing was said. There was no haggling.

After dinner, the three men made their way over to the 'titty' bar, as Richards called it. Wayne had tried to talk them out of going, but Richards and Bobby wouldn't hear of it. Both men had their reasons. Bobby loved to look at naked women, and Richards loved to look at the aroused men looking at naked women. The club was located a mile from the restaurant and only a few blocks from the NAGS office building. Once inside, Bobby paid three men, sitting at a table next to center stage, $200 to move. They eagerly accepted the money and found a table in the back. Before long, Bobby's $20 tips had every girl on the stage playing to him. Bobby was happy, the girls were happy, and Richards was happy. With so many girls showing their wares so close to their table, men began hovering around their table. This delighted Richards who managed to nudge up against the bulge in the on-lookers' pants as he excused himself numerous times to go to the restroom or the bar for another drink. He also managed to cop a few 'accidental' feels as he pushed his way back to his table after rewarding one of the female dancers on stage for their performance with tip money given to him by Bobby.

While on one of his frequent "missions" to the bar, poking his hardened member against the unsuspecting crowd who were gawking at the featured dancers, he felt a tap on the shoulder. He had been caught! His excitement turned limp. Maybe he had rubbed against someone once too often or too hard. He decided to ignore the second tap until he heard his name called. *John!* He turned and was extremely relieved and delighted to see a familiar face, a former acquaintance - someone who happened to be on the same type 'mission.' After a big hug, the two friends retreated to the rear of the club where they found a secluded table, ordered a few drinks, all on NAGS' tab and began catching up on old times. Less than an hour later, Richards, profusely thanked his hosts for such a great time, gave them $30 for his portion of the tab and left with his friend. Wayne stayed with Bobby until about 3 a.m. Wayne tried to drink away the dreadful events of the past few days, and Bobby tried to drink himself into the pants of any of the dancers that would have him. Neither man achieved their goal, so they left the club... frustrated.

With Bobby passed out in the back seat of his car, Wayne drove straight to his Georgetown residence, deciding it best to go straight home rather than to swing by the Watergate Apartments to drop Bobby off. Less time on the roads. Although he had drunk a lot, he didn't feel intoxicated. In retrospect, he regretted not having called a cab. Had the police pulled him over, he most certainly would have been given a DUI and hauled off to jail, an embarrassment that neither he nor NAGS could afford, especially with the impending court case and all the positive publicity they had gotten out of the Margie Hamilton murder. He had been lucky, and he knew it. But wasn't it about time he had some good luck?

Morning had come early, but Wayne stayed in bed as long as he could, trying to sleep but finally decided it wasn't going to happen. Throughout the night, or what was left of it, his mind kept replaying the events of the previous days, trying to remember the lies they had told, and how everything would eventually play out. It was all bad.

He was thankful that last night, actually early this morning, even in his diminished capacity, he had remembered to make the coffee and even set its timer for 9 a.m. Coffee made the morning tolerable. After downing his first cup of coffee, he poured a second. Out of habit, he flipped on the TV and tossed a couple of bagels into his toaster oven. The TV's sound was muted but the familiar morning duo on the local Fox channel WTTG were all excited, yapping about something. He never turned on the sound unless he saw something that piqued his interest.

Wayne could hear Bobby's loud and nonstop snoring coming from the den. He had not made it to the guest room. To his credit, he *had* made it into the house which was a miracle in itself considering the condition he was in. He was still fully clothed and still wearing his overcoat. Somehow, he had managed to remove his boots and to set his LBJ on one of the nearby wing chairs.

On most mornings, much earlier than this, and after a good night's sleep, Wayne would relax, read the Times and enjoy his coffee. Not today. And the way things were going, maybe never again. However, it was obvious that nothing was bothering Bobby, not if his relentless, incessant snoring was an indication. Finally, Wayne couldn't take it anymore and headed to the den.

"Bobby! Wake up! It's time to get up! Breakfast is ready! We've got things to do, places to go, people to meet! Chop! Chop!"

Bobby opened his eyes, saw Wayne, smiled then closed them.

"Bobby! Let's go! Move it!" yelled Wayne. When he saw Bobby's eyes open, stay open, then give him a thumbs up, he headed back into the kitchen. He pulled the cream cheese out of the refrigerator and was thickly applying it to his bagel when he saw a picture of Jamie Barnes on the TV, then pictures of Jim and Elaine Barnes. Automatically, he picked up the TV controller and turned up the volume. He assumed they had just reported how Jamie Barnes had killed both his mother and father and then committed suicide - just the way Bobby planned. The TV picture switched to a reporter outside of Elaine Barnes' home who was interviewing a witness, a heavy-set lady in a full-length fur coat, holding a white dog.

Wayne listened intently to the lady as she described Barnes' wayward son - how he had been outside yelling the night of the murder. Once the reporter finished his interview, they flashed a picture of Jamie Barnes on the screen again.

"... so please keep in mind that he's probably armed and dangerous," wrapped up the reporter.

What? What did he say? Armed and dangerous? It couldn't be true. Obviously, he misheard the reporter. Then the reporter repeated himself. Wayne dropped his bagel and raced into the den, yelling!

"Bobby! Bobby! Where are you?"

"In the crapper," responded Bobby from the hallway bathroom. "What's got you so unraveled this early in the morning?"

Wayne headed to the hall and started talking outside the bathroom door while Bobby relieved himself of the many drinks from last night.

"We've got a serious problem! A really serious problem. Your *shoot from the hip* plan has just fallen apart. Hurry up and get out of there. We need to talk!"

"Good God, man. Can't anyone have some private time around here?" asked Bobby as he jerked open the door then flung the hand towel onto the sink. "What the hell has gotten into you?"

"Jamie! He's alive. I just saw it on TV. The news. They think he killed his parents."

"Are you sure?"

"They said it twice. *Armed and dangerous.* You think a dead man can be armed and dangerous?"

"Aw shit! That stupid fuck. I knew he'd screw up everything. I shoulda given him more whiskey and stayed there until he croaked. So the police have him in custody? What's he saying?"

"You're not listening. They don't know where he is. They only said he's armed and dangerous."

"OK. That'll work," said Bobby calmly. "We call our attorneys and see if we can put a reward out for *his* ass and make it big. Say, $150,000. That'll have every bounty hunter within a thousand miles looking for him. And they don't usually take prisoners."

"Bobby! This isn't the Wild West. I don't…"

"Would you *please* just call our lawyers. They'll know how to handle this," interrupted Bobby.

"God! What an unbelievable mess. I knew I should have called the cops in the first place. We're way over our heads. This is going to blow up in our face. I can feel it. We should have stuck with *my* plan. We should have left Jim at the lodge. You should have never killed Elaine. What the hell were you thinking?"

"Are you finished?" asked Bobby. Then without waiting for an answer. "OK. My turn. If the police capture Jamie, all the evidence points to him. I made sure of that. Nothing, and I mean absolutely nothing points to us. Jamie can say what he wants, but he's a crackhead. Nobody's gonna believe anything he says. They have their man. The gun that killed Jim is at Jamie's house along with Jim's body. The poker iron that killed Elaine has his fingerprints all over it. And as far as the cops know, Jamie was the last person to see Margie alive. We're in the clear. There are *no* loose ends. I repeat. No loose ends. It's perfect with Jamie dead *or* alive."

"I wish I were as confident as you, but I do see loose ends."

"Like what?" asked Bobby, peeved.

"Like…" Wayne tried to think. "Like the clothes. Yes. The clothes. The overalls and boots we left at the lodge. They have Margie's blood and DNA and *our* DNA. They point directly to us. They need to be destroyed."

"That's it? That's all you can come up with?"

"No. And my computer. My plan needs to be erased and the disk destroyed."

"Good God, Wayne. You're fucking paranoid. Look. Why don't you go to the office, take a fucking hammer and beat the shit out of that computer like I did Elaine? That'll take care of that problem. And while you do that, I'll run up to the lodge and take care of the clothes. That'll get me out of your hair and vice versa… at least for a few hours. I think we need a break from each other."

For once, Bobby was right.

Chapter 80

Saturday, December 30, 2006, 9:18 a.m. EST

Jamie awoke with a start, totally disoriented. Having lived over half of his life on drugs, the feeling wasn't unusual. He did a quick visual tour of the room from the plush leather chair that had been his makeshift bed and instantly recognized the lodge's massive stacked stone fireplace. The fire had died out earlier that morning with only smoldering red embers, ashes and the smell of old smoke remaining. His sleep had been restless as he tossed and turned throughout the night, one that was filled with nightmares. Now awake, the truth was more horrible than the abhorrent dreams. His mother was dead and he had killed her.

In the past, every time trouble found him, he found his Dad and he would fix it. He would sermonize, cajole, beg, praise, ridicule, post bail, hire lawyers, hire psychologists, hire psychiatrists, whatever it took. Even lie to Elaine, if necessary. But this time he didn't need him or his advice and counsel. He didn't need to talk to anyone. He knew what he had to do. Amazingly, he felt relieved and comforted by his decision and the fact that he had made it himself.

Before losing his resolve, Jamie jumped up, did a quick pit stop, and headed to the kitchen for what would be his last ever breakfast at the lodge – a hastily brewed cup of coffee and a small bag of Famous Amos chocolate chip cookies. His and his Dad's favorite. He wasted little time finishing his Spartan breakfast. Afterward, he hand washed his cup and spoon and put them away. He hurriedly slipped on his Dad's large overcoat, turned out all of the lights in the lodge, closed the door behind him, and headed to the barn. Even in this freezing temperature, the Mercedes started quickly and easily.

It wouldn't be long before the Mercedes was nice and warm. Jamie looked around the interior of the car. It was such a beautiful car. It made him realize how good a life he had as a youth, the luxuries he had taken for granted, and how he had wasted his life, all for the sake of drugs.

But his drug days were over. And so was his life. He had so many regrets, especially the way he had treated his parents. Yet even in the darkest of times, he knew they still loved him - in their own way. His Dad had his sermons; his mother had her tough love. His Dad was permissive, lenient; his mother was strict, detached. His Dad had his 'I love you, son' and hugs; his mother had her 'Why can't you just grow up?'. In the end, they both wanted the same thing for their defiant and aimless son: responsibility, accountability, dependability and a life without drugs. That never happened. It wasn't their fault. He had always been told that until he hit rock bottom, he could never begin the road to recovery. But for him, rock bottom had been a moving target. Maybe death was his rock bottom. Like killing his mother. But more than likely, rock bottom was an eternity in Hell. He checked the fuel gauge. Half a tank. That was enough.

Chapter 81

Saturday, December 30, 2006, 9:57 a.m. EST

"God, that was brutal!" exclaimed Daniel as he and Johnny made it back to their desk and Bennie to his car. Having to work one Saturday a month was bad enough, but throw in a meeting with Vernon, *and* the commander only added insult to injury. The meeting had lasted longer than expected. Vernon wanted to hear everything - the evidence, witnesses, lab reports. Everything *including* Daniel's, Johnny's and Bennie's concerns. The commander remained silent. Again, not a good sign. In the end, however, everyone agreed that Jamie Barnes was their man. Especially with the fact that Jamie's fingerprints were on Elaine Barnes' murder weapon. With the BOLO on James H. Barnes III, every law enforcement agency located in their geographic region had a picture of the suspect on their computer along with the silver Mercedes, licensed NAGS 2. Hopefully, an arrest would come soon.

While at the meeting both Daniel's cell phone and Johnny's vibrated a couple of times. Both men ignored the calls as a courtesy to their supervisors. After they returned to their desk and checked their messages, they read that Nate Freeman, aka Skinny, had been arrested. Two officers had spotted Freeman giving out 'samples' to students at a nearby elementary school playground. They arrested him without incident and seized as many of the 'samples' from the kids as they could. A search of Freeman's vehicle, a 2006 Black Cadillac Escalade, produced a leather briefcase, a 9mm handgun with its serial number filed off, a portable safe on the passenger's side floor, and two car seats strapped to the back seat. According to the officer's arrest report, Freeman said that he had just dropped his kids off at a nearby daycare center when he saw kids at the nearby elementary school smoking weed. He said he was just trying to 'bust' them, make a citizen's arrest, take the drugs away from the children. The 'samples' were not his. The report said that Freeman denied knowing there was a gun in the car. If so, he said someone else must have left it there, or it was planted. The briefcase contained four packs of rolling papers, two packs of Camel cigarettes and three fake IDs, all with Nate's picture. Within the hour,

Nate had been processed and was in one of the interrogation rooms waiting for Johnny and Daniel's arrival.

Both detectives badged in through the security door to the basement and headed to the interrogation room. Looking through a two-way mirror, they could see Nate, nervously rubbing his hands on his pants legs, then his face then back to his pants legs.

"No good cop, bad cop for him. Just bad cops," offered Johnny, looking at Daniel who understood. Nate had been on the streets too long *not* to know the routine. Plus, he was on five years' probation. Another blip on his record and he was back in the slammer to finish the five. Both men entered the room. Johnny sat in front of Nate while Daniel stood with his back to the door.

"Nate, you know why you're here?" asked Johnny.

"Yeah. Something about me selling weed to kids. I told the cop I ain't doing that shit anymore. That I was just trying to be a good guy. You know. Take those drugs *away* from them kids. I learnt my lesson. Got jail time to prove it. Plus I got kids of my own, you know?"

"Do you *know* a Jamie Barnes?" ask Daniel ignoring Nate's earlier response.

"Never heard of the dude," answered Nate, his eyes staring at the table, never giving eye contact to Daniel or Johnny.

"Can you explain why your prints are all over his car?" Without waiting for a reply, Johnny continued. "Ever hear of Otto Max?"

Nate knew Otto Max. He was a competitor, always hitting on his customers.

"I might know something if we can forget about this little weed incident," smirked Nate, nodding his head profusely.

Johnny was fuming inside but kept professional.

"I think we've had enough today. Nate, you were caught selling drugs to minors. You were caught with a 9mm in your car, and you're on probation. Daniel, do you have Nate's probation officer's telephone number?"

Daniel held up his notepad for Nate to see.

"Now, you don't have to go off on me like that. I were just being funny. Yeah, Yeah, I know the dude," answered Nate now ready to throw Otto under the bus. "He lives somewhere near Capitol Street. His real name is Antoine Johnson. Me and him went to school together.

He likes to call hisself Otto Max 'cause he sells cars. Thinks he's a fucking big shot. And that *ain't* my gun."

Both detectives could feel the animosity in Nate's words.

"Where were you Wednesday morning, between 7 a.m. and 1 p.m.?"

Nate thought for a minute, then smiled showing off one of his gold front teeth.

"I was in traffic court. Got there about 8. Didn't leave until 1:30. Anything else?"

"What about Wednesday night, between 6 and 9 p.m.?" Daniel hoped that Nate was one of the two drivers in the surveillance tape.

Nate looked at the ceiling as he pondered the question and the answer. "Me and Roberta… my wife. We went to some friends… Jimbo and Willamena Brown. Watched football. Yeah. Saw the Florida State, UCLA bowl game. Florida State came back in the 4th quarter to beat the shit out of the Bruins. I forgit the score, but I won $25 off Jimbo. You call him. Axt him. I was there all night. At least until 1 a.m. I don't know what you're trying to pin on me but I ain't your man. I'm clean through and through," Nate said smugly.

Daniel left for a few minutes while Johnny continued to ask Nate questions. When Daniel returned, he whispered into Johnny's ear. "Looks like Nate's telling the truth about the traffic court. And the address for Otto Max is valid. I've sent a patrol car out to pick him up. I think we need to focus on Otto. Oh. I also called Nate's parole officer. He wasn't the least bit happy. I guess ol' Nate is about to get free room and board at taxpayer's expense for a while."

Both detectives looked at Nate and smiled. Nate didn't smile back.

Chapter 82

Saturday, December 30, 2006, 10:48 a.m. EST

Middleburg, Virginia's Police Department is located in an old c.1939 red brick building complex on S. Madison Street, just around the corner from the famous Red Fox Inn and Tavern. The main entrance to the building is only accessible by walking down two flights of stone steps and then taking a short walk through a courtyard. The police share the building with the city's health department. The interior design of the building is similar to a 'dogtrot' or 'breezeway' house where rooms are on either side of a hallway/breezeway that run the length of the house. The police occupy the first three rooms to the right of the long hallway. The first room is their administration office, the public's first point of contact. A Dutch-style door, with the bottom half locked and the top half wide open, separates the general public from the work area. People seeking police assistance are directed to that door. Unless someone saw the police department's small sign or the occasional police squad car parked out front, they could easily mistake it for a dress shop, florist, dental office, even an upscale restaurant. It looks nothing like its big-city cousins. Today, however, there were no squad cars parked out front. Only a large silver Mercedes.

.At an old wooden desk in the administrative office sat an attractive young redhead, feverously working on some paperwork. She was smartly dressed in her freshly starched black uniform and had her hair neatly pulled back into a ponytail. Normally, there was one other staff person on duty during the 8 to 5 shift. But today, because of the year-end holidays and the need for all personnel to be available for New Year's Eve duty, she was holding down the fort alone.

The petite redhead's phone rang just as a handsome young man wearing a much too large trench coat came to the door and poked his head in. She answered the phone and immediately placed the caller on hold. She then spoke to the young visitor.

"Hi! If you don't mind signing in," she said, then pointed to a clipboard on top of the door's shelf. "I'll be with you in just a minute."

She stared momentarily at the young man to make sure he understood, then returned to the caller.

"Hey, Amy. Geddings here," answered the caller. "Just wanted you to know I'm going to be a few minutes late. So don't panic."

"I thought you were doing a 3 to 11," replied Amy Carlson, Administrative Assistant.

"Not today. Chief wants me to pull an 11 to 11."

"You gonna be able to stay awake that long?" laughed Amy, then hung up before Geddings could reply. There was no panic.

Meanwhile, Jamie signed in as requested then printed his name and address in the appropriate areas. Under 'Police Matters' there were four check blocks: *Parking Tickets, Traffic Violations, Post Bail, and Others - Include Brief Description.* Jamie checked the *Others* block and wrote 'Wanted for murder in Washington DC.' He couldn't bring himself to write 'Wanted for murdering my mother.' He then sat down on one of the long wooden benches. A huge weight had been lifted from his shoulders. He had done it. His life as a free man was over, but he was doing the right thing. His Dad would be proud.

A recently discarded newspaper lay folded near him on the bench. He leaned over and picked it up. He needed something, anything to occupy his mind and help him from changing it. When he unfolded the paper, his eyes zoomed in on the headlines, 'Double Homicide in DC!' A picture of him, his mother and... *his father* occupied the entire top half of the front page of the *Washington Post.* In disbelief, he read the first paragraph that detailed the family slaughter that had him identified as the possible butcher. As he tried to read, he began to hyperventilate causing him to feel dizzy and nauseous. His heart was racing. The words began to blur but not before he saw: *Be on the lookout for... Last seen... Driving a Mercedes NAGS 2... Armed and dangerous... Possibly high on Drugs... Loner...* He didn't need to read anymore. His father and mother, dead! Both murdered by him!

"No! Oh God, No! No! It's not true! It's not *TRUE!*" he yelled out, throwing the paper to the floor, his raised voice startling the young redhead who quickly rose to see why the commotion.

Before she could say or do anything, Jamie had left, running out the door and up the steps to the street. The redhead ran after him but could only manage to see the young man as he drove off in a big silver car, license plate NAGS 2.

Chapter 83

Saturday, December 30, 2006, 11:01 a.m. EST

Only after Jamie had driven straight up South Madison Street, made a left on Washington Street, past South Pendleton Street, and then a left onto The Plains Road did the reality of what he had just read hit him harder than any drug he'd ever taken, spinning his mind out of control. He could still see the headlines in the paper, the pictures of his parents and the picture of him from his driver's license. How could it be? Tears that began with a trickle, steadily ramped up until they felt like a tsunami washing over his face. Driving became impossible with the constant flow of tears, the erratic heaving of his chest, and the gasping for air. The sleeve of his Dad's overcoat only provided temporary relief, for as soon as he wiped his eyes, they immediately demanded more attention. Finally, to the relief of the car behind him, he pulled off to the side of the road and parked. The flood of tears lasted for about five minutes then replaced by fear. He was now all alone. He had no one to turn to, no one to love him. He felt empty. Even in the worst of times, he always knew his parents loved him - especially his Dad. And now they were gone. He was in a void. Everything seemed to be spiraling out of control. His mother and now his Dad. Gone.

Once he had control of his tears, his angst, his emotions, and the intermittent heaving and waves of nausea, he shifted the car into 'Drive' and pulled back out on the highway. He didn't know where he was going or what direction the car was heading. He was just driving. Questions began to whirl around in his mind. How did his Dad get killed? When? Where? He could kick himself for not having taken the *Post* with him.

He needed answers. And he wouldn't get them sitting in jail. He needed time to think and a place to hide. It wouldn't be long before every law officer in the State of Virginia, Maryland and the District of Columbia would be looking for him. Obviously, his house was not an option. And going back to the lodge was out of the question with him having left his name at the Middleburg police department. Even a second-rate cop could make that connection.

As he drove, he found himself constantly looking in the rearview mirror as much as he looked out the front windshield. There wasn't a lot of traffic on the road, so every car that came from the opposite direction posed a threat. By now the police probably had the Mercedes' license tag. He needed to ditch the car or at the very least switch license plates and soon.

About fifteen minutes out of Middleburg, he saw his answer – a car sitting off the side of the road with a frozen rag hanging out the window - obviously abandoned. A heavy layer of snow covered the entire car suggesting that it had been there a while. Jamie parked behind it and turned on his flashers. There was no telling how long the car had been there or when the owner might return with help, so he knew he would have to act fast but not so fast as to arouse suspicion. Casually he got out of his car, walked to the back of the abandoned car and checked to see what tool he needed to remove its license plate. He did the same with the Mercedes. Both were fastened with flathead screws. He popped the trunk of the Mercedes and found his Dad's roadside emergency kit. Every car in the Barnes' family had one except his 1992 Cadillac which was lucky to have a spare tire. Using the flathead from the kit, he removed the license plate from the abandoned car and attached it to the Mercedes. He then buried the NAGS 2 license plate in the snow in a nearby field. Within minutes he was on the road again.

To keep from mistakenly returning to Middleburg, Jamie never made two left, or right-hand turns in a row. Even so, he never felt comfortable as to which direction he was heading. With the sun blocked by massive snow clouds, it was impossible to determine if he was heading north, south, east or west. And to further complicate matters, all of the roads were beginning to look the same with their similar surroundings of vast snow-covered farmlands, horse pastures and countless acres of trees. He drove for almost an hour down two-lane roads, private roads, dead-end roads and roads that circled back giving him that feeling that he was permanently lost in a maze of Virginia back roads when unexpectedly, signs pointing to I-66 began to appear.

At the Old Tavern Road interchange just outside of The Plains, Virginia, Jamie turned up the ramp and merged into the steady stream of cars and trucks. He was glad to be on the interstate, intermingling with other Silver Mercedes. At one of the more popular exits on I-66, Jamie parked his car, ran in and purchased a Washington Post. In the comfort of his Dad's car, with the engine running, and the heater pumping out heat, he sadly read every word about how the police had found his dead parents – his mother brutally murdered in her living room and his father shot to death in a 4th Street home owned by the dead man and occupied by the son, Jamie Barnes. In the same article, it told of the death of Margie Hamilton with the suspect, Jamie Barnes, being the last known person to see her alive. The police declined to speculate if all three murders were linked, but they did say that James H. Barnes III, aka, Jamie Barnes, was a 'person of interest' in all three murders.

Jamie laid the paper down in the passenger's seat. He stared out the window, looking at nothing in particular, just space. Then hanging his head low and covering his eyes with his hands, he began to weep. A lot at first. But the tears soon began to subside as he began to feel anger boiling up inside of him. Not fear. Anger. Yes, he was a drug user. Yes, a bad son. Yes, a compulsive liar. Yes, a miserable loser. But a murderer? NO! And HELL NO!

Jamie threw the car in reverse, then before it came to a full stop, shifted into 'Drive' causing the car to spin in the slushy snow as he drove away from the service station and to his next destination: Washington, DC.

Chapter 84

Saturday, December 30, 2006, 11:06 a.m. EST

Minutes later, Corporal Ray Geddings slammed his car into 'Park' and ran as fast as he could into the Middleburg's police building. He was met at the Dutch door by Amy Carlson, Middleburg PD's youngest and prettiest administrative assistant/secretary.

"What do you mean a murderer came into the office?" he almost yelled.

"Just what I said. Look!" Amy handed Geddings the sign-in sheet pointing to the last entry. "And I saw this on the floor. It's him!" She showed him the newspaper with a small picture of Jamie Barnes under the larger pictures of his mother and father. Geddings looked briefly at the pictures then back at the sign-in sheet. He then grabbed the paper from Amy.

"See that's him... only he looked much nicer. No mustache or beard and his hair pulled back into a ponytail. He was very handsome, not like he looks in this picture. Oh... and I also got his license plate number."

"Oh, boy!" muttered the young officer as he perused the paper and quickly picked up on the fact that the elder Barnes had worked for NAGS.

"What?"

"Those two dudes that me and Al saw at the old Jackson house last Wednesday night... they work for NAGS! Hell, they *are* NAGS! I gotta go! I gotta check on them, make sure they're all right. I'll call if I need backup."

"What do you mean? I don't understand what you're saying. What does NAGS have to do with any of this? Hey! Don't you go running off without telling me what's going on!"

"Call Al! Tell him about the sign-in sheet. Tell him I've gone to the old Jackson house. He'll fill you in! Oh. And bag that pen that guy used when he signed in... for fingerprints!"

"What about the State Police?" asked Amy as Geddings ran out the back door.

"You call 'em. Tell them what you told me."

Before Amy could get another word out of her mouth, the young corporal, only two years on the force, was headed out of town, siren blaring.

Chapter 85

Saturday, December 30, 2006, 11:48 a.m. EST

Bobby was in no hurry to get to the lodge. Maybe Wayne was worried about the stuff they had left up at the lodge, but he wasn't. As far as he was concerned, next week would have been just fine. But rather than fight over something so trivial, he gave in. Let Wayne win his little battle. Keep both men happy. Plus, it would give Bobby a needed hiatus from Wayne's neurotic doomsday prophecies.

Before leaving Washington, he returned to his Watergate apartment where he showered and put on a fresh change of clothes. The yellow crime scene tape that crisscrossed Jim Barnes' apartment door was impossible to miss. It stood out like a neon sign. Just like dogs, the police had their way of marking their territory.

Right off I-66, he found a Starbucks where he stopped for an apple fritter, a cup of strong coffee, and a Washington Post. The bold headlines were hard to ignore. As he sat at his table slurping coffee, he read every article related to the three murders. While his 'plan' hadn't gone exactly as he'd hoped, from what he read, it didn't matter. The press, the police, and the public already had Jamie tried and convicted. And with a $150,000 reward on his head, he was a dead man walking. So what if his plan wasn't as meticulously laid out as Wayne's, it worked. Unlike Wayne's plan which was rigid almost to a fault, his was based on common sense that allowed for adjustments on the fly. In the corporate world, where you could manage, predict, pressure, terminate, organize, bribe, whatever, Wayne's planning methodology was best. But this wasn't the corporate world. Wayne was so out of his element. Plus he didn't have a U.S. Senate seat to lose. Bobby did. So they were going to do things his way and it was working.

Bobby continued to mentally berate Wayne all the way to the lodge finding fault with almost every aspect of Wayne's plan. The rebuke immediately ceased when he saw the police squad car parked out in front. Bobby rushed up the porch steps just as the front door swung open. Coming from the lodge to greet Bobby was one of the cops that he and Wayne had met Wednesday night.

"Man, I'm glad it's you!" exclaimed the officer as he holstered his gun. "I know you don't remember me, but I'm Corporal Geddings. Me and my partner met you and your friend here a couple nights ago."

"What do you mean you're glad it's me? Why are you here? How'd you get in?" asked Bobby in rapid-fire succession as he walked past the officer, into the lodge, and stared directly at the kitchen, and in particular the appliances. To his relief, all were closed.

Corporal Geddings followed him in. "Well sir, the door wasn't locked, so I just let myself in. I feared that maybe that Barnes fellow might be here. One of the ladies in the office saw him this morning and I immediately thought about you and your friend. I was worried he might have come up here and kilt y'all like he did all them others."

Bobby stopped and turned to the officer. "What you mean that one of the ladies in the office saw him? Him? You mean Jamie Barnes?"

Bobby was mad and upset, and the young officer knew it.

"Yes. Him. The Barnes kid that kilt his parents. Anyways, Amy… Amy Carlson. She works in the office. She saw him. He was at the station house. He signed the log-in sheet. I saw it myself. Amy said she recognized him from the picture in the newspaper. And you know something else? He wrote down on the sign-in sheet that he was wanted for murder. Can you believe that?"

Bobby looked confused.

"Wait a minute! Jamie Barnes *came* to your office, *told* you that he was wanted for murder and *no one* locked him up?" asked Bobby incredulously, his anger steadily growing and showing. "Talk about incompetence!"

"*Sir.* Maybe I'm not making myself clear. When the suspect arrived, *no officer* was there. And he left before I got there. Maybe he got cold feet about turning hisself in. But Amy, the lady at the office, she got his license plate number. NAGS 2. There's a BOLO… be on the lookout on that car and tag. So that's why I came here as fast as I could. To make sure you two were safe. I would think you'd appreciate our concern."

Bobby didn't know exactly what was going on but one thing for sure, he needed the cop out of the lodge and now. So far, no harm had been done.

"Well, Officer… er…" stammered Bobby looking for the officer's name tag, "Officer Geddings, I'm sorry you went to all this trouble for nothing. As you can see I'm all right. Nobody killed me." Bobby laughed trying to calm his and the officer's anger. "In fact, I wasn't even here last night. And neither was Mr. Peters, the other gentleman you met. After your visit Wednesday night, he was so shaken up, we left right after you did." He then began to usher Geddings toward the door.

Geddings turned and looked at Bobby, pushing Bobby's hand away.

"Well, if *you* weren't here, *somebody* was. Everything points to the Barnes boy. Look at the fireplace, it's still smoldering. And there's something else I found that's just not right." Geddings headed to the kitchen. He pointed to the coffee maker and continued, "Look. The grounds are still wet. And there's more."

Then Corporal Geddings walked over to the microwave and, using a paper towel around the handle so not to destroy evidence, opened its door. He pointed to the blood-splattered white jumpsuits and caps. "I found this when I went to reheat my coffee. I know that you or your friend didn't leave them. I'm thinking it *has* to be that Barnes fellow."

"I'm not a detective, but it sure looks like you're on to something," commented Bobby as he patted the officer on the back. He had a real problem on his hand and he had to contain it.

"Let me show something else I found!" said young Geddings who moved over to the stove and opened the oven, again using a paper towel. "Looky what we got here!" he exclaimed. "Now who in hell's name is gonna put a couple of pair of boots in the oven? I'm not the brightest cop on the beat, but like you said, I do believe I'm on to something. Might even have something to do with that boy murdering his parents. And, with two pair of everything, I'm a-thinking we're talking about an accomplice."

"So have you called anyone to let them know what you found?" Bobby asked as he walked back into the den, followed by Geddings. "You know, evidence like this has to be handled with extreme caution. It can't be contaminated. You haven't contaminated it, have you?"

"Oh, no sir. I know all about handling evidence. I'm supposed to use latex gloves but they're in the squad car so, instead, I used paper towels when I opened the oven and microwave just in case there's some prints. *And* I was just about to call the State Police when you drove up."

"So, did you call anyone back at your office to let them know that you saw me drive up? That I was OK? Not that I'm that important, mind you. But you *did* come all the way out here to check on me."

"Well, I called Sergeant Frankel soon as I got here. He's the other officer you met the other night. I told him that everything was OK. That nobody was here. That he didn't need to come. But I probably do need to call him now to find out what to do next."

"That's what I would do," replied Bobby quickly considering his options.

Corporal Ray Geddings pulled out his cell, turned his back to Bobby for a little privacy and began to dial. Before he could press the final digit, Bobby, who *was* wearing gloves, buried the nearby fire poker into his skull. Young Geddings crumpled to the floor with blood gushing from his head. Bobby jerked out the poker and with a second blow, guaranteed the young corporal would never make sergeant.

Bobby threw the poker down next to his victim then checked for any bloodstains on his pants legs, shoes, gloves, and overcoat. It was a clean kill. While the blood seeped out from under the officer's head, Bobby quickly gathered the tarp from the dishwasher, the two jumpsuits and caps from the microwave, and rubber boots from the oven, and headed to the front door. Before leaving, he turned to do a final visual check of the lodge. That's when he saw the officer move, just slightly. But he moved. Maybe it was an involuntary muscle twitch or jerk, or maybe he was still alive. Regardless, he couldn't take a chance. Laying the armful of incriminating evidence on a nearby chair, he slowly walked over to the young officer and pushed him with his foot. Seeing no movement, he reached down, unholstered the officer's gun, unlocked the safety and fired a bullet directly into the back of what remained of the officer's head. He then locked the weapon and shoved it in his overcoat pocket. There was no doubt in his mind that the officer was now sufficiently dead. And for all practical purposes, so was Jamie Barnes - cop killer. If the bounty hunters didn't kill him, the police would. Jamie's chances of being taken alive had just taken a sudden nosedive.

Along the Lee Jackson Memorial Highway, on his way back to Washington, Bobby pulled off to the rear of a service station and deposited the two jumpsuits and caps into a trash bin. At a second service station along Interstate 66, he rid himself of the two pairs of rubber boots and tarp.

As much as he hated to admit it, Wayne had been right about going back to the lodge.

Chapter 86

Saturday, December 30, 2006, 1:37 p.m. EST

"Well, you were right, as usual," said Bobby speaking into his cell phone as he crossed over the Key Bridge from Virginia into Washington, DC.

"Why? What do you mean?" asked Wayne who automatically shut the door to his office ensuring his privacy even though no one else was at the office.

"You know. Those boots and jumpsuits. It's a good thing you insisted on me going up to get them today."

"Why? You get that same worried feeling I had?"

"No. Nothing like that. It's just that when I got there, we had a visitor."

"What? Oh my God! Who? Nobody was supposed to be at the lodge. Nobody was scheduled…"

"Don't get your panties in a wad. It was only one of the cops that we met last Wednesday, you know, when the alarm went off. Anyway, he *greeted* me as I walked through the door."

"Why? What happened? Did the alarm go off again?"

"No. We never set it. But evidently, Jamie stayed there last night. Used the lodge as a hideout. From what I gather, he went to the police and, based on what the cop told me, was going to turn himself in. But, instead, he just left. Maybe he got cold feet or whatever. Anyway, the cop came to the lodge to make sure we were safe. Make sure we weren't dead."

"Dead?"

"Yeah. I guess he thought we were still there. The cop wanted to make sure that Jamie hadn't *kilt* us," replied Bobby, mocking the officer's dialect.

"Well, I hope you got rid of everything."

"Oh yeah. I dumped everything into a couple of different trash bins on the way back. But I did have a slight problem at the lodge."

"What do you mean? What kind of problem?"

"I probably shouldn't tell you because I know how you worry, but sooner or later you'll hear it anyway."

"Hear what?"

"Jamie killed the cop that was up at the lodge."

"What! What are you talking about?"

"The cop found the boots and stuff in the kitchen before I got there, so Jamie had to take him out. No loose ends, you know what I mean?"

"What do you mean Jamie had to… OH! MY! GOD! NOT AGAIN!" yelled Wayne almost hysterical. "Please tell me you're joking!!"

"Wayne. I don't joke."

"Bobby, you're… you're crazy. This has gone too far. Way too far. We need to go to the police."

"Wayne, shut up and listen to me. Jamie killed that cop. He had to. Now, you get a grip on yourself. Everything's OK. Look. I haven't had lunch. I'm real near Clyde's in Georgetown. If you haven't already eaten, why don't you meet me? I'm starving, and I'm craving some of their meatloaf."

Wayne couldn't believe what he was hearing. "How can you even think about eating? My stomach's in knots. This is just too much. Too much. I…"

Bobby interrupted Wayne before he could complete his thought. "Wayne, you started this mess. I'm finishing it. Everything is going to be all right. Just calm down. Keep your cool. Chill a little bit. Look. Jamie is as good as dead once it's known that he killed a cop."

"But you killed the cop. And Elaine."

"Yeah. And you killed Jim and Margie. So we're even. Nothing is going to happen unless you start freaking out. Just don't do anything stupid until I get there. OK?"

"Yeah. OK," answered Wayne, and hung up. But he wasn't OK.

So I guess we're not meeting for lunch, thought Bobby.

Chapter 87

Saturday, December 30, 2006, 2:58 p.m. EST

Like every other detective in large metropolitan police departments, Johnny and Daniel never experienced a shortage of work. Crime never took a holiday or vacation. While the Barnes and Hamilton murders had the eyes and ears of their boss, the commander, the chief, the mayor, and the ever-hungry media, the two detectives still had other cases to solve. With no apparent leads to the whereabouts of Jamie Barnes or Otto Max, and waiting for information from outstanding search warrants, they turned their attention to other unsolved crimes.

Both men were deep in concentration, reading through documents, making notations, filling out paperwork when Daniel's phone rang. Every time one of the detectives' phones rang, it was like a crapshoot. Sometimes the calls were winners - suspects ready to confess, new leads for dead-end cases, and sometimes even arrested suspects. But more often than not, they were losers - new homicide cases adding to their ever-increasing workload, disappearing witnesses, or worst of all, legal maneuverings that freed the guilty.

"Detective Whitehead," answered Daniel who remained silent until the call ended. Throughout the call, Johnny looked at Daniel giving him the *'What's happening? Who's that?'* look. Daniel held up his *' Wait a minute finger'* and shaking his head at the same time.

"What was that all about?" Johnny asked as soon as Daniel hung up the phone.

"It's Vernon. There's been another murder. This one's in Middleburg, Virginia at a hunting lodge owned by *NAGS.* Can you believe it?" asked Daniel, and then without waiting for a reply. "It gets worse. It's a police officer. And they believe that Jamie Barnes is responsible. So Vernon wants us to assist, like now. Bennie's already on his way. Middleburg's captain, William Allen, is expecting a phone call from us. ASAP. Oh, and get this. The FBI is being brought in on Monday, so all the higher-ups want us to wrap it up before that happens. Bad publicity and all that nonsense. Like we can't do our jobs without getting the FBI involved."

"Oh for crying out loud!" lamented Johnny, choosing to keep his thoughts to himself.

Within minutes, both detectives were on a conference call with Middleburg's Chief of Police, William Allen, Sergeant Al Frankel and administrative assistant, Amy Carlson. Daniel had his legal pad out, and Johnny had his notepad and micro-recorder. After brief introductions, Chief Allen gave a 20,000 foot summary of what transpired at the police department and at the lodge. He then asked Amy to give a more detailed account of Jamie Barnes' brief visit to their office.

Amy leaned toward the microphone, cleared her throat and began.

"He was a nice looking guy, not like the photo in the newspaper or the BOLO. But it was definitely him. Jamie Barnes. He's also on our surveillance video. Anyways, when he came into our office, I was on the phone with Corporal..." Amy paused to collect herself. ".... Corporal Geddings. I ask him... the Barnes fellow, to sign in. And he did. Then... before I had a chance to even get up from my desk, he starts yelling and runs out the door. I followed him up to the street and saw him drive off in a silver car heading up Madison Street. The license plate on the car was NAGS 2." She then spelled it out for the two detectives. "I checked the sign-in sheet after I got back to the office and immediately called Ray... er...Corporal Geddings and told him what had happened and what the Barnes fellow had written on the sign-in sheet. That he was wanted for murder in Washington. When Ray got to the office, he looked at the sign-in sheet and left immediately, telling me to call Sergeant Frankel, the Virginia State Police, and to bag the pen Barnes used for fingerprints, which I did. That's all I know."

"Thank you, Amy," said the chief, kindly. "Any questions?"

"Yes," quickly answered Johnny. "Amy, you said that the suspect, Jamie, started yelling. Do you remember what set him off and what he yelled?"

"Sort of," responded Amy as she looked at her page of handwritten notes. "He started yelling something like *It's not true.*' He yelled it a couple of times. But I'm not sure what caused him to start yelling like that. Maybe it was the newspaper with his picture in it. I can't really say. He just did, then he left. He didn't look like he was on any drugs... you know how drugs cause you to do weird things. And he didn't look like one of those homeless guys who start yelling things for no reason. That's all I know. Is that any help?" Amy felt embarrassed that she couldn't fully answer Johnny's question.

"Yes. Very helpful. You did great. Especially getting the license plate."

The chief looked at Sergeant Frankel and nodded. Amy settled back in her seat as the sergeant leaned in toward the conference phone and began to speak.

"This is Sergeant Frankel. I'll pick it up from there. Like Amy said, she called me and told me what happened. Immediately, I knew what Corporal Geddings was thinking. This past Wednesday night, we got a call from the Loudoun County Sheriff's Department asking if we could check out a possible security breach at the old Jackson's place, now owned by the North American Gun Society. NAGS. All of the Sheriff's Department's officers were tied up with a big tractor-trailer wreck on I-66. So Corporal Geddings and I went to the lodge instead. Everything checked out fine. The two gentlemen who set off the alarm were NAGS employees. Mr. Robert Armstrong and Mr. Wayne Peters."

Johnny and Daniel looked at each other in surprise at the mention of Armstrong's and Peters' names, with Johnny shrugging his large shoulders.

Frankel continued. "Because these two gentlemen were NAGS' employees and this Jamie Barnes, his daddy also being a NAGS' employee, Corporal Geddings decided to drive up to the lodge to check on Mr. Armstrong and Mr. Peters, make sure they were all right. I was just about to head up that way myself when Ray called me and told me that everything was OK. That nobody was there and laughed when he said that nobody was dead. Dammitall! I shoulda gone to check on him." Sergeant Frankel's voice broke and he paused a moment to compose himself. "Ray… Corporal Geddings said he just wanted to check out a few things and would be back at the office within the hour. When I called him on his mobile at about 12:30 to see if he wanted to meet us for lunch, he didn't answer. I tried a couple more times, and again no answer. So I got worried and drove up to the Jackson place to check on him. It's about ten, fifteen minutes away. That's when I saw him… lying next to the fireplace. Oh God! This is so hard!" said the big man, choking back the tears.

"That's OK Al," consoled Chief Allen. "We all miss him."

The sergeant waited a few seconds then continued. "Anyway, I saw him lying next to the fireplace and thought maybe he had fallen. So I rushed over to see if I could help. That's when I saw the fire poker lying next to his head with blood all over it. And his gun was missing.

His head was such a mess, I couldn't tell if all the damage had been done by the poker iron or if he had been shot or... or maybe both. Anyway, I checked his pulse just to make sure he... Then I called the Chief. Right now, we have Corporal Latham and a couple of guys from the sheriff's department keeping watch. Everything's just like it was when I got there. I didn't touch anything except the front doorknob and Ray. That's all I got to say other than I want that vicious son-of-a-bitch put out of his fucking misery! What kind of animal..."

Middleburg's Chief immediately jumped in. "Thank you, Al. You know we *all* feel that way. Detectives, I'm sorry if our emotions got the best of us. This has been really hard on us. Ray was family."

"There's no need to be sorry. We completely understand," countered Daniel. "Over the years, we've lost a number of our guys, and we know the feeling. Based on what you've told us, and what's happened here, Jamie Barnes is most likely our killer, but until we hear his side of the story, until all the evidence is in, we have to keep an open mind. I do have a couple of questions for Sergeant Frankel."

Frankel quickly responded. "Yes sir and I apologize for my outburst, but I loved that boy like a son. I went to school with his Mom and Dad. Saw him grow up. He played ball with my boys. Oh, Jeez," said the sergeant, fighting off his emotions.

Daniel waited a few seconds before asking his question. "Now you said that a Mr. Armstrong and Mr. Peters were at the lodge, the Jackson house, this past Wednesday?" asked Daniel looking at his notes.

"Yes, sir."

"Did they say why they were there?"

"Yes, sir. They said they were there for a little R & R."

"Do you know if they stayed at the lodge after you left?"

"You mean overnight? I don't know. But if I had to guess, I doubt it. The Peters fellow looked kind of shook up. All I know is that Corporal Geddings called me around noon to tell me that nobody was at the lodge and the door was unlocked."

"Johnny? You have any questions?"

"None that come to mind but I'm sure that'll change."

"Chief Allen, Sergeant Frankel, Ms. Carlson. You've all been most helpful. Detective Williams and I will be at the crime scene shortly. I would appreciate it if Sergeant Frankel could meet us there. Our forensic expert, Dr. Benjamin Archer, has already left and should be there within the hour. The FBI is also involved so they may be calling you to ask questions. I know I don't have to ask, but please call us if *anything* comes to mind."

Daniel and Johnny hung up their phones and looked at each other.

"Well, that was interesting," surmised Daniel. "Another nail in the coffin for Jamie Barnes."

"Yeah. That's what bothers me," added Johnny. "It's too perfect. What also bothers me is this whole Middleburg police thing. He goes to the police department, signs in as a wanted murderer then yells, *It's not true!* Then for no reason, leaves. The next thing we know is one of their police officers is dead. This whole thing is too bizarre for me. Like a bad movie."

"Yeah, like a bad movie. But, you know, sometimes we're handed an easy case where there is absolutely no question as to who the bad guys are and... Wrinkles? You've got that spacey look. What's going on it that little brain of yours?"

Johnny didn't answer immediately but continued in his thoughts for a few moments. Then...

"You're right. I'm probably reading too much into this whole thing. It's just that I have this fear that we are overlooking something. My mind keeps going back to what Kyle Hamilton said. That Jamie was the kindest, most gentle person, you'd ever want to meet. These murders were definitely not committed by a kind, gentle person. They were committed by someone evil, someone with no conscience. A psychopath."

"Johnny, I agree with you. But we can't ignore the evidence. Everything points to him."

"I know. I know. Look. If it's OK with you, do you mind going over to Middleburg by yourself? Bennie will be there. I mean, what more could you want? I have a few things I want to work through. You know, go over my notes, the ME reports, whatever. Maybe look at these cases from a different angle, if there is a different angle. Could be everything circles back to Jamie."

Daniel left for Virginia without Johnny.

Chapter 88

Saturday, December 30, 2006, 3:03 p.m. EST

The caller-ID on Kyle's cell phone displayed 'Unknown' as it rang. Normally, Kyle wouldn't have answered it, but with his mother's visitation set for Sunday and the funeral, Monday, he decided to answer just in case it was one of his mother's friends needing directions to the church or the funeral home or possibly some other information.

"Woody?"

"No. This is Kyle Ham..." Kyle stopped in mid-sentence. Only a handful of people ever called him 'Woody' and he recognized the voice on the phone.

"Oh my God! Lefty? Is that you?"

There was no response at first. Then, "Can we talk? Are you by yourself?"

It was Jamie Barnes, known in his younger golfing years as 'Lefty' because he had played left-handed.

"Yes! Yes! I'm by myself. Where are you?"

"I'm here in Washington. That's all I can tell you. I want you to know that it wasn't me. I didn't kill your Mom. I loved your Mom. I hope you believe me."

"I do. I believe you. I told the police the same thing. I told them there was no way."

There was a long silence.

"Jamie? You still there?"

Silence again. Then muffled sobs. "I can't believe my Dad is dead. Oh, God! Oh, God..." Jamie's voice cracked and tapered off as he tried to talk.

"Did you..." Kyle attempted to ask, but Jamie interrupted him.

"Oh noooooooo! I could never, never hurt him. I loved him so much. Oh, God! What am I going to do? I'm *so* alone."

"You've got to call the police. Turn yourself in. I know two detectives…"

Jamie interrupted. "*No!* That's not going to happen. The police think I did it. So they're not looking for anybody else. I'm the 'person of interest' as the paper says. But I know I didn't kill your mom or my Dad."

"Jamie. What about…"

"Mother? They also say I killed my mother, but I don't know. I'm so confused. I wish I could tell you that I *wasn't* responsible. But the night she was killed, I was stoned. All I remember is that I went to our house and mother let me in. The next thing I know is I wake up the next morning and find her in the living room, *dead.* But I swear in God's name, I don't remember doing it. Everything points to me so I must have done it. But everything also points to me that I killed my Dad and your Mom. And I *know* for a fact *I didn't.*"

"Who do you think could have done it? You don't owe anybody any money, like your drug dealers, do you? Like they were out for revenge. Something like that?" Kyle asked.

"No way! I've been pretty stupid all my life, but I know better than to mess with them. I've seen firsthand what they can do when they feel they've been screwed over. It's scary!"

"Well, you can't just sit around and let whoever did this put the blame on you. You need to turn yourself in. Tell them your side of the story. Let them…"

"No! They'd never believe me."

"Well, I believe you."

"That means a lot to me, Kyle. You've always been a friend. How could I have messed up my life so? Oh, God. Look. I need *you* to call the police. Tell them that I called you. If you don't, you're an accessory. *That* can't happen. Tell them that I did *NOT* kill my Dad or your Mom. If they ask for this number, you can give it to them, but no one will answer. The phone's disposable and I'm tossing it after I hang up. One other thing. I need an hour's head start before you call them. I want to talk to a man named John Richards. He's a congressm…"

"I know him!" interrupted Kyle. "He and two guys from NAGS came by Mom's apartment to see me and Aaron. They wanted to set up some kinda memorial or something like that for Mom. Aaron saw right through them. Shut 'em up. You think Richards is somehow involved?"

"I don't know. I overheard this guy named Armstrong, who works with Dad, say that Richards might kill everybody. And then I found some pictures of him... Look. I gotta go. He just pulled up."

"He? Who pulled up? Richards? Armstrong? Wait. Wait. Don't do anything stupid."

But Jamie had already left.

Chapter 89

Saturday, December 30, 2006, 3:18 p.m. EST

Congressman Richards used his ample butt to close the rear door of his car, as both his hands were full. In one hand, he held a small bag of groceries, and in the other, he had a firm grip on a bottle of Chateau Montelena 2004 Cabernet Sauvignon - a most exquisite red wine and one of his favorites. Richards was not normally a happy man. Happy didn't have a place in his disposition or personality. But today was different. He found himself sporting a smile and humming his favorite song, 'It's Raining Men.' He still couldn't believe his luck! I mean what were the odds of him bumping, both figuratively and literally, into an old friend of his at that god-awful strip club. Someone he hadn't seen in over four years

His friend, Darryl Coleman - a muscular, brown hair, brown-eyed, manly-looking man, and a lawyer by trade - was at the club with a group of his younger associates. Like the congressman, Darryl was not officially out of the closet, and only a few people suspected he was gay even though he was 49 years old, had never been married, and had never been seen out in public with a woman except in groups. Both men had left separately from the strip club after a few more drinks but met up again at an underground gay spot known only to the elite Washington gays. There, they talked about old times and caught up on what had been happening in their lives. For the life of him, the congressman couldn't remember why he and Darryl had never become partners. He was sooooo good looking and sooooo intellectually entertaining, not like some of the male bimbos he had dated in the past. The evening had ended with Darryl accepting an invitation to an early Saturday night dinner at the congressman's house.

The snow was lightly falling causing the congressman to watch his every step as he made his way to the front door of his stylish townhouse. Richards loved how it covered the dirt and grime of the city and made everything beautiful. He cautiously set the bottle of wine on the front stoop freeing up his hand to unlock his front door. Turning off the alarm, he set the bag of groceries on a foyer table and glanced over at his antique English Briggs grandfather clock to check the time. He had lots to do, but it was still early. He wanted his dinner to be perfect for Darryl. Mentally he reviewed his menu - Oysters Rockefeller as the appetizer with Steak Diane as the main course ending with Crème Brulee. His mouth watered just thinking about it and Darryl.

Richards quickly returned to the front door to retrieve his prized bottle of wine. As he stooped to pick it up, he heard the rush of snow-crunching footsteps approaching him. When he looked up, he saw a very handsome young man, wearing an ill-fitted overcoat, almost on top of him. His face was familiar. He had the look of one of the thousands of Capitol Hill staff workers, but his face showed an anger that alarmed Richards.

"Get in the house!" said the young man quietly but firmly, and pointing what appeared to be a gun in his overcoat pocket towards Richards. "Do it now! And don't say or try anything or I'll shoot you."

"Do you know who I am?" blustered Richards.

"Shut up and get in the house!" Replied Jamie in a hushed angry voice and raised his left coat pocket even higher as he spoke.

Richards began backing into his house, keeping an eye on the young man and alternately keeping an eye on what appeared to be a gun in the man's coat pocket. His backward movement abruptly ended when he unwittingly bumped into the foyer table catching him by surprise and causing him to drop his bottle of cabernet. The bottle landed first on Richards' foot causing him to wince in severe pain and then hit the hardwood floor where the neck of the bottle shattered causing its expensive contents to begin spilling out onto the floor and under the foyer's expensive Oriental rug. Instinctively, Richards reached down and quickly righted the broken bottle.

"You... Stupid... Imbecile! Look what you've done," bellowed Richards, either having completely forgotten or simply ignored the fact that the young man had threatened to shoot him. "You know how much that bottle of wine cost? And look at my rug! Shit! Shit! Shit! OK! What the hell are you doing here? What do you want? If it's money...."

Then suddenly, he recognized the intruder whose face had been plastered on the front page of every daily newspaper and viewed as the lead story on every major TV news channel. His demeanor immediately changed from indignation to fear.

"I know you! You're Jim Barnes' kid. Oh God. Don't hurt me. Pleeeeese. Pleeeese!" he begged, dropping to his knees, shaking.

"Oh shut your whining! And get up," barked Jamie as he slammed the front door shut. "I'm not going to hurt you." Once he could look Richards in the eye, he moved closer to the congressman and asked, "Why did you kill my Dad? Was it because of this filth?" He then shoved an opened, large brown folder towards Richards' face.

The accusation caught Richards totally off guard, replacing his short-lived fear with shock then outrage.

"What the *hell* are you talking about? *You* killed your dad. *You* killed all those people including that old lady, Millie, or whatever the hell her name is. Not me!" Richards then surprised Jamie by grabbing the top of the folder. Jamie instinctively jerked back causing the folder to fan open and a number of the photos to spill out onto the floor with a few falling into the pool of expensive cabernet.

"Oh my God!" shrieked Richards as he saw the pornographic photos of him with other men in different stages of undress and homosexual activity. "Where'd you get these?" he asked as he knelt down and began shuffling through every picture including the soggy ones in the wine spill, shaking his head in disbelief.

Jamie said nothing but watched as Richards gathered up the photos and then snatched the brown folder from Jamie's hand.

Then looking up at Jamie with his eyes shooting daggers, Richards hollered, "I SAID, WHERE DID YOU GET THESE?"

"AND I ASKED WHY'D YOU KILL MY DAD?" retorted Jamie, yelling back at Richards just as loud, then stuck his hand back into his overcoat pocket raising what appeared to be a gun as high as it could go.

"LOOK, YOU ASSHOLE," bellowed Richards and then in a lowered know-it-all tone. "I've been around this town long enough to know when someone is bluffing, and you're not very good at it. If you've got a gun, you better fucking use it now before I call the cops!" He then turned his back to Jamie and started walking toward the kitchen.

"No. No. Don't call the cops. Please. See, I don't have a gun!" Jamie then pulled his left hand from his coat pocket then patted the pocket down to show that nothing was there. "See?" Then to further reassure Richards, who had turned around and was returning to the foyer, Jamie pulled out the pocket liner, again revealing nothing. He then started backing up to the front door. As he retreated, he said apologetically, "I'm sorry. I shouldn't have come here. Obviously, I've made a really bad mistake."

He turned, reached for the front doorknob and had the door partially opened when he saw Richards' hand shove it closed. Then Richards slid in between Jamie and the door pushing him back into the foyer while yelling in his face.

"WAIT A FUCKING MINUTE! YOU CAN'T JUST BARGE INTO MY HOME. ACCUSE ME OF MURDER THEN LEAVE. WE'RE GONNA FINISH WHAT YOU STARTED. NOW, WHERE DID YOU GET THESE FUCKING PICTURES?"

Frightened by Richards' violent outburst, Jamie began talking as fast as he could, telling him what he knew in hopes of calming him down. "They were in that folder at my Dad's apartment. In his safe." Jamie pointed to the folder that Richards was clutching.

"Why'd he have these? Where'd he get them? Why do you have them?" asked Richards in rapid succession.

"I… I don't know where my Dad got them. All I can tell you is what I overheard from a guy named Armstrong. He works with my Dad."

"I know who he is," interrupted Richards. "Tell me more."

"Anyway, he… Armstrong was in my Dad's apartment talking to someone on his cell phone. I can't remember everything he said, but I do know he *specifically* mentioned your name and how he said you would *kill* them all if you found out about the folder. So I assumed that included my Dad. I found your address inside the folder, so that's how I knew where you lived."

"I'm confused. Why would Bobby Armstrong give *you* this folder?"

"No. He didn't give me the folder. I doubt he even knows I have it. He didn't even know I was in the apartment. I was hiding in the bathroom."

"OK. I'm really confused now. What were you doing hiding in the bathroom?"

Jamie paused before saying anything else, embarrassed to tell Richards that he was there stealing money from his own Dad.

Then resolutely, "I was getting some money out of my Dad's safe in his apartment… in his office. Your folder was also in the safe, on top of the money. I took it out so I could get to the money. That's when I heard someone coming into the apartment. It was Mr. Armstrong. When I closed the safe, I forgot I had left it out. So I shoved it under the sofa. I didn't want Mr. Armstrong to know that I was there or what I was doing so I hid in the bathroom. He never saw me, but I saw him through the door crack. He was on his cell phone, talking to someone and that's when I overheard him."

"And that asshole Armstrong said that I would kill them if I ever found out about this folder?"

"Yes, sir. Kill *everybody* is what I think he said."

"Well, he's fucking right." Then Richards thought for a second. This had blackmail stamped all over it.

Continuing. "So because my name was mentioned by Bobby Armstrong, you presumed that I killed your daddy?"

"Yes, sir. I'm sorry. It's just that I miss him so much and…"

"Look. I might be a lot of things but a murderer I'm not. I don't even like guns. Never even owned one. Furthermore, from what I read, your father was murdered this past Wednesday. I wasn't even in Washington until late Wednesday night. But I don't think I need to *prove* this to you."

"No. No. I believe you," answered Jamie, at a loss as to what to do next. Everything seemed to point to Richards. It seemed so logical. The contents of Richards' folder were so vile, so damning, it was a career killer if it ever fell into the wrong hands. And Armstrong had specifically mentioned Richards' name. Yet he believed Richards.

"Look, son," Richards said reverting to his congressman's persona, "if I were you, I would turn myself in to the police. Let them do their job."

"No sir. I can't do that. I've read the paper. They think I did it. I think I'm gonna check out some of the other folders. See if there's a possible connection there."

"Wait! You've got other folders? Folders, like mine?"

"Yes. Maybe a dozen or more. In my car."

Richards seemed surprised. "These other folders, they have pictures like mine?"

Embarrassed, Jamie replied, "I've only looked in a few but yes sir, they also have pictures of… of…"

"Naked old men?"

"Men and women. And people snorting cocaine and stuff."

"Son, you need to go to the police. Give them those folders. They'll find out who killed your daddy. There could be a link between what's in those folders and these murders. But it's *not* me. Anyway, that's what I would do. But somehow I don't think you will. But if you do, I would appreciate it if you left my name out of your conversations and I won't mention that you forced your way into my house."

"Yes, sir."

Nothing else was said. Jamie turned and left. Richards didn't stop him this time.

Richards immediately headed to his office where he lustily reviewed each one of the photographs before shredding all but two – pictures of him with some young blond ponytailed male bimbo in front of the fireplace at the NAGS lodge. He placed them face down in his IN/OUT box hidden by his copy of the appellate court documents on gun control. As upset as he was about the secret photos taken of him, he couldn't help but get turned on by what he saw. His friend, Darryl, couldn't get there soon enough.

Chapter 90

Saturday, December 30, 2006, 3:48 p.m. EST

Richards' first call went to Wayne Peters' cell phone. He got voicemail. His second call went to NAGS headquarters. He got the answering service who, in turn, called Wayne Peters' office, then cell phone, then home phone. No answer anywhere. Congressman John Richards was not a happy man. His third call went to Bobby Armstrong's cell. Bobby picked up on the first ring.

"I want to see you and Peters RIGHT! FUCKING! NOW!" yelled Richards as loud as he could into the speakerphone on his desk.

"And a fine afternoon to you, too, congressman," laughed Bobby, trying to calm Richards down. Having calls like this from the congressman were not unusual. Everything was always an emergency with him. *What a fucking asshole.* "So what's got *your* panties all in a wad?"

"Bobby…" Richards paused in frustration. He needed to gain control of his emotions. If he played his cards right, he could use this to his advantage. Without question, he needed NAGS support and their thousands of members in his district. But NAGS needed him and his political clout even more. Re-elections were around the corner. His numbers were slipping. With more money in his political coffers, he could stay in office until he decided to leave. And NAGS had lots of money. Obviously, the photos were their insurance that certain politicians, judges, rich people, powerful people, and rich *and* powerful people who supported NAGS never strayed. And he was one of those powerful people. Powerful but not rich. Now that he knew about the folders, that changed everything.

"John? You still there?"

Again silence. Then Richards spoke.

"You won't believe who just paid me a visit at *my house* this afternoon."

Bobby was at a loss. He hated it when Richards played games with him.

"George W?"

"So, do you also have pictures of him, too?"

"Huh? Pictures? What are you talking about?"

"I'm talking about Jamie Barnes. *He* just paid me a social visit about 10 minutes ago. He…"

"Holy shit!" interrupted Bobby. "Jamie Barnes? You're lucky the son-of-a-bitch didn't kill you. Have you called the police?"

"And tell them what? That he came by to accuse *me* of killing those people. That I did it to get back some pornographic pictures of *me* taken at *your* lodge? You think I need that kind of publicity?"

"What? What pictures?"

"DON'T MAKE ME OUT TO BE A FUCKING FOOL, YOU ASS! You know damn well what I'm talking about. Those horrible, horrible pictures that YOU, PETERS, BARNES, OR ONE OF YOUR FUCKING MINIONS TOOK OF ME WITHOUT MY KNOWLEDGE." Richards then lowered his voice. "You, Peters and I need to talk... ahem… about reparations."

Bobby realized it made no sense to continue denying knowledge of the pictures. All it would do would be to piss Richards off even further.

"You're right. We need to talk. Look, I'm only about five minutes away from your house. Wait right there. Don't do anything rash."

"If you have any duplicates, get Peters to bring them when he comes. I want them all, and that means memory sticks, CDs. Everything. And by the way, *I'll* decide what I want to do… rash or otherwise."

Congressman Richards then shut off his speakerphone before Bobby had a chance to reply. He was done talking and listening. He was now in a position to be demanding.

Chapter 91

Saturday, December 30, 2006, 3:56 p.m. EST

Within ten minutes, Bobby Armstrong stood at the front door of Congressman Richards' opulent townhouse. He could see an eye peering through the peephole of the door after the first knock. When it vanished, the door slowly opened.

"Not taking any chances?" laughed Bobby as he walked past the congressman and into the living room.

"This is no fucking laughing matter. Where's Wayne? When's he coming? I want him here, too!"

"Wayne's not coming. I'm a big boy. I can handle this. Where are the pictures? Let me see them."

"I destroyed them," Richards blurted out without thinking, regretting his words as soon as he said them.

"Really? Oh! That's too bad. *No* pictures?" scoffed Bobby. "So what is it you wanted to talk about?"

"Don't take me for a fool, you insolent bastard. I've always worked with you and Wayne, never asking for *anything* in return other than your support. And look at how you repay me. Are y'all that fucking paranoid?"

Bobby remained silent, evaluating the situation. Nothing good was going to come of this. He let Richards continue his banter.

"I am *fully* aware that I am not the only victim. Jamie had several other folders of people just as important as me. I saw them," he lied. "Think how disastrous it would be to you, Wayne and NAGS if I went public. Your organization would be ruined by all the lawsuits. Including mine. Not only that, you could say goodbye to that toad of a wife of yours, not that she's any great loss, *and* your senatorial bid. Could I be harmed if I were outed? Maybe. Maybe not. Being gay is not the curse it once was. And you know how the voters rally behind the wounded. So having said all of this, this is what I've decided to do. Are you listening?"

"This is all about money, isn't it John? About reparations, as you put it," asked Bobby completely aware that Richards had the upper hand.

"Isn't everything about money?"

"You got a point. So what are we talking about?" Then shooting him a lowball number. "Would a hundred grand ease your pain? The brown bag kind. Untraceable. Non-taxable."

"I'm not a greedy man. A hundred grand? No. No. No. I was thinking more like five million in an offshore… er… retirement account. That seems like a reasonable start. *Plus,* the maximum campaign contributions from NAGS, its employees, and its members that can be legally given to my upcoming campaign. I feel that's only fair for all the humiliation I've suffered," answered Richards who then pulled a Kleenex from his pocket and wiped his brow in mock anguish.

"And that will satisfy you?"

"That and one million annually in the same offshore account as a contingency fee. And by the way, this is not negotiable. This is my final offer."

The smug look on Richards' face was more than Bobby could handle. He was fuming inside. It took every bit of his self-control to remain calm. He hated Richards. Always had. He was such a pompous ass. NAGS, Peters and he could handle his threats of lawsuits and financial ruin. That was business as usual for the three. But for the ass to threaten his marriage and much more importantly, his Senate bid? That moved Bobby beyond his tipping point. Beyond his point of no return. They needed Richards' support and influence. But not that bad.

"Do you know that before Jamie came here, he killed a cop at our lodge in Virginia?"

"What?" asked Richards, taken off guard by Armstrong's sudden change of dialogue. "What does *that* have to do with anything?"

"I just thought that you might want to know that he used this gun," smiled Bobby sardonically as he pulled out Corporal Geddings' revolver from his overcoat, unlocked the safety and fired point-blank into the congressman's surprised face. A second bullet was not needed, but Bobby did it just for the pleasure of doing it.

What do you think of those reparations, you greedy bastard?

Chapter 92

Saturday, December 30, 2006, 3:58 p.m. EST

Forty minutes was long enough. In retrospect, he should have called Detective Whitehead immediately.

Daniel's cell phone rang just as he turned left off of E. Washington Street and onto S. Madison Street in downtown Middleburg, Virginia. He was only two blocks from the city's police department. He answered immediately.

"Detective Whitehead, this is Kyle Hamilton. I hate to bother you, but I thought you needed to know that I just talked to Jamie."

"What!" exclaimed Daniel, almost jumping the curb as he parked his car.

"I just talked to Jamie Barnes."

"You sure it was him and not some nutcase calling you?"

"Oh no, sir. It was him all right. He asked for 'Woody,' not Kyle. Nobody but my high school golfing buddies ever called me 'Woody.' Just like nobody ever called Jamie, 'Lefty' or Billy Saperstein, 'Ziggy' or…"

"Did he tell you where he was?" interrupted the detective.

"Here. In Washington. But no address."

"So, why'd he call you?"

"He wanted me to know that he didn't kill my Mom or his Dad."

"That was it?"

"No, sir. He wanted you, the police, to know it, too. He also talked about his Mom. He said he wasn't sure if he killed her or not. That he was stoned but didn't remember doing it. I told him he should turn himself in but he said that the police wouldn't believe him."

He's probably right, thought Daniel. "Did you get his phone number?"

"He told me he was using a disposable phone, but I have the number for you if you need it." He then gave the detective the number.

"Great. So was that all he said? "

"No, sir.   Before he hung up, he said he was going to talk to Congressman Richards, the guy who came by our house the other night."

"Richards? Oh my God! Did he tell you why?"

"No, sir. He hung up before I could say anything else."

"If he calls again, give him my number or Johnny Williams. We need to talk to him before he gets hurt or possibly killed. I know you think Jamie is innocent but, and this is for your ears only, a Virginia police officer was just found murdered at a lodge owned by NAGS. They think Jamie did it. And to make matters worse, if things could get any worse, NAGS has upped their reward to $150,000. With that kind of money on his head, it has the eyes and ears of every bounty hunter within a thousand miles. And considering he's armed and dangerous, I doubt he'll ever make it to court alive, especially once it's known that he's also a cop killer."

"Can NAGS do that?"

"I'm sure whatever NAGS did, they did with the approval of their lawyers."

"Oh my God, you're scaring me."

"It is scary. Even *without* the reward or bounty hunters, I'm concerned that even our city's finest would have no qualms about putting him down if given the opportunity. So if Jamie calls again, you need to do what you can to get him to call us, or better yet, turn himself in. And *do not*, and I repeat, *do not* agree to meet him unless we're with you."

"Yes, sir."

Daniel hung up and immediately called the US Capitol police who are charged with the protection of the members of Congress. Then he called Johnny Williams.

Chapter 93

Saturday, December 30, 2006, 4:04 p.m. EST

Johnny Williams had just crunched down on his next to the last bite of a Snickers bar when his cell phone rang. He couldn't drive, hold the candy bar, and answer his phone at the same time, so he shoved the rest of the Snickers bar into his mouth, chewed a couple of times and then answered his cell.

"Detective Williams," garbled the detective with his name so muddled that it sounded like a foreign language.

"I won't even ask what you're doing," responded Daniel, laughing. "Just listen." Then he proceeded to tell Johnny about his conversations with Kyle and the Capitol police.

"Why Richards? His mother, father, yes. Margie and the Virginia cop, maybe. But Richards? I can't even begin to figure that one out. Surely, you don't think Jamie would harm a *congressman*, do you?"

"I hope not but the way things are going… By the way, the Capitol police have our numbers. They'll keep us informed."

"So where are you now?"

"Parked out in front of the Middleburg's Police Department. About to head inside. What about you? What are you working on?"

"I didn't come up with anything, so I've decided to start back at the beginning. At NAGS headquarters, the last place that Margie Hamilton was seen alive. I'm supposed to meet Peters at four. But now I'm not sure that this isn't just a friggin' waste of time."

"Wrinkles, ever since we started working this case, you've not been happy the way it's been going, with everything pointing to Jamie. I say stay the course; go with your gut feel. But keep your eyes open. Don't be a hero. We don't know what's up with Jamie and he could be anywhere."

"Hero? Me? Look. I'm too old and too close to retirement to be a hero."

Chapter 94

Saturday, December 30, 2006, 4:07 p.m. EST

Although he knew it was only in his mind, the ring tone on his cell with calls from Bobby always seemed louder and more vitriolic than other callers.

"What do you want now?" asked Wayne, impatiently, having had enough of Bobby Armstrong.

"I called you from Clyde's, but you didn't answer. Thought you might change your mind about lunch. Where were you?"

"Out."

"Out where?"

"Do I need to start reporting to you everywhere I go? But if you *must* know, I walked over to Glen's to pick up a sandwich. I needed to think. What you did in Virginia has overwhelmed my senses. I'm at a loss... I..."

"Speaking of losses. You're not going to like this. John Richards. He's dead."

"What?" asked Wayne, certain that he had misheard Bobby.

"John Richards. Murdered. Dead as a doornail. Jamie's done offed a congressman. Even used the gun he took from that poor dead cop at the lodge. All I can say is good riddance to..."

Wayne was listening but his head was spinning as Bobby continued to ramble. *Oh God! Not again!* Images of Elaine, the Virginia cop, Richards, Margie, and Jim began to flash through his mind. Suddenly, he felt sick to his stomach. Before he could make it to the toilet in his office bathroom, he began to heave, throwing up his partially digested breakfast and lunch everywhere - the bathroom floor, sink, and toilet.

Once the dry heaves subsided, Wayne rinsed out his mouth, then the sink, washing away as much of the vile contents of his stomach as he could. Then he took a paper towel, wet it down with hot water and wiped his face, trouser legs, and shoe tops. It wasn't perfect, but he didn't care. Not anymore.

He headed back to his office, grabbed his cell phone and began to yell at Bobby until he realized that he had hung up. His hands shook as he redialed Bobby's cell.

Bobby could hardly get 'Hello' out of his mouth when Wayne began yelling at him again, pacing back and forth in front of his desk as the words ripped from his mouth.

"WHAT IS WRONG WITH YOU? HAVEN'T YOU KILLED ENOUGH? HAVE YOU LOST YOUR EVER-LOVING MIND? GOD ALMIGHTY! WHAT ARE WE GOING TO DO NOW? WHAT? WHAT? WHAT? I KNEW I SHOULD HAVE GONE TO THE…"

"WOULD YOU SHUT THE *FUCK* UP!" yelled Bobby so loud that it halted Wayne in mid-sentence. Then Bobby lowered his voice. "Richards had the folder with all those naked pictures of him. Somehow he got it from Jamie. He was going to blackmail us. And I can tell you from experience that blackmail never ends. It's the gift that keeps on giving. Richards wanted *reparations,* as he called it, to the tune of five million upfront, and then 1 million annually. How long do you think he would be satisfied with that? I didn't like the terms. So I killed him. I used the gun that I took from that cop in Virginia. The police are smart enough to make the connection of the spent shells to the cop's stolen handgun. That and I'm fairly certain they'll find Jamie's fingerprints on something, somewhere in the weasel's house. And if not, they'll figure it was an intruder or someone with an ax to grind with Richards. Maybe one of his queer friends. But there's no way they would ever think it was us. After all, Richards was one of our most ardent supporters."

"Us? You killed him, you son-of-a-bitch!" thought Wayne.

There was a long silence on the phone as Wayne tried to regroup. Unlike Margie and Jim, he had not seen the bodies of Elaine Barnes, John Richards, or the Virginia policeman. So while he knew they were dead, it was more surreal than real. Words, not actual people.

"Bobby, this is pure lunacy. So we'd have to pay Richards a few bucks to keep him quiet. So what? It's only money and not even our money, at that. He would have been worth every dime. Now, what do we do? What's your plan to replace him? Oh, that's right. You don't do plans, do you?" asked Wayne, with sarcasm dripping from every word.

"Look asshole. If *YOU* had done the proper planning when you decided to fire Barnes, none of this would have happened. For the love of God, who in their right mind would shit-can someone right after his mother dies, his wife divorces him, and at Christmas time. What *moron* would have ever *PLANNED* it that way?" snapped Bobby. "If that had been me, I would have probably tried to shoot you, too."

Wayne didn't respond.

Bobby continued. "This is what I want you to do. I want you to prepare two different press releases depending on who the cops come up with as their prime suspect. If it's Jamie, make sure you double the current reward amount. If it's anybody else, just put up an extra ten grand. That asshole Richards wasn't worth any more than that. You got it?"

Wayne again remained silent.

Bobby ignored Wayne's snub and carried on the conversation. "Then I want you to hit home *really* hard with our *rebranded* campaign of 'If Congressman Richards had been able to carry a gun in Washington.' That way we don't need that dead bitch *or* her two ungrateful boys. You hear me?"

"Bobby, I'm tired. Tired of lying. Tired of you killing people. Tired of covering up. I don't want to do this anymore. All I can say is you're one crazy son-of-a-bitch."

Without waiting for a reply, he slapped his cell phone shut, walked behind his desk and collapsed into his chair. Within seconds his cell phone began to ring. He didn't have to look to see who it was. Instead of answering it, he turned it off. Then he took the receiver off the landline and stuck it in his desk drawer. Still, in disbelief, he clasped his hands in front of him and just stared out into space. He was lost. There was no plan that would remove him from this miserable situation. At least, not any that he liked.

Only the ringing of the front doorbell woke him from his trance-like state of mind.

Chapter 95

Saturday, December 30, 2006, 4:10 p.m. EST

Johnny Williams waited almost a good five minutes at the front door of the NAGS headquarters building rapping on the door and ringing the doorbell multiple times before he heard the unlatching of the two deadbolts and door lock. When the door opened, a haggard-looking Wayne Peters greeted him.

"Sorry, I'm a little late. I had a hard time finding a parking space," said Johnny.

"Oh no! I must have shut the parking gate. I'm so terribly sorry. My brain is a little scattered. Follow me upstairs."

Little was said as the two men made their way up to Wayne's office. Johnny removed his overcoat, laid it across the back of one of the wing chairs and sat down in the other. Wayne sat on the corner of his desk nearest to Johnny trying to create a more informal setting.

"So how can I help you?" asked Wayne, his mind swirling with the events of the past few hours.

"Mr. Peters. To be perfectly frank, I'm not sure why I'm here."

"Well, that makes two of us. I assume this is about Margie's and Jim's murders. From what I read, I thought you were looking for Jamie Barnes. That he was the one responsible. Have I missed something here?"

"No. Not really. It's that, and this is not to leave this room, some things just don't add up. Everything seems to point to Jamie. But being a policeman for nearly thirty years, I've developed kind of a sixth sense when it comes to solving crimes. And right now, I feel that I need to look in a different direction. My partner, Daniel Whitehead… he listens to me, but doesn't feel the same way."

Another direction? That's all Wayne heard. His mind was now reeling. He hoped the detective didn't see the internal panic that was now gripping him. All he could think about was Elaine, the dead cop,

John Richards and now *another direction.* Where was Bobby? He was the one who created this mess.

Johnny continued. "When I feel like things have taken a wrong turn or I'm not happy with the direction the case is going, I like to start back at the beginning. Having said that, from what I remember, you were the last person to see Jamie before he supposedly went on his killing spree. Is that correct?"

Wayne didn't answer. He needed his 'Bobby' notes. He should have reviewed them before the detective arrived. But his mind was preoccupied with Bobby's most recent atrocity.

"Mr. Peters?" asked Johnny, offended at Peters being so inattentive.

"Oh. I'm sorry. I… uh… I'm not sure. He was here. That's for sure. And Margie offered him a ride. That's all I remember."

"What was his demeanor? Was he angry or agitated?"

"Uh… yes… no. I mean no. He was his normal self."

"And what was that?"

"Why are you asking me these questions?"

"Mr. Peters. I'm just trying to do my job. If you don't mind, I would appreciate it if you would please answer the questions."

Was it time? Should he tell the detective everything he knew? Cut his losses? Let Bobby pay for his sins, and he do likewise? After all, Bobby was the evil one.

Before answering, Wayne shook his head to these thoughts. He had come from nothing. His parents were poor; he'd put himself through college working crap jobs that nobody wanted. And now he had reached the pinnacle of his career. NAGS was his life. He couldn't do it. He just couldn't give everything up.

Finally. "Anytime I saw Jamie, he always seemed happy, regardless of the circumstance."

"Was there anybody with Jamie the day he came by the office?"

"No. Not that I was aware of."

Johnny glanced at his old notes, then back at Wayne. "Why did Margie Hamilton need to give Jamie a ride home if you gave him gas money? I believe you said a couple of twenty's? Why wouldn't she just take him to a gas station?"

"How the hell would I know?" asked Wayne angrily his voice elevated causing Johnny to give him a stern look.

"What about Jim Barnes? When did you last see him?"

As hard as he tried, Wayne couldn't remember what he had told the detectives. In an attempt to give himself more time to gather his thoughts, he stood, walked around to the back of his desk and slowly sat down in his chair.

"I… uh… I can't exactly remember. I think it was… uh… oh yeah! It was here. It was here. He came by on the same day that Margie gave him a ride… home… I think."

Johnny didn't remember Peters being so indecisive, agitated and nervous during their last interview.

"Why did you place Jim Barnes on administrative leave?"

"What does that have to do with all these killings? That's confidential information. You already know who killed these people. Why…"

Before Wayne could complete his sentence, a muffled ring from Johnny's cell phone came from his overcoat's pocket interrupting the comeback question. Johnny quickly retrieved the phone and glanced at the caller's name. It was Daniel.

"I'm sorry, I need to take this call. In private," apologized Johnny who flipped open his phone.

"Detective Johnny Williams," answered Johnny, very professionally as he walked outside Wayne's office and sat down in the desk chair that had once been Margie Hamilton's.

"Johnny. More bad news. Congressman Richards is dead. Shot in the face. Probably with the gun taken from the dead patrolman."

"Unbelievable!" muttered Johnny under his breath.

Daniel continued. "I hear that Richards' house is crawling with Feds. So don't be surprised if we get a call from the captain. Maybe the commander. I'm sure we're about to take a back seat on this one, and nobody will be happy."

"I know. I know," responded a dejected Johnny Williams.

"And that gut feeling you had that Jamie might possibly be innocent? You can throw that feeling right out the window. Up at the NAGS lodge, Bennie said he found tire tracks in the barn that could belong to a large car, like a Mercedes. *And* he found digging holes in the barn's floor similar to those found in Jamie's basement. He also found fingerprints everywhere including the poker iron that was used to kill the police officer. We'll know soon enough if they're Jamie's. But if you want my opinion, I believe the fat lady has sung and already gone home. I say case closed."

"You were right all along on this one. Just like everybody else. I don't know why I can't just go with the flow. I guess the feeling in my gut was hunger pangs. I'll wrap up things here with Peters and get back to the station. Maybe get something to eat. Or better still, just go ahead and retire."

"Johnny, don't get down on yourself. Your gut instincts have been right more than they've been wrong. Look, I've got to run. Gotta let the locals know that the Feds are coming to town."

Johnny headed back to Wayne's office, stopping at the doorway.

"You got a restroom I can use?"

Wayne looked up from his computer where he had been feverishly studying his 'Bobby' notes.

"Yes. First door on the left."

"Thank you. Just wondering. By any chance was this Margie Hamilton's desk?"

"Yes. Yes, it is... er... was," stammered Wayne obviously saddened by the thought.

"Figured so by all the pictures of her sons."

Wayne went back to viewing his computer screen, and Johnny turned to his left and walked to the first door past Margie's desk and opened it.

"Well isn't this just par for the course," grumbled the old detective. "A friggin' closet." He closed the door and immediately reopened it.

Oh my God! What do we have here?

Johnny quickly closed the door and walked back into Wayne's office.

"Mr. Peters. I just got a text from the captain," he lied. "He needs me back at the station. Pronto. If I need you for anything else, I'll call. But I doubt it. Seems like Jamie's killed again."

There was no response from Wayne. He didn't need to ask who it was.

Johnny turned and headed for the door when Wayne called out.

"Detective Williams! Your coat! Don't forget your coat."

"Oh! Thank you! I must be getting old. How could anybody forget their coat in weather like this?" smiled Johnny.

Chapter 96

Saturday, December 30, 2006, 4:14 p.m. EST

After leaving Richards' townhouse, Jamie needed some time and a place to think. He drove around until he saw the Safeway grocery store on Wisconsin Avenue where his mother used to shop. The store's parking was behind the building, away from any patrolling cops which was good. The bad. The lot was almost full, as many shoppers were picking up groceries for their traditional New Year's Day meal. Luckily, he found one of the few remaining open spots in the far back and pulled in. On the rear window deck of the car, he found one of his Dad's old golf hats. He put it on and pulled the visor down to shield his face. To further limit his exposure from passerby shoppers, he slumped down in the reclined seat as if asleep. Seeing a young executive in a Mercedes waiting for his wife to pick up a few items at the Safeway was not unusual in the Georgetown area.

His thoughts immediately turned to Richards. His visit with the congressman had not gone as expected. In fact, it had gone rather badly. In hindsight, did he really expect him to confess even if he had killed his Dad? What was he thinking? But Richards had a point. The clue to the murders might somehow be connected to the folders. He had looked at the contents of every folder. They all contained pictures. Very important men, mostly naked and taken with other naked men or women engaging in sexual activities. A few of the pictures showed them snorting cocaine. All pictures were taken at the NAGS lodge. The folders were the one common thread. While Richards seemed to be the most likely suspect because of what Armstrong had said on the phone about him wanting to kill everyone, he had been wrong about Richards. Or at least he thought he had been wrong. He certainly didn't want to make that mistake again. He needed help. But the only people that could help were dead. Except for Kyle. He could help. With his last remaining disposable cell phone, he punched in Kyle's number. A woman with a soft, sweet voice answered. Moments later, Kyle answered the phone. Jamie could sense a chill in his friend's voice.

"Look, I hate to bother you, but I really need to talk to someone," pleaded Jamie.

"Well, I think *you* need to talk to the police. Not me," answered Kyle frigidly.

"I can't. They won't believe me. All they see is some whacked-out rich kid who's gone on a killing spree."

"Well, haven't you?"

"Oh, Kyle. Not you, too," said Jamie, despondently.

"Look. I did what you asked me to do. I waited before I called the police. And when I did call, I find out there's been another killing. A police officer in Virginia. At your Dad's lodge. And they think you did it. So I think it's time you turned yourself in."

"What? What do you mean another killing? Who?"

"A cop up at your Dad's lodge. But you should know that!"

"Another murder? At the lodge? And they think I did it? Oh my God. Why is this happening to me? Woody, I didn't do it! I didn't. You've got to believe me," pleaded Jamie.

"I want to believe you, Jamie. You know that. But… Look. You've *got* to turn yourself in. They… NAGS has a really large reward out for you. Detective Whitehead is worried that if the bounty hunters don't kill you, the police will. Especially now that they think you killed a cop."

"But I didn't kill him. You've got to believe me."

"Jamie…" Kyle didn't know what to say. He wanted to believe his friend, but it was so hard.

"Can you just listen to me? Please?" Jamie elongated the word please to make his point.

Kyle's silence seemed to last forever. Then…

"OK. But I'm going to put you on speakerphone. I want my girlfriend, Katie, to listen. Maybe she can help. Is that OK?"

"Thank you, Kyle. Thank you."

After Kyle's brief introduction of Katie, Jamie told them everything. Sneaking into his Dad's apartment. The money. The folders. The pornographic pictures. Armstrong. Richards. His visit with Richards. Everything.

Wow was all Kyle could say, still not sure he believed his old friend.

Then Katie spoke. "The people in these folders. Did you know them?"

"I recognized a couple from their pictures in newspapers. The rest I didn't know. But what I forgot to tell you is that in each folder, there was a page that had all kinds of information about that person. Like name, address, job, family information, phone numbers. Even a short kind of history of the person. Also on the sheet was a list that had dates, names and picture numbers. I think the names must be the other people in the pictures," concluded Jamie.

"Just think if any of these pictures got out to the public, it would ruin these people's lives," said Kyle.

"I think you're on to something," said Katie. "Maybe someone at NAGS was blackmailing these people, and your dad found out. Maybe that's why he was killed. Jamie, you're at risk. Other people at NAGS could be at risk. You need to come here, to Kyle's apartment. That way you'll be safe. We can get Detectives Whitehead and Williams to meet you here. They'll listen. I promise. You show *them* the folders, and they'll find out who's behind all these killings."

Kyle was nodding and mouthing *Yes* as Katie pleaded with Jamie.

"Katie. Kyle. Thank you for believing in me. You don't know how much that means to me," replied Jamie. Then he hung up. He knew where he was going next, and it wasn't to Kyle's apartment.

Chapter 97

Saturday, December 30, 2006, 4:18 p.m. EST

The first phone call Johnny Williams made, after he left the NAGS headquarters building, was to secure search warrants for the NAGS Dupont Circle office, the Watergate apartment complex and Wayne Peters' home. The second call he made was to Daniel - all from the comfort of his heated car as he sat across the street from NAGS HQ. This way he could talk and keep an eye on the building to make sure Peters didn't leave with his newfound evidence.

"You ready for this?" asked Johnny as soon as Daniel answered his phone. "My gut was right! I found the coat! Margie Hamilton's coat! At least I'm ninety-nine percent sure it's hers. A brown suede coat with a fur collar."

"You're kidding!"

"Nope. Found it in her closet *at work*. So what does that tell you?"

"Are you going to tell me or do you want me to guess?"

"I think we got one big ass cover-up going on here. I'm not sure who killed whom but I feel quite certain it all started here. At NAGS."

"You're still at NAGS?" asked Daniel.

"Yep. Across the street. Not letting any of those douchebags abscond with that coat or anything else."

"Surely you don't think that Peters or Armstrong is responsible for these murders?"

"I'm not sure *who's* responsible. I doubt it's Armstrong. I checked my notes, and according to Peters, Armstrong wasn't even in town when Margie Hamilton and Jim Barnes were killed. So I don't see how… Speaking of the devil, Armstrong's pulling into the parking lot right now."

"You sure it's him?"

"Yeah. You know any other idiot that would drive around in *this* town wearing a cowboy hat? And you're not going to believe what he's driving?"

"You're kidding me. The Impala on the surveillance tapes?"

"You got it. I'm telling you, something's rotten here in Bismarck,"

"Denmark."

"Huh?"

"Nothing. So if this is a cover-up, what about Jamie. He's the one whose fingerprints are everywhere. By all appearances, he's our murderer. Where does he fit in?"

"Off the top of my head, I'd have to say he *is* the murderer. He could have come to see his father, at his office, mad about something. High on drugs. Needing money. Whatever. They argue. Then in a fit of anger, he pulls out the gun he'd stolen from his father and shoots him. Then on the way out of the building, he shoots Margie Hamilton and steals her car. Peters panics. Instead of calling the police, he calls Armstrong. They decide that having someone shot at their office is too much bad publicity, especially right before their court case. So Armstrong flies here to help Peters get rid of the bodies and they plan a cover-up. They carry Margie's body over to the dumpster and abandon her car somewhere else to make it look like a carjacking. With Jim Barnes, a second carjacking would be too much of a coincidence, so they dump his body over at Jamie's house. Let the boy take the fall since, after all, he shot him in the first place. What's Jamie gonna say? I shot them, but they did the cover-up?"

"Wrinkles, that's *so* far out in *left* field, it actually makes a lot of sense. Even Elaine Barnes and the dead cop, here, fit in with your story. But what about Richards? What's the connection there?"

"I have no idea," answered Johnny. "Maybe the Feds…"

"Wrinkles. Hold that thought! I need to make a call to Kyle. It's something that he said that I need to confirm! Don't go *anywhere!* I'll call you right back!"

Johnny snapped his phone shut, flipped on the windshield wipers to knock off some of the accumulated snow, and sat back in his seat with his arms folded trying to put all the pieces together. Regardless of the scenario, everything still pointed to Jamie.

Johnny's mental exercise was interrupted when he saw a large silver Mercedes pull into the NAGS parking lot.

Chapter 98

Saturday, December 30, 2006, 4:25 p.m. EST

"Thank God you called," answered Kyle. "Did you see my message that Jamie called again? He…"

"Is Jamie left-handed or right-handed?" interrupted Daniel.

"Left-handed. That's why we called him 'Lefty.'"

"Any chance that he's ambidextrous?"

"Oh no. Once he tried…"

"Thank you, Kyle." He hung up and called Johnny.

The call went to voicemail.

Chapter 99

Saturday, December 30, 2006, 4:25 p.m. EST

Jamie found the key to the side door of the NAGS office building on his Dad's key ring and let himself in. Just in case he needed a fast exit, he left the door ajar, just as he had done with the parking gate. He carried with him as many folders as he could, leaving the rest locked in the trunk of the Mercedes. Once inside the building, he did a cursory look around to make sure no one else was there. The place seemed empty.

As he made his way to the foyer, he heard voices coming from the 2nd floor, soft at first, then much louder. Argumentative. The voices of Bobby Armstrong and Wayne Peters. As he quietly crept up the stairway, the voices became more intense. Once he reached the top of the stairs, he stopped for a moment to gather his thoughts as to what he was going to say when he entered Peters' office. He knew his presence would be a shock to the two men and that he would somehow need to quickly reassure them that he meant no harm. He hoped they would see by his behavior that he was no killer. That he was *looking* for the killer.

Jamie took a couple of deep breaths and, when the shouting between the two men stopped momentarily, he took advantage of the lull to enter Peters' office. Wayne was standing behind his desk with his hands resting on the back of his chair while Bobby stood in front of the desk, arms folded. He was still wearing his overcoat. His LBJ lay on top of Wayne's desk. The angry look on both men's faces was disturbing.

"I'm looking for the person who's willing to kill for these," blurted out Jamie, holding up the folders.

Peters' mouth flopped open in complete surprise. Bobby turned, stared, and then grinned.

"I am not a killer. I just want information," continued Jamie nervously.

4:26 p.m. EST   Meanwhile, Johnny used his car to block the entrance to the NAGS parking lot and then called for backup.

Afterward, he quietly made his way into the building through the unlocked side door. From the foyer, he heard voices coming from upstairs. Most likely, Wayne Peters' office. He silently walked over to the stairway and began to make his way up the steps. The loud voices in the upstairs office easily masked the noise of the creaking steps.

4:26 p.m. EST "Please don't be alarmed," warned Jamie. "I'm not here to harm anyone. I am not armed. See?" Jamie opened the right side of his coat, then shifted the folders to his right hand, and opened the left side of his coat so that the two men could see that he came unarmed.

Wayne wasn't afraid of Jamie. He was afraid *for* Jamie.

"Oh please don't hurt me! Please!" quivered Bobby feigning a nervous tremble in both hands that covered his mouth. He smiled at Wayne whose eyes shot daggers back at him.

"Bobby, don't patronize the boy. Don't you think we've done enough to him?"

Jamie was totally confused. Nothing was going like he'd thought. Why weren't they afraid? Hadn't they put a large bounty on his head?

4:27 p.m. EST Johnny paused every three or four steps to get his breath and to listen to the ongoing dialogue. He was just as confused as Jamie. It was not what he had expected. Once he was eye level with the 2nd floor, he ever so quietly reached into his coat pocket, pulled out his miniature tape recorder, hit 'record' and slipped the lanyard attached device over his head. Silently he unholstered his revolver and disengaged the safety.

4:27 p.m. EST "Wayne. Zip it. I'm just having a little *fun* with the boy. Jamie, why don't you have a seat," commanded Bobby, pointing to the leftmost wingback chair.

4:28 p.m. EST Johnny moved to the far right of the steps and then tiptoed across the landing area to the exterior wall of Wayne's office where he eased his portly body as close to the entry door as possible without being seen or heard. His mind was now a quagmire of disconnected facts. The cover-up was definitely a possibility. But had Jamie initially been a part of the cover-up? Had he turned rogue? Or had Wayne and Bobby thrown Jamie under the bus? All were possibilities. He decided to listen further before making his move.

4:28 p.m. EST   Jamie obediently sat down in one of the wingbacks unable to process what was happening.

"Mr. Armstrong? I just wanted to talk about…"

Bobby's intense stare stopped Jamie in mid-sentence. He then turned to Wayne.

"Can you believe our luck? I mean even *you* couldn't have planned this any better. *And,* the young man has been kind enough to bring us back our missing folders."

"What the hell's wrong with you?" asked Wayne, taken aback by Bobby's behavior.

"What's wrong with me? Wayne. We've got a mass murderer sitting right here in our office. We can't let…"

"I'm no mass murderer!" yelled Jamie, attempting to stand, interrupting Bobby. "You've got this all wrong! You've…"

"Goddangit! Would you just shut the fuck up, you stupid twit? And sit *DOWN!*" demanded Bobby whose red-angered face was now within inches of Jamie's. The boy quickly reclaimed his seat. Bobby, who then returned to an upright position, spoke calmly and much slower, "I want to have a conversation with my associate if *you* don't mind."

He then turned back to Wayne.

"So as I was saying before I was so *rudely* interrupted, I think it's time to put an end to this killing madness. We have right here in our hands the proverbial golden goose. We can't let it slip away. The police and probably the Feds are looking for this young man. He's killed his parents, an old lady, a cop and now a congressman. It is our civic duty to put a stop…"

"No! No! No! You got this all wrong. I'm no killer," Jamie said angrily, again rising from his chair.

4:29 p.m. EST   Johnny was stunned. Nobody knew about Congressman Richards' murder unless…

4:29 p.m. EST   "SIT DOWN!" ordered Bobby loudly. "DO NOT, AND I REPEAT, DO NOT INTERRUPT ME AGAIN! Goddangit! If you had only stayed dead."

"Bobby, *I've* had enough of this," barked Wayne. Then turning to Jamie, he continued, "Son. You're not guilty of killing anybody. Not your parents, not Congressman Richards or that cop in Virginia. And certainly not poor Margie. Why don't you leave before…"

He stopped mid-sentence when he saw Bobby pull out a pistol from his overcoat pocket and pointed it at him, then Jamie.

4:29 p.m. EST   Shocked by Wayne's confession, Johnny inched toward the door ready to pounce when Bobby started talking again. Not knowing that Bobby had a gun and that Jamie's life was in the balance, Johnny decided to listen a little more hoping to fill in some missing blanks. Like what happened. Motive. Organizers. Accomplices. He eyed his recorder. It was doing its job.

4:30 p.m. EST   "You think you've had enough?" asked Bobby, pointing his gun towards Jamie's head. "Well, by God, I've had enough, too. Enough of you and your fucking cockamamie plan that never worked. If it hadn't been for me, we'd have cops all over our ass."

"Bobby. *Listen* to me," urged Wayne.

"Wayne. Dammit. Sit down and shut up!" ordered Bobby, turning his body so he could see Wayne and Jamie. The fury in his voice and the haphazardly way he was pointing the gun alarmed Wayne. So he sat.

Then Bobby continued. "Here's our final plan. One that will work. See, Jamie boy… he needs money. He's gotta get out of town, out of the country or he needs drugs… whatever. His sources have dried up. Dead, actually. He has keys to Jim's car so he also has keys to the office. So he sneaks in planning to rob *us*. He knows that we have money and there's money in our vault. He finds us in your office and pulls out his gun… you know the one he used to kill Richards and the cop. Anyway, somehow we get into a fight, I grab the gun from him and shoot him as he charges me. See it's so simple. Not like that complicated, convoluted, fucked up plan of *yours*."

Jamie is too dumbfounded and frightened to respond or move.

"Bobby! No more killings! I can't take it anymore. You've put this boy through enough. You're crazy! I'm calling the police," responded Wayne while picking up his cell phone.

"Oh *fuck*. Change of plans. He kills you first!" Bobby swiftly points the gun at Wayne and fires two rounds. One to his body and one to his head. Wayne is dead. The force of the bullet causes his body to slam against the back of his chair, and then recoil towards the desk, his head striking his computer keyboard - one last time.

With Jamie next, Bobby quickly turns back to see the boy springing from the chair, flinging the folders at the deranged man, some hitting him in the face and arm, one knocking the 'LBJ' to the floor. In the melee, Bobby fires two rounds at Jamie. The first barely misses; the second grazes the young man's neck, causing him to fall to the ground. Before Bobby can fire a third and unhindered shot, he sees in his periphery a large black man charging into the room, gun raised.

It was the last thing that Nelson Robert Armstrong would ever see. Johnny's bullet strikes Bobby right between the eyes and knocks him to the ground causing him to land on his 'LBJ,' crushing the hat and, without saying, his Senate bid.

4:33 p.m. EST Johnny holsters his gun, rushes over to Jamie and slowly helps him up and over to a seat in the closest leather wingback chair. From Wayne's desk, he grabs a handful of Kleenex and applies them to the neck wound. Jamie instinctively presses them tight against the wound. He manages a smile. Johnny plops in the other wingback and returns the smile. Hung around the detective's chest is his micro-recorder, still recording. He presses the 'Stop' button. The faint sirens from DC's finest can be heard in the distance and are growing louder. Nothing is said between the two men. They both know it's over. Seven people are now dead, including four employees of NAGS, a wife of a NAGS employee, a Virginia policeman and a U.S. congressman, and the only people who know what really happened and why are among the dead.

Johnny pulls out his last Snickers. He offers it to Jamie who declines. As he munches on the candy bar, he pulls out his cell and turns it on. Two text messages. One from Daniel. *Your gut is right. Don't do anything foolish!* The other from the captain. *The Feds are in. We're out. Call me.*

Chapter 100

Tuesday, January 2, 2007, 10:18 a.m. EST

An opened FedEx box sat on George Henry's desk. It had been sitting there since December 31, 2006. All packages and letters sent to the Law offices of Henry, Chapman and Parker were now screened and opened by security in their basement level mailroom ever since the mail-bombings and ricin incidents at other law firms in the District. Even the *Open upon my death* label on the outside of a smaller box contained inside the larger FedEx box had been ignored as it too had been opened. Security did not care if the sender was dead or alive. Their job was to protect the employees of their firm.

Henry found the contents of the smaller box disturbing. Besides an opened notarized envelope, the box also contained a Ziploc bag revealing a 9mm handgun and two shell casings along with a computer CD. These were not items normally sent to a divorce lawyer.

As Henry read the letter which security had dated and time-stamped, everything in the box made sense. It answered a lot of questions about the previous week's tragic events that dominated the headlines of the local and national news media. As requested by the writer of the letter, the entire contents of the box was to be hand-delivered to either Detective Whitehead or Detective Williams of the Washington Police Department.

Henry read the entire letter twice making sure he completely understood the originator's intent. Then as directed in the letter, he took pictures of it and the contents of the box. Satisfied he had carried out his duties as lawyer and friend of the sender, he called the police.

Henry had known Wayne Peters, the writer of the letter, for almost ten years. He was Wayne's friend and personal lawyer.

Epilogue

Monday, December 24, 2007, 6:45 p.m. EST – Christmas Eve
One year later

Almost a year has passed, yet the pain lingers. I am not looking forward to tomorrow or any future Christmases as they will never be the same. While I can look back and see the bad, I can also see the good. The bad, you already know. Now I will tell you the good.

Vernon Martin, a captain in the 5th District, DC police, retired in August after 33 years on the force. He was a fair and honest leader, earning the trust and loyalty of his peers and subordinates. His career was distinguished by numerous commendations as well as bullet wounds. He and his wife have since left Washington and moved to the Outer Banks in North Carolina to be closer to their grandchildren. His handpicked successor was Daniel Whitehead – a popular choice with everyone, including the Mayor. He would have become the youngest captain, ever, on the D.C. force but turned it down to stay in the field with Johnny Williams who continues to talk about retirement, eat Snickers and harangue his old friend and colleague, Bennie Archer. Bennie also chose not to retire. He is still working as lead analyst for all the DFS teams.

Winston Blackwell III has been working with a mission's group from Margie Hamilton's church, helping to rebuild the Gulf Coast. It's been keeping him busy, and he has met a lot of wonderful people in the mission's group and church.

Aaron Hamilton continues to work the same long hours with the same ambitious goals as he had before his Mom's death. But he has learned to balance those long hours with long periods of time off. He spends the majority of that time with Kyle. He even started taking golf lessons and playing on Saturdays with Kyle and Katie. He knows that he will never achieve their same level of expertise, but that wasn't his goal. His underlying objective was to spend more time with his brother and to reestablish the closeness they had as youths.

Kyle Hamilton proposed to Katie Chandler six months to the day after their first date with her parents' presence and blessings. The wedding is scheduled for next April, the week before the Masters. A honeymoon is planned in Charleston, South Carolina. After the honeymoon, the newlywed couple will spend the following week in Augusta, Georgia. Aaron has secured two Masters' clubhouse tickets, a suite at the Marriott Hotel, and dinner reservations at La Maison on Telfair, Bistro 491 and the White Elephant Café – his wedding present to the bride and groom.

Tomorrow, Kyle and Aaron Hamilton will be celebrating Christmas with Katie and her parents at her parents' home in Maryland. It won't be the same without Margie. But Margie will be in their thoughts and prayers as they remember the good times and celebrate the future.

They have been kind enough to invite me for Christmas Dinner although it, too, will not be the same – not with both my parents gone. Kyle and I have renewed our friendship. We've played a few rounds of golf. He's much better than he would have you believe and I'm much worse than I ever believed I could be. He, Aaron and Katie have been an inspiration. They have helped me believe that I can change my life, and I feel that I'm making a turn for the better.

With the support of my friends, I checked myself into a rehab facility in Virginia. Removing the drugs from my body and their crippling effect on my mind has been easy compared to freeing the eternal guilt that I carry for having caused so much angst to my parents while they were alive. And it is especially heartbreaking to know that they went to their graves never having seen the man they desperately wanted me to be. When I look back, I see that my life was filled with sadness and depression. Yet, the future fills me with fear, anxiety, and hope. So I just try to make it through one day at a time. Recovering addicts will understand what I mean.

While in rehab, I was able to complete my GED – a high school equivalent diploma. Then with the help of Winston Blackwell and Aaron Hamilton, I applied and was accepted as a conditional student, albeit an old student, at the University of Virginia. Both Aaron and Mr. Blackwell are alumni of UVA and are generous benefactors. Going back to school has been very difficult considering the amount of time I have been away from any formal classroom education. But, with every passing day and with my parents in my heart and mind, I am inching my way out of that big hole I dug for myself.

As part of my therapy, one of the rehab counselors suggested that I start a journal of my thoughts – to help me understand why I am the way

I am. It helped me cope with the stress of losing two parents. It helped me win the battle over the need for drugs. In the process, I found I enjoyed writing. So with encouragement from my friends, Kyle, Katie, Aaron and Mr. Blackwell and to make sure the truth is made known to all, I authored this book. I pray to God that my parents are proud of the man I have become.

P.S. George Henry, Wayne Peters' lawyer, turned over the contents of the FedEx box to the detectives. Anal to the last, Wayne Peters' letter gave a complete timeline of everything that had transpired, who did it, and why it was done. He also confessed to the cover-up and the withholding of evidence. He identified Bobby Armstrong as the killer of Jamie Barnes' mother, Elaine, and the young police officer in Virginia. Since the letter was written before Congressman John Richards had been murdered, Peters' letter did not include any information about that murder. But the FBI matched the bullets that killed the congressman to the ones from the gun that Armstrong possessed, the one he had taken from the dead Virginia police officer.

The letter also asked that the reward money be distributed equally among the Hamilton, Barnes, Geddings and Richards families. The letter also asked the new leaders of NAGS not to challenge any lawsuits filed on behalf of the aggrieved.

The CD contained Wayne's original plan and the 'Bobby' plan, neither of which worked.

Once the truth about NAGS involvement with the cover-up and the death of so many people was made public, the organization took a major hit in their membership. All new leaders were elected, but the damage was done. Fair-weather members were the first to leave, followed by many hardcore members who felt betrayed. But NAGS will survive and eventually rebuild its membership. Even in its darkest hour, the U.S. Court of Appeals ruled in favor of the Appellants which is what NAGS had so dearly coveted.

The End

John Thomas

United States Court of Appeals

FOR THE DISTRICT OF COLUMBIA CIRCUIT

Argued December 7, 2006 Decided March 9, 2007

No. 04-7041

SHELLY PARKER, ET AL

APPELLANTS

v.

DISTRICT OF COLUMBIA AND

ADRIAN M. FENTY, MAYOR OF THE DISTRICT OF COLUMBIA,

APPELLEES

Appeal from the United States District Court

for the District of Columbia

(No. 03cv00213)

Acknowledgements

I would like to thank my wife, **Lou**, my daughter, **Shannon Waites**, my friend, **Dick Sands**, my sister and brother-in-law, **Susan** and **Rod Burney**, nephew, **Dr. Owen Burney**, and my best friend since the third grade, **David Paul Burnett** for pouring through this novel looking for errors, omissions, *discrepancies* and just bad writing. They have been very helpful, supportive and honest!

Also, a big thanks to **AJ Panebianco**, Chief of Police, Middleburg, Virginia, his staff, and the tourism department for being so kind and helpful to me, listening intently while I rambled on.

Any resemblance between the fictional characters in this book and my friends and previous co-workers is intentional. Please forgive me if I have offended anyone. This novel is a work of fiction. Any names, characters, events (other than the actual Shelly Parker, et al., appeal), actions by police, detectives, medical examiners, government works, timelines, and plot are purely fictional. I have never been behind bars, never fired a gun except in basic training at Fort Benning, GA, (excluding my BB gun), never been in the 5th district's police department or in a morgue. So bear with me for my ignorance in these areas. I have tried to keep technology relevant to what was available in 2006. So flip phones were the norm. GPS tracking and triangulation were in their infancy. Again, any errors were purely unintentional.

Thank you for reading my book. I hope you enjoyed it as much as I enjoyed writing it. If so, please read my next book, *The Innocent Thief* due out April 2022.

John Thomas